Praise for *The Forest of Hands and Teeth*:

'A bleak but gripping story of survival and the endless capacity of humanity to persevere. Poignant and powerful, fresh and riveting'   *Publishers Weekly*

'Mary is a powerful, sympathetic heroine with plenty of depth and complexity, which will draw readers into her struggle for freedom'   *Waterstone's Books Quarterly*

'What makes this captivating, apart from the beauty of the prose, its wonderfully measured pace and neat plot twists, is the tension between Mary's dreams and the ever-present knowledge of the evil surrounding the village. For once, the hype surrounding a novel is not exaggerated. *The Forest of Hands and Teeth* is unputdownable'   *Guardian*

'*The Forest of Hands and Teeth* is original, gripping and rich in metaphor. In the cluttered zombie fiction market, it stands out like a living creature among reanimated corpses'
                          Financial Times

'Ryan writes with an infectious style that draws the reader in, buoying them with momentum at the right moments before delivering sequences of tense action. It's a very effective style and one that will surely resonate with fans of similar novels. A worthy and highly recommended read'   *Sci-Fi Now*

'Opening *The Forest of Hands and Teeth* is like cracking Pandora's box; a blur of darkness and a precious bit of hope pour out. This is a beautifully crafted ___ ___ ___ ___g, powerful novel'   elissa Marr

THE
DARK AND
HOLLOW
PLACES

▼ ▼ ▼

CARRIE RYAN.

The right of Carrie Ryan to be identified as the author
of this work has been asserted by her in accordance with
the Copyright, Designs and Patents Act 1988.

First published in Great Britain in 2011 by
Gollancz
An imprint of the Orion Publishing Group
Orion House, 5 Upper St Martin's Lane, London WC2H 9EA
An Hachette UK Company

This edition published in Great Britain in 2012 by Gollancz

1 3 5 7 9 10 8 6 4 2

A CIP catalogue record for this book is available
from the British Library

ISBN: 978 0 575 09485 7

Printed in Great Britain by
CPI Group (UK) Ltd, Croydon, CR0 4YY

The Orion Publishing Group's policy is to use papers
that are natural, renewable and recyclable products and
made from wood grown in sustainable forests. The logging
and manufacturing processes are expected to conform to
the environmental regulations of the country of origin.

www.carrieryan.com
www.orionbooks.co.uk

For my sisters, Jenny and Chris –
We'll have each other, always

▼ I ▼

This city used to be something once. I've seen pictures of the way it gleamed—sun so bright off windows it could burn your eyes. At night, lights shouted from steel like catcalls, loud and lewd, while all day long white-gloved men rushed to open doors for women who tottered about on skyscraper heels.

I wonder sometimes what happened to those women when the Return hit—how they were able to run and survive with such absurd contraptions strapped to their feet. How different the world must have been before—safe and comfortable.

The City's nothing like that anymore. Now, bare beams scrape the sky like splintered finger bones. Half the high-rises have fallen, and scavengers pilfered the intricately scrolled ironwork long ago. There's not much of anything left anymore, just the fear that seeps foglike through the streets.

Fear of the Recruiters. Fear of the Unconsecrated. Fear of tomorrow.

Even so, this city's been my home. Other than the village I lived in as a child, this is the only world I've known. It's sharp-cornered and raw but it's a refuge for those with a burn to survive. You pay your rents, you follow the rules and you do what it takes to keep living.

Which is why I find myself on the Neverlands side of the Palisade wall that cordons off and protects the Dark City as the last dregs of evening slide across the sky. This is the place where Elias would go when he was desperate for money, desperate to trade so we could pay our rent and stay in our tiny flat for another year. It's the place where anything can be found for the right trade, and where, after the blade of my only knife broke this afternoon, I've come for help.

Clutching the replacement blade tightly, I've started to cross over one of the bridges strung between two buildings when I hear a deep rumbling cough. It's approaching dusk and storm clouds hover over the river, causing the light to drip a dull green. I shuffle faster toward the next roof, determined to get back to my flat in the Dark City before full night, but as soon as my foot lands on the rickety bridge connecting the buildings a voice calls out, "Wouldn't do that if I were you."

I freeze, the frayed rope railing in one hand. I've been alone long enough to have learned to look out for myself, yet something about the warning makes me hesitate. Just as I start to take another step the voice says, "Look down," and I do.

The alley a dozen stories below is dim and choked in shadows, but even so I see something moving. A moan floats up, echoing softly between the buildings as it rises. The sun breaks through a narrow gap in the clouds and the light reflects down the alley, glinting briefly off what looks like eyes and a row of cracked teeth.

As my gaze adjusts I can make out dozens of clawing fingers reaching for me amid a pile of broken bodies that should have died from their fall but didn't. Or maybe they did die and infection's brought them back as plague rats. I shiver, disgust rolling through me.

Carefully, I inch back onto the roof, noticing how the wooden boards I was just about to walk onto are rotten. One step more and I'd have been down on that heap as well.

"You're the first one to listen to me and not take a dive," the voice says, and I spin, pulling my new knife between us. A woman sits tucked between two crumbling stone chimneys. In her hand she clutches a charred wooden pipe that feebly chokes out smoke.

I glance around the roof, expecting some sort of trap. The woman gestures toward my knife. "Don't bother," she says. "Just me up here."

She puts the pipe back in her mouth, the end of it burning a bright red, and in that instant I get a clear look at her face: thick dark lines painted around eyes smudged by tears or sweat or both. Then the ember fades, pulling her back into shadow.

But not before I see the raw circle around her wrist, festering with infection. The flesh edging the wound puffs and oozes, and I recognize it as a bite. I pull my knife back up between us, refusing to let it shake.

I'm usually pretty good at avoiding any confrontation with the Unconsecrated. No matter how careful you are, there's always the risk that something will go wrong and they'll get their teeth into you one way or another.

The woman shrugs and inhales. The light makes her skin glow again and I watch how her hand trembles. Cracks etch through the powder she used to make her old skin appear blushing and fresh—it looks like a fractured mirror instead.

I think of my own face, the scars overlaying the left side of my body like a thick spiderweb. Her cracks can be washed away. Mine can't.

It's easy to see that she's close to the end—when the infection will kill her. I glance down again at the pile of bodies below, their feeble moans filtering into the night. She'll be one of them soon. If she's lucky someone will take care of her before she turns. If she isn't . . .

I swallow.

With a sickening heaviness in my stomach I realize I'm the one who's going to have to kill her. It makes me feel off balance and I take a few steps away from the edge of the building, suddenly unsettled by such height.

The last of the evening light slides down my body, a final brush of heat, before disappearing for what will be yet another night of forever. The woman's eyes aren't on my knife; instead they focus on my face.

She inhales but her chest barely moves. She considers me a moment, staring at my scars. "There are men who like 'em like you—messed up," she says, nodding. Her gaze slips past me back down the island toward the ruins of the bigger buildings of the Dark City in the distance.

No they don't, I think.

She exhales a wavering line of smoke. "But more 'n likely, they're the ones that want to do the messing." She pushes a thumb into the corner of her mouth, as if tidying up a lip stain that she's no longer wearing, the gesture a habit of so many years that's become useless.

I should say something. I should be comforting or

consoling or helpful. This woman's infected and she's facing the final moments of her life and I realize how utterly useless I am faced with the enormity of what's going on. Instead I clear my throat. How in the world would I know what could give this woman comfort?

I look back across the roof where I came from. It would be easy for me to just retrace my steps—leave her for someone else to deal with. But that seems unnecessarily cruel. After all, I'm alone on this island like she is. Maybe if I were in her position, I'd want someone to listen to me at the end.

She picks at the edges of the bite, pressing against the angry red infection lines streaking up her arm. "You got a man?" she asks. "You in love?" She sounds nervous, like she's uncomfortable. Like she understands what I'm going to do and she's just extending time a bit.

Her interest takes me aback. I try to say yes and no at the same time and instead it just comes out as a grunt. "I have a . . ." I stumble over the word, then mouth "brother." It's the lie Elias and I have told everyone to make our living together in the Dark City simpler. We've said it so long it feels like truth.

"He joined the Recruiters," I say instead.

"When?" Her eyebrows pinch together.

The question has weight to it—if he joined up before the Rebellion it means he wanted to change the world into something better. If he joined up after it means he's a masochist who gets high on the power of controlling people with no hope.

"Three years ago." I've rarely had to say it out loud. Had to acknowledge how long he's been gone. Before, I could just go from day to day: tomorrow to tomorrow to tomorrow without having to bundle them all together in heaps to represent weeks and months and years.

The woman laughs, her wet mouth open and lip curled in where she's missing a few teeth on the left side. She doesn't even have to say how absurd the hope in my voice sounds. We both know the survival rates of the Recruiters before the Rebellion: one in seven. Only that one ever makes it home after his two-year term is up, and Elias should have been back a long time ago.

Anger darts through me. Maybe that's what she wants. To make it easy for me to thrust the knife into her chest. Make me want to feel the jolt of the blade grazing over her ribs and the squelching heat of her blood. I take a step toward her, narrowing my eyes. She's as good as Unconsecrated, and I've put them away before.

She just slips the stem of the pipe through the gap in her teeth and inhales, burning a red glow between us. "Oh, honey," she finally says, but it's not judgment I hear, it's pity.

It unsettles me, and I turn to the side so she can't see the expression on my face. Even so, her gaze traces over my scars again, one by one. She tilts her head as if trying to piece them together in some sort of pattern.

"Oh, honey," she says again, and I know it's for the misery of this moment. "You been waiting for him all this time?"

The concern in her voice sounds like the way a mother would talk to a daughter, and this opens up a fresh ache inside me. I nod.

"The City's dying," she says. Her voice is calm and gentle. Soothing. "You should leave. Find a new life." She drags the thin strap of her shirt up over her shoulder but it just slides down her arm again.

I shrug. "This is my home," I tell her. I know I sound defensive.

There's silence between us for a bit. Not real silence—that doesn't exist—but as quiet as it gets in the Neverlands with the moans drifting from the alley and the sound of someone yelling the next block over.

"I had a man once that I stuck around for," the woman says. She pokes a toe through the tip of her worn shoes and I wait for her to tell me more, but instead she just contemplates her foot awhile and then shrugs.

"Some men have a strange idea of what love is." She pushes a strand of greasy hair back behind her ear and I see bruises dotting her neck.

What she doesn't understand about me and Elias is that I promised him I'd wait for him to come back, and leaving would mean he's dead. I know there's nothing else that could keep him from coming home to me. The evening he left he said he'd find me again, and I believe him.

But a dark thought seeps into my mind, one that's been curling around the edges of my consciousness for months: Elias left my sister alone in the Forest of Hands and Teeth when we were kids. Why would I ever think that he wouldn't leave me?

The woman stands and I whirl to face her, pulling the knife back between us, ready to end it. She doesn't come closer or threaten me in any way. She just flips her pipe over and knocks it against one of the chimneys, spirals of embers twirling and fading around her legs and feet.

"Did you ever think about what you really wanted your life to be like? Like when you were a little girl?" She moves toward the edge of the roof. The darkness seems to stretch forever.

I think about the village where I was born. Where I had a

sister and a father and a community of people who loved and took care of me.

That. That's what I want my life to be like. Not this city. Not these scars. Not this loneliness. I remember the moment in the Forest when my sister fell and scratched her knee and how bright the blood looked. How desperately the dead clawed at the fences while Elias and I walked away from her.

But I tell this woman none of those things. Instead I shake my head. "No."

Her face falls a little as if she was expecting a different answer. "Ever wonder what you'd do if you knew you were going to die?"

"We're all going to die eventually," I tell her.

She smiles, more like a wince. "I mean if you knew when," she clarifies. "If you only had a few days." She inhales, sharp, and adds, "A few moments."

I shake my head. It's a lie, but I don't want this woman to know me any better than she already does. Being here for her death—that's already more intimacy than I've shared with anyone in years. I don't want to like this woman—I don't want to care about her—because then this moment and the one that's coming next will hurt too much.

I refuse to have feelings about someone when I know they're going to leave me. I feel sorry that I can't offer this woman something different, but I have to protect myself more than I have to protect her.

Her eyes begin to glisten and her shoulders shift as she pretends to laugh. "Oh well," she says, waving her dirty pipe in the air as if it could clear it all away. "Oh well," she says again, barely a whisper.

She begins to shake. I've seen it before, the infection

taking a firmer grasp, burrowing in deep for the kill. Any moment she'll collapse, her body giving out and dying. And then she'll Return, clawing for my flesh.

I move toward her, knife tight in my hand, but she jerks her head, waves me away with a fling of her arm. She's standing on the ledge of the roof. Below us the plague rats moan.

"I just . . . ," she says, raising a hand to her head, patting her hair into place. She presses her lips together, her nostrils quivering as she takes a deep breath. "I just wanted someone to remember," she says then. "I just wanted to be beautiful to someone, just for a little while."

And before I can ask "Remember what?" or "Remember who?" she tips forward and jumps. The rushing air pulls her hair from her face, and her body twists like a ribbon caught in a breeze for a moment before she tumbles into the darkness.

She doesn't even scream.

I don't have to run toward the ledge to know what happened to her. I hear the thump of her body hitting the concrete below. The sound of bones breaking, of her skull shattering.

I drop the knife and press my face into my hands, dig my fingers against my forehead, as if that will hold me together. I shouldn't have been the person here at her death. I don't even know the woman's name or who to tell that she's gone.

And suddenly I realize just how much her situation echoes my own. How no one would know or care if the same thing happened to me. How unlikely it is that any of the few neighbors remaining in my corner of the Dark City could even recall my name, much less notice if I went missing one day.

I've never felt so alone in my life. Sure, I've spent the last three years on my own but I've always focused on surviving and waiting for Elias. This woman's done something to me, though. She's made me recognize a kind of gap inside, and now I don't know if I'll ever figure out how to close or fill it.

Finally, I raise my head and notice a bundle left in the nook between the two chimneys where the woman was sitting. Numbly, I pick it up. It feels wrong to sift through the contents, but that doesn't stop me.

Her few possessions amount to not much more than half-empty cases of colored powders and stains. Makeup that could never come close to hiding her age or the desperation seeped into every line on her face.

I trace my fingers through a vermillion red, something about the tone of it calling to me. Then, tentatively, I press my hand against the chimney next to where the woman sat, tracing a red slash across the smoke-blackened bricks.

Digging through the pots, I find a blue that I smudge over the red and then black around the blue. Eyes, lips, hair, chin: Bit by bit I create a portrait of the woman. Not the way she was at the end, crouched in the shadows, but how she looked falling, with her wide smile and the knowledge that her misery was ended.

Plague rats moan in the alley, and from a window below me I hear men laugh and women joke. The air's thick with the smell of their sweat and need as they find solace together while I hunker in the night drawing the woman. I make her beautiful, make her flying through the air as if gravity would never dare to sully her with its grasp.

It's a rush. I feel like I'm reclaiming the control the woman stole from me. And when it's over and I step back I realize that at some point I stopped painting the stranger and started painting myself. But not how I am now, not scarred, with stringy blond hair that tangles in front of my face. How I could have been if I'd never left my sister in the Forest that day.

The woman asked me what I wanted in my life if it could be anything. I haven't given any thought to what I want in a long time, outside of longing for Elias to come back. When we first arrived in the Dark City I'd have said I wanted to go home to my village in the Forest but somewhere along the way I've forgotten that. I've let the day-to-day existence of life blind me to dreams.

Just like this city, I used to be something once. I used to be a girl who liked to get out of bed every morning and who understood passion. Yet for the past three years—longer than that, even—I've been frozen, incapable of accepting that life around me has shifted without my consent.

Exhausted and lost in thought, I push away from the wall and start making my way back to my flat, needing the familiar surroundings to remind me why I'm still here.

Why I've allowed myself to stay stuck waiting.

The darkness of the night settles heavy on my shoulders as I retreat toward the Dark City. I scamper over bridges and wade through the line of people waiting to cross the Palisade wall into the City proper. I feel invisible, everyone around me wrapped up in their own problems, not caring about an anonymous girl with her gaze trained on the ground.

I scramble past the debris pile of what used to be a wing of the building housing our flat and climb down the fire escape, slipping through the window into the emptiness of my home. Bare walls, scarred floor, dust coating everything.

Nothing personal except for the quilt twisted at the bottom of the bed, where it landed after I kicked it off this morning. I wrap it around myself, burying my face in the tattered cloth that was once bright. That once held his smell.

Usually sleep comes fast and easy. Usually I want nothing more than to be yanked into the featureless dreams, but not tonight.

Tonight I think of the woman. The stars spin outside, chasing dawn across the sky, and sleep never comes. Only the cold emptiness of the flat.

No other heartbeat to keep me company. No voice to keep away the blackness of night. Nobody to share the length of days with.

And I realize that I've been spending too long trying to forget that I've lost the part of myself that used to belong to someone else. That I once held my sister's hand and sat on my father's lap and knew my neighbors' names. I've filled that place with an emptiness, and the woman tonight made me see that that hole inside me is from Elias and that I've waited for him to come home long enough. He's gone. And I'm alone. Crouching here in my empty flat, listening to the moaning of the City dying around me, I remember what I want.

I want to find my way back home, to my sister and my family and my village in the Forest of Hands and Teeth.

▼ II ▼

There are only two ways off the island: boat or bridge. The boat docks sit on the southeast side, deep in the protected range of the Dark City. A series of gates and fences blocks the City from the docks, and Recruiters patrol with dogs that can smell infection to ensure that no vessels carry it into the City.

The few boats remaining after people fled during the Recruiter Rebellion are fiercely guarded, and I know it would be almost impossible for me to book passage on one. Which means that if I'm going to really do this—leave—I'll have to travel by foot like everyone else who wants to get off the island. And the only bridges in and out are far north in the Neverlands.

I start my journey in the late morning after a sleepless night standing on the roof of my empty building waiting for dawn. I stared at the few remaining lights flickering in the skyscrapers along the bottom edge of the island and tried to find the strength to leave it behind. Elias fought so hard for our flat in the Dark City, scraping together the exorbitant rent just for the promise of safety, and I feel wrong abandoning it.

What if he comes home tomorrow and I'm not here? What if he's just over the edge of the horizon, dreaming of me, fighting his way back to me?

But then I remember that woman. Her falling through the air. If I only had a few days left to live would I spend them like her, huddled on a roof, waiting for a stranger to stumble upon me?

And the answer is no.

By the time I arrive at the Palisade wall it's early afternoon. No one challenges me as I make my way through the series of gates separating the Dark City from the Neverlands. It's only those coming the opposite direction—those trying to gain access into the Dark City—they care about. People leave every day.

The journey through the Neverlands is uneventful as I stick to the well-traveled avenues, keeping safe in the crush of people scurrying about. Streets of broken buildings spread out around me, dark alleys with sinister promises that I walk past gripping my knife tightly, promising a fight if anyone tries to mess with me.

There's already a line at the bridge when I arrive in the late afternoon, the process of leaving the island a slow and sometimes arduous one. No one meets my eyes. No one glances at me or cares, even when they brush past to shove their way forward, knocking against me as if I'm invisible. It's easiest when I keep my hair pulled over my face, my head tilted forward as if I'm examining the ground.

My scars make me stand out—they mark me as a distinct

individual, and I've learned well enough that it's better to stay inconspicuous, especially since the Rebellion. The Recruiters like to make examples of people, and their methods have grown crueler and harsher day by day. It used to be their cruelty was a form of keeping order, but now with the Protectorate no longer around to hold them in check, it seems more like some sort of sick pleasure.

I've heard rumors of Recruiters enslaving women who catch their eye and taking anything that isn't theirs. There have been even worse murmurings: black-market dealings in the dead, people disappearing, heads staked throughout the City as proof of Recruiter power. Things I choose not to contemplate but that have convinced me to avoid causing trouble as much as possible.

Around me people shuffle anxiously. Some of them carry bags and one or two push a cart piled with crates. Those are the ones I try to stay away from—they'll only attract attention from the Recruiters interested in looting, and there's no one to stop them.

The main bridge spanning the river between the Neverlands and the mainland is cut into sections by thick metal walls, each with two doors: one for those leaving the island and one for those entering. Running along the center of the bridge is a metal fence separating the coming from the going. A bell rings, the doors slide open and people pool from one lock into the next, and then the doors close and we wait, trapped in a pen until the bell signals again.

People push past me, elbows digging into my arms and back. I'm wearing most of the clothes I own: thick trousers under a skirt, three shirts layered over one another and a worn coat hanging down to my thighs. A small pack holding my old quilt rests against my lower back, and I've tucked my knife against my hip. I was afraid anything else I packed might be taken. The layers of clothing make my skin slick with sweat as the sun beats down, the day unseasonably warm for winter.

The door to the next airlock slides open and a man steps in front of me as I start walking through. He knocks me back and just as I catch myself from falling, palms flat against the steel wall, I see her through the metal dividing fence, walking toward the island.

Or rather, I see me.

The crowd grumbles as I hesitate in the entrance, trying to catch another glimpse of the girl. Eventually someone shoves me hard in the back, but I refuse to budge, bracing my hands against the door. My eyes skim every face, wondering if I was mistaken, but then I see her again just on the other side of the fence, entering the space I'm leaving. Her hair's long and blond, almost burned white by the sun.

She walks with her chin tilted up as if she's never had to worry about anything. As if she has no sense of the danger her clean, healthy looks invite. No one shoves or trips her, she just glides along as if expecting the world to make room.

Her eyes slide over the crowd, skipping right over me as if I don't exist.

Of course, that's why I keep my face hidden in my hair. It's why I hunch my shoulders and wear drab colors. I'm supposed to be invisible. It's who I am.

But not to her. Never to her. She should be able to find me in the deepest darkness. She should feel me there in the crowd the same way I feel her.

She's my sister. Her face as familiar to me as my own because it *is* my own. My chest tightens and I have a hard time gulping enough air. I'm dizzy, gripping the doorframe to steady myself, and the person behind me uses the opportunity to force me through.

I turn against the crowd, trying to wrestle my way back, but they're insistent and overwhelming. They push forward, flowing through the door in an unending stream as I struggle.

Nothing feels right about this moment. I fight for another look at the girl, knowing I must be mistaken. Even so, a prickle of hope starts to swell inside.

I want to scream—to draw attention to myself—but the warning bell rings and the crowd surges forward and then the doors groan shut and the girl I saw is gone.

I stand frozen, trying to understand what just happened. Trying to breathe. Trying to put the pieces together in my head. Even from such a quick glimpse I could tell that she had my face. My nose. My green eyes. She even had my wrists and chin and ears and neck and hair, if I spent time outside in the sun.

She had everything but my scars.

None of this makes sense—can't make sense—but I don't care because I desperately want it. For years I've replayed the moment Elias and I left Abigail, my twin sister, behind in the Forest of Hands and Teeth. I see her trip, see the blood trickling down her leg, catching in the downy hairs of her five-year-old shin. I remember the hesitation I felt, the intense desire to keep exploring mingled with rage that my sister was crying and fear that she wouldn't go on any more.

I remember walking away from her. We thought we'd just go a little farther, just around the corner.

We never saw her again. We got lost, couldn't find our way back and ended up here.

Over the years I've dreamed of her a dozen different ways but I've only known one truth: that I left my sister crying and terrified in the middle of a path in the Forest because I was being selfish.

I left my sister once and I can't do it again. I can't give up this chance that she's real and safe and within my grasp.

I fight my way back to the door, start banging against it, but a Recruiter grabs my hands and twists my wrists painfully, his fingers digging into my skin. "Wrong way," he says, pushing me back to the crowd waiting at the other end of the holding area, waiting for the bell to sound and the door to open so they can move forward on their journey across the bridge to the mainland.

"I have to go back," I tell him, trying to rip my arms free.

"Not the rules." He narrows his eyes, causing wrinkles to spread around his cheeks. His shirt's dirty and reeks of smoke and overly ripe perfume. "Unless you have something to trade for it." He tugs me a little closer until I have to look up at him, my hair falling back from my face.

He takes in my scars, his lips pressing thin. He drops my wrists.

I hear the bells ring down the bridge, hear the doors sliding open and know that she's getting farther away from me. "You have to let me go," I shout at him.

"Get to the end and then you can come back. This side is one way only—off the island," he says. He can't help but stare at my scars, a look of disgust in his eyes. "Either way, keep moving forward. That's the rule."

I see the door begin to grind open behind him, the creak of old gears and rusty metal separating me from my sister. He pushes me away from it, away from her. Away from the Neverlands and farther out over the river toward the mainland.

People flood in around me and press tight, making it hard to breathe. They crowd against me, just wanting to get to the other side, and I'm causing trouble and getting in the way.

I'm drawing attention and attention isn't good. But I refuse to give up. Already she's out of my sight. Already I may never find her again. The Recruiter must see the resolve in my eyes the moment before I move, because his muscles tense, ready for me. I'm just about to lunge at him, just about to fight my way through the door, when we both hear the fierce growling and barking of dogs and then the explosion of the alarm blaring over the bridge.

Every door rolls shut, the heavy metal pinning one poor woman's fingers against the jamb, causing her to howl in pain. The Recruiter forgets about me and leaps for a rope ladder, climbing to one of the lookout posts at the top of each wall.

All around me people press against the side of the bridge, trying to see what caused the commotion, shouting at each other in confusion. I elbow my way through them, keeping low until I can shove my head through the gaps in the railing. The sound of dogs barking, their growls deep and ferocious, underscores the wailing siren piercing my ears.

It's almost impossible to figure out what's going on, but there's clearly chaos at the checkpoint on the island end of the bridge. A few Recruiters gesture wildly and I watch as they push a young man to his knees against the metal wall circling the shore of the island. Dogs lurch at him, their backs spiked with rage.

He pulls something from his pocket—some sort of disk that looks like one of the old Recruiter IDs—and holds it out to them. One of the men snatches it and frowns, disappearing into the guardhouse as the young man kneels, his hands held up as if trying to entreat the guards who pull knives from their belts. The dogs smell the infection—they won't allow him onto the island. He's too dangerous.

The siren eats away at the air, cutting off everything except the sound of the woman still screaming as they try to pry her fingers from the steel door. Everyone around me jostles, all of us straining to see what will happen next.

A large man, his Recruiter uniform crisp and clean with a red sash across his chest, storms out of the guardhouse, towering over the young man. The Recruiter's mouth moves but none of us can hear what he says and the young man keeps shaking his head, his hands raised palms-out.

Just then a blur bolts from the crowd at the edge of the bridge. It's my sister. She's running at the large Recruiter, tangling her arms around his neck. He twists, batting her away, but in the split second of distraction the young man lunges to his feet and throws himself against the metal wall, feet scrabbling as he clambers to the top and slides down the other side along the river.

Chaos erupts, Recruiters running to climb after the young man as others on the bridge take aim with their crossbows. Around me people scream and lunge out of the way but I stay kneeling, watching the young man scrabble along the shore while bolts pepper the ground around him.

"Got him!" one of the Recruiters shouts. The young man stumbles, a bright red streak of blood along his arm where a bolt clipped him. He loses his balance and starts to slip toward the river running under the bridge. And with a splash, he's gone.

Everyone around me holds a collective breath as they wait for his body to break back up to the surface. Except me. I'm staring at the girl—at my sister—the one who is me. Abigail. She's crouching where the young man knelt just before he ran. Thin lines of blood well along her arm where her sleeve was torn in the scuffle, and she holds her fists to her temples. One of the dogs thrusts his nose against her elbow and she leans on him as if she has no idea what to do next.

Two of the Recruiters slap hands as they walk past her and she raises her head. They must tell her what happened as they haul her to her feet, because she opens her mouth, and even with the havoc flaring around me I can hear her screaming in rage. It reverberates inside my head as if it were my voice and my throat and my pain.

I will her to look at me. To turn her head and glance my way. I beg her with my mind to see me. To know I'm here. But she doesn't move. Her gaze never wavers from the towering metal wall where the young man just stood.

Below me the ripples on the river die out to a calm smooth glass. The man never comes to the surface.

▼ III ▼

The siren eventually cuts out and the Recruiters order everyone to line up so they can search us. They go from section to section with the dogs, trying to determine if any of the rest of us might be infected like the young man.

By the time I'm released everything's in disarray and I'm able to double back toward the Neverlands, but when I finally make it off the bridge I can't find my sister anywhere. I race to the wall where I last saw her and press my hand against the cold rust-pocked metal, trying to feel her.

Not too far away a group of Recruiters huddle in a circle around a low fire, laughing and passing around a clay jug. I square my shoulders and as I approach, one with a thick white mustache breaks away, stopping me before I get too close. I'm acutely aware of the way they all stare.

"What are you looking for, hon?" he asks, his voice a mixture of warning and stern amicability.

"What happened to the girl?" I keep my chin up, my hair

tucked behind my ears. I feel wide open and vulnerable but I have to know if he sees what I saw: if he notices the resemblance or if I'm just believing what I want to. That my sister is still alive. That I didn't leave her to die in the Forest after all.

But like everyone else, his gaze fixes on my scars and then bounces away again, to the water and the bridge and the wall and the ground. Everywhere but at my face. He's an older man and a look of kindness still hovers around the tilt of his mouth.

"She was a friend," I prod.

He reaches down and tugs on one of the ears of his dog, which leans against his leg, tail twitching lazily. "I wouldn't worry about her." I can tell this isn't what he means; he's telling me I should forget about her. He shrugs and still refuses to look at me directly. "They might let her go, but . . ."

I don't want to think about the "but." I can't. "Please," I beg, hating the taste of the word but knowing I'll do what it takes to find my sister. I even let my eyes water, hoping tears will help my cause.

"They'll take her to the headquarters on the Sanctuary," he says eventually. "That's my guess. I'd also guess you won't be seeing her again." He pauses before adding, in a lower tone that doesn't carry far, "Don't go looking for trouble."

It's clear he's trying to tell me that hanging around the group of Recruiters any longer will be inviting trouble. With a nod I turn back to the crowd, allowing myself to fade into forgotten people whose shoulders slump and gazes dull as I try to figure out what to do now. How to find my sister, if that really was her.

I was so close to leaving. So close to saying good-bye to all the pain and misery this place has caused me. A tension pulls along my neck as I realize everything's changed again. I can't go—not yet. Not when my other half might be here.

There's no point in searching for my old village in the Forest if my sister's here on the island.

Letting my hair fall back in my face, I thread through the crowd as it thins, people wandering different directions. Most of them will stay in the Neverlands, the broad swath of crumbling neighborhoods that comprise the north end of the island.

I make my way south toward the Palisades—the thick layer of walls and defenses that separates the Neverlands from the Dark City. It used to be that the Dark City was the safest place to live other than the Sanctuary, where the Protectorate was housed before the Rebellion. But now the City's just as barren and worn down as the rest of the island. Without the Protectorate there's no authority to control the Recruiters, to manage the formerly vast array of patrols that secured the Dark City's borders and kept the streets clear of infection. Now there's no check on the Recruiter power.

Those with connections fled in the wake of the Rebellion. Others seeped into the sprawling underground network of black markets in the Neverlands. The rest of us remained out of some sort of desperate hope that maybe one day things would right themselves and we could go back to living life the way it was before.

But of course we're only deluding ourselves by staying. Between the Unconsecrated and what's left of the Recruiters, the City's not safe anymore. And there are only two options for a girl with no connections like me: Figure out how to take care of yourself, or find someone in the black markets to take care of you.

I've never liked the kind of protection they've offered, so I've spent the last three years completely on my own.

As I walk toward the Palisades, clouds gather over the mainland, wind rushing along the river and twining through the narrow alleys, whistling against windows busted out so long ago that weeds spill over the ledges and trail down broken facades.

In my mind I keep replaying the moment on the bridge when I noticed my sister; I keep picturing her face. Her expressions and the way she carried herself. But the farther I move from the river and the bridge, the more I begin to doubt what I saw.

I left my sister alone in the Forest, and I've spent the last decade of my life alternating between assuming that she got lost like Elias and me and died or that she somehow made it back to the village and has lived there safely ever since. Either way, I can't imagine how she could have ended up here on the island.

Could the girl just be someone who looks like me? Who merely has hair like mine? It's not like it's rare to have blond hair. It's not like I have any extraordinary features that make me stand out in a crowd. Other than my scars, of course.

Laughter trails down the alley behind me, snapping me from my thoughts. I cross my arms over my chest and pull my coat tight, hunching my shoulders. It's colder here in the shadows, the pinch of winter settling between the cracks.

Someone calls out and I walk faster, staring at my feet and trying to train my senses behind me. Just as I reach the corner there are more shouts and the sound of feet running.

I spin back into a broken doorway and fumble for the knife in my pocket. There's a group of three men down the road circling a bone-thin girl who barely looks old enough to be a teenager and a tall lanky boy who doesn't seem much older, both wearing dingy gray tunics that flutter around their knees. One of the men lunges at the boy, throwing a punch, and they tangle. The girl backs away, her eyes wide and lips trembling.

In the shadows of the alley our gazes connect. She's shorter than I am, petite with slim shoulders and a pointed chin. One of the men reaches for her, wraps a hand around her upper arm, and she cries for help. Her gaze pleading for me to do something.

I grip the knife so hard my fingers ache. The men can't see me here, huddled against an old concrete pillar just out of their line of sight. The girl fights against her attacker's grip, screaming now. The boy reaches for her but he's on his hands and knees on the ground, the two men alternating kicks to his ribs.

My teeth hurt, I'm clenching them so tight, and my heart pounds furiously. I should help them. There's no one else around and it's not hard to see that the boy and girl are severely outmatched.

I could sneak along the edge of the alley and try to surprise the men. I could run and search for someone else. I could throw something.

But none of these things would really help—they'd only serve to draw attention to me as well, and I know better than to invite trouble.

I'm rooted in place, unable to make up my mind to help, when two Recruiters stumble past me, their focus on the scuffle down the road rather than on me, crouching in my ragged clothes.

"What's going on?" one of them shouts in a booming voice. The men scatter away from the pair, leaving the girl shaking, her companion on his side on the ground, groaning as he clutches his abdomen.

She looks at the Recruiters as if they're her saviors. My stomach turns.

"Thank you," she starts to say as the two Recruiters split apart, one moving to either side of her. "Those men, they told me they know about a place to buy fresh meat, but . . ." Her voice trails off as one of the Recruiters places a hand on her shoulder, his thumb curling over her collarbone.

"You two Soulers?" he asks. He and his fellow Recruiter trade a look as if they've just found treasure at the bottom of a garbage bin.

The girl swallows, wide eyes dancing between the men. Her chest rises and falls, sharp and quick like a bird. Reluctantly, she nods, and the Recruiters grin widely.

"We've been looking for some of you," he says. "Man in charge has a few questions he wants answered. Though I don't see there being any rush."

A rage burns inside me. There used to be a time when the Recruiters were worth something. When they actually protected the people rather than preyed on them. The smart thing would be for me to fade back into the shadows and sneak away. It's safer for me to just forget this girl and boy who were stupid enough to trust a stranger.

I've never been anyone's savior—I've barely been able to keep myself alive, much less anyone else. But then I think about my sister and how I left her in the Forest.

Shifting my weight, I start to move away from the group, when one of the Recruiters reaches out and flicks at the girl's stringy ponytail, then wraps it around his fingers and tilts her head back.

She doesn't scream. She probably understands there's not anyone she could call for help, not anymore. The boy on the ground tries to crawl to his feet but the other Recruiter just places his foot on his back, pushing him down.

At that moment I realize I can't abandon her. I take a deep breath and hold my mouth against my arm. Slowly I exhale, moaning deep and long like the Unconsecrated. The Recruiters' heads snap up and tilt to listen.

I moan again, the sound urgent and rife with need. My skin prickles at how convincing I am to my own ears. How pained and wounded my voice seems. The moan bounces between the buildings, making it impossible for the Recruiters to pinpoint.

Three times I inhale and exhale, then I dash into the street, breathless. "Run!" I scream as I sprint toward them. I glance over my shoulder as if expecting plague rats to stumble after me.

I've known panic in my life. I've known a deep clawing fear that crawls along the spine and roars blinding loud. This is what I call on as I race toward the little group, as I yell that they must go and go right now.

I grab the girl's hand in mine and pull the boy up by the collar of his tunic. I drag them behind me, darting to the left as we leave the alley and weave around buildings to put as much space between us and the Recruiters as possible.

We run until my legs burn and my throat is raw and I half believe my own terror. The girl tugs at me when I slow. "What about the Resurrected?" she pleads, her eyes wide, and I have to remind myself that she doesn't know I made it all up to save her.

The boy bends over, hands braced on knees as he tries to catch his breath, his face broken with pain.

"It's okay," I tell her, holding her close against my side. "We're fine. I was just trying to distract them from you. You're okay now." I'm surprised at how much their safety actually matters to me.

The boy looks up, trying to focus. "You're sure?"

The girl shudders. They have no reason to trust me, which is the way it should be. They need to learn that no one—no place—in this city is safe anymore.

"What's your name?" I ask her.

"Amalia," she says.

I think about my sister and the way she looked when Elias and I left her in the Forest. Her knee was bloody from where she'd fallen and scratched it. The scent was driving the Unconsecrated around us into a burning need. They pushed against the fence for us, moans curdling up long-dead throats.

How easy it would have been for me to have made a different decision. To have taken her hand and led us both home. How long I've tortured myself for choosing to follow Elias down the path away from her.

"Where do you live?"

She starts to turn and point but the boy grabs her hand and pulls it down. He stands as straight as possible, his arms pressed to his side where he was kicked. "We can make it," he says, trying to sound as though he's strong enough to take care of the situation. It's easy to see neither one of them has eaten in a while—cheeks sharp and eyes smudged with bruises.

"They said they were looking for you—why?" I ask, still not sure I should leave them on their own.

They glance at each other, clearly warring over what, if anything, to tell me. "They've been after all the Soulers," the boy finally says. "We don't know why. We just know that they've taken the ones they find."

The clouds hugging the mainland have shifted over the

island, dropping the temperature, and I'm finally glad to be wearing so many layers. Amalia hugs her arms around herself and I pull a scarf from my neck and drape it over her head and shoulders. The boy pulls her against him.

"I can walk you home," I offer, not sure how much help I'll be against another band of Recruiters, but at least we'd have more numbers between us.

"We'll be okay." His voice is firm, though I still see the hesitation in his eyes. The lingering terror of what almost happened to both of them.

But what else can I do? And so I nod and turn back toward the Palisades, hoping that somewhere out there a stranger might take pity on my sister and ensure that she's safe and alive.

▼ IV ▼

The incoming storm erases the lingering daylight early, and wind smelling of fires and rot curls down the street, seeping through my clothes. Even though I try to make my way back to the Dark City as quickly as possible, I'm still stuck weaving through the Neverlands when night falls. Feet shuffle down an alley nearby and I shiver, rushing toward the nearest fire escape so I can climb up to the roof to escape the claustrophobia of crumbling walls.

It's safer up high at night, less possibility of the wandering dead sneaking up on you in the darkness.

My sister is near, I think as I hurry toward the Palisades. Abigail's here just across the river at the Sanctuary. I close my eyes and try to feel her. When we were kids I thought we had some sort of connection, a thread that tied one to the other. If she was sad I could sense it—any intense emotion would reverberate through me no matter where I was in the village.

It was like we shared everything: one heart, one soul, one

breath. But standing here in the Neverlands I can't feel her. There's too much despair to pick out that of one girl.

I cross a rickety bridge and it bucks under my feet with the force of someone else's weight. The ropes creak and protest as another person leans against them for support. I pull the knife from my pocket and pick up my pace, skirting an abandoned roof garden and scurrying over another bridge. This is not the place to run into a stranger—no good can possibly come of it.

But the steps keep following me, gaining ground in time with my heartbeats. Keeping my head ducked low, I round the corner of a storage shed and glance back over my shoulder. The person following me is tall and broad, loose clothes draped over his lanky frame and face wrapped in shadows. His hands tense by his sides.

I press my lips together and take a deep breath. To my left shouts ring out from a broken window, people yelling and screaming at each other, and I use the distraction to start running. In my mind I see a crude map of the Neverlands, the pattern of bridges connecting the buildings, the fire escapes leading down to the streets and the places that are too dangerous to venture into.

Just as I'm scampering across a wide low roof another form materializes out of the dark. "Hey, what's the rush?" he asks, starting toward me with a leer on his face.

I feel so stupid for being here at night. For thinking I could be invisible. In the old days I was always safe enough in the Neverlands—it was the place for people like me: outcasts, smugglers, the desperate people who lived on the fringes of the Dark City.

Sure, I'd get propositioned, but my scars have always kept

most people away. Things have been changing too fast and I've refused to notice that it's become so dangerous here, even for me.

The man coming toward me whistles to someone and suddenly there are three men falling into step, one of them blocking the bridge on the other side of the roof, trapping me.

The night suddenly feels like it wants to swallow me whole. I swipe my knife widely, trying to cut a clear space between us.

I curse myself for not having left the island this afternoon. I should have kept going across the bridge and never looked back.

The men circle me, tighter and tighter, closing in. I flick my eyes around the rooftop, trying to figure out a way off. But there's nothing. They have the bridges and fire escape covered. I tighten my grip on the knife and plant my feet, bending my knees for balance.

"This one wants to fight," one of the men says. I can't keep them all in front of me no matter how hard I try. I spin around but there's always someone behind me. Then arms close around my chest, pinning my elbows to my sides.

Everything explodes inside me with the need to survive and escape and the terror-fueled realization that I might not be able to.

I twist my wrist, flicking the knife up hard, aiming for his shoulder. He ducks but still I feel the blade nick his skin. He grunts and releases me, pushes me away from him, hooking his foot around my leg so that I stumble.

Before I can regain my balance he's standing over me and he lashes out, kicking my hip. Pain erupts through me, making me suck in a deep breath as the horrible throbbing stabs reverberate with every beat of my heart. I crumple to my hands and knees, dropping the knife as I splay my hands to break my fall. He grabs my shoulder and flips me onto my back so hard that all the air in the world leaves my body. I buck, trying to inhale, but he places his knee on my chest, crushing me.

This is it, I realize. This is the end of me. This man might choose to kill me or keep me alive but either way, who I am is done. A sadness begins to seep through me, a deep regret for all the time I kept my gaze focused on the ground rather than the sky.

But then an acid burns up the back of my throat, a rage coursing through me. I'm not willing to give up that easily. If I were I'd have died years ago.

Blood trails from the man's shoulder and I focus on that, watch it darken the sleeve covering his arm and spiral over his wrist. I beat at his leg with my fists, trying to find the tender spot between muscles that will make him stop. Trying to breathe. Spots sparkle around me, bright flashes of light that scream in my head.

"Can we sell her?" I hear one of the other men ask. "Is she worth anything?" He walks toward us, hovers over me.

The man with his knee on my chest takes my chin in his hands, turning my face into the light. I bare my teeth. "She's got a good fight in her," he says. "And I'm sure we can find someone who'll want to add to those scars."

I turn my head fast and catch the man's thumb in my mouth, sinking my teeth into his flesh as hard as I can. Tasting blood. He rears back, the pressure on my chest lessening as he yanks his hand free.

I roll away just as he swings and his fist brushes my cheek

before slamming into the roof below us. He's about to lunge for me when we both hear something that doesn't fit in with our desperate surroundings.

Singing. Three figures, a man with a woman under each arm, stumble toward us over one of the bridges that creaks and sways under their combined weight. The man's belting out an off-key tune, his words interrupted by hiccups, and the women move their lips, trying to sing along, but their words are nothing more than slurred mumblings.

I open my mouth to scream for help but one of my attackers clamps his hand over my face before I can get the words out. He pulls a dagger from his side and pushes it against my ribs and I stop struggling. Slowly, he drags me back from the edge of the roof, toward the darker shadows cast by the storage shed.

The threesome lurches across the bridge from the neighboring building, the women almost falling and the man having to pull them up, laughing loudly at their uncoordination as they weave toward us. I'm desperate to catch his eye, hoping that he isn't too drunk to understand what's going on. Isn't too out of sorts to help me. Or to care.

But his gaze only lands briefly on each of the men, not even noticing me standing here enraged and in desperate pain. The women hardly glance up, stringy hair covering their faces. The large man who pinned me down steps toward the group, blood glistening on his fingertips.

The drunk women both stumble again, and the man holds them tight against him, pressing their faces to his shoulders as his voice booms over us. "Don't suppose one of you's looking for a woman tonight?"

The women tug at him and he careens across the roof,

closer to the men blocking me. He laughs, head thrown back and neck exposed to the bare light of the moon. When he's done catching his breath, he leers at the thugs. "I seem to have more than I can handle here," he says with a wink. "I'm only one man, and I've perhaps celebrated a bit too much tonight, if you catch my drift." He laughs again, swaying as the women tug at him.

The thugs glance at each other and I feel the one holding me hesitate, feel him pull his blade away from my ribs ever so slightly, and at just that moment, the drunk man's eyes hit mine so sharp and clear that I have to keep myself from catching my breath in surprise.

He mouths one word: *Run*.

I blink and the man's back to being drunk. He lets his head loll around on his shoulders and stumbles again. "You see, I'm a sharing man. That's my motto. Share the love," he says.

And as the thugs stand there, clearly confused, the man shoves the women toward them. One of the women falls into the arms of the big guy who pinned me down and he catches her instinctively. She looks up at him and opens her mouth and then a clear bright moan slips from her throat as she sinks her teeth into the man's flesh.

V

The large man screams and reels away and the other two men rear back in panic. But it's too late. The Unconsecrated women smell their blood and are after the kill. One of the women snags another man's coat and tugs, dragging him down and falling on top of him.

I lunge toward my knife, wrapping my fingers around the handle just as the drunk man grabs my arm and pulls me to the fire escape at the edge of the roof, shoving me down the steps. The only sounds shattering the night are the men screaming above me, the women moaning and the drunk man telling me to run as my feet pound down the rusty stairs.

An alarm begins to ring out and I hear other people shouting as they pour out of buildings with weapons bared.

I hit the ground and the man grabs my free hand, jerking me out of the alley and down another street. Chaos erupts all around us and the stranger keeps us hidden in the shadows, where the crumbling walls block the moon.

He asks only once if I'm okay to keep running and I nod, cold air searing my lungs as I try to catch my breath.

His hand grasps my own tightly, pressing me back when we approach intersections to make sure the way forward is clear. More alarm bells start to ring, the night growing crowded with shouting.

Ahead of us a group of Recruiters rounds the corner, shoulders set and gazes intent. They're wound tight, weapons flashing, and I try to tug my hand from the stranger's. I need to get away from their advance.

But the man doesn't release his grip, which causes my own internal alarms to spike. He saved me on the roof, he's protecting me even now in the streets, but he's still a stranger.

"This way," he says, pushing me down an alley. I dig my heels into the ground, protesting. I'm not sure I should follow him, not sure I can trust him, but the Recruiters are nearing and the sound of moans echoes down the street and so finally I relent.

It's a narrow alley, almost pitch-black except where the moon glints off shards of glass still stuck in broken windows. "A dead end," I whisper as a wall rises in front of us. Dread starts to leak through my system.

"You trapped me," I growl, spinning toward him and raising my knife, ready to fight.

The Recruiters hover at the mouth of the alley, calling for us. I start to back away from the stranger, looking for any means of escape. More moans sound in the distance.

A streak of flame lights the sky several blocks away, illuminating the alley, and I see the stranger hunched over a pair of metal doors set flush with the ground. He's prying at a chain wrapped around the handles and finally he tugs it free, throwing open the doors.

There's nothing but darkness beyond, the gleam of the first few steps of a staircase leading down and down. I refuse to move.

The stranger takes the steps, his legs disappearing into blackness. I stare at him. The old subway tunnels aren't safe and it would be stupid to follow him. I glance at the buildings crouching over the alley but none has a fire escape. My choices are to follow him or take my chance with the Recruiters, already shouting as they race toward us.

The stranger holds out his hand, urging me into the darkness. One choice is a known danger, the other unknown. I hesitate, trying to figure out a third option, but there is none.

Cursing under my breath for getting into this mess, I start down the stairs, tucking the knife into my pocket so I can press my hands against the wall to guide me. The stranger pulls the doors shut behind us, sealing us together in the emptiness. For a heartbeat we stand there, silent and still. And then the Recruiters beat against the doors, and without waiting I race down the stairs, the stranger not far behind.

A sharp pain radiates along my hip where the man kicked me on the roof and my throat feels raw from running through the cold night. It's pitch-black, and even though I strain my ears, all I can hear is the echo of our pounding steps and the clamoring of my heart.

At the bottom I hit a set of metal bars blocking the entrance to the old station, but I find a gap, wiggle through and keep running until the darkness is too much. Eventually, his steps slow to a stop behind me and I push on a little longer, putting some distance between us as I try to figure out who this person is and how I can stay in control of what's going on.

I try to swallow the fear that flooded my veins as I was being chased, but the dark is closing in on me and it starts to suffocate my mind. I begin imagining other sounds than the scraping of our breaths, squeaks and moans and the grating of flesh over concrete. I can't figure out what's born of fright and what's reality, and I shake my head to clear it.

The blackness is a living thing that whispers in my ear as it strokes my arms and brushes over my hair. It tries to wrap itself around my body, tries to drag me down to the ground and bury me, and I fight against it, waving my arms until I find a wall.

It's not safe down here. Back before the Recruiter Rebellion, the Protectorate tried to keep the subway tunnels clear—tried to patrol them and chase out those who used the underground network for black-market goods between the Neverlands and the Dark City. But even the Protectorate couldn't monitor the entire grid of crisscrossing passages, and it's always been rumored that there are caved-in sections. Sections still filled with plague rats, downed until they sense human flesh.

I shiver, the air damp and colder than outside, the walls slick with half-frozen condensation. There's an almost imperceptible draft flitting across my cheeks. And in the distance water drips into a puddle, every drop creating a distinct ping that echoes over and over. The stranger's breathing slows to normal even though I'm still gulping at the air, little hiccups shuddering through my chest. I hear him step toward me, feel him coming near and I throw up a hand, ready to ward him off.

I still don't understand what happened back on the roof. How he was able to walk so casually with those two Unconsecrated women.

Why he bothered to save me. *Me.*

"Who are you?" I ask, my voice strained and overly loud as it bounces sharply off the tiled walls.

"I'm not going to hurt you," he says. He sounds too close

and I take a few steps away, putting distance between us. It's impossible to see anything down here—the darkness is absolute—but my other senses kick in. I can smell him, the tang of his sweat with an undercurrent of fear and adrenaline. I can hear the sound of each inhalation, the way he holds his breaths and exhales slow and long.

I can feel the heat of him.

"Who are you?" I ask again, trying to sound hard and unafraid.

He shifts, the sound of fabric sliding along the wall. "My name's Catcher," he says, his voice nearer than it was before. I take rapid steps away until I hit another set of bars with my back. I sidestep, stumbling over something that clatters in the blackness, metal against metal.

"Are you okay?" he asks. "Did they hurt you?" There's anger in his voice and he's moving toward me again.

I think about the large man kicking me, swinging at me, kneeling on me. *Yes,* I want to tell him. *Yes, they terrified me. They made me feel small and weak and I'm not used to that.* I despise those feelings.

"No, it feels good being kicked," I say instead, infusing the statement with as much sarcasm as possible. Slowly I slip my hand into my pocket, hoping he can't hear me shift. I slide the knife out. Simply holding the familiar handle bolsters my courage, makes my breathing come easier. I'm finally in more control of this situation.

I hear his sharp inhalations, feel his exhalations across my skin. He's close, too close, and I raise the knife in front of me. "Back off," I tell him.

"It's okay, Annah," he says.

He holds his breath as mine comes out in a loud whoosh. He knows my name. How does this stranger know my name?

And suddenly I realize that my instincts were right and I may be in more danger here than I was aboveground. Here I'm trapped.

I keep the knife in front of me, running my other hand behind me along the bars until I find a gap I can slip through. I swallow, trying to steady my erratic heart.

"I'm not going to hurt you, Annah," he says. "You don't have to be afraid of me."

I laugh at him. "Why should I believe you?" I ask, swiping my arms out in front of me until I find the cool tile of the wall again. I fumble along it, sliding my feet over the ground as silently as possible. It falls away beneath me and I teeter for a moment before I regain my balance. My heart thunders in my ears, making it impossible to hear if he's following me.

Cautiously I feel through the air with my toes until I find a step and then another. As I descend the air grows even thicker, wrapping me in its embrace.

"Annah, I know who you are," he says, his voice closer.

I say nothing, just continue to grope my way down the stairs, putting distance between us so that I can think.

He releases a puff of air in what sounds like frustration. "I know who you are because Elias told me about you."

I freeze, all words trapped in my chest. It's odd to hear a stranger say his name and a little tremor of pain flutters through my chest at it. I clench my teeth, swallow the emotion back down.

It's so quiet I can hear as he shifts in the darkness. "He told me to come find you," he adds.

"How do you know Elias?" My voice trembles, making me sound weak. I bite my bottom lip, needing to regain control over my body, my thoughts.

"You can trust me," he continues, taking another step forward. But he must not have realized that he was standing on the edge of a staircase. He must not have known that the ground drops away, because I hear the surprised gasp as he starts to fall. I hear him scramble to catch himself.

And then he tumbles into me, and our bodies tangle around each other as we careen down the rest of the steps. We land hard on a cracked concrete floor, lights exploding in my head as it smacks against the wall. Catcher falls on top of me and I feel the knife still clutched in my hand slice through his skin. Feel the wetness of blood on my fingers.

"Oh my G-God," I stammer, choking in the darkness. Catcher grunts and slides off me and I drag myself out from underneath him, our legs still snarled.

I drop the knife, feeling the slick of blood coating my skin. "Oh my God," I say again. "Are you okay?" There's so much blood I'm terrified I've killed him and my stomach twists with a frantic dread.

I reach for him, grab him and run my hands over his body, searching for the wound. "Oh my God, I didn't mean to. Are you okay? Catcher, are you okay?"

He doesn't say anything and the realization that I may have murdered someone starts to make me dizzy. I don't know whether I should leave him and go to the surface for help or stay here. I skim my hands up his legs and over his hips, trailing them along his chest that thankfully still rises and falls.

"Catcher," I shout at him, needing him to be okay. His skin's hot where I touch him and he winces as my hands slide over his forearm, blood dripping from his wrist. I fumble in my pack for the quilt, shredding a strip from it and pressing it to the wound.

He grunts and rolls away from me but I keep my hands locked on his arm. "You're hurt," I tell him, relief rushing through me that he can move.

He pushes at me but he's still disoriented from the fall.

"You're hurt," I explain again. "Just hold still and let me stop the bleeding. I don't know how deep the cut is. There's too much blood."

He jerks up and swings at me, throwing me back from him. "Get away from me," he roars. My ears ring with the sound of his voice that still echoes up and down the staircase. I sit frozen, my hands grasping at the darkness.

My breath hitches. I'm confused and don't know how to respond. I reach for him, just slightly, and I hear him back farther away. "Don't touch me," he growls.

His words sting and a low rage begins to build inside me. "I was only trying to help," I lash out at him, any relief at his recovery now gone.

I grope in the darkness for my knife and when my fingers accidentally brush Catcher's leg, he pulls away. "I said: *Don't. Touch. Me.*" He grinds out the words, harsh and commanding.

Every one of my scars feels like it's on fire, a scalding blush burning my body. Angrily, I fold the remnants of the quilt and shove it back into my bag, yanking it closed.

Without a word I stand, dizzy and disoriented, and feel my way forward along the wall until I find another set of stairs. My worthless eyes blur with tears at his sudden and unexpected censure but it doesn't matter in this darkness. I fumble down the steps away from this stranger and his anger and heat. Away from the way he makes me feel.

"Annah," he says, a tinge of apology and wariness in his voice.

I keep walking, my hip aching where I was kicked and my head throbbing from where I hit it during the fall. The pain becomes overwhelming and I stop and take a deep breath and then stagger away from the sound of Catcher.

He shuffles around on the landing, muttering curses, and I hear him start after me. But I push deeper into the darkness. The stairs end and I stumble on solid ground, not knowing where to turn, where to go next. It's disorienting having no idea where the walls are or where the platform ends—where the tracks are. I'm lost in a sea of black nothingness that crawls along my skin. Catcher trails after me, his footsteps never far behind.

"You said Elias sent you. Where is he?" I hate asking but I have to know. I cross my arms, needing something to hold on to. The darkness makes me dizzy. My head throbs, pounding from where I hit it. I shake it, trying to stop the spinning, but it just makes my brain hit against my skull with an agonizing thud.

Catcher comes near but doesn't touch me. I hear his breathing, feel his heat. His earlier words echo in my mind, making me feel stupid and worthless, and I dig my fingers into my arms, fighting against the unwanted emotions.

"He's still with the Recruiters," Catcher says. My heart jolts, a fluttering pain. My chin trembles.

"He's okay?" I can only whisper the words. If I say them out loud, I might scare the hope away.

"He promised he was on his way to the Dark City," Catcher answers, and I squeeze my eyes shut and press my palm to my mouth, trying not to let this stranger hear the way my body shakes with relief.

I don't say anything in response, wondering if I can trust

him. If Elias trusted him. The floor seems to tilt under me and I can't tell if it's because of the sparks in my vision or that the ground beneath us is uneven. My stomach starts to roil, my head throbbing harder.

"I'm sorry, Annah," he finally says, his voice softer. He moves closer to me but keeps some distance. Still, his warmth makes me shiver. My body starts to tip and I throw out an arm to stay steady and balanced.

"It's just . . ." He hesitates. I hear what sounds like him running his hands through his hair. I try to remember what he looks like from the brief glimpses on the roof. The gleam of the moon on his neck when he threw his head back to laugh. He's taller than I am, I know that. I can picture his broad shoulders, long fingers that he cupped around the Unconsecrated women's arms.

Nausea inside me grows too full, the blackness spinning around me faster and faster. My stomach heaves and I swallow, press my palm harder against my mouth, trying to keep from throwing up. The dark is too heavy. I feel as though I'm drowning.

I can smell his blood on my hand, feel it drying and cracking on my skin. It's like a metallic sheen on the back of my tongue. I double over, retching.

"Annah," Catcher shouts, lunging toward me. He wraps his arm over my shoulder and I fall against his strength, my legs losing all sensation, my fingers going numb.

I retch again, my back arching as I heave, my mouth filling with saliva that starts to choke me. I gasp for air, my body feeling like it's floating. Bright spots flare in my vision, almost beautiful, like stars with darker voids swallowing them.

"Annah," Catcher yells again, holding me close. I slip along him, falling to the ground as the world tilts and sways and I don't know what's up and what's down. My head screams pain, my skull too small to hold it all in.

He lays me on my back and runs his hands up my body, over my arms and legs and finally along my neck until he's cupping my cheeks in his palms. His pulse beats against my skin, hot. My eyes flutter, the heat so nice. Something to focus on. Something to curl up against as chills spike through the rest of my body.

"My blood," he says. He's leaning over me, close now. I can feel his breath, taste the desperation in his voice. "Did you touch it?" He holds my cheeks tighter in his hands, his fingers arching under my neck. "Annah, this is important. I need to know."

My eyes roll back in my head but it doesn't matter. They were useless anyway. I much prefer the colors dancing in my mind. A woolen fog seeps in around me, blurring the pain and tempting me to dream.

"Annah!" Catcher calls to me, his voice loud but so far away. It slides along my consciousness, fading into the sound of water rushing and the wind howling. I want to raise my hand to his cheek. I want to tell him it's okay. That it's pretty here in my head and it doesn't hurt. But instead I just let the black wash of waves roll over me and drag me under.

▼ VI ▼

When I wake up there's light and the crackle of a fire. I open my eyes and stare at an intricately carved ceiling of interwoven bricks arching overhead. The flames flick oranges and yellows over them, shadows stretching and snapping. Smoke curls through a small vent, disappearing into the void above.

We're still underground at an old subway station somewhere in the Neverlands. I'm lying on my back on the platform, the quilt from my bag spread over me, its smell familiar and comforting. I let my head fall to the side, wincing as a dull ache throbs along my spine.

The stranger, Catcher, sits on the other side of the fire, staring at nothing. He's so lost in his own thoughts, his own world, that he doesn't realize I'm awake. I let my gaze wander over his features: sharp jaw, blond hair, brown eyes so dark they seem almost fathomless. His knees are bent with his elbows draped over them, a strip of cloth wrapped around his lower arm from where I cut him when we fell. Bruises from our tumble down the stairs already bloom under his skin.

There's something about him that seems familiar, and I search my mind trying to figure out why. Generally I don't bother with other people, don't care what they look like or who they are. Everyone around me's always a stranger.

It's safer that way.

And then I realize what it is. "You're the one from the bridge." Belatedly it hits me what that means: He's infected. I scour his face with my gaze, trying to detect how far along he is—how close to turning. But his skin's flushed with health, his eyes clear. He looks nothing like the woman on the roof, only heartbeats away from death.

His eyes flick to meet mine. "How're you feeling?" he asks.

I push myself up until I'm sitting, the quilt falling from my shoulders and pooling in my lap. I shiver, feeling dizzy and sick, but I shove the sensations away. "You're the one who climbed the wall and fell in the river. They thought you were dead. You should've drowned."

He drops his head a little, rubs the back of his neck with his hand. It's such a familiar gesture that I stop breathing for a second. It's something Elias always used to do. To buy time, to think, to figure out a way to swim through the awkward moments.

"I didn't," he finally says, and I almost want to laugh at his non-answer. But before I can react, before I can say anything or ask him to explain, he's moving around the fire until he's crouched in front of me.

He reaches out a hand, places it along my cheeks, rests his wrist on my forehead. I feel each scar on my face under his probing fingers. I yank my head away, setting off a sharp throb down my neck and a pounding against my skull.

"Your skin's hot," he says. His eyes are wary, his lips pressed thin.

"I've been lying in front of a fire," I tell him testily, moving away and pulling the quilt up like a barrier between us. "Of course I'm hot. That happens with flames."

He glances over my shoulder into the darkness with such intensity that I almost turn around. And then his chin drops to his chest. "Does it feel like . . ." He's looking up at me as he struggles for the words. "Does it feel like fire in your veins?"

His question doesn't make any sense to me. "What are you talking about?"

He focuses on his hands. "Inside," he says. "Does it feel like you're dying? Being eaten by heat?"

I push myself to my feet and stumble away from him. "What kind of question is that?" A wave of nausea hits me again and I press a hand to my stomach, the other to my head, trying to stop the world from spinning. I blink rapidly, Catcher and the light blurring and then sharpening.

"Annah—"

"No," I cut him off. "I don't know you and you don't know me. Why are you asking me these things? What's going on?"

He stands up, arms by his sides as if he's trying to prove he's not dangerous. I don't fall for it. I scour the station, trying to figure out where I could run to get away. My stomach heaves again, throwing me off balance, and I stagger.

He steps forward to help me but I hold up my arms, warding him off. "Stay away from me," I growl.

Something hardens in his eyes. "I need to know if you're infected," he says, his tone blunt.

It takes a moment for my mind to process the meaning of his words but they don't make sense. "Why would I be infected?"

"Because you're clearly sick—you can barely stay on your feet. There's something wrong with you and you touched my blood when we fell," he says matter-of-factly.

I frown. I've seen plenty of infected people—like the woman from last night. I know what it looks like and I know how it's caused and there's no way that's what's wrong with me. I haven't been bitten; therefore, I can't be infected. "Why would your blood have anything to do with it?"

He stares at me for a long time, his jaw clenching as if he's frustrated at my lack of understanding. "Because *I'm* infected," he finally says.

I nod slowly and cross my arms over my chest. "I know. I saw what happened on the bridge. But I'm fairly certain you can't pass the infection until you're dead, and as far as I can tell, that hasn't happened to you yet."

I realize suddenly how flippant I sound. While I've *known* he's infected, I haven't really thought about what that means to him. That he's dying. The man standing in front of me, who looks strong and healthy and handsome, will be dead in a matter of days. I'm used to people becoming infected and dying and Returning—it happens all the time in the Neverlands and it's contained pretty quickly. It's something we're used to seeing—something *I'm* used to seeing. Just not to people I know, since I make a point to know no one.

What a waste. And then a small voice whispers in my head that I'm trapped underground with an Infected. That this is serious—I don't know exactly where I am, where he carried me when I blacked out. I don't know where my knife is.

Catcher's infected and I don't really know how much time he has, which makes him dangerous, and once he dies he'll come for me. Like with the woman last night, I might be the one to have to kill him. He could even turn Breaker if there aren't other plague rats around that he can sense, and I'm not sure my little knife would be a match for that kind of speed and ferocity.

Anxiety begins to burn under my skin and I start feeling restless—my legs itching to run even though the rest of my body feels weak. "I'm not infected," I assure him.

Something shifts in his eyes and he turns away but not before I see sadness flooding his face. "We can't be sure yet. It could still be inside you," he says.

I walk past him back to the fire and kneel next to my quilt and bag. I feel a little woozy and press my hand to the ground to steady myself. My fingers shake as I pretend to fold the quilt while I look for my knife.

I hear a clatter behind me and then metal sliding over concrete as Catcher drops my knife and kicks it over to me. I stare at it before glancing up at him.

"You're not going to need it," he says, still keeping his distance. "At least not against me. I'm not going to turn—I'm immune."

I wrap my fingers around the handle, flicking my thumb over the blade. Fire shines along the metal without a trace of his blood. He cleaned it after I passed out. "You're immune to being stabbed?" I ask.

A small smile flickers over his lips. It's lopsided, one side of his mouth ticking higher than the other. It's gone as fast as it came and it leaves me slightly off balance. He looked so different, so much younger and relaxed.

He looked almost normal.

"I'm immune to the infection," he clarifies. "Or rather, the infection doesn't kill me. I've been this way for months." He spreads his hands out to either side as if to display how healthy he is.

I narrow my eyes at him. What he's saying doesn't make sense. "I've never heard about there being any immunity," I tell him.

He shrugs. "It's not that complicated—I got bitten late in the summer," he says, almost nonchalantly. "It's winter and I'm not dead yet. It never killed me. I'm infected but I'm immune, which means I'm basically like a living Mudo—you saw that yourself last night on the roof."

His tone seems so casual, but there's an undercurrent running beneath his words, an emotion I can't pinpoint. It could be rage or desolation, but something tugs on each syllable, making his words heavy. He even holds his body rigid as he waits for my response.

It's hard to believe that what he's saying could be true, but at the same time he's right: I saw him on the roof with the two Unconsecrated women. They didn't seem to care about him at all and there are no visible bites on him from them.

I stare at my hand clutching the knife. Catcher might be immune—he could be telling the truth—but he's still a stranger, and strangers are dangerous.

"Not many people use the word *Mudo* to describe them." It marks him as an outsider the same way everyone knew Elias and I weren't originally from the Dark City because we called them Unconsecrated instead of plague rats or one of the other terms.

"I'm from down the coast," he says. "A place called Vista on the edge of the Forest."

My skin breaks out in goose bumps at the mention of the

Forest. It makes me think of Elias and then of my sister, Abigail. She helped Catcher escape on the bridge. Which means he knows her. Slowly, I raise my head and meet his eyes, trying to figure out how to ask the right questions.

"I just . . ." He pauses and licks his lips as if he's nervous. "I just need to know that you're okay. You had my blood all over you and I don't know . . ." He lets the words trail off. "I don't know if I can pass the infection. If being immune means that the infection inside me is somehow different and I could still infect others. I've been careful not to find out." He holds himself steady, trying not to show the uncertainty and fear that threads through his voice.

I can remember the taste in my mouth at the bottom of the stairs: metallic and earthy. I remember the feel of my blade over his arm, the slickness of his blood on my hands. I remember pressing those fingers to my lips to stop from heaving.

There's no trace of blood on them now, and I realize he must have washed me after I passed out. A strange sensation sparks in my stomach at the thought of it, at his tenderness and consideration.

But then my mind clears. I was asleep and he had his hands on me. I rub my free hand up my arm, not sure what to think about this information.

"I'd know if I was infected," I say firmly enough to convince both of us. Though there's a tiny bit of dread in my mind now—worry that what he's saying might be true and even now the infection is taking hold.

I've never really allowed myself to think about what it would feel like. I've imagined being dead, being one of the Unconsecrated. But I've always avoided thinking about the time in between—the knowing part of it. I wonder what that must have been like for him: the feel of the dead teeth, the realization that everything was over.

Catcher's still staring at me, almost as if he cares about me, which doesn't make sense and makes me uncomfortable. He doesn't know me and I don't know him. I shouldn't feel safe with him. I shouldn't still be here. I should kick his knee out and run for the surface, but I don't do any of these things because I still haven't figured out who this guy is and how he knows both my sister and Elias.

"I'm fine," I tell him, snapping the words.

Relief washes over his face and he turns away, trying to hide it. Trying not to show me how afraid he was. "Are you sure?" he asks, his voice weak.

I nod. "I hit my head when we fell. I'm dizzy and nauseated. But I'm not infected."

He squeezes his eyes shut, pressing his fingers to them. I feel like I'm watching something I shouldn't, seeing a part of him that's too personal for a stranger like me.

I glance away and clear my throat, needing to break the silence and desperately wanting to figure out what's going on. "Why were you on the roof last night?"

He raises his hand to his neck again and I almost scream at him to stop it, stop reminding me of Elias. I even take a deep breath, ready to say something when he runs his fingers over his head, through his hair.

"You looked like you needed help," he says. I scowl. It's another non-answer, and I'm starting to realize he's good at those.

"How did you know who I was? Or do you make it a habit to rescue any damsel in distress when you come to a new city and almost drown?" My words echo slightly, tracing up and over the soaring arches above us.

I want him to admit he knows my sister. That he sees past my scars to the similarities between us.

He walks over to the little fire, keeping distance between us when he sees me tense my hand around the knife. It's clear I still don't trust him.

He crouches and I watch him through the flames. "I saw you when I was running from the Recruiters and I followed you."

Chills ease over my skin again and my breath comes a little shallow. I'm glad there's a fire between us. "Why?"

He hesitates and I can tell he's weighing what to say next and I wonder if it's all going to be carefully crafted lies. "Because I promised Elias I'd find you," he finally says.

This is all too strange and convoluted. It doesn't make sense. "You mentioned Elias earlier." I pause, hoping he'll fill the silence.

When he doesn't I press, "Where is he? How do you know him?" The words come so fast I trip over them, frustrated at not knowing what to ask. "I don't understand. How did you even know it was me you were looking for?"

He stares at me then, his gaze even more intense than the flames. His eyes trace over my face, down my body. There's something in his look I don't understand, something painful and awkward. I see him follow the lines of my scars.

I'm used to it, so used to the gaping stares, that I don't notice them sometimes. It's just a part of my life. But this man, here in this moment, makes me remember every line on my body. Makes me feel every scar as if it's a fresh wound, festering and raw.

I wanted him to recognize me because I look like my sister but I realize that's not how he knew who I was. "Oh." I mouth the word, unable to put sound behind it. I cross my arms. "The scars." The walls I use to protect myself inside falter and I close my eyes and try to build them back up higher than before. But some of the pain and ugliness seep through.

Sometimes—rarely—I'm able to forget what I look like and it's embarrassing to realize that this is how Elias would describe me. Of course it is—"Look for the angry girl with the scars down the left side of her body" is easier than "Look for the girl with the dirty-blond hair who never lifts her eyes from the ground."

I rub my chin against my shoulder as if I could scratch the vulnerability from the moment. I then shift until the tip of my knife scrapes against the ground—a reminder to both of us that I still have a weapon. I still have some control.

Catcher looks like he wants to say something but he presses his lips together until they burn white. I clear the awkward silence between us by asking the obvious question. "So why'd my brother tell you to find me?"

He looks down at me. "I know he's not your brother, Annah."

▼ VII ▼

I jump to my feet and start walking toward the darkness swallowing the tunnel at the end of the subway platform. No one's supposed to know Elias isn't my brother. No one *could* know that unless they were from our village or one of us told them. And we vowed to never tell. It's just easier to let people believe what they want and it makes his protection of me more secure.

I clear my throat but the words feel trapped. How does he know he's not my brother? What has Elias told him about me? What else does he know? What was he doing with my sister? Where's Elias and why hasn't he come back? I feel like Catcher's playing some sort of game with me and I have no idea what the rules are.

Frustration makes my shoulders tense and my head throb. I stop at the edge of the platform, staring out into the dark that eats the light from the fire behind me. It's colder away from the flames, the last trace of warmth leaching quickly from my clothes as the chill attacks my skin through seams and holes. I pull my coat tighter around me. It's easier to talk when I don't have to see Catcher's face. When I don't have to keep him from seeing the uncertainty in mine.

I don't like others knowing my business, especially strangers—I like to be the one who controls what people get to know about me and when.

My stomach growls. "We should go," I tell him. "Start figuring out a way to find my sister." It's well known the underground tunnels aren't safe. When the Unconsecrated don't sense a living human nearby they collapse, almost like an insect going dormant, waiting for food and the ability to infect. Everyone knows there are pockets of plague rats down here waiting for someone to stumble upon them.

For as long as I've lived in the City I've heard the rumors of tunnels so deep that the dead lie asleep, waiting for the barest scent of living flesh to wake them and cause a surge to the surface.

Every few years there's a fresh outbreak in the Dark City, half the time rumored to have started in the Neverlands and the other half begun underground. I'm not one to test the theories. It might not be too safe up on the streets but at least there's light and air—not walls curling around you like a coffin.

"These the same stairs we came down?" I ask, moving toward them. Catcher nods but doesn't follow. I turn; he can only see my profile of clean smooth skin. I think about him on the bridge with Abigail—the way she saved his life.

"Do I look like her?" I ask, the words slipping out before I can stop them. My fingers clench around the ragged hem of my coat. I can't resist knowing. "Like my sister," I add, as if he didn't understand.

Catcher approaches me, each step a distinct echo in the dim chamber. The firelight jumps over his skin, shadows flickering around his eyes. He stops just out of reach. For a moment he stands there and breathes as the muscles along my neck tighten.

I blush. What do I care if I look like her or not? "Never mind," I mumble, turning back to the darkness and the stairs.

"Yes and no," he says.

"Let me guess," I snort, spinning toward him. I raise one finger and press it to the smooth side of my face. "Yes." I raise my eyebrows as I move my finger over to the scars. "And no."

"That's not what I meant," he says, inching in closer.

I back away. There's still too much I don't know in order for me to trust him. To allow him this near.

"You're just different people," he says, trying to explain. "Different personalities. It's reflected in what you look like."

"Whatever," I say, waving my hand in the air as I start up the stairs. It was a stupid question for me to ask.

His footfalls follow me in the darkness and I feel calmer and more in control now that I'm invisible. Our breaths fall into a rhythm with each step, our hands gliding up the rusty railing bolted into the wall. Soon the movement chases away the chill of the tunnels, a clammy sweat trickling down my back.

"I think it's time you told me what's going on," I say as we near the top.

He hesitates, breaking stride. "What do you want to know?"

I stop and he stumbles against me, his hands sliding along my arms to steady himself. His touch is warm, almost to the point of hot. He jerks back and mumbles an apology. I ignore it.

There's so little light that I can barely even see his outline. He's become nothing more than the sound of his breathing, the rustle of his clothes and slide of each footstep. It feels almost intimate, being so aware of the noises he makes, and I become uncomfortable.

I pull farther away from him, the heat radiating from his body fading with distance and the cold taking its place. "I want to know why you act like you know me. I want to know why my bro— Why Elias told you to find me. I want to know what's going on with my sister and what you're doing here. With me."

He shuffles, shifts his weight from foot to foot and then sighs. "I know Elias because he came to kill me when I was infected. And when I didn't turn, he was the one who told me about the immunity."

I start to say something but he cuts me off. "And I know your sister because I grew up with her."

This is too much too fast and I sit, my feet propped on the step below. His fingers brush against my hair and cheek and then along my shoulders as he moves his hands through the air to find me. He sits next to me, the heat of him wavering around us. I touch my hand to the stairs, needing to ground myself, to stop the spinning.

"You grew up with Abigail?" My voice is nothing but a puff of air in the dark. "But . . . you're not from the village." I try to think about what he would've looked like when we were younger. When Elias and Abigail and I played tag in the fields. I don't remember anyone our age named Catcher and it makes me feel uneasy. How could he know my sister otherwise?

Catcher shifts. "I'm from Vista, remember? Not your village." His voice reverberates from the wall as if he's looking away from me, staring into the void below. "Her name's Gabrielle now—Gabry."

The floor's grimy under my fingertips, thick with dirt and dust. The air down here tastes stale and old like we've disturbed the past. I squeeze my eyes shut, trying to put all these pieces together. "I don't understand."

"Her mother found her in the Forest when she was young. She couldn't speak—couldn't remember her name. So her mother called her Gabrielle and raised her in Vista, on the ocean down the coast. Gabry didn't even know anything about it—didn't remember the Forest at all until her mother told her a few months ago."

I try not to think about leaving Abigail behind when she skinned her knee, but hearing about the Forest, about her being lost, all I can see is the blood trailing down her leg, the way she begged Elias and me not to leave her behind. She was so scared and I just left her there. Alone in the middle of the path.

I've spent my entire life with that moment crowding my nightmares. Remembering the sound of the Unconsecrated thrashing at the fence for her. The smell of Elias's fear and determination.

It's haunted me. Tormented me. It's who I am: the girl who left her sister behind in the Forest of Hands and Teeth.

I never knew if she died because of me. Or if she found a way back. Day after day and week after week, I've agonized over her fate—I even welcomed the slash of barbed wire over my skin when the accident happened because it made me not look like her anymore.

I clutch the back of my head with my hands, fingers digging into my scalp as I bury my face in my knees. It never occurred to me that while all I could do was remember, my sister could forget it all. That she could have found a way out of the Forest like Elias and I did, but end up with a life so different from mine.

She grew up next to the ocean safe and loved by a mother. That was why she could keep her head raised high when she crossed the bridge. That was why she didn't hunch when I saw her, why she didn't recognize me.

I could see in her everything that I ever wanted to be. I saw what I'd lost, what I could never have. She didn't recognize herself in me because she could never imagine what it would be like to have lived my kind of life.

Knowing this makes me feel empty. This other half that's walked like a shadow through my life never knew I existed.

"Does she know I'm here too? Does she remember anything about me?" I hold my breath, waiting for the answer.

My lungs start to ache.

"She knows you're here," he finally says. "Elias told her," he adds softly. "But she doesn't remember anything from when you were kids together."

My own sister doesn't remember me. I've spent my life trying to atone for what I did to her and she doesn't even remember.

"I have to find her," I whisper. "They said she might be at the Sanctuary. I have to find a way to get there."

Catcher shifts next to me, his hand bumping against my knee and then sliding up my arm to tug at me until I let him wrap his fingers around mine. "*We* have to find her," he says gently.

I'm startled by the quiet strength of his grip. By the resolve in his voice. It terrifies me because it makes me want to lean on him and let him prop me up. Let someone else be strong and in charge.

For a moment, I indulge in this thought; indulge in the feel of his hand holding mine. Then I jerk away and stand up.

I've let myself believe in someone else's strength before. When Elias left, I promised I'd never put myself in that position again.

"Let's go, then," I say, racing up the stairs fast enough that he can only follow one step behind.

▼ ▼ ▼

It's daytime aboveground, and when I throw open the doors and we reel out of the darkness, the bright glare of snow sears my eyes. Catcher stumbles after me, both of us holding arms in front of our faces against the blinding light of the morning. A stinging cold wind roars down the alley between two buildings behind us, instantly penetrating my layers of clothes and causing me to shiver violently.

Pulling my coat tight and wrapping my arms over my chest, I let the wind shove me toward the mouth of the alley. The tips of my hair whip around my face and force me to close my eyes as the howling fills my ears, blocking out any other sound: the crunch of ice underfoot, Catcher's footsteps behind me. Every movement is an effort. The storm rushes at us until we finally stumble around a corner and into a crowded intersection of one of the main Neverlands roads.

Someone in the crowd blunders against my shoulder, knocking me off balance, and I stumble sideways. Hands grab at me, and at first I think it's Catcher trying to help me regain my footing, but the tugging becomes insistent like an aggressive beggar, causing my feet to slide over a patch of ice coating the ground.

I jerk my arm free, my elbow connecting with the beggar as I fall. The impact with the ground makes me bite my cheek, filling my mouth with the taste of hot metal. "Get off me!" I shout with a gurgle just as the beggar lands on me, pushing me back until my head smacks the ground.

There's a sharp pinch along my arm and I struggle to draw a breath, fighting the lump of sour-smelling clothes twisting on top of me.

"Stop!" I shout, feeling blood from my shredded cheek leak from my lips and down along my jaw. The person on top of me becomes frantic, elbows punching my chest as he lifts his head from my arm and lunges toward my face, desperate for something he must think I have.

My mind's a moment behind. As his teeth veer toward my cheek I'm belatedly aware of two things. First, the man is Unconsecrated, and second, he just bit me. That's what the pinch on my arm was.

Horror floods me. It incites a panic I've never felt before. I lash out, retribution in the face of death, punching at his face and kicking at his torso.

Even so, he's heavier than I am, and gravity pulls him closer. I twist my head away, trying to scramble from underneath him. "Catcher!" I scream, desperate for help. The frozen ground numbs the back of my arms. It's impossible to find traction. I can't dig my feet in, I can't buck the plague rat off.

I push my fingers into his eyes, trying to keep his lips from my flesh, but nothing stops him.

My arm throbs where he's already attacked me and useless grunts slip from my mouth. I'm choking. This isn't the way I'm supposed to die. I've fought too hard. I've resisted the Unconsecrated for too long for this to happen now.

I growl and sob as his mouth brushes my ear, tongue trying to fold me between his teeth. To bite. To infect. That is all that matters to this monster. I'm nothing to him but the absence of infection—something clean that must be sullied.

His teeth scrape my skin, once more and then again.

▾ VIII ▾

I twine my fingers through the Unconsecrated man's hair,
trying to pull him away, but it's too short and I can't get a
decent grip. Just then, his head shudders in my grasp and he
collapses on top of me, immobile.

For one moment I wonder if this absence of feeling is
what it means to be Unconsecrated. If this is death. And then
the body on top of me shudders again and I scramble from
underneath him, pushing myself as far away as possible across
the ice-slicked ground.

My back hits a wall and I shove myself standing. The
storming wind pauses and its absence is filled with moaning
everywhere at once, ripped from mouths and carried away as
the howling wind rises again. Bodies and bodies and bodies
stumble down the street, a trickle around me, a river several
blocks away and a flood in the distance. They push against
rotted doors and crumbling walls that keep the living se-
questered, and start to pile beneath windows, fingers reaching
up and up.

At first it doesn't make sense—I can't comprehend it. I've seen outbreaks before but nothing like this. There are too many of them.

To the north a building roars with fire while people run over trembling bridges to safety. The air's thick with panic— the sound of it all whipped together by the rising storm so that the only noise is a screeching wind.

The true tidal wave of dead is blocks away, but rivulets of Unconsecrated have already pooled through the streets around us, stumbling and straining for the living.

A line of crumbled bodies arcs around me like a barrier. I stare back at the man who attacked me and there's a wooden bolt jutting from his head. Another flies through the air, catching an Unconsecrated child midstride. It collapses only a few feet away, and I follow the trajectory of the arrow up to a narrow window high in a building several doors away, where I can just see the tip of a crossbow.

I raise my hand in thanks just as Catcher emerges from the growing tide of Unconsecrated, reaching for my hand. A bolt slams into his upper arm, throwing him against me. I open my mouth in horror as blood splatters from the wound, frosting the snowy ground red.

His weight pushes me against the wall with a thud and Unconsecrated ooze around us. There's a sound like the scraping of metal and I realize Catcher has dropped a machete at my feet. Blood runs across his elbow and over his empty fingers from the bolt still lodged in his upper arm.

"Let me help—" I try to tell him, reaching to pull it free, but he shakes his head and twists the wound away from me.

"The machete," he pants, and I shift my weight underneath him, reaching for the large blade. Catcher's eyes are bleary, wide with pain and shock. He blinks rapidly, trying to focus on me. "The tunnels." His teeth are clenched and the words come out clipped and harsh. "We can get back to the tunnels."

He breaks off the length of bolt, tossing the spiked chunk of wood to the ground before lurching toward the Unconsecrated lumbering our way. I press against the wall and lash out with my machete as he shoves the dead back, grunting from the impacts that jar the remnants of the bolt still protruding from his arm.

There are so many of them creeping around us, all I can do is swing the machete indiscriminately. I scream, fight raging through me, as I take off fingers, slice through flesh, kick at knees. Anything to keep them away from me. We make it back into the alley just as the current threatens to overwhelm us and we find that it's still clear, no living around to draw the dead in. Catcher pushes me toward the tunnel entrance and I sprint, feet skidding through frozen slush as the wind tries to throw me back.

I fight the buffeting air, clutching building walls for traction until I get to the dead end. I throw open the doors leading down into darkness and hesitate. "Come on, Catcher!" I shout at him. I can barely see the top of his head in the throng of Unconsecrated pooling around the intersection of the alley and the main road. At first I think the Unconsecrated have him. That they won't let him go.

"Catcher!" I yell. The Unconsecrated are already stumbling toward me, following the trail of blood from my lips. I swipe my hand over my mouth, smearing red on my palm. My heart screams in my body, my muscles straining with the instinct to defend myself.

Slowly pushing against the storm, the dead advance as if

they've never known urgency. And they don't need to. They'll just keep coming. They'll always press forward. I can kill the first few, but it won't take long for them to overwhelm.

They come at me with teeth bared, some with bloody lips where they've already found a living person to bite and infect. Catcher threads his way through as if he's one of them.

My heart lurches at the sight of it: him there among them. Them not even noticing. It's jarring: He's alive, they should be scrambling for him, and yet they don't. He walks through the throng as though he's used to being surrounded by their moaning death, and it makes me realize that this is his reality.

He's the line between the living and the dead. He is both and neither at once. He belongs nowhere, and now I understand his hesitation when we were down in the tunnels. I recognize the way he holds walls between him and other people because I'm the same way.

"Faster!" I shout at him, afraid that he'll be too late. He starts to jog, arms up against the biting wind, fighting to cover the distance between us and leaving the dead to stumble after.

My hand's curled tight around the sharp edge of the metal door guarding the stairway. One side of it's scarred and dented while the other's still smooth and shiny. As I turn to the darkness I catch my reflection: wide eyes, blood smeared around my mouth. I grip the machete tighter, instinct screaming that it's an Unconsecrated staring back at me.

I can't catch my breath, startled terror zinging through my body. What if I *am* one of them? I relive the pinch of the Unconsecrated biting my arm, the feel of the edge of his teeth against my ear.

Catcher finally makes it to the entrance, grasping his arm where the shaft of the bolt still protrudes. Blood trickles over his fingers as he gently nudges me to the stairs and closes the doors, throwing us back into the pitch-black. Cutting the vision of myself as one of the dead away.

"Annah," he says. I feel his hand wave through the air, seeking me, but I ignore it. Instead I race down the steps, gripping the railing to find my way back to the fire and the light.

Catcher calls after me but I don't slow. My heart's roaring in my chest, my thighs aching, but none of that matters.

Back on the platform the fire's nothing but embers, and I blow shaky breaths over them until one of the half-burned bits of wood catches and sparks.

My fingers shake as I fumble with the buttons of my coat, ripping it from my body and then yanking off my sweater and the shirt and tank beneath until there's nothing covering my torso.

"Annah, what's going on?" Catcher shouts as he jumps the last few stairs and runs into the weak ring of light.

As soon as he sees my nakedness he jerks away from me, throwing his good arm up over his eyes and twisting his head away from my pale bare skin. "Annah?" Concern threads through his voice. It's clear he thinks I've gone insane.

Frantically I run my hands over my arms, prodding and poking at the flesh as I twist to get a better look. I don't feel any breaks in the skin but I can't be sure. I run to Catcher and thrust my arm in front of him.

"Is there a bite?" I demand, breathless.

"Annah, what's—"

"Is. There. A. Bite!"

His eyes go wide and then he takes my arm lightly in his scalding fingers, running them along the contours of my muscles as goose bumps spring to life in the path of his touch.

"No, not that I see," he says gently.

"What about here?" I ask, tilting my head so that my ear and neck are under his gaze. I feel each exhale of his breath as his touch flutters up along my hairline, tracing the curve of my ear, slowly. Methodically.

"No." It's a whisper, his lips almost—but not quite—pressed against the base of my skull the way I thrust myself at him.

I stand there a moment longer, the heat of him pulsing around me in the dim cold underground air. I turn, just slightly. Inch closer to the warmth. When he inhales, his chest brushes against my shoulder, his coat scratching my bare chest.

"You weren't bitten," he adds softly, breaking the silent tension between us.

Relief soars through me. I collapse, wrapping my arms around myself and rocking, my fingers clutching my naked shoulders. Tears course down my cheeks and drip, rosy red after trailing through blood, from my jaw to the cracked concrete of the platform.

I was dead. I was so sure of it. I'd felt the sear of Unconsecrated teeth. How is it possible I'm not infected?

I'm sobbing and shaking from the release of the terror that froze me deep within. Catcher kneels, pulling me to him, and I bury my face in his chest and let the sweet solace of life course through me.

"I'm not infected," I say, still incredulous.

He runs his fingers over my hair, cupping my head so easily in his hand.

"I don't understand." I try to gather my emotions back inside myself, afraid of having let them run free for so long. I pull away from him and swipe at my eyes and that's when I remember the bolt lodged in his arm.

Dried blood pools at the base of it, crusted black in the firelight. "Oh, Catcher," I say, reaching a hand toward him, horrified at the sight of the angry wound.

He jerks his fingers around my wrist, stopping me. "Don't touch it," he says, his eyes turning hard and pleading and full of pain. My mouth opens to protest. "Please," he adds before I can speak. Then he gently nudges me back into the darkness.

I try to pull my arm free of his grip, to move closer, but he's too strong. I'm intensely aware of the fact that I'm not wearing any clothes from the waist up—all the scars and twisted skin visible—but his injury is more important. "You're hurt."

He still doesn't let go and seems oblivious to my nakedness as he moves me away from his bleeding arm. "You know this feeling of being alive—those tears you just cried because you're not infected?" When I don't answer his grip tightens until I nod my head.

"That's the feeling you need to hang on to," he says adamantly. "Because that's not a feeling *I* can guarantee you."

I don't like that I'm unable to escape from his grasp. I don't like how vulnerable it makes me feel. "If you were dangerous you'd have killed me by now," I tell him, still struggling. I almost believe what I'm saying.

His eyes narrow. "It's not an *if*, Annah, it's a reality. I *am* dangerous. I'm infected. This blood"—he holds his injured arm away from me—"it's infected."

We've already had this argument and so I just glare at him and say, "Fine. Keep the stupid bolt in your arm for all I care."

He actually smiles, which softens the moment between us.

He holds me a minute longer and as if by instinct, his eyes sweep along my neck and across my collarbone, careening down my exposed body. It lasts only an instant, almost as if it were involuntary, and I tug my arm free from his relaxed grip, immediately missing the heat of his skin against mine.

I turn sharply and start pulling on my clothes, waiting for the sound of him to release the breath he'd held when he glanced at me.

"I'm sorry," he says softly. I close my eyes. Is he apologizing for yelling at me or gaping at me? For my nakedness or the ugliness of my body?

I deflect his attention away. "You'd better figure out what to do about that thing in your arm," I tell him. "You don't want an infection." Before he can say anything I hold up a hand to stop him. "I don't mean Unconsecrated infection, I mean a blood infection. That arrow looks pretty dirty, and who knows what kind of bugs it got into your system."

I finish buttoning my coat and turn to face him. He's staring toward the dark mouth of the tunnel at the far end of the platform. His eyes glisten, but before I can ask him why, he shakes his head, grabs the bolt and jerks it free. His choked whimper echoes in my ears and I flinch at the pain. Then he groans and falls to his knees, the bloody arrow slipping from his fingers and landing on the broken concrete. I rip some cloth from my quilt and place my fingers over his shoulder, letting him lean on me as he ties the strip around the wound. This time I'm the strong one.

IX

"What happened up there?" I ask after he's tied off the bandage and pulled away from me. "I've never seen that many Unconsecrated before." I walk closer to the stairs, wondering how long it will be before the pressure of so many dead against the metal doors at the top causes them to buckle and collapse.

"The horde." He sounds indifferent as he sits and rubs a chunk of ice between his fingers to wash away the blood.

I move back to the tiny fire, huddling in close to chase away the damp cold, hoping the light will erase the terrors floating at the edge of my thoughts. "Horde?"

Water drips from the bony knob of his wrist, leaving a trail of pink across his skin. "The horde. The one from the valley in the Forest." He's speaking as if what he's saying makes sense but it doesn't.

"They didn't warn you?" he asks, incredulous.

"Who warn us?" The air down here is frigid and each exhalation puffs like a cloud from my lips.

He pushes to his feet and starts to pace. "Millions of Mudo headed for the City. Already here apparently. How did the Recruiters not prepare you for this? They had to have known." His eyes are wide, the ice forgotten in a puddle.

"I don't understand what you're saying," I tell him, my chest fluttering with fear.

"Annah, those dead up there—that's just the beginning. There are millions, more than you can even imagine could exist. That's why Gabry and I were in such a hurry to get to the City and find you—so we could get you out before the horde hit."

"That doesn't even make sense." I'm shaking my head. "I was just at the bridge to the mainland—*we* were just there and there weren't Unconsecrated. How did they get across the river? How did they get over the walls? It's only been a few hours."

He crouches in front of me, rests two fingers on my knee, two bright points of heat seeping through the layers of my clothes. "You were knocked out for a long time, Annah—you slept even longer. It's been more than a day since the bridge."

I push away from him, an explosion of movement, and stalk to the edge of the platform. "Okay, fine. So it's been a day. That's still not enough time for what we saw up there. Those streets were almost overrun. That can't happen that fast. It just can't."

He doesn't say anything to contradict me. He doesn't have to. His expression says everything and I spin to the darkness of the tunnels, reeling. There were so many dead. It was like walking into a swarm of gnats on a hot summer evening. They were everywhere.

Slowly Catcher walks over to me. "There are enough of them that they can almost fill the river—clamoring over each other before there's time for them to sink. They've probably already overrun the bridges. They'll overrun *anything* in their path." His voice is gentle but his words are not. "They pile on top of each other against the walls—they'll push any barriers down. A horde that big . . . it's like pouring the ocean into a jar except the island is the jar. There's nothing that can hold it back. It's impossible to comprehend unless you've seen it."

But what I don't tell him is that I *have* seen a horde. I press my palms into my eyes until it hurts, trying to erase the memory, trying to push it down but still it comes.

I was a kid, lost in the Forest with Elias after leaving my sister. I remember how much my feet hurt, how sore my legs were and how proud Elias kept saying he was of me because I was still walking, because I was trying so hard to be a big girl. I remember him holding my hand, helping me up the mountain path, and the fences on either side, always the fences that went on and on and on.

I remember when we got to the top. How Elias froze, holding me behind him. It made me angry. He'd told me I was a big girl so I peeked my head around him until I saw what he did. It was beautiful, mountains stretching out in front of us for as far as you could see.

But that wasn't why Elias stopped. He was looking down. Into the valley. I followed his gaze and saw the path winding into the trees, the hint of a road wrapping around the mountain partway down. He tried to turn me away before I saw the rest. He even grabbed me, pushing his hand over my eyes, but it was too late. I'd seen them in the valley. The people strewn like wilted flowers. There were so many that a line from a song we'd been taught came to mind, about the lilies in the valley.

"How are there so many?" I'd asked Elias. I'd never known

that such a massive number of people could have ever existed in the world.

His face was white, his fingers cold and shaking. "We have to turn around, Annah. We have to go back. Now." His voice was low.

I swallow as I remember that feeling, that shock as I realized the scope of the Unconsecrated. Until that moment I'd never comprehended that many in one place. I'd seen them against the fences, pawing against the metal links trying to get into the village. They'd followed us along the path, always moaning and reaching.

But never had there been so many. There were more bodies in that valley than stars in the night sky.

Elias had grabbed my hand, but to comfort me or him I still don't know. "They're downed. We can't let them sense us or they'll wake up and then I don't know if we'll be able to get away."

I sat, refusing to move. "We can't go back, Elias," I had whined. I was tired and hungry and sad and upset. So disappointed. I'd felt like we were close but here was another obstacle that meant we'd be trapped in the Forest forever. My lip began to shake. "We already tried all those other paths. They were locked and you said this was the only way." I began crying, I couldn't help it.

Elias sat down next to me. Pulled me to his side, tucking my head to his chest, where I could hear his heart pounding and the way his breathing hitched, so I knew he was crying too.

It was afternoon and dark clouds pushed around the horizon. He sighed. "If it rains hard enough, maybe we can make it without them sensing us and waking up," he finally said. "We'll just have to wait here for a few days and see."

So we'd spent two days on the top of that mountain, trying not to stare down into the sleeping horde. Then on the third evening a storm gathered and started out small but by morning was so furious that we could hear the crack of trees falling and the groan of the metal fences shifting.

The mountain edge was crumbling beneath us as we climbed down to the road. When we got to the bottom, we ran along a brick wall and then sprinted over the bridge that bucked and swayed from the wind howling down the valley. Thunder and lightning raged around us, the rain so heavy we could barely breathe. It felt like the entire world was tearing apart.

The last I'd seen of the horde had been when a crack of lightning struck the bridge, buckling it just as we reached the other side. Cars exploded in sparks and fell into the valley, illuminating the slumbering bodies below before crashing to the ground.

I drop my hands and square my shoulders—shoving the memory from my mind. I'd escaped them once before and now I would have to do it again. "We're trapped in the tunnels." Already I can hear the moans filtering down the stairs. "It won't be long until they're everywhere."

"You said you knew where Gabry is and we can't leave her. We have to make sure she's okay," Catcher says, as if he thinks I'm on the verge of giving up.

It takes a heartbeat for me to remember, again, that Gabry is my sister. That she's no longer Abigail. Thinking about her being out there somewhere with the dead flooding the streets causes my throat to close up. I've left her defenseless once before and I won't do it again.

My mind whirs over what to do next. I pace along the edge

of the platform, the fire behind shifting and sending sparks into the air. "Even if we surfaced here we'd still be in the Neverlands, and the bridges don't connect the entire island anymore," I think out loud. "We'd have to cross the Palisade wall on foot, and I don't trust the Recruiters to let us through or for it not to be overrun already."

"Can we take the tunnels?" Catcher asks, and of course it's the obvious question.

I stop and stare at him for a moment. The tunnels connect the entire island like underground rivers. The Protectorate used to keep them patrolled and used wheel walkers to keep the pumps running so they didn't flood. The tunnels have always been off-limits and dangerous but have only gotten worse since the Rebellion: aside from the caved-in sections I've heard that some areas are underwater. It's a labyrinth that might just swallow us whole.

I remember the last time I came underground and feel my scars tighten—each one a reminder of just how dangerous these tunnels can be.

"It would be a risk," I finally say. "A huge one. I'd be guessing which way to go. There could also be Unconsecrated down here, and unless smugglers still use this tunnel a lot, the dead could be downed and we won't even know until we stumble onto them."

Catcher winces and I realize belatedly that the Unconsecrated wouldn't sense him. They'd only sense me. I open my mouth to apologize but he waves his hand to brush it away.

"Would there be fewer in the tunnels than up in the streets?" he asks.

I stare into the darkness and then back over my shoulder

to the stairs. Already the moans are sounding louder, as if they've breached the outer door. "It's impossible to know," I tell him honestly.

"Are you willing to take the risk?" I can tell that Catcher doesn't know how I'll answer the question and it reminds me that we're strangers to each other. I wonder how much of my personality he thinks he understands because of my sister.

I wonder if when he sees the smooth side of my face he forgets that I'm not her.

"I'll do anything to save my sister," I tell him. And when I say it out loud I know it's true. It's the only way I can think to finally forgive myself.

X

Catcher breaks off a thick shaft of wood from one of the subway ties and wraps the remnants of my quilt around it. He lights the tattered cloth from the fire, creating a makeshift torch. It glows a warm red, not giving much light but enough for us to see our feet and avoid the debris scattered along the old tracks.

I hold the machete Catcher found aboveground tight in my chapped hand as wind swallowed by the tunnels moans like the dead. I huddle deeper in my clothes, bracing against the cold, almost positive the Unconsecrated have broken down the door to the stairs and are shambling after us, their footsteps lost in the echo of our own.

With every step I think about the bodies that could be strewn about in the darkness. The forgotten dead, now in a quasi-hibernation, just waiting to sense me and wake up. Chills chase each other up the back of my neck and along my arms. It's better down here than out there, I remind myself, to stop the fear paralyzing my mind.

"What's she like?" I ask Catcher, trying to distract myself from the way the tunnel furls tightly around us, forcing us to move forward into the possibility of more danger than what we're leaving behind. "My sister," I add.

Catcher walks slightly ahead, torch held high. "Gabry's . . ." He trails off for several steps and I glance at the way his shoulders tense as he concentrates. "She's strong. Dedicated and loyal."

There's admiration in his tone but also an underlying current of melancholy.

"Were you good friends with her?" My voice trembles through my chattering teeth.

He stumbles and because I'm following so close behind I press my hands against his lower back to keep from careening into him. His heated skin blazes through his clothes—so delicious in this freezing darkness. Before I can stop myself I press my palms harder against him, curling my fingertips into the warmth and smiling.

"You okay?" I ask when he doesn't resume walking. There's an odd expression on his face and he looks away from me before I can figure out what it is.

"There's something you need to know," he says.

I realize I've pushed tighter against him. It's like leaning toward a fire on a frozen day—the way it eases through you, unwinding muscles and loosening joints.

I'm surprised at how comfortable I am with him already, how he doesn't quite feel like a stranger anymore. "What?"

And then he twists away from me, taking his heat and the glowing ember of the torch with him. The meager light glistens from rivulets of water wandering along the old tracks on the ground.

"You need to know that I'm broken," he says.

It's not at all what I'm expecting. I frown, showing him I don't understand what he's saying.

"I just . . ." He seems to struggle with the words. "I need you to know that I'll help you find Gabry. I'll make sure you're both fine and safe but that's all. After that I'm gone. I can't . . ." He runs his hand through his hair, making it spike up like a halo. "I can't be or do anything more."

His pronouncement makes me feel cold and ugly. Unwanted. And this infuriates me because I promised myself that I'd never put myself in this position again—a place where I could hurt because of someone else's decision.

Not after Elias joined the Recruiters and abandoned me.

I stare at him, to the point where he seems to become uncomfortable. I want to ask him why he thinks that would matter to me. I want to tell him that we're all broken, that *I'm* broken. But instead I shrug like I don't care and say, "Okay."

I realize as the word falls from my lips that it's a lie, which only fuels my irritation at both him and myself. I stomp past him, brushing his shoulder with mine as I take off down the tunnel. His steps echo behind me when he follows, the feeble light from the torch he carries just barely tempering the black emptiness in front of me.

I've always liked the darkness anyway.

▼　▼　▼

The longer we're underground, the more heightened my senses become. When we near an abandoned platform at a station the pressure of air whispering over my exposed face changes, lightens. In the depths of the tunnels the air is a searing cold, the forgotten warmth of fall leaching from the walls, heating everything just enough to keep water trickling around us, not yet frozen solid into ice.

Even so, I press as close to Catcher as I dare because of his radiating warmth and the meager glow from his torch. When the flame threatens to sputter out I rip lengths of material from my skirt—the extra layer of clothes a nice defense against the cold but not as important as light.

Sound down here is also tricky. Sometimes there's a shuffle that could be feet sliding over old concrete and other times there's the hurried chirping of animals that have made their home in the dark passages.

Every noise makes me jump, turn my head. My heart beats louder than any of it and I have to constantly tell myself that we're okay. That we'll be to the surface soon enough. That I've survived in this city alone for three years and I'll make it through this as well.

But all that does is keep the panic from taking over completely—it still itches around the perimeter of my mind.

"Think this is far enough?" Catcher asks as the ceiling thrusts up, curving into the blackness of a gaping station.

I shake my head, my arms wrapped tight around my chest from the cold, my teeth chattering. I imagine the island above, the warren of twisty Neverlands streets crowded with buildings trailing toward the broad bare expanse of the Palisade wall. It doesn't feel like we've walked far enough to have crossed fully underneath it.

"One more, I think. Just to be safe."

Catcher nods and keeps pushing forward. Out of the corner of my eye I think I see something shifting deep on the platform, uncurling and stretching toward us. I tighten my grip on the machete. Running would only drain our strength—as long as we keep walking we can outpace the dangers down here.

We just have to keep going.

As we continue, the sound of dripping grows louder, more

insistent, like a tripping heartbeat. Murky water starts to splash under our feet, cresting over our shoes and eventually up to our shins. Our steps become loud sloshing sounds that drown out everything else.

My skin tightens into goose bumps, the heavy weight of sodden pants dragging at my hips. On the surface thin slivers of ice fracture and disappear like eggshells cracking as we pass. The water keeps rising—it's up along my thighs and then I'm standing on my tiptoes to keep it from brimming over my waist, my body jerking with the cold.

"Wait," I call out to Catcher, my breath whispery and shaking through chattering teeth. He stops a few paces in front of me and turns, the low burn of his torch throwing an orange glow over his cheekbones.

I gesture at the water, a darkness swallowing my lower body. "What if there's Unconsecrated in there?"

He holds the light closer to the surface as if it could illuminate what's below. "They'd be downed," he says. "You should be okay."

"Should?" my voice squeaks. After the close call from before, I'm not willing to take the chance of being bitten by some plague rat floating underwater.

"They can't smell or sense the living in the water," he says but I'm shaking my head.

"Unless I bump into one of them," I protest. "That's not a risk I really want to take. Even if *you* brush them they won't . . ." I wave my hand at him, thinking about earlier when he stood in the midst of the crowd of dead as if he were one of them.

He looks at me for a moment, his forehead furrowed, and then he frowns as he realizes what I mean.

It's freezing and my muscles won't stop cramping. Ripples

bloom in the water around me as I shift and jolt to keep the blood moving through my body.

"Carrying you won't be easy with my arm," he says. "You could float but in this cold and with your hair being so long . . ."

I cringe at the thought of Unconsecrated hands twisting through my hair, winding it around their fingers until they'd pulled me under to feast.

Catcher sloshes closer, his movement kicking up waves that pulse around my hips. He turns away from me and leans over slightly, gesturing toward his back. "Can you climb on?"

I stare at him a moment, the expanse of shirt pulled tight over skin. I hate that I need his help like this, but I'm not stupid enough to shrug off his offer. The best chance I have of making it through the water is to rely on him.

Inhaling a sharp cold breath, I bend my knees, sending the frigid water level cresting up to my waist. Then I jump, my momentum so slowed by the sludge that I sort of fall and slide against Catcher's back, scrambling to grip his shoulders and wrap my legs around his waist.

He stumbles a little, my extra weight throwing him off balance, and then tucks his hand under my thigh to help settle me into place. I sink into him, laying my cheek on the smooth spot between his shoulder blades. His body is so warm it causes me to shudder, the heat spreading along my legs and up my stomach and chest.

I sigh, threading my arm up over his shoulder to pull myself closer. He still smells like the outside, like the Forest. As he trudges through the darkness the water sloshes around us both and his body rocks. I squeeze my legs around him tighter, linking my feet together just below his abdomen.

"This okay?" I ask and my mouth hovers next to his ear. I sense more than feel the hairs along his neck prickling, almost brushing against my cheek. He grunts an answer and keeps walking, the slushing sound of his legs cutting through the water echoing around us.

I feel the twitch of his muscles and the beat of his pulse thrumming just under his skin. He rests his arm on my knee, the wound from the bolt tied tight and the blood washed away. I can't stop my mind from being hyperattuned to every detail of this moment. Wondering if he's aware that his fingers trail along the narrow band of skin between the bottom of my pants and top of my sock. They drum lightly against me like drops of water falling to the ground.

I feel like I should say something. The silence is too familiar. I'm not used to touching people, to having them touch me. But anything I could say would be either too mundane or too personal. And so I let my cheek rest in the crook of his shoulder blade and allow my body to mold to his as he plows forward.

I close my eyes and imagine the sun. I imagine a field of flowers and no sounds on the breeze other than the call of birds and hum of insects. No death. No running and hiding. No fear. And then I imagine Catcher next to me, the steady drum of his touch around my ankles, moving up toward my knee.

I draw a sharp breath, startled at the direction of my thoughts. My neck flushes, the heat of it creeping up over my jaw and along my cheeks. I'm glad Catcher can't see me.

He tightens his grip. "Stop squirming," he says, which mortifies me even more. "It's getting shallower," he adds as he stumbles from the water up toward the higher and drier ground of a station.

He lets go of me just as the surface clears his knees and I wriggle down, splashing when I land. I scramble toward the platform and hoist myself up, keeping my back turned the whole time so he can't see my blushing face.

Suddenly, I feel awkward. As if I should say something about what just happened, but I'm not used to talking to people so all I can muster is "Thanks."

Out of the corner of my eye I see him grimace as he uses his injured arm to help lift himself up. "Whatever it takes to survive," he says, pulling himself to his feet.

It's stupid of me to want him to say something more, to acknowledge the intimacy of the last few moments, and I realize he's right: we do what it takes to survive. His carrying me wasn't a tender moment, it was simply what needed to be done.

I should know better than anyone that this life isn't about feelings; it's about making it through alive.

I wrap my arms around myself again, digging my fingers into my shoulders to conserve what heat is left from his body. My pants are sodden and heavy, my feet almost numb. "This should be far enough into the City," I say, and nod my chin toward the stairs ascending into the darkness.

He starts walking toward them, the light still gripped tight in his hand.

I follow, pulling the machete from my belt. "When we get outside we'll need to find the closest fire escape and climb up to the bridges," I tell him. "Judging from what we saw in the Neverlands it might not be long until they breach the Palisade wall if they haven't already."

He says nothing, just nods again and takes the steps two at a time, so I have to scramble after him to keep within the meager light. My thighs quickly start to burn, my body exhausted and starving as I struggle against my heavy water-logged clothes.

But at least the physical strain is almost enough to over-power the thoughts spiraling through my head, the remnants of what it felt like to press against his back and the smell of the crook of his neck and the fact that he's barely said five words to me since he let me go.

Finally, by the time we reach the metal door barring the street, I'm ready to leave all that behind and face whatever lies outside. I have to be.

▾ XI ▾

Catcher eases through the door first, and I can see around him that there's panic in the streets. He pauses and I dash past him to the closest fire escape, jumping for the ladder that's just out of reach. He nudges me aside and pulls it down before shoving me up it.

Around us I hear the City in uproar: people shouting and bells ringing. The wind smells like smoke, and I'm almost terrified by what I'll see when we reach the roof and can take in the full scope of what's going on around us.

Fetid water trails down my legs with each rung I climb, and I'm pretty sure it's dripping on Catcher as he follows me up to the landing. I pause to readjust my grip on the machete and start up the stairs before Catcher pushes me aside, taking the lead.

"I can take care of myself, you know," I snap at his back as I follow him up, our steps reverberating through the rusty metal stairs.

His shoulders tighten in response but he keeps going. At the top he hesitates, peering over a once-elaborate but now-broken stone cornice circling the building. "It's clear," he says, struggling only slightly this time as he uses both his arms to haul himself up and over onto the roof.

I follow, landing beside him with a squelch as water leaches from my shoes. That's when I get a clear view of the Dark City around us and the Neverlands beyond. Or rather, what's left of them.

At night when I couldn't sleep I used to imagine what this city was like before the Return. There are a few artifacts left over from the before time. The Protectorate once used an old building as a museum of sorts, as if seeing what life was like before would be an incentive for us to work harder toward a similar future.

One year for my birthday Elias gave me a pass to the museum. I remember taking care the night before to wash my hair and braid it so that it would frizz around my head like a golden crown when I awoke and unwound it. I was nervous going into the museum—I was alone since Elias wasn't going to spend the credits for two tickets, and I remember tugging the ends of my hair while I waited in line.

I still believed in the Protectorate back then. Believed what they told us about what was best for us and our way of life. Recruiters stood at the doors to the building, their black uniforms so clean and crisp against the grime of the City. This was well before the Rebellion so they were our regal protectors then—respected and trusted.

They marched us past the exhibits quickly, nudging me along when I wanted to stop and gawk. And then some girl started screaming about something, throwing a tantrum, and it distracted everyone else and held up the line so that I suddenly could take all the time I wanted wandering from room to room, examining what existed before.

The walls were covered with photographs: shiny bulletlike machines that sped through the tunnels called subways, sloping parks with families picnicking while kids clutched balloons. Buildings that stood tall, the glare of light bouncing off them so bright that even from the dingy picture I wondered how people back then didn't go blind.

Every detail of the museum awed me. After that visit I became obsessed with trying to understand what this city had been. I wanted a museum of my own—artifacts to decorate our flat's bare depressing walls. But most of all I wanted to know what happened to this place when the Return hit. What did it smell like? What did it sound like? How did any of it survive?

That was when I first went down into the subways, hoping there'd be clues of what came before, lost in the darkness. I pushed farther and deeper than I had any right to go—than was reasonably safe if you could ever call the tunnels safe at all.

The pit of barbed wire was a trap from the Return—a tangle of razor-sharp wire strung up to catch and maim Unconsecrated, not a little girl so many generations later.

I shudder, remembering the penetrating bite of each keen edge. The sound of Elias's panic when he came searching and found me bloody and broken.

Now, standing on the roof and looking down, I understand just a taste of what the Return must have been like. The fires that gutted rows of buildings and tore a gash through the old park. The sound of terror as people screamed and the dead moaned. The sight of people running through the streets that could never be safe again.

Without thinking, I slip my hand into Catcher's. Just needing something human to anchor me in the horror of the moment. His fingers wrap around mine, squeezing tight.

The north end of the island, the Neverlands past the Palisade wall a few blocks away, is almost impossible to see through the haze of thick roiling smoke. The wind twists and pulls flames into the sky, trailing dark clouds out over the river. The bridges leading to the mainland are stuffed with what must be Unconsecrated—so full that bodies tumble over the railings, careening down onto the river below.

But they don't strike water because the river is a frothing mass—dead churning and sinking only to be replaced by another and then another. The bodies packed so tightly they form almost a solid platform for the ones behind to walk across. They crash against the shore, the walls on either side of the bridge breached and crumbled, not even slowing the onslaught. The far mainland shore writhes with them all, trees snapping and crashing under the barrage of so many arms and legs and hands and feet.

Streams of the living force themselves south along the bridges strung from roof to roof. Even from here I can see how they push and shove, trying to make it to the Palisade wall so they can cross into the Dark City where Catcher and I stand.

Except the bridges aren't meant for so much weight—for such panic. They sway, some of them snapping, and spill their occupants into the rolling sea of dead below.

And that's what it's like in the streets: an ocean of dead. Bodies tumble over and around each other. In some places they pile against the buildings, trying to push their way toward the people they sense inside. Others group under the bridges, their arms raised, waiting for the living to rain down.

The worst part is the tidal wave of dead surging toward the Palisade wall—slowly and inevitably. Recruiters line the top of the thick wall, shooting at any body that tries to cross over, be it living or dead. The Unconsecrated shove against it, their moans a roar of desperation.

Suffusing everything are the screams of the people. Shouts for mercy as the Recruiters fire bolt after bolt into the crowd swarming the wall, trying to find any weakness to make it across. More Recruiters join the fray, their faces pinched in concentration.

Catcher tugs my hand, trying to pull me from the edge of the roof. No place is safe in this city—anywhere on the island—at this point. The Unconsecrated can't climb the wall, but their numbers are piling against it so deep that they just crawl over one another. Like a rushing river hitting an obstacle, soon they'll crest the top and flood into the Dark City, if they don't push the wall down first.

We may be out of harm's way now, but that won't last long.

Yet I can't take my eyes off the chaos of the Neverlands. Fires consume the bridges, eating along old ropes leaping from building to building, tearing through box-shaped structures and blowing out the few windows left. Flames pepper and snap as they find old tinder.

I look behind us down the length of the Dark City and it's like a mirror of the Neverlands: bridges stuffed with people pushing toward the docks, which are already swollen and overwhelmed. Boats dot the river, some of them half empty and others capsizing under the barrage of too many trying to climb aboard. People dive into the half-frozen water, swimming desperately toward anything that floats.

My stomach tightens and acid eats up my throat as I realize just how dire the situation is. The main bridges to the mainland in the north are already drowning in Unconsecrated, panicked escapees folding under the onslaught. The water underneath churns with the dead, the bodies so numerous they can almost walk on top of one another before sinking.

"We have to find my sister," I finally say, the thought of her kick-starting my mind away from the horror of what's going on, giving me a goal—something to focus on so that I'm not pulled under in the tide of panic.

"How?" Catcher stands facing me. He looks as helpless as I feel.

"I don't know." I start jogging across the roof, dodging around old barren gardens thick with dead weeds. I vault a low wall onto the next building and thread my way toward the bridge at the end of the block.

"Where are you going?" Catcher shouts, following me across the spindly bridge, the boards under my feet almost rotten.

"Home," I call over my shoulder as I race south. This corner of the City was practically abandoned even before the horde hit, and most everyone who tried to scrape out an existence here already left after the Rebellion, when it became pointless to pay such high rents to live in a city that no longer promised safety and order.

We cross past a few panicked families, their backs loaded with bags of supplies as they rush from roof to roof toward the docks to the southeast, the only hope of an escape. "What do we do?" they ask, their eyes wide and terrified, but I don't know what to tell them and so I just keep running.

All they have to do is look around them to see how hopeless the situation is.

The building with my flat is an old high-rise. It used to occupy an entire block until half of it crumbled a few years ago, leaving me the only occupant after everyone else moved away. Trees already struggle up through the rubble pile, winterburned vines twisting through rooms now exposed to the elements.

I race across the roof, skirting the edges of my garden as if it matters whether I trample the fragile buds. Once at the fire escape I make my way down to the fifth floor, not even pausing before I step through the window.

My mistake is in thinking that things would be the same as I left them only a few days ago. My mistake is in not checking to see if the flat is empty. In barging in without a weapon drawn.

For assuming that the panic of the horde would mean that people were consumed with tasks more important than breaking into places that are not their own.

I see the figure standing by the bed at the back of the long narrow room and my heart skips. I pause, and the sudden change in my momentum causes me to stumble, my balance thrown off.

His body is wrapped in shadows, the meager winter light from the window not penetrating deep enough to illuminate his features. He stands with all his weight on one leg, and his once-black shirt is now frayed and gray, the cuffs at his hands ragged. His fingers clutch into fists.

"Annah?" White clouds slip through the frozen air as he exhales my name.

I close my eyes. I will my heart to stop beating and my blood to stop pumping so that nothing can distract me from the full measure of the sound of him calling my name, his voice soft as his lips form around the sounds and syllables.

It can't be true. It can't be him. I know this deep inside, and I understand the realization that this person in my flat is really a stranger will be one of the most painful I'll have to endure.

But for just this moment I want to believe. I want to imagine that even while the City falls apart outside, something can still be hopeful.

"Elias," I breathe.

▼ XII ▼

His eyes grow wide and mine fill with tears. In an instant, I see all the ways he's changed over the past three years, every feature hazily familiar. Where his hair used to be long enough to tuck behind his ears, now it's short, as if his head's been shaved recently. Three faint remnants of scratches run down his cheek, so light I'd probably not have seen them if I weren't staring at him, examining him so closely.

My heart quickens as the reality of the situation washes over me.

Elias. This is my Elias. He's here, right in front of me. I stare at him, at the curve of muscle over bone that protrudes too far. The way his cheeks seem a little sharp, and barely visible lines furrow between his eyes. He's at once the boy who left me behind and yet someone else entirely. Someone new and almost scary.

Suddenly I wonder what changes he sees in me—if I'm the girl he remembers or if I've changed as he has. My stomach feels fluttery at the way he stares at me, taking me in.

In all my dreams of him coming home again, this is how it happens—me and him alone in the flat. Safe together.

He's just moving toward me when Catcher stumbles into the room, placing his hand on my back to avoid knocking into me. I know the instant he senses someone else in the flat because he steps forward and in front of me, his fingers reaching for my arm to push me toward the window and safety.

Elias halts, taken aback. "Catcher?" Confusion spreads across his features and Catcher stiffens.

And then before anything else happens, before I can touch Elias and pull him into a hug to make sure that it's really him and he's really here safe and alive, he grabs Catcher. "Where's Gabry?" he demands, looking out the window past both of us as if expecting her to follow.

It's like I don't exist, hidden behind Catcher's back. I step around him and watch as Elias grips Catcher's shoulders hard. Catcher winces, the wound on his upper arm fresh under the bandage. He eases out of Elias's grasp.

"Where is she?" Elias asks again, his voice taking on an edge of hysteria. I'm stunned by the look on his face, the barely controlled panic.

I move forward, place my hand on his arm. "I have to find her," he says to Catcher as if I'm not even there. "I promised her I'd find her."

The tension between them almost crackles. They're squared off, facing each other, and I brace myself.

"The Recruiters have her," I tell Elias.

He stares at me a moment as if he doesn't understand and then shoves a hand in his hair and wraps the other behind his neck. Such a painfully familiar gesture that my chest burns. He paces back toward the shadows of the room.

I follow, hovering behind him. "It happened yesterday." I look back at Catcher for confirmation. After being knocked out and spending so much time in the darkness of the tunnels, I'm still confused about how much time has passed.

"The day before," Catcher corrects me.

"I was on the bridge and saw it happen. They were both coming into the City and the dogs smelled his infection. The Recruiters had him, but she distracted them long enough for him to get away and they took her."

Elias faces the wall at the back of the flat, his forehead pressed against it. I'm just about to lay my fingers on his shoulder—anything to try to comfort him—when he lashes out, swinging at the wall so hard his fist crashes through it.

Jolted, I shout his name and reach for his hand. Blood already trickles over his knuckles and smears along the cracked plaster. I've never seen Elias violent before, not like that. I've seen him fight Unconsecrated and fight to protect me but never violence just for the sake of it.

Something cold tightens inside me as I realize how much a person can change in three years.

"Elias." I say his name the way I would to a wounded animal, trying to soothe. He looks up at me, the pain in his eyes deep. "We'll find her," I tell him, because I don't know what else to say to make it better.

He takes a step toward me and then I'm in his arms, his hands pulling me tightly to him as if we can erase the time and distance of the past. "I missed you, Annah," he says, his voice muffled against my hair.

I tilt my face into the crook of his neck. He is everything familiar and yet I can tell how our bodies have changed and grown. How we don't fit quite like we used to.

"I missed you so much," he adds, and all I can do is nod, because if I say anything my voice will crack and he'll know I'm barely able to control the emotions building up in me.

Catcher clears his throat. He's standing by the window looking out into the narrow alley between our building and the row over. "We should figure out what the next step is, because that Palisade wall won't hold back the Mudo for long."

I pull away from Elias, feeling suddenly out of place. The narrow room seems small and cramped with two large men in it. Elias looks around, his gaze lingering here and there, making me wonder what memories are playing out in his mind.

"So the Recruiters took Gabry when she crossed into the Neverlands?" he asks, and I nod.

"One of them said she'd be taken to the Sanctuary," I add.

Elias kicks at the wall, growling with frustration.

"But aren't you a Recruiter?" I ask him. "Can't you just demand to see her?"

Elias takes a deep breath, pinching the bridge of his nose. "This isn't what I expected to happen. It's just that if we go to the Sanctuary . . ." He pauses and looks at Catcher. "We'll be trapped."

I frown, confused. The Sanctuary is a smaller island out in the river, and because of its size and location it's safer and easier to protect and defend. The Protectorate used to control it, and it's where the most important people lived until the Rebellion, when the Recruiters infiltrated and took it over.

Only the most elite members of society have ever been allowed on that island, even now. "What do you mean, *trapped*?" I ask, the possibility of going someplace safe making my heart pound with hope. "Wouldn't the Sanctuary be safer than the Dark City? We'd have a better chance there."

Calmly and evenly, Elias says, "The only way we'd be able to get on that island is if we had something to trade."

I look back and forth between Catcher and Elias. Something's going on that I don't understand; some sort of silent battle of wills.

"I have some tokens," I start to say, "and I might have some other valuable stuff if I just—"

Elias shakes his head. "That's not what they want."

"I don't understand," I tell him, frustrated. "What else could they want?"

Elias just looks at Catcher and finally Catcher says, "Me. They want me." He turns back to the window, placing his hands on the sill. His fingertips dig into the rotten wood.

Elias slumps to the bed, distractedly rubbing one of his legs as if it bothers him. Their silence is too much.

"Someone has to explain to me what's going on here," I demand.

Catcher doesn't move. Doesn't say anything.

"How much do you know?" Elias asks.

"Nothing!" I snap back at him.

He sighs, stretching his neck in an attempt to relax the muscles. "Catcher's very valuable," he says. "The Recruiters desperately want him because he's immune, which means he can go anywhere. Do anything. Get anything."

I nod. "He told me about that."

"Right. Well, they were chasing us—me; Catcher; Gabry; her mom, Mary; and her friend Harry—because they wanted Catcher. But it's not just him they want because they can't really control him. His whole value is in going out and getting supplies, but they need a reason for him to come back. So the way they'd control him is by imprisoning people he loves. It's a guarantee that he'll always return."

I stare at Catcher's back. His shoulders are hunched, his body curved over itself. Once again I realize how much of a burden his immunity really is.

"So you're saying they'll let us on the island and into the Sanctuary because of Catcher?" I ask quietly.

Elias doesn't respond at first but then says, "Yes. Catcher's our only way to get to Gabry."

"But you're a Recruiter," I protest, because it can't be true. "They have to let you into the Sanctuary."

Elias shakes his head. "They don't. I mean, they might if I bargain with them, but they don't have to accept you. They *won't* accept you unless . . ." He swallows, refuses to look me in the eye. "They'll only let you on the island because you're a woman and they'd want to take advantage of that. I wouldn't let that happen to you."

"Oh." I stare down at the floor, understanding. A layer of dust coats the scarred wooden boards. I was never very good at keeping the place clean. It makes the room feel abandoned.

The sound of the Dark City raging filters through the open window along with the smell of smoke. We're running out of time to figure out what to do next. I think about my sister alone at the Sanctuary with no one to protect her—not only from the dead but from the living as well.

"There has to be something we can do," I murmur. I feel so useless, my mind spinning but finding no solutions.

Catcher lets out a long breath. "Let's go," he says. He steps onto the fire escape, his feet on the rusted metal a loud rattle in the quiet room. "Let's make the trade."

I wait for Elias to protest but instead he slumps in relief, pressing his hands to his face. Frowning, I stare at him as I hear Catcher climbing to the roof. A part of me wants to comfort Elias but he's not the one who just agreed to hand himself over as bait to the Recruiters.

I turn and chase after Catcher, still trying to figure out a way to work everything out and failing. Around us the City continues to fall apart: billowing smoke clouds hovering over the Neverlands, alarm bells blaring. The crowds pushing at the docks to the east have swelled and we can hear the shouting from here.

Catcher stands surveying it all. I want to tell him he doesn't have to do this, but I know that would be a lie. We both need my sister safe, and handing him over is the only way. And so I ask him, "Are you okay?" even though it's a stupid question.

He shrugs. "It's like I said before. We do what it takes to survive." He sounds so emotionless that it makes the air around us feel that much colder.

"We can try to figure out another way," I offer.

He turns to face me, his expression resigned. "There's no other option, Annah. They have Gabry and they have safety from the horde. The only way we can all survive is if I trade myself to them."

I take a step toward him. "Maybe you should worry about yourself more than us."

He looks at me for a moment, his eyes tracing along my scars. I raise my chin, refusing to glance away.

"Maybe I am," he says.

His words make me shiver, but before I can ask what he means there's a tremendous crash and a chorus of wails behind us. I spin around and see a massive section of the Palisade wall only a few blocks away crumbling, debris from its collapse spiraling up to the sky and tangling with the broiling smoke from the fires.

And then they come, stumbling from the cloud of dust and dirt: Unconsecrated. At first it's just a few, but then there are more and more, struggling across the rubble and flooding into the streets. Slow but steady they flow like blood from a seeping wound.

Some are short and some are tall. Some men and others women. Some wear clothes from olden times and some are naked, their bodies striped with wounds. But all moan with gaping black mouths. All claw at the air, reaching and needing. Some of them shuffle on broken limbs, arms gnawed away, with stringy gray tendons swinging with each step.

There are more than I could ever count and I know this is just the beginning. Soon the entire City will fall to them. I stare and wonder how we've survived as long as we have against such an inevitable destruction.

▾ XIII ▾

Elias scrambles onto the roof. "We have to go," he says, a little breathless. "Now."

I nod, unable to take my eyes from the sight of so many Unconsecrated only a few blocks away.

"This way." Elias grabs my hand and tugs me toward a rickety bridge spanning the alley to the next building. Through grimy windows I see families shoving clothes and belongings into bags and reaching for weapons.

I struggle to remember the names of the terrified faces, of the little girl screaming as she clutches a ragged doll and her brother sharpening blades while their parents race to pack. These people are my neighbors—faces I see almost every day and yet never talk to. It seems too easy to leave them behind, which feels wrong and unsettling.

But I'm not sure I can save myself, much less anyone else.

The Dark City explodes around us as we run, news of the horde fording the river spreading everywhere. I hear screaming mixed with the shrill sirens alerting residents of the breach. Everywhere is panic, no one knowing what to do or where to go.

The bridges are chaos, people shoving one another as they flee the dead. I watch people tumble off roofs and scream for help as the Unconsecrated slowly fill the streets. They claw at windows and brick walls and moan and snatch at everything around them.

Elias runs in front of me, a strange, awkward, limping stagger, and Catcher follows behind as we scamper along the tops of crumbling buildings. Families climb fire escapes, joining us in a flow of refugees streaming toward the docks on the southeast side of the island. It becomes more difficult to keep track of Elias and Catcher and not to get lost in the crush of panic.

Long lines begin to crowd at the bridges, which are too narrow and fragile to take that many people at a time. The bridges were constructed long ago out of whatever material could be scavenged and are for people to travel back and forth between the roofs of buildings, to avoid the potentially dangerous streets. They weren't made for this. Some snap and fall apart, spilling people to the ground, stories below, where hungry dead attack them, tearing at their limbs as they scream and fight. Any survivors may as well be dead. It will only take one bite to turn them Unconsecrated.

It's hard to avoid looking, impossible not to watch the struggle taking place so many flights beneath us. I try to focus on Elias's back and the feel of Catcher and his heat behind me, but the sounds and the smell are too much—the metal taste in my mouth and the screaming of the living.

Someone pushes up against me, knocking me down, and

someone else steps on my hand, the weight grinding my knuckles. I scream and lash out. A third person reaches for me and at first I think he's trying to help me up but then he wrestles for my machete, trying to pry it from my belt.

As I'm twisting away from the man's grasp, Catcher swings at him, fist slamming into his jaw without hesitation. The man stumbles back and Catcher lifts me up as we press forward into the crowd.

In some places children stand motionless, wailing for mothers they can't find. In others men stand along the edges of roofs and stare at the Neverlands as if they can't believe what's coming. As if they can't fathom so many dead.

People beg for help, wanting to know what they should do and where they should go, but I don't know what to tell them and so I say nothing. It's like being caught in a deluge, following the crowd east as the buildings around us grow taller, some of them only rusted-out husks of what they used to be. Old steel beams spire above, their ragged ends sharp and broken.

Midway across the island, the bridges snake erratically around obstacles, weaving several blocks south before turning back east. Most everyone is heading for the docks farther south, but the Sanctuary is on an island directly east of the Dark City, which means we're forced to shove across the crowds to head in that direction. It's impossible. People scream at us, one man even swinging at Elias before we give up and descend a fire escape to the street. Down here it's easier to move faster, fear driving the masses to the air.

A few blocks away I hear the pounding scrape of Unconsecrated feet. There are so many of them that the ground shudders, their moans so many voices that it creates a discordant vibration through the air. It's louder than the most violent rainstorm, a thundering hissing mass of bodies and need.

Elias tries to run but he's clearly in pain, his steps more like lurches. I offer to let him lean against me, but he refuses. Even though it's cold outside, especially in the shadows of the towering buildings, sweat drips down his face and darkens the back of his uniform.

There are fewer people on the streets but still they stream around us, some heading in the same direction we are and others away, making for the docks farther south. Every face is pinched tight, and above I notice frightened eyes watching us from behind tattered curtains gripped tight in white-knuckled hands. People willing to stay and fight, taking their chances in the City rather than running like the rest of us.

There's only one access point to the Sanctuary—an old cable-car line—and the closer we get, the more crowded the streets become with voices shouting for help.

At the base of the cable car the mob thickens, people shouting and pushing toward the gates blocking access to the platform and the car itself. Recruiters line up along the fence stretching to either side of the gates, indiscriminately shooting bolts or lashing out with wicked-looking blades at anyone who gets too close.

Tension coils in the air, the smell of blood and bodies thick. People pump their fists, scream for access to the Sanctuary or for the Recruiters to do something to stop the tide of dead creeping through the streets.

Elias slips through the gaps in the mass and I follow, pressing between bodies. I try not to think that in a short while all of them will be dead. Most of them turned Unconsecrated.

They'll be husks of what they are now: the same fierce yearning turned sinister. Though a part of me wonders how thin the distinction between living and dead is in this mob—how quickly they'd turn and kill for the chance at survival.

Catcher trails after me through the crowd, the tips of his fingers pressing my lower back lightly so that he doesn't lose me—a reassurance that he's still there. Elbows dig into my ribs, and some people hiss as I force my way through, but I ignore them. When we near the front of the pack the Recruiters guarding the gate brandish loaded crossbows and yell for us to step back.

There are already a dozen dead bodies littering the gap between the mob and the fence, and a handful of people hover over the injured. I stop in place but my body keeps vibrating. Everyone's so frantic it's only a matter of time before the panic ignites.

Elias steps forward, holding his hands open and to his sides to show he's also a Recruiter and unarmed. He tries to shout over the screaming mob, but his voice disappears in the roar of the others. Finally, the Recruiter by the gate motions Elias closer.

Catcher holds tight to my shoulders as we watch them confer. The Recruiter shakes his head and Elias's gestures become more adamant and fierce. He's turning away, his face red and furious, when down the platform a door to the cable car opens and a large man steps out.

He's wearing a Recruiter's uniform—not dingy and frayed like all the others, but crisp and clean with a red sash of fabric over his chest. He strides toward the fence, all his focus on Catcher.

His mouth moves as he shouts an order, and I think he's

telling the guard to let us through, but I can't be sure. The crowd surges and screams, shoving against us. A girl next to me stumbles and falls, but before I can help her up she's trampled and I'm pushed too far away.

Catcher shoves me to the gate, a throng of Recruiters trying to keep the swarms of panic-stricken people at bay. They begin to climb the fence, not caring about the curls of barbed wire on top. I can't watch as they tangle through it, as bright stripes of blood stretch over their skin.

My body seizes at the memory of the razor wire's pain on my own flesh. At the burn and sting. Catcher punches a man trying to pull me back from the gate, trying to take my place. People scream and wail in my ears and claw at me as the gate slips open a crack.

Recruiters reach through, yanking me past the fence, and then Catcher's after me. It's too much for those left behind. They sense the opportunity and pounce, tearing at the fence and pounding on the gate.

The Recruiters open fire, not caring who they shoot. I see one Recruiter lighting what looks like bottles of alcohol, tossing the makeshift bombs into the crowd. The flames lick and spread. People try to beat them out but there's no room and bodies flare and flail.

I'm pushed along the platform, no longer paying attention to who's grabbing me and why. Rough hands shove me into a car that's already moving, the steel cable pulling it up and away.

Safely inside, the din of the riot drowning all sound, I press my face against the window and watch the shore recede. The few Recruiters left are unable to beat back the tide of panicked people and are soon engulfed.

Some of them leap for the cable car but we're already too far away, the metal box swinging side to side as we're pulled slowly over the river. I feel the steel cable shuddering under our weight, the entire cab stuffed with Recruiters.

I look around desperately and then I sense the heat of Catcher against my back. "We made it," he says into my ear and his hands find mine. My body trembles, overwhelmed by our narrow escape. By the number of people left behind.

Men around me shift out of the way as the large Recruiter with the red sash pushes his way toward us. He stops in front of our tiny trio and I twist to face him. He looks at Elias and then at me and finally at Catcher, and his face breaks into the grin of a predator.

"Nice to see you again," he says.

"Conall." Elias's voice is strained. "You promised we'd be safe."

I glance at the faces around us, everyone tense after the ordeal on the dock and many still clutching weapons tightly. It's very easy to see that these men belong to Conall and will do anything he says.

We are utterly at their mercy.

"You made the right decision," he says to Elias. "You promised him to us and you delivered." And then he turns and shoves his way to the other end of the car.

I'm left staring at Elias, shock making my breath run shallow and my head light. "You set us up?"

Catcher's hand tightens around mine. "Not right now, Annah," he warns.

I stare at him in disbelief. "But that man said Elias—"

Catcher shakes his head once, sharp, and then his eyes scan those around us. All the Recruiters listening in.

I glare at Elias and then turn back to the window, preferring to watch my city fall than look at a traitor.

We're just approaching the midpoint of the river when the horde stumbles onto the cable-car landing we just left. People jump from the platform, trying to escape, but it's no use—the water's half frozen and there's nowhere for them to go.

Boats dot the surface of the river, some struggling toward the Sanctuary but moving away when they see the line of Recruiters patrolling the wall that rings the island, ready to shoot anyone who approaches the shore.

The scope of what's happening begins to sink in. This was my home. The Dark City, the Neverlands—this island—has survived against the Unconsecrated since the Return. Generation after generation has struggled and fought—protected and held on.

And it's all gone. Just like that. In less than a day.

I press my forehead to the chilled glass, my breath puffing cloudy circles, obscuring the chaos I'm leaving behind.

What if this is it? What if we're only staving off the inevitable?

As if he's reading my thoughts, Catcher moves closer against me. But his heat can't penetrate the cold terror invading my heart and freezing through my veins.

▼ XIV ▼

I know the Sanctuary based on what I could see of it from the Dark City: a small island sitting in the middle of the wide river with a thick stone wall circling the shore. At either end there are clusters of tall narrow skyscrapers and sprawled in between is a long low building painted a dull gray.

When our cable car lands on the platform in the wall it's to the gray building we're taken. A handful of Recruiters confiscate our weapons and huddle around us as the sounds from the Dark City float across the river on the icy wind: screaming, moaning, panic.

I want to point out to them that they don't have to worry about us leaving—there's nowhere for us to go—but instead I shove my hands deep into my empty pockets and hunch my shoulders against the cold.

Inside the gray building it isn't much warmer, just dim, without many windows to let in natural light. The floor is dirty, the walls grimy, and everything smells faintly of sewage and garbage. I try to take shallow breaths as Conall, clearly a high-ranking Recruiter, silently leads us down twisty corridors and past rows of empty rooms. Some of them are totally bare; others have papers or broken furniture strewn about. Everything heavy with the weight of abandonment.

I don't know what I expected—the opulence of the former Protectorate or at least the spoils of the black market. It makes me wonder if perhaps the Recruiters are just like the rest of us in the Dark City: barely surviving.

Eventually we enter a dark hallway where thin shafts of light barely shine through dirty windows on one side and a series of closed doors line the other. Conall opens one of them and nods for Catcher to enter. He hesitates, glancing back at me.

"There are details to be worked out," Conall says. "Until everything's in place, we'll not have you wandering around the island."

I can tell Catcher's uneasy but he does as he's told and enters the room. Conall shoves Elias in after him.

"Wait," Elias shouts, rounding on the door. "What about Gabry? You said I could see her!"

"All in due time," Conall says evenly, slamming the door before either Elias or Catcher can do anything to stop him.

I'm left standing in the hallway with Conall and three other Recruiters. Elias and Catcher pound on the door but it holds firm. I swallow, thinking about what Elias said about why Recruiters would want me on the island.

I refuse to let them see my fear. "What are you doing?" I ask evenly. My pulse hammers through my body as I straighten my back and raise my chin, waiting to see what will happen next.

"We've got other plans for you." Conall eyes me up and down, gaze lingering on my scars with an expression of disgust. "You look nothing like her," he adds, and then turns back down the hallway, indicating that I should follow. I can't help it—my face burns with embarrassment, and any fear I may have felt is replaced by a comfortably familiar rage.

I follow him up several flights of stairs, our footsteps echoing loudly in the narrow concrete stairwell. The farther we get from my friends, the more my steps want to falter. I'm used to taking care of myself, I think over and over again just to keep my hands from trembling.

We come to a door leading outside to the roof and my hackles rise when Conall shoves me through it. I stumble and fall on my knees, gravel digging through my pants and stinging my palms, surprise striking me speechless. I scowl at the man over my shoulder.

"Ox wants to talk to you," he says, nodding toward a figure standing on the edge of the roof facing the Dark City. Conall's glare traces over my scars again and he shakes his head, lips pursed, before going back inside and banging the door shut.

I get up, slowly, and wipe my hands on my coat. Wind streaks across the river, nothing to block it as it whips against me, invading every seam until my clothes are useless at buffering the cold.

Flames still eat at the Neverlands, and a part of me wishes the warmth could carry this far. I'm so tired of being cold. I'm so tired, period. And hungry. And dirty. And angry.

I stand there, refusing to walk across the roof. It's the only act of rebellion I have left. The man, Ox, looks over his shoulder, sees me and strides over.

"You must be the sister," he says. "Annah."

He's a large man: thick neck, shaved head, muscled arms and wide shoulders. He's much taller than I am, and I feel tiny and delicate but not in a good way. Instead I realize that if he wanted, this man could toss me from the roof with one hand.

But there's no malice in his eyes and so I nod.

"I'm Ox," he says, and I nod again. I think about throwing open the door and storming back down the steps but there's nowhere for me to run. No way Ox couldn't catch me. I'm completely at his mercy.

We all are. I remember the rumor of all those skulls staked around the City by the Recruiters, erected after the Rebellion to show their might. With one command mine could be one of them.

Silently, Ox and I stand side by side staring at the Dark City. Clouds have blown in, low and pregnant with snow. People still pile into the river trying to escape, and the Recruiters stationed along the perimeter wall of the Sanctuary are busy shooting anyone who tries to swim or boat ashore. I watch as they take aim at a group of boys crawling their way to the island across the cables. Even from up here I can hear them placing bets on which will fall first—on which boy to aim for next.

Half of their bolts go wide, but enough hit home that one by one the boys plummet into the freezing river below, their fingers clawing at the surface for a while as the water burns red with their blood.

Perhaps Elias and Catcher and my sister and I *are* safe here, but I wonder if it's worth it, seeing all it takes to protect us. Besides, just how long will this protection last anyway?

"It's beautiful, isn't it?" Ox asks, and his unexpected statement leaves me disgusted.

"It's horrible," I spit out. "All those people—they're terrified. They have nowhere to go."

He reaches out a hand and tilts my chin until I'm no longer looking down at the desperation in the streets but out at the line of buildings. They stand strong and still like soldiers marching against the wind, prepared to fight yet another storm.

I jerk my chin out of his grasp and dig my nails into my palms, trying to keep control of my scattered thoughts. The Dark City's impressive but I wouldn't call it beautiful, not with it filled by so much death.

"Sometimes I wonder what it would have been like before, all lit up at night," he adds. Surprised at his sentiment, I glance at him from the corner of my eye. I'd always wondered the same thing, wondered how people could get anything done in life back then when they were surrounded by so much color and light.

I realize that he's looking not at the Dark City but at me now, and I narrow my gaze at him. Let him know I'm someone who survives having half her body split open. Let him think he doesn't scare me.

"It seems so gray now," he says, not taking his attention off me. "Don't you think? Duller. In need of something more. Someone who can see the beauty of it, at least what it used to be."

I pull my elbows in tight against my body and stare at the skyline. The rise and fall of the rows of buildings. I think about the canyons between them filling with Unconsecrated. I think about the way we all live, every day a struggle to make it to the next.

How useless it feels sometimes.

"What are you doing with my brother, Elias?" I finally ask Ox. "What do you want from us?"

His mouth twitches as he rolls onto the balls of his feet. "You're not really his sister, are you?"

I know he's waiting for a reaction and I refuse to give him one, but still I can't stop wincing slightly. It's unsettling having so many strangers know the truth about Elias and me. We've played at being brother and sister so long.

He stretches his hands behind his back, the image of a commander. "Thing is, I know a lot about you, Annah. And I know a lot about Elias too."

"There's no reason to know anything about me," I tell him as I shift away.

But he stops me, grabbing my arm. I jerk back but he won't let me go. It's not until I stop struggling that he loosens his grip. "I know my men chased Elias and Gabry and the Immune through the Forest. I know that Elias sacrificed himself so that your sister and the Immune could get away."

I wrench my arm free. "His name's Catcher," I snap.

Ox throws his head back and laughs. I scowl. "That's all you have to say about it?" He wipes at his eyes, damp with mirth-filled tears. "You know how I know Elias isn't your brother? Because that would make Gabry his sister too, which would be pretty sick since he's in love with her."

My throat closes.

Of course I knew he cared for her. That was evident when he punched the wall when he found out the Recruiters had her. But I wasn't willing to admit to myself it was *love*. I refused to even let it occur to me that it could be love.

It shouldn't matter that he loves her. He left me three years ago. That alone should have made me realize that he didn't love me and never would.

But I'd hoped. I close my eyes and force my shoulders to remain strong and straight. It's one thing to know a truth in your head but another to understand it in your heart. I've known that Elias wasn't mine to love and I would never be his. But my heart has always wanted to believe differently.

I think about Abigail when I saw her on the bridge. Her clean hair and smooth skin. Of course it would be her he loves: my sister. My twin. The girl who's just like me in every way except that she's soft where I'm hard and she's hot where I'm cold and she's pretty while I'm hideous.

She's perfect. And I am not.

When I open my eyes Ox is staring at me with a knowing look, as if he can read my mind. It makes my stomach roil. I don't like this stranger thinking he understands me.

I jut my chin out. "Where is Abi—" I swallow the name I was about to say. "Where is my sister?"

He raises an eyebrow at me as if this is a game and I've just stumbled right where he wants me. "She's here," he says, waving his hand in the air. "She's fine. She caused a scene on the bridge from the mainland and Conall brought her back here knowing Elias would eventually figure it out and take care of the rest."

I press my lips together and stare back over the river to the City, watching how the clouds are slowly eating away at the top stories of the tallest buildings. Soon the snow will fall, turning it all into one bright blank canvas.

How long until every inch of it's stained with blood?

"You're a fighter," he says. There's respect in his voice, and it warms my skin, but other than that I don't respond.

He leans forward and braces his hands against the short wall ringing the roof. "You can't have survived in this city without fighting." He glances at me. "Especially as a woman alone."

I ignore him, but he keeps talking as if trying to provoke a reaction from me.

"If there's anything I know about fighters like you, it's that you won't give up. I know that even right now you're thinking of ways to get out of this. To get the upper hand. Maybe figure a way off this island."

He's completely right but still I say nothing.

He shrugs: "If I were you I'd be doing the same thing." Abruptly he stands back up, straightens his black Recruiter uniform.

"See, this is what you need to understand," he says, stepping closer, using his bulk to intimidate me. "I know how you think because I'm just like you: a fighter and a survivor. This is why you need to understand something: this is your last chance at safety."

As if to punctuate what he's saying, he places a heavy hand on my shoulder, and I jerk back, brushing his touch away. "I'm just letting you know where reality stands so you can make the right decision."

"You don't scare me," I lie to him.

He smiles, even chuckles, and considers me a moment before saying, "There's something you should see."

▼　▼　▼

Warily, wishing the Recruiters hadn't stripped us of our weapons when we landed, I allow Ox to steer me through cold gray corridors that twist and turn, taking us farther into the core of the mazelike structure. He never hesitates, just weaves around corners and down steep stairwells with me following and trying to memorize the pattern of turns.

He pauses in front of a plain door that looks no different

from any of the others and pushes it open, stepping back for me to go in first.

The room's pitch-black, no windows or light source of any kind that I can tell, and I hesitate in the entrance. Ox slides past me, letting the door slowly swing shut until it falls against my back, only a narrow sliver of illumination from the hall penetrating the darkness.

I swallow and try to breathe evenly, not wanting him to notice my fear that maybe I've gotten myself into worse trouble than I realize.

Next to me I hear him fumble, see the sparks from a flint and then a tiny warm glow. "Shut the door," he says, cupping the flame in his hand. I hesitate, staring back into the empty hallway, watching my breath frost in the flat light. Wondering if I should make a run for it after all.

But then I glance around me at the room and my heart stills. Slowly, carefully, I reach out my fingers and nudge the door closed with a click.

Ox moves farther inside, lighting more lanterns scattered along tables of varying size as he goes. The flames fight against the dark, the room growing brighter, and as it does, what covers the walls becomes clearer: maps.

Maps of cities and countries—of the whole world. Maps of everywhere, and they all sparkle under the growing light as if live stars reside within. Mesmerized by the gleam, I walk over to the closest wall and find that the maps are peppered with pins, their metallic shafts glittering.

It's amazing and beautiful and overwhelming all at once.

▼ XV ▼

Ox stays on the other side of the room, far away from me, and I take his distance as permission to explore. I run my fingers over the pins, entirely fascinated by what I'm looking at. There are countries I've never heard of, with lines criss-crossing and scratched out to show new borders.

"What is this place?" I ask, moving to the next map, inspecting the curve of a shore along some ocean, the pins sticking out like tiny metal trees.

"War room," he says. "The Protectorate controlled it. Recruiters didn't even know about it until we took the Sanctuary." He leans against a table, his hands curled around the edge of it, one foot crossed over the other. He looks relaxed but I can tell by the way he holds himself, the tension in his shoulders, that he's just trying to pretend he's calm. To pretend that me being here doesn't bother him.

I make a full circle, staring at each wall—the world spread flat for my eyes to travel. I end up in front of a magnified section of the map that shows the Dark City, the rivers surrounding it and the land stretching beyond that. To the west and south on the mainland there's a huge barren section bordered by a thick black line. I trace my finger along it.

"That's the edge of the Forest," he says evenly, as if he doesn't know what the significance of that is for me. I don't bother to enlighten him.

He riffles around on a table behind him and picks up a small jar of pins. He pours out a handful and I see they all have colored heads on them: red and green and yellow and blue.

"The Protectorate spent a lot of time sending scouts all over the world to figure out what and where was still alive, and this is where they kept all that information. When we took over we found their records." His expression is unreadable in the dim light—sad? Resigned? Angry?

"There's a key to the map." He fumbles through the pins and holds up one with a green head. "Green means Protectorate-controlled. Red is infected and blue means they lost contact and don't know the status."

Ox turns his hand, letting the rest of the colorful pins fall back into the jar, some cascading to the floor below and scattering along the water-stained concrete.

Like everyone else, I knew the Protectorate sent Recruiters out to fight the hordes, trying to reconquer land. But I had no idea they had so much information about the entire world. I feel like I've been starving and someone just set out a buffet in front of me. I start to spin back to the map, to take it all in, when Ox grabs my arm.

For the first time I realize how haggard his face is, how bruised the skin under his eyes. "This is what you need to know, Annah." He physically turns me until I'm staring at the map, his grip tight.

"A black pin means there's nothing. Overrun by the dead. Gone. Never heard from again."

I stare at the wall, eyes traveling from pin to pin. Almost all of them are black. "That can't be right," I say. The entire country—the entire world—is covered with black pins.

Ox drops his arms, moves away from me, every gesture screaming exhaustion. He knows what this means—has known. It's what keeps him from sleeping and eating.

It means most of the world is gone.

I struggle to focus as I step closer to the map, searching for evidence that I'm somehow wrong. That not everything is gone. I scan the walls from pin to pin, trying to find some color in the emptiness of the black. And then I see it: a tiny green pin down the coast from the Dark City, on a peninsula jutting out between the Forest and the ocean. I reach a finger toward it but then hesitate, eventually letting my hand drop.

"What's going on?" I ask him. "What is this?" My voice is shaking, my entire body trembling.

He says nothing and I turn on him. "Why did you show this to me? I don't understand." I want to fight, to prove this man and this map wrong. I'm not willing to believe any of what Ox is telling me.

"This is the world, Annah. This is where we are now." He shoves himself from the desk and I notice he winces at the effort of it. Slowly, he walks to the wall and pulls out a pin from the middle of the country. "This was a city. At the Return it had a population of five hundred thousand. After the Return they tried to hold on. They were overrun fifty years ago."

He drops the pin and pulls out three more nearby. "These were tiny suburbs around it, little enclaves that were holding on and then the walls gave out."

Running his hand over the map, he dislodges the pins, and

they scatter to the floor with tiny metallic plinks. "All these places—these were survivors. These were people trying to make it and eventually failing.

"This one." He holds another underneath my chin. "This fell only a year ago. And this one"—he takes another—"barely lasted the Return."

"How do you know these things?" I whisper.

He slams a hand against the wall. "This is what the Protectorate did. It was their job to keep it all together. To know where the safe zones were—to figure out how to survive. We have their books and their notes. We have their maps and letters. We know everything they knew about trying to make this world work so we could live in it."

I back away from him slowly, putting the heft of a table between us. "Maybe there's some place out there that's not on the map." I scramble for some ledge of hope to hold on to—some proof that we're not all slowly disappearing. "Maybe there's still somewhere safe the Protectorate kept secret. They had to go somewhere after the Rebellion."

I sweep my arm around the room at desks covered in paper. "Maybe they got information about somewhere that beat back the Unconsecrated—we just need to figure out what it is. Maybe it's still in here." Ox simply shakes his head as I start tearing through the desks looking for something, anything.

Finally, he puts a hand on my arm as I'm sifting through pages, tossing them onto the floor—some of them so old they crumble in my fingers. "It's impossible in this world." He says it gently, but there's an undercurrent of anger, frustration and despair.

"We're surviving," I protest, not wanting to believe what he's saying. Wanting him to be wrong.

He looks at me, so sad. "That's what I brought you here to

see," he says. He walks over to the map where our island is clearly visible, a green pin stuck firmly in the lower end of it for the Dark City and another pin to the north for the Neverlands. A thick line bisects the two where the Palisade wall was built between them long ago.

He sorts through the pins scattered on the desk until he finds two black ones and sticks them both in the island. One for the Dark City and the other for the Neverlands. It's such a final gesture that I can barely breathe. In a second he's wiped out almost everything I've ever known.

He then collects a handful of silver-topped pins. "There's one more color," he says, pushing pin after pin into the map, all through the Neverlands and the river and across onto the mainland.

I don't even have to ask. I know what he's doing. "Silver means horde," I say evenly. "It represents the horde."

He smiles bitterly. "Not *the* horde," he corrects me. "*A* horde." He turns back to the wall, shoving in more pins. "This one's from the beginning, right after the Return. They thought they could try to stop the infection if they led the huge hordes of dead into the Forest and closed them off. Contain them all. We've been fighting other ones for decades, slowly whittling them down. This one we just ignored. It was in the Forest, they were downed and there weren't people around to waken it. . . ."

I press my cheek against the chilled wall, not even listening to him trace the route of the horde from the valley in the Forest toward the Dark City. Not telling him that I saw it as a child. My skin feels flushed, like a fever. This is all happening too fast—my mind can't keep up anymore.

Finally, I realize Ox is silent. He shifts on his feet, coming to stand beside me. When I look up at him his expression is sympathetic, as if he understands my confusion and heartbreak. It's hard to remember that he's my captor now.

"It can't all be gone," I whisper, needing to believe this is some sort of complicated ruse designed to throw me off and make me docile.

He shakes his head, and I can tell that the maps are the truth. I can see in his own face the pain of this reality.

"That's why I needed you to see this, Annah. You're a fighter, like I am. But you need to know that there's nowhere else for you to go even if you're able to escape. If you want to survive, then you have to fight for this Sanctuary alongside us."

He lets the final pins drop to the floor, silver flashing, as I try to catch my breath and stop the tears from clawing up my throat.

"We need Catcher," he continues. "Our survival depends on his ability to go out into that world and bring back supplies and food. *You* and Gabry and Elias are here to make sure he comes back, because if he doesn't, then we have no use for you anymore. You'll just become a drain on our resources."

He leans toward me. "I don't like trouble—I don't like dealing with it because it's nothing more than a distraction." The tendons along his neck strain. "And so there's something you need to remember: we only have to keep around one person Catcher cares about to control him. And right now we have three."

Slowly, deliberately, he reaches out a finger and trails a scar that runs along my jaw. I try to jerk my head back but I'm pressed against the wall. I bat his hand away and he smirks, knowing he's gotten to me.

"If he stops caring about you, you become useless to us.

Well, to me. Perhaps some of my men would find a use for you. And if you start to cause trouble trying to escape or having a bad attitude that brings morale down . . ." He pauses, a wide grin breaking over his face. "Then we'll get rid of you.

"Remember this: Catcher is what matters. You're just ancillary to that end."

I cross my arms over my chest, trying to force more distance between us. His point made, he takes a step back, his shoulders relaxed as if he hasn't just threatened me and my sister.

"No matter what you're thinking right now, I'm not a bad person," he says. I snort in response, rolling my eyes, which causes him to laugh. "I'm a fair leader—that's how I got to where I am. But I'll give you another warning: be careful around my men. Some of them are good and honest guys and some aren't. The thing is, they know I always side with them, and you should too."

With that he claps a hand on my shoulder, squeezing hard to remind me of his strength. "Welcome to the Sanctuary," he rumbles, then turns and starts through the door.

"Wait," I shout, chasing after him. "What about my sister? I want to see her and Elias and Catcher."

He pauses and glances out one of the windows lining the other side of the hallway before pointing to a door at the end of the corridor. "Follow the stairs up to the main level and through the glass door. It'll lead you to the courtyard—you'll find them there."

As I race up the stairwell I hear Ox laughing behind me, but I drown him out with my pounding feet. I climb the last few steps and run toward a door with a narrow window set along one side. The glass is yellowed and aged, laced through with metal wires. It makes everything outside look like an old photograph.

Through the window I see Elias sitting on a bench, Catcher standing on the far side of the courtyard, his back to both of us. My heart rushes with relief, my breath coming in ragged gasps. I'm just about to turn the knob and bolt outside when Elias jerks his head up, his body freezing.

A door opens to my right and a girl races out, white-blond hair trailing behind her. Her squeal of joy is muffled by the thick window between us but nothing dulls the look on Elias's face.

The pure joy and adoration.

She throws her arms wide and he reaches for her, grabbing her around the waist and spinning her so that her legs kick in the air. He stumbles under her, losing his balance, and they fall into a thick patch of snow-dusted grass, her landing on top of him with her body pressed against his.

That's when I get a clear look at her face: it's mine. It's me. My blood refuses to pump, my mind to process what's going on, my lungs to draw breath.

I watch myself lean over Elias, clean hair falling over my shoulder and skirting the edges of his jaw. Him reaching up a hand to tuck it behind my ear. My fingers touching Elias's cheek and him smiling, his eyes seeing only me.

There's nothing in the world except for me and Elias.

Except it isn't me. I'm here in the hallway. I'm just a spectator as he reaches up his hand to her left cheek. Traces his thumb along the edge of her lip.

And because it isn't me on top of him, because it isn't me he's touching, there are no scars. The skin's flawlessly smooth.

Because he's not touching me. He's touching my sister, Abigail.

Then and there my heart shatters—shards of it slicing through my skin, razor sharp along each and every scar covering my body.

Abigail smiles, her expression purest joy, and Elias can't help but grin back at her, his eyes bright with love as he pulls her face to his and kisses her.

It's passion and need and worship as his hands tangle in her hair and she grabs for his shoulders.

It's white-hot pain searing through me. He nibbles at her ear and she swats at him, laughing, and he grabs her hands and pulls her to him again. Pulls her fully against him. Over him and along him. I can't hear the words he speaks to her, murmurs in her perfect ears, but I can feel the weight of them. Like they fill my hollow chest and drag me down.

He places his hands on either side of Abigail's cheeks. His eyes eat every inch of her and he pulls her to him again, brushing his lips along her forehead and down her hairline. Over her ear and along the underside of her jaw until her mouth hovers over his.

I can't breathe. Can't move. Can't feel anything in my body because everything's numb—except for the broken pieces of my heart. I feel as if I've been turned to dust, ready to be blown apart and scattered far away.

I tell my legs to move but they won't. I beg my eyes to close but they refuse. I plead for this all to be a mistake. For Elias to be somehow confused—that it's really me he thinks he's holding—but then his lips form the name: "Gabry."

At first I don't understand the sound's coming from me—an impossibly loud wheezing sort of keening—but Catcher hears it, across the courtyard, Elias and my sister between us. He looks up at me through the window.

I realize that, like me, he's been watching the lovers—a desperate look of repressed desire marring his features. He starts toward me and that's when Abigail's head snaps up and her gaze collides with mine.

Of all the times I dreamed that my sister could still be alive, all the nights I stayed awake wishing on stars and praying to any god that would listen that I would someday see her again—that she was safe and warm and loved—I never imagined it would be like this.

▼ XVI ▼

I spin around and run. My feet slide over the concrete floor as I careen down hallways, randomly turning left and right, not caring about the footsteps chasing me.

Finally, I find my way outside, the bitter cold hitting me like a wall. Images and memories hurtle through my head: flashes of Elias and my sister overlaying memories of Elias touching me the night before he joined the Recruiters, his hand on my cheek, his fingers finding every part of me.

His lips touching hers. My sister's mouth so close to his.

And my sister. Myself. Alive and here and soft-looking and pretty. My sister, whose eyes glistened with so much joy at being by Elias's side.

I don't even know what I want anymore. I used to want Elias home. I used to want the promise of safety and security but the Sanctuary feels more like a prison. I used to want to know my sister was alive, but I never expected that she would be that part of me that no longer exists.

Snow's begun to fall from the heavy clouds and it stings my eyes, swallowing the sound of my steps. The entrance to a low squat building rears up before me and I slam against it, almost falling inside into pure darkness. Blissfully, I let it consume me.

I fumble forward, not caring that I can't see, not caring that my feet stumble over uneven ground. I just need to move. I can't stop my teeth chattering. The cold air seeps around me but even so, sweat breaks out along the back of my neck.

Behind me the door creaks open, a shaft of light cutting into my solitude. A figure just like me in so many ways hesitates before slipping inside. I want to tell her to go away. I want to tell her to leave me alone. But this is my sister. This is myself—missing for so long.

She's so perfect. She's what I desperately wanted to see in my own reflection but never did.

She's also the reason I'm here in this city. The reason Elias and I were lost in the woods. The reason I've been alone for so long. If she hadn't let Elias convince us to go through the forbidden gates and explore the paths in the Forest. If she hadn't skinned her knee and refused to go farther. If Elias hadn't been so afraid of getting in trouble because she'd gotten hurt.

She's always been the reason my life fell apart so long ago. Why I can't even remember the sound of my father's voice.

She steps in after me and I retreat deeper into the darkness, weaving from side to side as I push away from the walls. I just want to be home. I want to be surrounded by my things and the long-faded smell of Elias and the way everything was.

I need time to think and figure out what's going on before I face her but she calls my name and even though I don't want to, I stop. There's a small click and then a whirring sound. A moan penetrates the darkness and Abigail's footsteps falter. My heart lurches as hands grab and tug me back to the entrance. My sister trying to pull me away.

The metallic creaking noise grows louder, steady and rhythmic, and then a light struggles to life. I wince under the sudden glow, throwing up my hands to protect my eyes and stepping instinctively into the shadows. Tucked in an alcove just off to my left, a young Unconsecrated man reaches for me through the bars of a wheel. With each step he takes toward me, the wheel turns, keeping him in one place.

He'd walk forever toward me if he could but all it does is turn the wheel, which winds a crank that powers a small string of lights reaching along the hallway wall. It reflects off icicles dangling from the ceiling, making it feel like we're caught in some sort of absurd ice castle.

"Just a wheel walker," I murmur to my sister, slipping from her grip. The Protectorate used them to power lifts and lights. Instead of stocks or jails, they'd tie rule breakers to a chair in front of the wheels: temptation to keep the Unconsecrated walking. "They're trapped—can't hurt us."

I shiver as his moans tremble around us. I can hear the sharp breaths of my sister behind me, the panic she'd felt at the Unconsecrated coming out with each puff of air.

A part of me wants to turn around and comfort her but I don't. I'm not used to people getting through my barriers. Usually I just lash out, force them away. But I can't do that with her. And I'm not ready to let her see my scars up close. To let her see the resentment I feel, which makes me even more petty and horrible.

Her shadow falls against the wall and I watch her raise a hand toward my back. Watch her fingers hover near my shoulder and then fall away.

"Annah?" My name's a whisper. There's no judgment or malice in her voice and it makes me feel even more selfish and cold.

I close my eyes. She used to be my other half but now she only makes me think of the worst parts of myself and I'm too wretchedly ashamed to face her. I left her alone in the Forest. I blamed her for being weak rather than blaming myself for being selfish—that's what makes it even worse.

"Annah," she says, her voice a little stronger. "It's . . . it's me." She draws a breath. "It's your sister."

As if I wouldn't know her.

"Please, Annah, please look at me."

The Unconsecrated man moans and reaches, chains around his wrists rattling against the steel bars of the wheel he's trapped inside. The lights connected to the turning gears hover and buzz, growing bright and dim and blazing back to life again as he lurches forward.

I wish he'd stop. I wish it would all stop. That the dead could just give up. Turn around and go back to their homes and leave us all alone. Then I could stay huddled here in the darkness and I'd never have to face my sister—would never have to see her expression when she sees my face.

I open my mouth to say her name but I freeze, suddenly unsure what to say. *Gabry* doesn't feel right—she's always been Abigail to me. "I don't know what to call you," I whisper awkwardly and I glance down at my hands, at the shadows they make, and heat crawls up my chest and along my throat.

"Call me your sister," she says. And then I can hear the smile crossing her face, feel it brightening the hall behind me. "Your big sister."

And I can't help but laugh because it feels so like my hidden memories of *her*. I'd forgotten that as kids she'd lorded her superior age over me, even though it could only be counted in minutes.

She laughs too and I drop my chin to my chest, covering my face with my hands as my laughter turns to tears. All the guilt and shame and anger too much for me as my shoulders hitch with sobs.

She doesn't hesitate but pulls me to her, taking my head and pushing it into her shoulder, her arms circling my back. I weave my arms around her and it's like nothing's changed.

We still fit together—two mirrored halves.

I close my eyes against the twisted joy and pain and try to control my breathing and swallow my sobs but I can tell that she's shaking too. I can feel her tears trailing over my skin.

Finally, she pulls away, her fingers tight around mine. She's staring at my hands and she traces a thumb over my scars. I stay utterly still and hold my breath, waiting for her to say something. She finally looks up at me, her eyes following the fissures across my face. "Elias never mentioned . . ." She trails off and I look back at our hands. At how smooth and perfect her skin is. Especially against mine that's so marred.

It's strange to hear her say Elias's name. To think about them talking about me. For so long it's felt like he's belonged only to me—a desire so intense and hot burns inside me to know what they said. To know how Elias spoke about me.

I want to know why he didn't mention my scars. Is he just so used to them that he doesn't see them anymore? Or is he ashamed? Suddenly I'm hyperaware of each line along my face and down my neck, trailing over my arms, hip and thigh. Twisting around my knee and ankle.

"What happened?" she asks softly. It's a question I've gotten so many times before and I always brush it away. But with my sister, I don't hear the horror in her voice. I hear only the sadness that something so painful could have happened to her twin.

I swallow a few times—I'm not used to anyone but Elias caring about me like that. Not sure how to handle it.

And then I tell her about Elias and me. About where we went after we left her on the path—how we got lost and couldn't find our way back to the village and eventually discovered a way out of the Forest and to the Dark City. How I fell into a patch of barbed wire when I was exploring the tunnels for artifacts and how Elias refused to let me go down into them ever again.

But I don't tell her why he left me. I don't mention the night he made me feel so beautiful and so ugly at once. Because I feel like to voice those words is to make them belong to someone other than me. Is to let them go into the world and never have the chance to get them back again.

My sister's eyes glisten as I talk, and sometimes she can't hold back the tears. And when I'm done she's silent and finally she says, "I'm so sorry. It's my fault. If I hadn't been so scared when we went on the path . . ." And then her face crumples and I pull her to me.

"We were children," I tell her. "We were barely even five." But I'm not trying to give her absolution, I'm trying to give it to myself. Because I'm the one who left her behind to almost die.

She shakes her head, pushing closer to me. "It's my fault, Annah," she says. "I forgot about all of it. I wandered for so long that I was almost dead and I forgot about it. I grew up never remembering—never knowing. Even when something did spark a memory my mother—Mary—she'd tell me it must have been a dream. I didn't even know about you until I met Elias. All this time and I never knew."

"It's all right," I tell her, testing the words in my mouth to feel if they're true. I pull back and place my palms on her cheeks, staring at her face. At what mine would look like if I weren't so scarred. I can't help but wonder what it was like for Elias to see her for the first time.

To wonder if he saw me. And I wonder if that's why he didn't come home to me. Because he found something better.

▼ XVII ▼

The Unconsecrated moans and reaches for us, stumbling around and around in his little caged wheel. I stare at his legs that will never stop so long as he senses human flesh.

"Are you okay?" I ask my sister, dreading the answer. "I saw them take you on the bridge. I was afraid they'd hurt you."

She shakes her head. "No, I'm fine. They just threw me in a room to . . ." She doesn't add that she was the bait for Catcher, and I don't press her.

"So, you and Elias, huh?" I try not to let the strain I'm feeling fill my voice.

The smile that stretches over her face is brighter than the lights lining the darkness. "I'm in love with him, Annah," she says.

I smile. Inside I feel ill. Sick at the memory of them together and sick at my own selfishness. I shouldn't have asked her about him. It was like sticking my fist into a wasps' nest: I knew what the result would be.

"And you grew up with Catcher?" I ask. I think about him standing in the middle of the Unconsecrated as if he were one of them. I think about the heat of him burning against my chest and thighs as he carried me through the dark tunnel.

I want to know more about him. I want to understand him.

She nods. "He was . . ." Her eyes lose focus for a moment and then she blinks fast. "He was my best friend's older brother." She walks closer to the Unconsecrated man. She's staring at him as if trying to figure something out, trying to see the person he'd once been.

"He changed after he was bitten." She laughs a little self-consciously. "I mean, of course he changed—he was infected and thought he'd die, but . . ."

I remember the moment I thought I'd been bitten when we were running from the horde in the Neverlands. The dread that all those years of fighting and struggling were suddenly worthless.

"How?" My voice comes out raw and I swallow before I continue. "How did he change? What was he like before?" It's cold in the darkness and I cross my arms tightly over my chest, trying to keep in the heat.

My sister reaches out a finger, pressing it to the metal wheel containing the Unconsecrated, letting its dull rim turn under her flesh. "He was happy before." She says it with such finality, as if his happiness existed in a past that is lost forever.

I frown. Hearing this makes me sad—more than sad, angry. Suddenly I realize how important his happiness is to me, which throws me off balance. "You don't think he can be happy again?"

She presses her hand harder against the metal wheel,

causing it to jerk and stop, the lights around us dimming. I want to grab her arm and pull her away but she seems so focused that I don't move.

"I'm not sure anyone can," she finally says. "Not anymore."

I let out a strained laugh. "I saw you and Elias just now. You can't tell me that's not happiness."

The Unconsecrated man moans and reaches for my sister, the chains holding him in the wheel rattling. I can almost smell the metal burning away the flesh of her palm, and I'm just starting to reach for her when she steps away and the wheel jerks forward, the Unconsecrated stumbling and falling.

The lights go out and we're dipped into pure darkness for a moment. "I'm the one who woke the horde," my sister says softly. She takes a deep shuddering breath and I don't know what to say, what to tell her.

Slowly, the wheel starts to move again as the Unconsecrated finds his footing. There's wheezing and creaking before the lights hum and begin to burn again with a low buzz. My sister holds one hand in the other, the palm red and smooth. In the dull light she turns to me, her eyes appearing hollow. "It's my fault they're coming to the City. I brought them here. I'm the reason the entire island across the river is gone. Dead."

I frown. What she's saying doesn't make sense and I shake my head, wishing I knew how to respond but unable to stop staring at her red palm.

It's as if she needs to confess. "Catcher and I were trying to escape and we crossed a bridge and the horde was in the valley and it was my blood . . ." She pauses and swallows. Turning back to the Unconsecrated, she says, "If I hadn't been there—if we hadn't escaped, they couldn't have followed us out."

In my mind I see the bridge she's talking about. I remember crossing it with Elias during the storm, the bodies littering the ground so far below. "It doesn't matter," I finally tell her. I wish I could say something better, something she wants to hear. "They would have come eventually."

"All those people." Her face is white, lips colorless. "They're all dying because of me." She looks at me, almost desperate. "How can I be happy finally being with Elias again when I've killed so many people?"

I stare at the dead man, who will always keep walking. So long as there are living he can sense, he'll be struggling for us. They'll push and push and drive us in retreat to the smallest places left in the world.

My sister trembles, tears trailing down her perfect cheeks. "We're all dying," I whisper. "Whether the Unconsecrated are in this world or not—we'll still be dying."

She looks at the ground, the flickering lights along the wall making the water dripping from her jaw glisten and sparkle.

Tentatively, I reach a hand out and grab her fingertips. I think of what I've had to do to get to this moment: the struggles as I figured out how to live alone in the Dark City without Elias. How I'd decided to fight rather than cower in the face of so much that frightened me.

"What matters is what we do with the life we have," I tell her. "We can't spend our days in fear."

"What if the Mudo take the Sanctuary?" Her voice warbles.

"Then we have to be thankful for the days we've had," I hesitate and smile, trying to make her think I believe my own words. "And then we run," I add, grinning wider.

She laughs then, and it's like a bright spark of joy spiraling around us. She's still laughing when the door opens and Catcher strides in. He glances between us, his steps uncertain.

"I was worried when you ran off and didn't come back." I can't tell which one of us he's talking to. I tug on the ragged ends of my hair, pulling it over my face like a curtain.

He seems rattled at seeing the two of us standing next to each other. My sister strides forward and places her hand on his arm. The light barely extends that far and I wonder if I imagine him flinching at her touch.

"You okay, Catch?" She sounds so familiar that it's easy to tell they've been friends for a long time.

Catcher glances over her shoulder at me and then steps away, gripping the back of his neck with his hand. She bats at his elbow. "You remind me of Elias when you do that," she says playfully, and his face seems to blanch a bit as he drops his arm to his side.

"He's looking for you," Catcher says.

Even though I can't see her face, I know it lights up. I can tell by the sway of her body and tilt of her head. "Where?" she asks.

"Back in the commander's office in the main building," he says. "They're finalizing details about where you'll be living."

My sister takes a step toward the door and then turns back to me as if remembering I'm still here. She parts her lips to say something but I cut her off. "Go on," I tell her, and she smiles, pushing out into the snowy afternoon and leaving Catcher and me alone.

I'm awkward around him. The last time we were alone together I had my legs wrapped around his waist, my face pressed between his shoulder blades. I blush, remembering the warmth of those moments. The way his muscles slid under my hands as he carried me through the flooded tunnel.

I clear my throat, trying not to shiver at the memory.

"I can try to get you another coat when I'm back in the City," Catcher says. He's standing at the edge of the darkness, the Unconsecrated man still walking in his wheel and the lights still flickering with a constant buzz.

"This is the only one I own," I tell him, picking at the worn fabric.

"I can get a new one," he says, and I try not to think about what that statement means. He'd skin for it—take it off some Unconsecrated. Which is probably where this one came from and why it was so cheap when I traded for it years ago.

"So they're sending you back over the river?" I ask. The thought of voluntarily going into the Dark City makes my skin itch. All those Unconsecrated. All the panic and hopelessness.

Catcher nods.

"Are you okay?"

He shrugs. "Like I said, we do what we have to in order to survive."

The flatness of his voice irritates me. Even though we haven't known each other for long, I thought we were at the point where we could be honest about the situation we're in together.

"Right," I say. "It's just about survival." I want him to contradict me. To say something—anything—but he simply nods again as if we're back to being complete strangers.

He's completely cut me off and it hurts, which makes me angry for caring in the first place. I stare at him a moment longer, the Unconsecrated moaning as he walks endlessly.

Catcher says nothing more, his gaze shuttered, and so I stride to the door.

"Good luck," I say, and as I pass him he shifts ever so slightly so that the knuckles of my hand brush against his. My step falters as I try to figure out if he did it on purpose. Unable to know, I push forward out into the freezing afternoon, letting the snow cool the heat of my face.

▼ XVIII ▼

Once outside I pause, trying to get my bearings. I have no idea where I'm supposed to be—where I'm allowed—and so I go back to the one place I know: the map room.

It's empty, the lanterns Ox lit still burning, and I stare at the walls. Black pin after black pin of hopelessness. Places that used to be. My head pounds and I realize my stomach's empty—I'm exhausted.

I lean against the wall and slide until I'm sitting on the floor surrounded by a world that once was. Ox's warning that we're all that's left circles my head, but I'm not sure I'm ready to believe that yet.

I'm not sure I ever will be. I close my eyes and remember what I can about the village I grew up in. It was so long ago, and my memories are mere suggestions of colors and scents and sounds.

The smell of the charred remains of the Cathedral that burned long before I was born, the sound of my sister giggling as we fell asleep at night, her hot sweaty hand resting on my arm. The grassy hill we used to climb so that we could stare over the treetops.

I shove my fists against my eyes as images from the past roll over me. The stupid fences that we felt the need to sneak past. The stupid stone my sister tripped over. The stupid me who chose to leave her there alone, preferring to follow Elias on more adventures that only got us lost.

Curling into a ball, back pressed into the corner of the room, I cover my head with my arms to block out the maps and the light and the thoughts of things past. But there's one memory that won't stop spinning through me and I grit my teeth as it unfolds, hating myself even as I relive it over and over again.

Once we escaped from the Forest and found our way to the Dark City, Elias began to call me his sister—it was easier for people to believe we were siblings who'd lost their parents to the Unconsecrated. People asked fewer questions and for the longest time it felt so natural that I began to believe it.

But in the months before Elias left for the Recruiters, something began to change in me. I started feeling embarrassed when he was in the room while I had to change. It was hard to sleep, I was hyperaware of the sound of his breathing at night, his shifting under the worn quilts. I started caring more about the scars running along my face and body, trying any concoction I could get my hands on in the black market to make them fade.

One night Elias teased me about the smell in the flat. I confessed it was a cream I'd traded for in the Neverlands to lessen the scars. He turned to me in the dim light, the moon somehow reflecting deep enough in the alley to illuminate us both.

"Oh, Annah," he said, his voice a whisper filled with an emotion that I couldn't identify but that made my stomach drop.

He reached out and with one finger he traced along the scars. The feel so different from anything else between us before. He started at my face, drawing his finger along each one, trailing down my neck. Pushing aside the collar of my nightshirt so that he could reach my shoulder, along my arm and down my side.

I tried to hold my breath but I couldn't; it came out shaking. So much building inside me, my skin so alive under his touch that I thought I would combust. Every time he reached the barrier of my clothes I thought he'd stop. I thought it must be some sort of dream. But he kept going. Along my hip, down my thigh. Curling around my calf and out to the very tip of my little toe, my feet arching under his touch.

By this time I was gasping and he was trembling. He pulled back and looked at me, the air so charged between us I felt like everyone in the world must be feeling this heat.

"You're so beautiful," he whispered then, and I felt tears pricking my eyes. Because I believed it. Because in that moment under the moon, under his gaze I felt it. As if just by his touch, he'd erased every scar that crisscrossed my flesh.

In that moment I felt like everything was alive. The world was new again and nothing but hope. When he pulled me down to the mattress and pressed against me, it was the first night in my life that I drifted into an easy sleep, a smile so wide on my face I was sure it would break me.

When I woke up, Elias was gone. He finally came home as the afternoon sun burned down around me, as my entire mind had been consumed with a frantic worry. In his arms he carried a Recruiter uniform. He'd signed up that morning and would leave for training in the evening.

Every day, the pain of that moment has scored through me. The humiliation and anger and misery and rejection. So many emotions that churn over me, always forcing me to feel it all fresh again and again—never in my life had I felt so ugly and unwanted.

And what took root that day has done nothing but thrive and bloom ever since.

▼　▼　▼

I've drifted so deep asleep that the shift of air in the room and the sound of footsteps doesn't wake me at first. It isn't until hands grip my arms that I'm able to struggle awake, muscles tense to lash out until I see who's holding me.

Elias. He kneels in front of me, shaking me gently. "Annah," he says softly. His voice makes heat flare across my skin and my stomach drop.

A look of relief flickers across his face when I open my eyes and he falls back until he's seated next to me, legs crossed, knee brushing my thigh. My mind flashes to the memory of him—the feel of his hands on my body—and I take a deep breath.

"I was terrified something happened to you," he says.

"I'm sorry," I tell him. "I didn't mean to fall asleep. I wasn't sure where else to go." There's only one lantern lit and it casts weak light around us, making it seem almost as though we're underwater.

After Elias left for the Recruiters I dreamed of this moment: him coming home. Me seeing him again, finally. I've had this conversation with him so many ways and in so many places. I've imagined his voice, his expressions, the feel of his hands along my body.

And yet I'm so lost. There's something missing between us—the quiet intensity that bloomed just before he left.

I want to talk to him, to tell him everything he's missed for the past three years. But when I open my mouth, nothing comes out. Because what *has* he missed? Endless gray days of monotony. Mondays gathering food, Tuesdays baking for the week, Wednesdays scavenging for goods, the in-between time nothing. Waiting. Fighting. Surviving.

What's different about me since he left? How can I explain how lonely and scared I was? How in the beginning I spent every hour wondering about him until that was all I was: endless hours of wondering about someone other than myself.

That I ate when I had to, not because I was hungry but because that was how I was going to stay alive and be there for him when he came back.

How long it took for me to stop thinking about him every moment of every day. How hard it was to push him far enough away that I could recover from his absence. How I vowed that I'd never go through that again.

"I thought about you," Elias finally says, and I crumble inside. I look away from him so he can't see it. I have to bite my lip to keep from making a sound.

"All the time, I thought of you, Annah." The edge of his hand brushes my hip as he shifts his weight, and I close my eyes.

In my most secret dreams, this is what he always said to me. But we weren't in some barren room in an old abandoned building, we were out in the sun on a grassy hill with white apple blossoms twirling around us in the warm wind.

My legs feel jumpy and I push to my feet, pacing back and forth between the scattered tables. Needing to get away from what's so familiar: the smell, the buzzing nearness. In my dreams this is where he'd take me in his arms. This is where he'd run his fingers over my face, magically smoothing away the pain of our past.

This is where he'd tell me he loved me and that he'd never let me go again. He'd tell me he's sorry, he never should have left. That I'm everything to him.

It used to be what I thought I always wanted. And him being near is too tempting, it's too easy to want to fall back against him even now when I know the absolute absurdity of it. He's practically a stranger to me and me to him.

I refuse to let him do this to me again. I won't keep wanting a man who can never be mine. I deserve someone who wants me as much as I want him.

Elias simply sits there, hands in his lap as he watches me pace back and forth. I can't tell what he's thinking or feeling and not knowing chokes me.

"Where have you been?" I finally ask, and the question comes out as a desperate ache.

"I was with the Recruiters," he says. He opens his mouth to say more but the sound just dies.

"I know, but . . ." There are too many ways for me to finish that statement. *But what took so long? But why didn't you come home earlier?*

But why did you leave me?

And I realize that I'm going to have to ask him, because otherwise I'll always feel this uncertainty. "Why did you go?" I whisper.

▼ XIX ▼

I feel it fresh all over again: the moment he said he'd joined the Recruiters and was leaving. How ugly and useless it made me feel.

He sighs, and when I look at him he's jumped to his feet and is standing by the door with his hand on the back of his neck. Only it's not his gesture anymore—it's Catcher's. I clench my teeth against the flood of emotions as thoughts of Catcher begin to invade the moment.

I refuse to let these men unsettle me this much. I'm stronger than that. I've *had* to be determined and independent—it's who I am now.

I cross my arms, waiting for Elias to answer. Finally, he drops his hand from his neck, rolls his shoulders as if to ease tension. "I was scared," he says. He shrugs and looks over at the maps covering the walls.

I'm silent, waiting for more.

"That's the reason I left at first," he continues. "I didn't know how to take care of you. I'd . . ." He swallows and I take a step toward him. "I'd failed you before."

"What do you mean, failed me?" I ask. He's now just a few feet away and he glances at me. His eyes flicker along my scars. It's so fast, such a small deviation of his gaze that I'm sure he doesn't think I notice.

But of course I do. It's the way people have looked at me most of my life. Usually I scowl back, but Elias knows me too well for that to work on him. I start to feel cold, my insides icy.

"It's my fault we went on the paths," he says. "It's my fault we left the village and didn't stay to take care of Gabry." His voice grows louder with each statement. "It's my fault you and I got lost in the Forest and barely found a way out. All of this—all of it!—is my fault." He sounds almost out of control and he takes a long breath before saying, "It's my fault you're . . ." He gestures at my face, trying to find the right word.

"Ugly," I say for him.

"You're not ugly!" he snaps. "You've always refused to believe that and I couldn't stand the pressure of having to believe it for you."

I jerk my head back, surprised at the outburst, but he keeps going, oblivious to the way his words tear through me. "You wanted me to be a hero and that's what I tried to be. That's why I left."

He rubs his hand across his forehead, his eyes closed tight for a moment. "I knew what we were doing to survive wasn't going to be enough—it was never enough. I had to find a way to make life better for us. I couldn't stand to just keep plodding along—I wanted something better. I was selfish."

I say nothing. Just stand there. I'd never thought of him as selfish. If anything, I'd never thought enough about what he wanted, who he truly was.

He lets out a long slow breath. "I was scared, Annah, can't you see? I left because of my own failing. Not because of yours."

I'm shocked by what he's saying. I'd had no idea. No idea he'd ever felt that way.

"I was never going to be able to be the person you needed." He sounds defeated and tired all of a sudden. "I wanted to come home and tell you that I'd taken care of everything for us. That we were safe and had a home and we didn't have to worry about skinning or going hungry or not having a roof over our heads or getting evicted from the Dark City. I wanted to be able to tell you that you were safe."

He grabs my shoulders and I wait to feel the heat before I remember that it's Catcher who burns me with his touch, not Elias.

"I did it for you, Annah," he says. He shakes me a little, as if he can force the words into my consciousness.

I stare at him. His eyes glisten and his lips tremble. I'd never told him he was enough for me. I was the one who failed him. Inside, I feel numb—so many emotions battling that they cancel each other out to nothing.

"Why didn't you come home?" I ask. "After your time was up with the Recruiters, why didn't you come home? It was only supposed to be two years and I waited for you and you never came home."

He lets me go and turns to the wall, staring at one of the maps for so long that I wonder if he even heard my question. "Elias?" I say, stepping toward him. Discarded pins crunch under my feet, scattering across the floor.

He shakes his head, keeping me at bay. "I didn't come

home because I never stopped working for the Recruiters." He reaches out, tugging on a series of black pins and letting them fall to the floor. "I still haven't."

I exhale like a laugh, fully understanding. "That Recruiter—Conall—he was right, wasn't he? When we were on the cable car and he said something about you getting Catcher to the island—he was right."

"It's not like that, Annah," he says, holding up a hand, but I shake my head.

"You betrayed him. Us," I spit at him angrily. "You said it was the only way—you made us think we had to come here in order to survive—"

"It *is* the only way for us to survive!" he shouts. A vein bulges along his forehead, his face red. "I had to find a way to keep all of you safe and this was it!"

I grimace, startled at his outburst, wondering who this person in front of me really is. Wondering if there's anything left of the boy I grew up with and once thought I might love.

"Please, Annah," he says. "You have to understand. I fought for the Recruiters against one of the hordes and we weren't making a difference." His voice is strained, desperate. "They say there were over eight billion people in the world when the Return hit—*eight billion*—and how many do you think died? Half? More? And now most of *them* are out there somewhere wandering around or downed, just waiting to infect us, and we were useless trying to kill them."

"But we've been fighting for generations—"

"You weren't there, Annah," he says. "This horde hitting the Dark City? It's tiny compared to some of the others."

I cross my arms and cup my elbows in my hands, not wanting to imagine it, not wanting it to be true.

Elias comes around the desk. "Ox made me a proposition," he says. "He offered me a chance off the fighting lines. They knew the Soulers worshiped the Unconsecrated, and they'd heard rumors of them having some Immunes that they treated like gods. He said that if I infiltrated the Soulers and figured out where the Immunes were, you and I could live in the Sanctuary.

"I knew those hordes we were fighting would come east," he continues. "I knew it was only a matter of time. I was trying to do what I thought was right for us—what it would take for us both to survive as we always have."

"This whole time it's been about Catcher?" I ask.

"No." He shakes his head. "That was pure luck."

"Then why didn't you hand him over when you had the chance? Catcher said you were running from the Recruiters. Why not just betray everyone then and be done with it?"

His shoulders sag and he won't look me in the eye. "Because they'd have used Gabry to control him and I wouldn't let them do that to her."

I laugh. I can't help it. "What do you think they're doing with her now?" I shout. "With all of us? They're using *us* to control him."

"I know," he whispers as if he's ashamed. "I tried to figure out another way. I really did. But with the horde . . ." His voice trails off. "After Catcher and Gabry got away, the Recruiters took me back to Vista and the town revolted against them, forced us all out, and so we came back here. I was hoping to get to you before Catcher and Gabry made it to the City. I was hoping to warn you—to figure something out. But they found Gabry and took her and then I had no choice."

He holds out a hand as if entreating me to believe him. "When I found out about the horde I tried to find another solution, but using Catcher was the only way to get you and Gabry into the Sanctuary."

"You did what it took to survive?" I hiss, throwing Catcher's words at him.

He just nods. "It's what I've always done, Annah. It's what *we've* always done."

I close my eyes and press my knuckles to my lips, trying to make sense of everything. Elias is right—if we'd still been in the Dark City we'd either be dead or stranded. But that doesn't make his lying to us—his betraying us—sting any less.

"How long have you been back?" I ask him. I don't open my eyes but I hear him shift, the metallic plink of a few pins rolling along the concrete floor. He holds his breath and I hold mine, waiting for the answer.

It takes five steps for him to cross the room. He takes my shoulders in his hands and waits until I look up at him. His colorless eyes are so achingly familiar. "This way we can survive, Annah. Isn't that what we've always struggled to do? Isn't that what I promised you in the beginning, that I would make sure we both survived? The Recruiters can do that. Catcher can do that for us."

He doesn't answer my question, which means that he's been in the Dark City for long enough. He could have found me and he didn't. That he wanted to warn me must have been just another of his lies.

I stare at him, at how he so firmly believes what he's saying. "I'm not sure I can survive at the expense of someone else," I tell him. And then I realize that there's one thing I've learned since Elias's been gone: "I can take care of myself." I try to ignore the way my voice shakes. And then I turn and walk out of the room, leaving him and the maps and the pins behind.

▼ XX ▼

I wander the dingy gray hallways, my stomach painfully empty as I follow the smell of food past barren rooms holding nothing but stale air and dust. It must be evening, the light through the windows fighting against snow-heavy clouds and reflecting dully off a thin layer of white coating the ground.

A few times I get turned around, all the corridors looking the same, but finally I find the source of the smell in a long narrow room stuffed with old tables. Most of them are unoccupied and I slip inside with my head tilted enough that my hair covers my face.

Even though I try to blend in with the wall, the few Recruiters slumped in the scattered chairs notice me. It's an uncomfortable quiet—forks paused midway to mouths, someone half standing with a dirty plate, all of them staring at me.

But I'm too starving to follow the voice inside warning that I should just leave. Trying to be as unobtrusive as possible,

I head toward a counter along the back wall that holds dishes of graying food: some sort of soup, some sort of meat, a few crumbs of bread. Hastily I fill a bowl, feeling the Recruiters' eyes following my every movement.

When I turn I don't know where to go. I start toward a small table shoved against the far corner but one of the men snakes an arm out around my waist, pulling me to him. My hip slides sharply along the lip of his table and I wince as I resist his grasping hands.

"We got room here," he grunts. His face is dirty, sauce from the meat crusted in the corners of his mouth.

"I'm okay," I tell him pointedly. In my head I hear Ox's admonition not to cause trouble and I look around the room to see if any of the other men care about what's happening. They're all watching but none moves to intervene.

"I could use some company like you," the man urges. His fingers bite into my lower back.

"No, really," I say firmly, not wanting him to sense my growing apprehension, "I'm okay." I don't like the feel of him, the smell of his breath mingling with the aroma of food that's stayed out too long.

"Pretty girl like you." He stands, reaching for my face. His chest rams the bowl of soup I'm clutching and it spills down his shirt.

I jump away, tensing as a sick feeling lurches into my stomach. I can see the rage boil inside the man as it climbs to his face in a red haze. "You bitch." He holds up a hand, knuckles angled toward my cheek. I flinch, recoiling into a ball, waiting for the blow and ready to roll away from it to lessen the impact. My own fingers clench into fists, but I know better than to strike and provoke the obviously stronger man.

All around us men stand, chair legs scraping across the concrete floor. None of them says anything or moves to step in.

"What's going on?" a voice bellows. From the corner of my eye I see the legs of a tall man striding into the room. When he comes into full view I recognize Ox. Relief teases the edge of my agitation. I start to relax my tensed muscles, letting out a long-held breath.

Ox looks at me and then at the man with his fist raised to strike. "Is there a reason you're about to hit this girl?" he asks.

The man doesn't lower his hand. "She spilled soup on me," he says, shifting so that Ox can see the stain.

Ox's eyes narrow. "Was it hot—you get burned?" he asks.

The man shakes his head no.

Ox shrugs. "If you're gonna hit her, then hit her. We've got work to do." Then he turns and walks from the room.

My heart freezes, my mouth open in shock. He was supposed to help me! Astonishment knots in my stomach as the man turns to me, leering. I start backing away, bitter-tasting apologies stumbling from my lips, but this only makes the man's leer grow.

My back hits another table and I push against it. Its legs groan and squeak as it slides over the floor, and still the man follows me—it seems as if he's reveling in my fear. I hold my arms up to block him but he forces them away until I'm kneeling, curled over myself, trying to make the most vulnerable areas of my body as tiny a target as possible.

"Next time a man asks you to join him, I suggest you respect that," he says. And then he brings his hand down, sharp and furious, across the right side of my face. Pain explodes, blasting through my skull, and I bite back a grunt as I throw my hands over my head to protect myself against another blow. I want to spring up, dig my nails into his eyes, but I force myself to stay coiled on the floor instead.

The Recruiter laughs and kicks the now-empty soup bowl I'd been carrying at me, then he calls to his friends and they all swagger from the room, leaving me huddled in the corner.

For a long time I stay there trying to catch my breath, which comes in wheezes and hiccups. Over and over again I replay the entire episode, trying to figure out how I lost control of it so fast. I curse myself that I wasn't stronger or somehow smart enough to manipulate the situation toward a better outcome.

Ox could have stepped in and stopped it but he didn't, and I realize he was telling the truth when he said he'd always side with his men and that it's my job to keep clear of trouble. When I'd told Elias that I knew how to take care of myself, I believed it. I've been taking care of myself alone for years—knowing to avoid the Recruiters and their cold cruelty. But I'm not sure I know how to do that anymore. Not in the Sanctuary.

Sick to my stomach, I find a rag to sop up the spilled soup and I try to eat a few bites of bread, knowing I need something in my system but choking on every piece that I force down my throat.

Finally, I slip from the room, glancing around each corner before shuffling down the hallways, staying pressed against the wall as if it could protect me.

I've never felt more cold and alone and tired. Hopelessness spirals through me, draining me of energy. Helpless tears cloud my eyes, but the rage that usually accompanies such feelings never comes. I'm used to anger—used to using it to fill me with fight to face another day or week or month. Yet there's nothing.

Listless and exhausted, I wander the corridors, trying to find Elias or Catcher or my sister, following stairs when they appear and letting gravity pull me where it will. My cheek throbs and I press it against windows, letting the cold of the night numb the pain.

I'm standing there, silent and lost, when I hear what sounds like cheering. It seems so out of place that I find myself following the noise, wondering what there is to clap about when the world seems to be pulling itself apart around us.

I turn a corner and there's a light glowing ahead, and I walk toward it hoping maybe Elias and my sister are there. The hallway opens up, widens with windows set into the walls—most of them broken or missing their glass. Instinct telling me to hide myself after the earlier altercation, I crouch close to the floor and peek my head over one of the ledges.

I end up looking down on a crowd of Recruiters huddled and sprawled along tiers of benches sloping to a concrete floor below. Some of the men stand with their arms raised, clapping and shouting. The air's thick with the stench of them, unwashed bodies and greasy hair.

Everyone's focused on one object: a large metal cage in the center of the auditorium. In the corner, several Unconsecrated trudge around in wheels powering lights strung across the ceiling under night-darkened skylights. They moan and reach for the living and I can see from here that most of them are missing fingers or even their entire hands.

I'm starting to back away when Conall climbs onto a platform balanced across the top of the cage. The Recruiters shout and jeer and eventually fall silent as he whistles.

"Tonight should be a good one," he calls to the crowd. "Place your bets."

A door off to the side slams open and the entire room goes quiet, everyone waiting but for what I don't know. Eventually, I hear someone wailing and then a young man stumbles into the auditorium. He's terrified, face drained white, eyes panicked as he scours the room.

My hands move to cover my mouth as if the crowd below could hear my strained breathing. Dread begins to unfurl in my chest.

The Recruiter who hit me earlier pins the man's arm behind his back as he cracks the gate to the big center cage open and tosses him inside. The Recruiters on the benches roar. The man turns back to the gate, trying to yank it open. He's screaming words I can't hear or understand over the shouting of the crowd.

He slams himself against the fence, trying to climb, but the top's enclosed with wire. Even from here I can see that he can't escape. He reaches his fingers through the links, his mouth moving and cheeks wet with a sheen of terror sweat, but the Recruiters nearby only laugh and taunt.

Just then a door in the far wall opens and the crowd dissolves into a raucous chant as another body is dragged toward the cage using chains attached to the end of rigid poles. The woman's tall with a shaved head, her body clad in the remnants of a white tunic. At first she seems confused, and for a moment I don't realize she's Unconsecrated. She stands there dazed as the scent of so many living overwhelms her.

And then, jerking at the restraining chains, she moves toward the cage, clawing at it. Her mouth is open, her teeth straight and white and biting at the air. The young man screams and throws himself away from her, scrambling at the fence and thrusting his hands through the links, trying to reach the lock or plead for help.

I stare, horrified. Unable to understand the cold cruelty of the men who throw open the gate to the cage. Who unleash the Unconsecrated woman, throwing her inside to face the helpless man.

He tries to climb up the side, but the Unconsecrated woman reaches for his foot, attempting to drag him down. The Recruiters only shout and jeer and one of them slices a knife along the man's fingers until he falls. Stumbling back across the cage, he stares at the blood that runs along his wrist and drips brightly to the floor. The Unconsecrated woman's face snaps up into the air and she rounds on him.

Slowly, she starts toward him, her steps a little uneven as she crosses the center of the large cage. The man backs away from her, his blood leaving a thin glistening red trail across the concrete. Of course she follows.

He bangs at the fences, screaming in terror. His fingers rip at the metal, not caring when the flesh tears from his palms or his pinky snaps. He races around and around, trying to keep clear of the Unconsecrated woman as he begs for help or mercy—for anything.

There's no way for him to escape. He's trapped. My body becomes nothing more than a thumping pulse, my heart pounding as I watch her pursue him slowly around the little cage. She's dead, she's uncoordinated, so he can easily out-maneuver her, and he jumps from her reach and dodges around her, always a step ahead.

At first it looks easy the way he stays away from her—he's faster and way more agile than she could ever be. But as the urgent minutes drag and multiply he begins to look worn out. Sweat causes his shirt to stick to his back even though cold winter air whistles into the auditorium from a broken skylight.

I realize just how sunken his cheeks are, and I wonder when he last ate or drank. How long he can fight before his body buckles in on itself.

And of course the woman keeps going. The man could run for days and she'd never stop. Eventually he'll collapse from exhaustion or starvation or dehydration—things that will never bother the Unconsecrated woman.

It's impossible to know how long she's been dead—days? Weeks? Months? The tunic she wears marks her as a Souler—a member of the cult that worships the Unconsecrated as the ultimate resurrection. The cult Elias infiltrated rather than coming home. Elias said the Recruiters had been rounding them up, and I remember how they'd been after the girl—Amalia—and the boy in the street the other day.

My stomach turns with disgust as I think about Elias being somehow a part of what's going on below. If he's somehow responsible for this Souler woman being here. For her being dead.

Soon the crowd gets antsy and begins to boo. They start chatting with one another, their attention waning, and I hunch under the windows, afraid one of them will glance my way. I want to crawl back down the hallway. I want to race out into the night and climb into the cable car and let it carry me away from this awful island and these horrible people.

Except that escape isn't an option, and even if it were I can't move. I'm stuck in place, unable to abandon this man's final brutal moments. I can only crouch here, listening to the moans and screams of the man as he begs for help.

Every time he pleads for mercy I shudder, bile burning the back of my throat. I can't believe the cruelty of what's going on. I can't believe anyone would consider this entertainment.

The timbre of the crowd below shifts, falls into chants and cheers. When I glance back over the ledge I watch as Conall motions to a man by the far wall, who ducks through a narrow door. Just as it's falling closed I catch a glimpse of what's beyond and it makes my body go numb. Lashed to the wall are more Unconsecrated—dozens of them straining and pulling against chains, their jaws tied shut with strips of cloth.

The Recruiter walks down the hall, strolling between the gathered dead as if he's a commander inspecting his troops, and then he stops and points and two other ashen-faced Recruiters scramble to pull an Unconsecrated from its restraints and wrangle it into the auditorium.

It's disgusting and horrifying and stupidly dangerous, but the rest of the men cheer at the sight of the new Unconsecrated, their voices reverberating off the walls as Conall grins maliciously and the plague rat is stuffed into the cage. It's two dead against one living.

Now it's harder for the man to get away. His movements become frantic and I dig my fingers into my thighs as I watch him try to dodge their stumbling attacks.

Slowly, inevitably, the two Unconsecrated pin the man against the fence. His desperate whimpers fill my head but there's absolutely nothing I can do to help him, which makes me feel complicit in this horrid spectacle.

He fights against them. Lashes out. He makes it around the edge of the cage a few times until he stumbles and the first Unconsecrated Souler falls on him. Her bite's not deep and for a collective moment everyone stares at the man's arm as he climbs to his feet and pushes away from her.

Like everyone else I hold my breath, waiting to see if he's actually been bitten. A flash of hope spreads over the man's face, searing through me as well. Then a tiny prick of red wells from his flesh and then another. The bite broke the skin. He throws his head back and wails as the Recruiters around the arena pound on the ground with their feet and clap their hands, drowning out the moans and the crying and even the sound of my own heartbeat.

I crawl to my feet and sprint down the hallway away from it all, their chants echoing as I careen around corners and slam into walls, trying to find my way out of the building. My vision is a blur but it doesn't matter in the darkness. I trip along the uneven floor and right when the door to the outside looms into view I fall against it, flinging myself out into the frigid night.

The sharp frozen air slaps me, blasting through my clothes, and my teeth instantly begin chattering. What little light exists is magnified by all the snow and I notice that footprints mar the thin layer of white, scuffling between the main building and the cable-car platform.

I follow them, my mind reeling over what I just saw. They were killing people for sport. For fun. I'd known the Recruiters had become vicious following the Rebellion but I didn't realize they were monsters. I didn't realize men could be this ruthless.

I fall to my knees, my stomach cramping, the tiny bit of food I'd eaten earlier fighting its way up. I heave and I heave, the sound of the man's terror screaming in my ears. The cheers of the Recruiters watching. The useless brutality of it all.

I wonder how much, if anything, Elias knows about this. If he knows what he's gotten all of us into. I try to figure out a way he could be a Recruiter but not know what every other Recruiter seems to be aware of. I don't want to believe he'd be okay with what they're doing in that cage, that he wouldn't try somehow to intervene.

The icy ground seeps through my pants and I use snow to wipe my mouth clean. I'm still reeling from everything I just saw and I don't hear the footsteps behind me until someone's fingers curl over my shoulder.

I scream, strike out with my arms, knuckles slamming into flesh. I push the body into a clump of snow-crusted bushes but he grabs me as he falls, pulling me on top of him, and it isn't until I feel the heat that I realize it's Catcher.

Words tumble from my mouth about the Recruiters and the cages and the Unconsecrated Soulers and the bodies, and Catcher holds me tight, whispering into my ears that I'm safe, that he has me, that I'm okay.

"You don't understand," I tell him, jumping to my feet. "The Recruiters are sacrificing people. They're throwing them into cages with Unconsecrated. We can't stay here. We're not safe—we can't be. We have to leave. We have to get Elias and my sister and find a way off this island."

He just sits there in the snow staring at me, a red welt rising along his jaw where I struck him. I don't know why he isn't moving. Why he doesn't understand the urgency. I spin away, so frustrated I can't even look at him anymore.

I hear him stand slowly, feel the brush of his fingers against my arm. "We can't, Annah," he says.

I jerk from his touch. "You didn't see it, Catcher. You didn't see how much fun they were having—the sick pleasure they took in what they were doing. How bored they were that the poor guy wasn't dying fast enough. They're horrible human beings who don't deserve to live." I'm shaking uncontrollably from the memories and the frozen night air.

His grip on my arm is strong, his fingers biting into me. "We can't go back because it's too late," he tells me. "There's barely anything left in the City. Pockets of people fighting. But no place as safe as this."

He looks almost like a ghost when he adds, "There's nowhere else to go, and even if there were, we're trapped. No way off the island."

In the distance I see lanterns burning on top of the wall ringing the Sanctuary. Watch the shadows of Recruiters as they stand guard, ready to shoot at anyone who attempts to land. I don't want to believe what he's saying. The City's always survived—it's been so permanent in my life that I'd never imagined it could disappear just like that.

"We can't stay here," I whisper.

He tugs on my shoulder until I'm facing him, my frosty hair hanging across my cheek. He tucks his finger around a lock, slipping it behind my ear. As he does so, the heat of his skin trails over my busted cheek and I wince.

"Annah, what . . . ?" His touch hovers over the throbbing pain. "What happened?"

I turn so that he can't see the welt. My breath comes out in puffs of crystalline clouds. The feeling of helplessness wells inside me, spills from my eyes.

"Who did this to you?" he whispers, and I can hear the rage in his voice that someone would hurt me.

I press my lips tightly together. He's right that the Sanctuary is our best hope of surviving. That the City is gone. I think of the map and all the black pins. "One of the Recruiters," I finally tell him. "It's not safe here," I add. "They're monsters."

Catcher trails a finger down my cheek, burning the path of one of my tears. His face is a war of emotions. "I'm going to keep you safe, Annah," he says. "I promise you."

I let him pull me to his chest, let him wrap his arms around me. I swallow back the words that choke me: that I'm not sure he can. Not after what I just saw.

▼ XXI ▼

Catcher leads me toward the north end of the Sanctuary. Most of the Recruiters live in the warren of shorter boxlike structures scattered around the headquarters—the main rambling building that contains the map room and the auditorium with the caged Unconsecrated.

Because almost everywhere else was deserted after the Rebellion, Ox allowed Elias to pick a place for all of us to live. He chose a middle floor in the tallest building, hoping that the effort of the climb would discourage most Recruiters from bothering us.

The rooms are small and dirty, long hallways connecting them. Catcher stands now in the doorway of the bedroom my sister chose for me on the corner of the building—a room with huge windows that open to a view of the fire-strewn Dark City and the curve of the black river.

It's a cozy room, sparsely furnished with a bed, table and chair likely left behind by the family of some high-ranking

Protectorate official who fled when the Rebellion broke out. I press a hand against the glass—a rare luxury in this world.

My reflection stares back at me: scars on one side, a raised red ridge on the other. I let my hair fall over my face as I turn toward Catcher. "I'm going to find a way off this island," I tell him, raising my chin in defiance.

His expression is steady, unreadable. He takes a long breath. "Please don't do anything that will get you in trouble, Annah. Not right now, when things are so volatile. We're safe—just let things settle down a bit."

"I'll be careful." His gaze darts to my bruising cheek and then away.

We stand there for a moment. It feels awkward again, as if we don't know how to communicate except in the face of trauma: running from Unconsecrated or Recruiters. We don't know how to just *be* around each other. How to talk about normal things.

We both fidget as this gulf of what might pass as normalcy widens between us.

"They're sending me back to the Dark City," he finally says. "Tonight. Now."

I nod. "Be careful," I tell him and this makes him smile. He pauses in the doorway like that, grin breaking over his face and hair flopped over his forehead, and something inside me jerks awake, a heat coursing through my blood. I feel my neck start to flush, feel it climbing over the tips of my ears, and I wonder if he notices.

His eyes widen just for a moment as if he feels the same thing I do. Then his grin falters and he slips into the hallway, leaving me pressing my hands against my stomach to keep the want from spreading too far.

I wake up the next morning to my sister's voice fluttering around my cracked door. I roll onto my side, gently prodding at my cheek with my fingers as I listen to her and Elias's conversation drifting down the hallway.

"I wanted to build something, Elias," I hear her say. "That's what we were supposed to be doing. Together. We were supposed to stop barricading ourselves off." There's such loss and pain in her voice that I wince. It never occurred to me that my sister had dreams like this—the same kind of dreams I once had. I realize then just how little I know about her.

I've spent all this time comparing myself to her that I haven't taken the time to try to see who she is as a person.

I hear a rustle of movement and imagine Elias walking over to her, wrapping her in his arms. "I know, Gabry," he says softly, his words full of understanding and love.

There's a pause before she continues. "Maybe we weren't ever supposed to survive this long in the first place. Maybe we should just be content with what we've accomplished since the Return," she says. But I can tell she's just testing the words. She doesn't really believe them. I smile a little—I know that tone well.

"Do you really believe that?" He sounds a little muffled, and I picture his lips pressed against her hair as he holds her tighter. I think about the way Catcher held me last night after I ran from the headquarters, how nice it was to sink into him and believe that his strength and promises could keep me safe.

I shake my head, hating how vulnerable the memory makes me feel.

"I don't know," my sister says, almost a whisper. "It's

just . . . What's the point of having fought this long if it all comes down to this? To being trapped here waiting for the horde to find some way across the river? What if this is all there is?"

There's a little more rustling and then Elias's voice is clearer, as if he's pulled away, as if he's looking at my sister's face. I imagine him resting a thumb against the perfectly smooth skin of her cheek. "Sometimes life isn't about the end," he finally says. "It's not always about tomorrow and the day after that—what we achieve over the years and how we leave the world. Sometimes it's about today."

I hear my sister start to interrupt him but he pushes on. "Any of us could die tomorrow regardless of the horde. We could get sick or be injured or anything else. That's the risk we take waking up each morning and stepping outside."

Another pause. Another soft rustle and his voice drops. I close my eyes, recognizing the tone. Hearing the smooth huskiness of his words. "Life can be about you and me and right now. If you want to build something together, we still can. And we can worry about tomorrow when it comes."

I wait to hear what my sister will say in response, but there's only silence. And then the soft sigh of a kiss that causes me to jerk my head back and slip quietly out of bed. I tiptoe down the shadows of the hallway, stopping just shy of the main room and peering at them around the corner.

For a moment I stand there staring at the edges of them that blur together. Inside wells a want so fierce that it threatens to consume me. But it's not because she's in his arms—it's because she can be so peaceful. As if she's not worried she'll wake up one day and he'll be gone.

I realize that's how it always would have been with Elias

and me if he'd come home alone. I'd always be waiting for him to leave me again, just as we left my sister in the Forest that day.

In the pale reflection of the morning sun, I watch the small rise and fall of Elias's chest pressed against my sister's shoulder. Watch the light trace over her smooth face.

I wonder if she's ever been cast aside. I wonder what it takes to believe in someone else's promises.

Clearing my throat, I push myself into the main living area where they've been standing. They jolt apart, my sister blushing prettily as Elias stammers good morning.

"We were worried about you," Elias says, and then my sister gasps, "Your cheek!" Her voice high-pitched, breathy. "What happened?"

I twitch my head, covering my face with my hair. "It's nothing," I mumble, moving toward a high table where a loaf of bread's been cut and laid out. I shove a piece in my mouth, thankful that it means I can't talk.

Elias comes over, spins me around to face him. Tilting my chin, he lets the light from the window wash over the bruise. "Who hit you?" He grinds the words out between clenched teeth.

I stare at him, astonished he doesn't know. "Some Recruiter." It should be obvious, but I can tell he doesn't want to believe it. I'm furious he didn't realize this would happen— two women on an island full of brutal Recruiters was bound to lead to trouble.

Finally he turns away, grips the back of a chair so tightly that his knuckles burn a bright white. There's a woodstove in the corner of the room and a log inside shifts with a thump, sending sparks through the narrow grate.

"Ox promised you'd both be safe," Elias says. "Do you know the Recruiter's name? I'll have to go tell him about this."

I laugh, tiny bread crumbs lodging in my throat so that I end up coughing. "Ox was there," I wheeze. "He could have stopped it but he let it happen." A cruel part of me revels in the way Elias's face drains of color as he realizes how ill-formed his treachery of Catcher has become.

"I'll talk to him," he says.

I shrug. "Ask him about the death cage while you're at it."

My sister's pouring a mug of hot water but freezes when I say this. "Death cage?"

I nod, letting any humor fall from my face. "We're not safe here. They're killing people for sport. I saw it happen last night."

"We're safer here than in the Dark City," Elias counters, starting to pace around the room. My sister finishes pouring the tea and with shaking hands pushes it toward me.

I step in front of him, blocking his way. "Did you know about it?" I ask. His expression closes down, turns flat. Astonishment crowds my thoughts.

"You knew," I whisper. I press my fingers to my temples, not wanting to believe it. Wanting him to deny it. But he merely clenches his jaw and stays silent.

"All the Soulers they've been rounding up—that's what they're doing to them. It's wrong. It's cruel."

I glance at my sister but she's just staring at the floor, not saying anything. "And you're okay with this?"

"No," Elias growls. My sister winces at his voice. "I'm ashamed. But you have to understand that some of those are good men. I fought with many of them—they're not all sick like that."

"They throw people in cages and then cheer when they're

too tired to run! They chant for death!" I scream at him, then catch my breath. Try to calm the spinning anger. "We can't stay here," I say, my tone more under control.

"And where do we go?" Elias shouts back, exasperated. He grabs the back of his neck. "You've seen the maps. There's nowhere else."

"What about the town Abigail grew up in by the ocean?" I ask.

Elias appears confused for a moment before my sister corrects me. "Gabry," she says. "My name is Gabry."

My cheeks warm and I stammer, "S-sorry." She shrugs, looking out the window.

"How would we even get there?" Elias asks. "Do you happen to have some sort of airplane or something? If you haven't noticed, we're on an island and it's surrounded by walls staffed with armed men. Beyond that's water teeming with the dead. We don't have a lot of options."

His voice boils with the same frustration that I feel. I throw up my hands. "Look, I don't know. I don't know how we get out of here, I just know that we have to. We're not as safe as we think we are."

My sister finally speaks up. "She's right," she says quietly. I glance at her, at the stubborn set of her jaw, which I know mirrors my own. I could hug her right now, but instead I flash her a small smile, which she returns.

Elias snorts and paces away from us both. "I'll talk to Ox about the man who hit you and about the death cage. If he wants Catcher to keep supplying the Sanctuary he has to keep us safe—*all* of us. In the meantime, I don't want either of you going near the headquarters alone, and preferably not without me. Now isn't the time to take stupid risks."

I bristle under the orders as if I haven't been taking care of myself for the last three years. I'm about to argue when my sister gives me a look and a tiny shake of her head. "We'll be careful," she says to Elias, placing her hand over his. At her touch he instantly relaxes, his expression softening.

"I don't know what I would do if anything happened to you," he tells my sister. His words are so infused with need and adoration that I cross my arms over my chest at the naked vulnerability of it.

And then he turns to me. "Either of you," he adds, and I bite the inside of my cheek, uncomfortable being loved so easily.

▼ XXII ▼

As soon as Elias leaves to go find Ox my sister turns to me and says, "So where do we start looking for a way out of here?"

I almost choke on my tea, I'm so surprised. She'd said she supported the need for us to leave, but I didn't expect her to be willing to go against Elias without my prompting.

She's got such a mischievous grin on her face that I can't help smiling back. "I have no idea," I admit. "It seems the only real way off the island is by that cable car, but it's guarded and leads to a platform crawling with Unconsecrated."

Her forehead wrinkles as she thinks. "No boat and no way to fly, so . . ." She wraps the leftover bread in a scrap of cloth, combing crumbs off the table into her hand and then tossing them in her mouth.

"That leaves the possibility of tunnels," I finish.

Her eyes grow wide and she covers her mouth as she coughs. "Dig a tunnel under the river?"

I laugh. "There are already tunnels under the Dark City and the Neverlands—part of the old subway system. There's a chance they extended them out to this island back before the Return. The only issue is trying to find the entrance, which could be anywhere but is probably in one of the buildings."

She leans back on the edge of the table, fingers drumming her lips. "So what you're saying is that we need to scour the island for something that might not exist?"

I nod. Put like that, the task seems impossible.

She sighs. "I'll get my coat."

▼ ▼ ▼

As promised we avoid the headquarters, which is easy since it's right in the center of the island. Instead we walk side by side as if out for a casual stroll. She tells me stories about growing up with a mother in Vista and I tell her anecdotes about Elias. For a few brief moments, life seems almost normal.

I can feel the eyes of the Recruiters stationed along the walls following us, though. They shout warnings to the boats bobbing in the river, evacuees from the Dark City on board begging for help. Unconsecrated that have washed ashore moan and scratch at the thick barrier. One of the Recruiters nicks his finger with the barb of an arrow and taunts the plague rat with it before putting the creature out of its misery.

I keep my fists in my pockets, wishing I had the comforting weight of a machete against my hip. Instead I have to make do with a small switchblade Elias found in our flat. Better than nothing.

Most of the buildings on this end of the island are abandoned, the Recruiters relegated to the barracks tightly clumped around the headquarters. We slip inside the first empty high-rise unnoticed and circle the main floor until we find stairs leading down to the darkened basement.

We stare at each other until finally I volunteer to go first. I trail my fingers along the cold wall as I carefully make my way down the steps one at a time, my surroundings gradually swallowed by darkness until I'm squinting for the barest hint of light.

"Maybe I should go find a lantern. I'm sure there's one left in one of the flats upstairs," my sister says, and she leaves me alone, stomping back up to the main floor.

I sit on the step, press my forehead to my knees and enjoy the chilled silence. A small gust of wind blows through the open door and over my back, rustling the ends of my hair. My toes tap a rhythm on the inside of my shoe, thumping in tempo with my heart.

It's difficult to tell how much time has passed. I count my breaths slow and sure, weaving them into the beat of my toes and urging my body to relax.

And then something shuffles below me where the light doesn't reach. A low rustle and slide like something being dragged across the floor. I jump up, jamming my shoulder against the railing, which throws me off balance.

My arms pinwheel the air for something to hold on to and just as I start to fall I finally grasp the railing, feeling it slide through my hands as my feet slip out from underneath me.

The metal-rimmed edge of the concrete steps slams into me as I tumble, pain digging into my hip and shins until I'm able to get a grip on the railing and stop my fall. I gasp for breath, trying to get my feet back under my body in the darkness, when I feel something brush my ankle.

I scream and kick out, hoping it's some sort of animal but knowing that it's not worth taking the chance. I drag myself up the stairs by the railing with one hand, and pull the knife from my pocket with the other, all the while screaming "Abigail!" hoping she's close enough to hear.

Something pulls me back to the darkness, yanking at my pants, and I kick again, twisting back and swiping the knife through the air even though I have no idea where to aim.

Just then a bright light appears at the top of the stairs and my sister comes sprinting toward me. She takes the steps two at a time, the circle of her lantern's gleam widening until I can see what I'm fighting: the torso of an Unconsecrated man, nothing left below his waist and a long gash across his neck as if someone tried to decapitate him but was unable to sever the spinal column.

Long skinny fingers twine around my foot, trying to pull me back and himself forward. He tugs and jerks, his grip so tight it's almost impossible to shake loose.

I lean against the stairs and kick at his face with my free foot again and again, feeling the crunch of his nose, watching his eye socket cave into his skull, the eyeball inside squishing like an overripe grape.

But still he fights—mouth opening and closing, sharp broken teeth glistening.

My sister makes it to my side and swings the lantern high before bringing it down hard on the Unconsecrated man's arm. Glass crashes and shatters. Flaming oil spills out, coating his body and spraying my pants. Quickly I beat out the embers on me before they can burn through the material and blister my skin.

The Unconsecrated man isn't so lucky. Flames devour his hair, eating away at his tattered old clothes and flesh. I gag at the stench of black smoke roiling up the stairs as I grab my sister's hand and haul her back up to the daylight.

Thankfully, the entire stairwell is concrete and the fire's contained to the plague rat's body, twitching and fighting against the consuming blaze. Up on the main floor I thrust my sister toward a broken window so that fresh air sweeps over us both.

We sit there panting, the two of us. I pull up my pants and examine the bruises already blooming across my shins from when I fell. My hands shake and my hair smells like burned meat, which makes my eyes water.

I wonder how long the man had been down there, downed until he sensed living human flesh. Perhaps he was a remnant of one of the wheels to power lights or lifts, but either way, if he'd bitten me and I'd bled out I could have been isolated enough in this basement to come back as a Breaker.

"You okay?" my sister finally asks after she catches her breath. I nod. "Next time perhaps we should take a lantern with us to begin with," she suggests, and I smile.

"A bigger knife too," I add, which makes her laugh.

We're both quiet a moment, still recovering from the incident. I slump into a broken chair, my sister sliding to the floor by my feet, her back braced against the wall. She takes my knife, absently wiping the blade across the thick hem of her pants to clean it.

Her face is twisted in thought and finally she sighs, setting the knife aside.

"What is it?" I ask her.

She glances up at me almost guiltily, and then back at her fingers fidgeting in her lap. "You love Elias." She says it as a statement, not a question.

My eyes go wide I'm so surprised. I look at her carefully,

wondering how she would even know to ask such a thing. I can't figure out what emotion's in her voice. If she's angry or hurt or sad or confused or amused. I can't tell at all what she's feeling and it frustrates me because we're twins. We're supposed to know each other almost better than ourselves.

"He was a brother to me," I murmur—a safe response. "Of course I love him."

"That's not what I mean, Annah," she says. That same tone. It stirs a memory of when we were kids, how she was always more serious about things than I was. I wonder if that's still true.

"You love him the same way I do now," she says. I can tell she feels awkward asking but even so she sets her jaw, waiting for the answer and not apologizing for the question.

I don't respond. My first instinct is to shout at her that there's no way she can love him like I did. That I know him so much more than she does. I grew up with him. I survived the Forest with him. I've lived with him since we were children, barely alive and struggling to figure out this world with no help. I've stayed up all night with him on the roof counting stars.

I know him better than he knows himself, and she can never be the same to him as I am. As I was.

But I don't say anything. Because I realize that these are things I *used* to feel. They're more of a habit now, born of so many years of waiting for him to come home. Of once thinking I needed him to be safe.

I'm not sure I understand what love is anymore. Seeing the way my sister and Elias are around each other, I'm starting to realize that it's so much more—so much deeper—than what I expected.

"Did he know you loved him?" she asks.

I think about the night before he left. Of him skimming his fingers over my body. He had to have known then.

I shrug.

She leans her head back against the wall, staring up at the ceiling soaring above. "He talked about you with such . . . fervor in his voice. He was desperate to find you," she says.

I can't help but snort, especially since I now know that wasn't the case. That he'd stayed on with the Recruiters rather than come home to me.

"You know he lied about that, right?" I ask her. "That he never came looking for me. He was with the Recruiters the whole time."

Her face clouds and she shrugs. "He did what he had to." I wonder if she believes her own words. Or if this is what you do when you love someone: accept their bad decisions along with their good ones.

"He called you beautiful and strong and sweet," she adds softly.

I keep my voice even and calm as my heart ricochets through my body. "He clearly lied."

She rolls her head along the wall until she's facing me. Her expression is somber and serious. "Do you hate me?"

Immediately I open my mouth to tell her no but I swallow the word down. Do I hate her?

Yes. I hate her for living a comfortable life. For falling that day on the path and letting me leave her behind. For growing up with a mother. For not having been tangled in barbed wire and becoming hideously scarred.

For showing me what I could have been if I hadn't turned cold and dark and hollow.

But of course none of that's her fault. She couldn't control the fact that she tripped that day on the path. She's not the one who forced me to walk away, who forced me to choose Elias over her.

"I don't hate you for loving Elias," I tell her truthfully. After all, we're twins—it shouldn't be a surprise that we've both loved the same man.

If I ever truly loved him to begin with.

She shifts until she's kneeling in front of me, and I still can't read her expression. She keeps herself so well guarded. I wonder if I'm the same way. I feel as though I'm a storm inside and the waves of it can be seen in my eyes.

"I want to understand who you are now, Annah," she says. "I've forgotten everything about who we used to be, but we're still sisters. We're *twins*. That means something to me. I want to mean something to you as well. I want to be friends." She lowers her eyes as if she's afraid of how I'll respond.

I stand up so fast that specks of light swim in my vision. I stalk across the room, needing distance. It's hard for me to catch my breath, my chest tight. I ache. So badly I ache.

My fingers tremble as I press them to my lips.

I hear her stand, hear her footsteps. "I'm sorry," she says softly. "I shouldn't have said anything, I shouldn't have—"

I shake my head, cutting her off. I want to tell her that I'm not used to being loved—I'm terrified of it. But she's my twin—I can't keep her at arm's length. It will be too easy for her to sneak past my defenses because she's so much like me.

"I'd like that," I finally manage to squeak out. I turn and see the relief on her face. "I've missed you," I add. "I'm sorry for leaving you." A lightness falls over me from saying it out loud, for finally apologizing.

She waves a hand through the air, brushing away my words, erasing the need for apologies, guilt and regret. I watch her fingers, thinking how alike we are, down to the smallest details. Down to the shape of our nails, our gestures and facial expressions. It's strange to see it after being apart for so long but at the same time there's a comfort in being near her again.

In knowing there's someone in the world who understands and loves me.

"We're sisters," she says simply, as if those words can seal the bond of all the mistakes of our past. As if it means that regardless of everything else in life we'll have each other, always.

"Yes," I say. "We're sisters."

▼ XXIII ▼

Over the next few days my sister and I continue to search all the buildings we can sneak into. We find nothing: no hint of a tunnel access or other inspiration for finding a way off the island.

During this time I don't see Catcher—not up close. Every now and then I may glimpse him unloading supplies from the cable car and then heading back into the Dark City. He looks more exhausted and worn with each trip.

I miss him.

My sister and I find a few odds and ends while scavenging through the abandoned buildings. She's collected a mound of old blankets and clothes she's been cutting up and arranging into a quilt, and after watching her for an afternoon, I've joined in, though it's clear I'm not skilled or detail-oriented enough to be any good.

Elias has been spending much more time at home with us, which means our movements have become limited—he hates the idea of us going outside and possibly stirring up Recruiter ire. While my sister seems content to sit and sew day after day, I'm not used to being cooped up inside. I can only stitch so much binding, and finally I tell them I'm headed to the roof for fresh air.

Our building is the tallest in the Sanctuary, so I have an unobstructed view of the world. It's close to evening, the clouds still belching snow while a clear strip of sky on the horizon burns a muted orange. It's a subdued cold, one so prevalent that it envelops me, slowly leaching the residual body heat from my clothes.

I stare across the river at the City. The fires in the Neverlands have mostly burned out, although several piles of rubble are still smoldering. In the Dark City itself a few buildings glow with life: people hunkered down against the horde. I wonder how long they'll survive—if this is what the City was like after the Return, a few sparks of life scattered like embers ready to burn again if only given the chance.

I wonder if they'll ever catch or just slowly shimmer out as winter and the horde march on.

Even from here I can hear the Unconsecrated, their collective moans drifting across the river on the frigid wind. Generally, cold weather should slow them down, but the City's always warmer than other places, retaining ambient heat trapped in narrow streets. And while the plague rats may be slower, they'll still overwhelm a human. There are just too many.

I lean against the wall of the structure enclosing the stairwell, letting it break the worst of the cold air blowing from the river. From here all I can see are the tops of the old skyscrapers in the City, and I blur my eyes, trying to visualize how it once must have been. Not naked steel but gleaming towers bursting with life.

The City must have held such promise then. So many hopes.

I'm yanked from these thoughts when the door from the stairwell opens and a figure moves out into the snow. I stay by the wall, hiding myself in the shadows. As soon as he takes a step I recognize Catcher. At the sight of him my stomach tingles, warmth flooding my body.

He glances around but doesn't notice me as he strides to the low wall at the edge of the roof. For a moment he glances across the river at the City like I was. And then he opens his arms wide and tilts his head back, staring at the sky while white swirls around him and the heat of the skin on his neck burns any ice that dares touch him.

He looks . . . beautiful. And as if he can hear my thoughts he turns, lowers his chin and finds me in the shadows. Snowflakes brush against his lips and melt. They catch in his hair and eyelashes. He smiles, his grin lopsided and free, and it feels like all this is just for me.

Heat radiates through my limbs. Nothing exists in this moment but the two of us and the clean crisp snow. It's too much, and I turn away from him, burying my face in the collar of my coat. But then something soft clips my arm in a powdery explosion.

I hesitate and another snowball brushes my side, falling apart on impact. Catcher holds up his hands as if to say he had nothing to do with it, but I can see that his fingers are red and puckered, wide troughs of snow dug up around his knees where he packed together the snowballs.

And then he laughs, the sound of it breaking the silence.

It's infectious, and soon I'm laughing too as I stoop and start collecting handfuls of powder, packing and smoothing them. Catcher scrambles to find cover but there's nowhere to go on the barren roof and I pelt him. He huffs with mock outrage.

It's his turn to chase me, and I shriek with laughter as I dodge his first attack, only to catch a snowball to my hip as I'm twisting to fire one off at him. We chase each other around in circles, scooping up snow and not even bothering to pack it before tossing it.

I'm out of breath from laughing and running and dodging. Snow crystals glitter around us, the frozen taste of them coating my lips. I give up all pretense of trying to make snowballs and just shovel snow at Catcher until he grabs me around the waist, pinning my arms to my sides. We're both crying with laughter as he spins me, the last gasp of the sunset light setting each flake into brilliant glowing color.

Catcher's cheeks are pink, his eyes bright and I can feel the heat radiating through his damp clothes. It's freezing outside and I want to push closer to him, to take that warmth into me. We're twirling so fast now that the force of it tries to pull us apart, but he holds me tighter, snowflakes spiraling around us. I let my head fall back and revel in the joy that erupts from every part of me for the first time in so long.

Finally, he stops and we stand there hiccuping and gulping frigid air. He reaches out absently and tucks a wet strand of hair behind my left ear, his fingertips just barely brushing my jaw. For a minute I forget to tense, forget to care that the hair was there to cover my scars, to hide me. For a minute I feel normal.

I don't let hesitation crowd my mind. Instead I let the buoyant freedom of the moment overwhelm me and I stretch up onto my toes and push my mouth against his.

I barely feel him under me, barely get a taste of the heat before he shoves me away. I stumble from the force of it, throw my hand against the wall behind me to catch myself. I'm so shocked I can't speak and he only stares at me, horrified.

"Don't ever do that," he wheezes. "Don't ever kiss me." He's wiping at his mouth with his hands as if my lips were poison.

I can't look at him. I turn away, mortified by his utter rejection.

Just like that, all the insecurities slam back into me. It's like walking down stairs in the dark and thinking there's one step left when there isn't—instead you stutter and fall off balance on solid ground.

For a moment I hope that maybe we can just pretend it never happened. That I didn't try to kiss him and that he didn't push me away. I want nothing more than for this to be possible but I know it's not.

I start for the stairwell door, my back stiff, but he stops me with his words.

"I'm infected," he says harshly. "I could infect *you*! Don't you understand that? Don't you even care about yourself enough to avoid that risk?" He paces, frustrated and angry, while I stand clutching the doorknob. I feel like nothing, as if I don't exist, and the taste of it is sharp-edged and bitter.

It doesn't matter why he can't kiss me—only that he's rejected me so thoroughly. I inhale deeply, welcoming the biting cold into my lungs. If only it could freeze me inside. I don't understand why I'm still out here, why I haven't stomped down the steps escaping from him and this moment.

"I care," I whisper, turning just enough to see him from the corner of my eye.

He stops pacing and looks at me, holds out a hand and then lets it drop. Emotions war across his face. "I'm sorry, Annah," he says softly. He's standing in the shadows, the remnants of the evening having faded while we were playfully chasing each other around the roof.

"You have to understand that I'm dangerous. It doesn't matter what you or I want. Don't you see that?" He's almost begging.

Not knowing what else to do, I nod.

"I can't do this," he says, but I hold up a hand to stop the excuses. I've let this entire evening spiral out of control. A control I've spent the last several years perfecting. I can feel the anger I've been holding back too long swelling.

Teeth clenched so that I don't say something I may regret, I whip open the door and step toward the darkened stairwell.

"Annah, wait," Catcher calls after me, but I don't listen. The rage simmers, rising up my throat like a hum. Words swirl in my head, hateful words directed at me and at him. This is who I am—broken glass and bile. I got too comfortable, let down my defenses.

"You don't understand." He chases after me, and just as I wrench the door closed he grabs it, holding it open.

I spin on him, eyes flashing. "I understand fine. I'm not good enough. Everyone wants Abigail. Beautiful, perfect Abigail and not me."

He reaches for me and I rip my arm from his grip. His eyes narrow with what looks like confusion.

"Her name's Gabry," he says, which sets my skin on fire as if I've been scolded.

I scream in frustration. "She's Abigail! She's always been

Abigail! That's who my sister is. Pretty, flawless Abigail while I'm ugly, scarred Annah."

He stands dead still, the snow swallowing all noise around us. I gulp in the frozen air.

"Why do you do this to yourself?" he finally asks, his expression a mixture of pity and concern. Heat pours off him and radiates in the air between us. I cross my arms over my chest and step down onto the next stair.

"Do what?"

He raises his hands as if to grab my shoulders and then pulls at the back of his neck instead. "Why do you always want people to see you as ugly?"

His words drain my anger, leaving only the pain behind. If all the air were sucked from the world and turned my body inside out, it wouldn't hurt as much as his words at this moment. "What?" I intend for the question to come out as a growl but instead it's only a whisper.

I step down onto the next stair and then another, but he advances, looming over me as I descend into the darkness. "You don't ever let anyone see who you really are, and whenever anyone gets close or even thinks about getting close, you thrust your scars in their face like they're some sort of badge. A way to ward people off. It's like you want them to see only the worst parts of you. Like you think you're ugly."

"I *am* ugly!" I roar at him. "What are you not seeing?" I scrape my hair back from my cheeks. "This isn't beauty!" I scream at him, tilting my neck to the light struggling through the door. He's now the one backing up the stairs and I keep climbing until we're out in the snow.

"Look at me!" I rip off my coat and then my shirt until I'm just wearing a short tight tank top, my skin on fire from rage.

The scars stand out like white streaks tearing my skin. Over my shoulder and down my ribs. Across my hips and snaking along my abdomen, trailing down into my pants.

"Annah," he says, holding up his hands and turning his head as if I'm naked.

"No!" I shout at him. "You wanted to know why I force people to see how ugly I am. It's because that's who I am. It's *all* I am."

I grab his hand and press it to my sternum. His touch is scorching hot and he closes his eyes.

"Annah," he says again, a plea and a warning.

"You *look* at me, Catcher," I growl at him.

He stares down at me, his eyes glistening. I'm panting with rage and humiliation and regret as it dawns on me what I'm doing.

Catcher's fingers curl against me ever so slightly, the pad of his thumb whispering along one of the scars on the top of my left breast.

I choke back the resentment that crawls up my throat as I yank myself away from him and grab for my shirt and coat. His hand still hovers in the air where my body used to be.

Furiously I turn around and shove my arm through the damp frigid sleeve of my shirt while I stumble away. I want to explain to him about all the times I've been taunted for the way I look. About the men who would see me walking through the City and who would shy away when they saw the scars. As if the marks made me worthless.

But how could he understand? He's beautiful, with high cheekbones and blond hair that falls over his eyes. A crooked smile that burrows inside even the coldest heart. Broad shoulders and long fingers and a heat that's all-consuming.

Nothing mars his face. His skin is smooth and warm and soft.

He doesn't understand what it's like for me to see my sister—so perfect in every way—and how Elias wants her and not me. As if I never could be good enough.

And now Catcher too.

"I think you're beautiful, Annah," he says.

I scowl. "I've heard those words before," I choke out, buttoning my shirt crookedly. I don't dare look at him. I don't tell him Elias told me that just before leaving me. Just before running away and finding someone else to love.

I throw open the door to the stairwell again, frigid snow seeping through my clothes and burning my skin. "It's nothing but a lie," I tell him. I make the mistake of glancing up at him as I stumble down the steps. He stands in the middle of the roof, his hand extended as if he can still feel my flesh under his own.

▼ XXIV ▼

I'm lying in my bed trembling with the emotions raging through me while I try to find warmth under a dozen quilts. I cringe as I remember the things I said to Catcher. As I remember twirling with him under the snow and how I ruined it all.

I don't understand how I can know so little about love and how it works. How I can be so bad at it when it's all I've ever wanted.

All I've ever known is about leaving or being left.

I'm beating my fist against a pillow in frustration when there's a knock at the door and my sister walks into the room. I can tell just from a glance that she knows something's going on.

Without a word she hands me a tin mug of steaming tea and sits on the chair by the window. The only light in the room seeps in from the hallway, yet even so I can see that her white-blond hair is braided, wisps escaping around her head like down feathers. I resist the urge to raise my hand to my own dirty hair and let the tea scald my tongue and burn its way to my stomach. Ever since she's been back, that little string between us has grown tighter—my awareness of when she's near and what she's feeling.

"You've been crying," she says.

Seeing her sitting there, I think about the Forest. Over and over again I think about her on the path. I relive walking away from her and leaving her. The bright red blood dripping along her shin and the sound of her voice calling me.

I see her falling and I'm not there to grab her before she hits the ground. If I'd just been standing next to her, if I'd just been there for her I could have caught her. I could have protected her. We could have made it back to the village and grown up safe and loved.

"What was it like to have a mother?" I ask her. Our mother died giving birth to us, so even if we had gone back we'd have never known her. It would have always been just the two of us and our father, Jacob.

Her eyes crinkle around the edges as she stares at me, her lips pressing a little tight. I've stared at myself enough times that I know every expression on my sister's face. She feels sorry for me.

She shrugs and looks away as if she's afraid telling me will only highlight what I grew up missing.

"Please," I whisper because I know my voice would crack if I spoke with any force.

She rubs her fingers along her lips. My own nervous gesture, except usually I trace the scars on my jaw.

"I miss her," she finally says. "Elias told me she wanted to come up to the Dark City with him to look for me, but they needed her in Vista. He said she was the one to lead the revolt overthrowing the Recruiters and forcing them from town. She's in charge of it all now—in charge of making sure everyone in Vista survives."

She looks down at her feet tracing invisible patterns over the floor. "Her name is Mary and she rescued me from the Forest. But she never told me that. I grew up thinking I was hers. I didn't remember anything from before—nothing. When I found out . . ." She shrugs. "I'm sorry." My sister's voice is quiet as she talks down toward her tea.

I narrow my eyes. "What do you have to be sorry for?" I ask, genuinely confused.

She takes a deep breath, her fingers tightening around the mug until her knuckles glow white. She finally looks at me. "I'm sorry I had a mother when you didn't. I'm sorry I had such an easy life growing up when you didn't." I'm about to interrupt her but she shakes her head as she takes a deep breath.

"I'm sorry I forgot about you. I'm sorry I didn't even know to go looking for you. I didn't even know to try to rescue you." She pauses, her shoulders hitching a little. "I'm sorry Elias fell in love with me and not you."

I wince at those last words but she's not finished. She comes around to sit next to me, setting down my mug and pulling my hands into hers. I can feel the heat from the tea radiating off her skin.

"I see the way you look at me now, Annah. I see the resentment in your eyes."

"Abigail—" I protest.

"It's Gabry," she says, her voice hardening. "And you know well enough that I can read every expression on your face the same way you can read mine."

I pull away from her and move into the corner of the bed, tugging the covers up around me. She faces me, hands balled into fists at her sides. "I'm not perfect, Annah. I've never been perfect. I've been a horrible person many times and—"

I can't help it; I start laughing. "You?"

"It's not funny!" she shouts, and I'm surprised by her outburst. She paces across the room. "You don't know what it's like to have forgotten everything. *Everything*. To find out that the life you thought you knew was a lie."

Her lips tremble and I can tell she's close to tears. I never realized how much this affected her. "You really don't remember?" I ask. "Any of it? Me? Our father? Elias and everyone else?"

She looks away from me but not before I see the way her eyes glisten. I lean back against the wall. What would it be like to lose your past like that? I try to decide if I'd be grateful to never know what it feels like to have had a place where I felt like I belonged.

If I didn't have anything to compare my current life with, would I be content?

"I'm not an angel," my sister says, her voice cracking. "I've done things I'm not proud of."

"We all have," I respond automatically. "That's the nature of the world we live in."

But she shakes her head. She opens her mouth as if to say something and then closes it, staring out toward the City for a long while. I listen to the rhythm of our breathing, the wind off the river buffeting against the building.

"Catcher told me about what happened between you two on the roof," she finally says.

"What?" I groan and bury my head in the quilts piled up

around me. My entire body burns with a mortified heat. "Why?"

The bed shifts as my sister sits next to me again, her hand trailing through my hair. "He's worried about you. He wanted me to make sure you're okay."

I squeeze my eyes closed, hoping to block all this out. "I'm fine." My voice is muffled. I'd prefer it if the bed could just swallow me whole.

My sister takes a deep breath. "There's something you need to know." Her tone is so serious it sends chills down the back of my neck. Slowly, I raise my head and push myself up. Her face is drained of color, tense lines crinkling her fore-head.

She stands and paces to the window and back again. "Catcher and I used to be together."

My eyes narrow in confusion. It's the accusation I'd thrown at Catcher on the roof but I hadn't really believed it. I'd just been angry and wanted to hurt him the way he hurt me.

"B-before Elias," she stammers. "Well, mostly before." Words tumble from her lips and she keeps pacing in quick lit-tle circles as if her body can no longer contain the energy inside.

"We'd always known each other—he was my best friend's brother—and I was fascinated by him and one night we kissed and then . . ." She swallows and I watch her throat tighten.

My own chest crushes with the weight of her confession. Jealousy builds up in my stomach at the thought of her and Catcher kissing. Of him running his fingers down her perfect face and how it must feel when he touches mine.

She stops moving, stares at me across the room. "And then he got infected and I did everything I could to be there for him. I disobeyed my mother's orders, I broke the town rules, I risked my life—risked everything for him."

What she says makes my heart pound slower, as if my blood's become too thick for movement. I press the back of my hand over my mouth, feeling ill. "So what happened?" I dread the answer.

She's staring out the window at the night and the reflection of her smooth skin appears warped and broken.

"He pushed me away," she says simply, a small shrug with one shoulder. "I met Elias. He figured out Catcher's immunity. I . . ." Her gaze deepens, lost someplace far away. "I got into trouble and we had to leave. We went back into the Forest and that was it."

She swallows. "I fell in love with Elias and realized . . ." She looks over at me and her cheeks pinken as she shrugs.

"Realized what?" I ask her.

Her face burns an even deeper shade of red and she squirms a little. She takes a breath and holds it before finally saying, "That perhaps the feelings I'd had for Catcher weren't that strong after all."

I frown. "Why?"

"Because I was willing to let him push me away. I was willing to let him go and I know now that I'd never be able to let Elias go." She hesitates and then adds in a firmer voice, "I'd fight for Elias in a way I was never really willing to do with Catcher."

And I realize something at her words: I wasn't willing to fight for Elias. Hadn't ever been. I'd let him walk away from me and join the Recruiters and I never said anything to stop him.

I stare at the way my sister holds herself as she watches me think, her body rigid, face strained. And I realize that she's actually afraid of me. Terrified she'll lose Elias to me. That he and I share something that she never could.

She's right, of course. He and I share a past of struggle and loss. We share the same guilt for leaving her in the Forest. We share the same memories and pain.

And we both share a love for my sister. Would Elias give her up for me if I asked? Could I ever ask it of him? Of her?

I think of Elias the night years ago that he made me feel beautiful. I think of the feel of his fingers along my skin. The words he whispered in my ear. I wonder if I could have said something to make him stay.

All these years I've wondered if I'd done something wrong. I've played that night over in my head a million times, willing it to end differently.

It'd never occurred to me that the years in between could change us so irrevocably. That I not only became a different person when he was gone, but that I also don't know who he is anymore.

And if I wasn't willing to fight for him then, when I thought he meant everything to me, why would I ever fight for him now when he's a stranger? When he loves my sister and she loves him?

"I'm not interested in Elias like that," I tell her. "He loves you, and even if I did have some kind of say in the matter, I'm not sure I could ever care for him the way you do."

Her whole body relaxes and tears glisten in her eyes. Her bottom lip trembles slightly. "Thank you," she whispers.

Just having said the words makes me feel lighter, as if I've let go of some dark gray burden.

"What about Catcher?" she asks, coming to sit next to me, the bed groaning under our weight.

"What about him?"

"Are you going to fight for him?" She tilts her head as if sharing a secret, a glint of mischief in her eyes.

I think about the look on Catcher's face when he told me I was beautiful. The horror and want and need. The agony. And then I remember what he said when we first met. "He told me he's broken. I don't know if he even wants me, or anyone else, for that matter."

My sister slips her hand into mine. "The broken ones need someone to fight for them even harder," she says, her thumb tracing over the scars on the back of my fingers.

◆ XXV ◆

"I don't know," I tell her, remembering how it felt when he pushed me away. I don't want to risk feeling that hurt again.

My sister shrugs as she stands from the bed. "You're the one who told me that we can't live our lives in fear," she says as she walks from the room. She pauses in the hallway. "By the way," she adds, "if you were wondering, Catcher told us he's heading to the City tonight. Said it would be a while before he made it back. He's probably already down at the cable-car platform by now."

It's a few seconds before I can move but I finally jump from the bed and hurry to the window, staring down at the river. Little bonfires burn along the wall, Recruiters huddled around them as they rotate off shifts protecting the shore.

I see Catcher making his way toward the cable car and my heart lurches. I wish I could be sure that he wouldn't reject me—not again. But I know I have to risk it—I have to see him before he leaves. I have to tell him I'm sorry for being so angry on the roof.

I have to fight for him.

Quickly, I pull on my damp coat and run through the flat to the stairs and out into the night. I race toward the platform, watching as Catcher strides to the car that will take him away.

"Catcher!" I scream, not caring that I'm drawing attention to myself. Not caring about anything but seeing him. Touching him. But he's already in the car, pulling the door shut. I stoop and grab a handful of snow. As hard as I can, I throw it at him and it explodes against the side of the car.

I grab another. "Catcher, wait!" But the Unconsecrated in her little wheel is already lumbering forward, grinding the gears that will propel Catcher away from me. I climb up to the launch platform as the car hovers over the middle of the river.

He stands looking out the broken back window, his hands tucked into his pockets and a small sad smile on his face. My breath hitches. I still have the remnants of a snowball in my hand, a streak of red from my thumb smeared across it where I somehow cut myself. I take a few steps toward the ledge and then I let it go.

It sails through the air and Catcher doesn't even try to dodge it but instead lets it hit square on his chest. Where his heart is. He doesn't move or do anything but stare at me. In the darkness his cheekbones look sharper under his skin and dark shadows fan around his eyes.

He looks exhausted and lonely and I ache wishing I could leap across the distance between us. To pull him to me and let his heat devour me.

I hold my arms out wide. "I'm sorry," I scream at him,

but I don't know if he hears me. Instead the car just continues to take him back to the Dark City, the cables jolting. I can see when it lands, see him stepping out among a sea of Unconsecrated.

"Catcher." My voice breaks. I want to tell him to wait. To come back. To simply let me touch him and look at him and make sure he's okay. I need to know that everything's all right with him and me and this world.

I just need to feel the heat of him.

But I don't know how to tell him all this. That I'm scared and I don't know how to be normal. I'm broken, just like him, and I'm not sure I can fix myself.

"Catcher." This time my voice is barely a whisper. "Please," I add.

He looks up at me, his face gaunt and oh-so sad and lonely. I want to know if he's been eating and sleeping and taking care of himself. I reach out a hand to him but he's so far away. He stands there, a rock in the river of Unconsecrated undulating around him. It's like he doesn't exist to them.

And then he raises one hand to his mouth, fingers touching his lips. I raise my own hand to my lips as he fades into the wash of death and disappears.

I stand there shivering, wishing he'd come back, but there's nothing. Just the dead struggling out onto the partially frozen river before the ice cracks and swallows them, lifeless fingers clambering for the stars.

"Doesn't look like he's too interested in you," a voice says. I turn to find a Recruiter climbing the platform steps. He weaves toward me. "His loss." His *ss* come out as a slurred hiss. He stops out of reach, his mouth breaking into a slow grin, then adds, "My gain."

I freeze. My eyes dart everywhere, trying to determine the best escape. The platform's long and narrow, stairs down to the island on one end and the other hanging out past the wall over the river. There's a rickety railing of sorts with a rope ladder leading down to the shore. But even if I were to crawl through it I'd just end up on the wrong side of the barricades with no way to get back inside.

Below me a few Unconsecrated who've found purchase on the tiny shore reach up for me. One of them's bald with a white tunic, like the woman in the cage inside the main building. Their moans rip away on the wind.

I shove my hands in my pockets, feeling the small lump of my switchblade there. It's not much and probably couldn't cause any mortal wounds, but it makes me feel calmer just holding the cold metal.

I shake my hair back from my face, knowing that the light from the fire at the end of the platform will highlight the scars along my cheek and neck. I hope it makes me look fierce—like a fighter.

The Recruiter's smile grows wider. "Not many women on this island anymore," he says. "Not ones you'd want to have a lot of fun with, if you know what I mean." My stomach turns as I think of the Unconsecrated woman in the death cage and the others lining the hall beyond. He hasn't moved any closer, just stands there knowing he's blocking my only escape. "I keep telling Ox he should parade y'all around more often but he seems resistant to the idea. For now."

My hand's wrapped so tight around the knife handle in my pocket that I can feel the designs etched into it. "I'm just on my way home," I tell him.

He laughs. "Aren't we all."

"Catcher's coming right back." I lift my chin. "He said this would be a short trip."

"Not if I don't set the crank on the plague bag down there he's not," the Recruiter says, gesturing at the Unconsecrated still turning the useless wheel, the gears disconnected. "Car's stuck on that side of the river until I say so."

I try to glance around discreetly and assess the situation. Except for a few other Recruiters huddled around their fires along the wall, we're the only two out here. I'm sure none of them cares about what's going on here—even if I screamed or called for help, I doubt anyone would notice. Which means I just have to get out of this situation on my own.

"Good night," I tell him pointedly as I keep my hands shoved deep in my pockets and move down the platform. I step around him toward the stairs but as I pass he grabs a fistful of my hair.

"Back off," I growl at him, but he doesn't let go.

"It gets lonely out here," he says, rubbing the ends of my hair along his jaw. "I just want to smell something clean and soft."

My mouth goes dry. "Let go," I bark, jerking my head away, but he yanks me until I'm arching my back, about to tumble over. He starts to move farther down the platform, pulling me into the darkness where no one will be able to see us. My feet scramble across the warped icy wood and I lash out at him, but I can't gain much traction.

"Let go!" I shout again, beating at him with my fists and clawing at his eyes. He only yanks harder until my neck feels about to snap and I'm finding it difficult to even breathe.

"We've been keeping you all safe here on this island. Don't you think we deserve some reward for that?" He winds his hand tighter through my hair, tangling it around his fingers.

I try to talk but he's pulling my neck back so far my voice comes out as a gurgle that makes him laugh. I swipe at him but he easily dodges. "I'm not going to hurt you," he says. "Not unless you want me to." He's pulled me to the very edge of the platform and starts to unwind the scarf from around his neck, keeping his grip on my hair tight enough that any movement is too feeble to make a difference.

It's when he starts to tug my arm from my jacket and ties his scarf around my wrist, looping the other end around the railing, that I realize just how far this trouble is escalating. That if I don't act quickly, I might not be able to stop him at all.

He reaches for my other arm and I wrench my elbow up, connecting with his jaw. He shouts and starts to fall backward, tipped off balance. He stumbles a step, dragging me with him, and then the railing collapses and he falls off the end of the platform. His weight jerks against my hair, pulling me to my side on the rotting wood as a blinding pain tears across my scalp and neck. Frantic, I loop my legs around one of the remaining railing supports to stop myself from sliding after him.

I can barely breathe under the agony of his weight dragging on my hair and I flail for some way to make it stop. With his free hand he scrabbles for the edge of the platform but the wood's old and wet with snow and crumbles under his fingers. "Help me!" he screams. Already I hear the Unconsecrated below shifting toward him, their footsteps a squelching crunch as they slog through frozen mud at the river's edge.

"Pull me up!" he shouts, reaching for me. The pain's blinding and I try to pry his fingers away but they're too tangled. I feel the hairs start to pull from my head, searing pinpricks of bright agony.

"Let go!" I cry, but he won't. I close my eyes and clench my jaw and fumble for the knife in my pocket, prying it open with my teeth. He's starting to jerk against me as he tries to pull himself up. Moans fill the air around us, blood from my scalp saturating the air.

I shove the blade through my hair, sawing as hard and fast as I can. Finally, there's so little hair left that it just pulls free, ripped from the roots with a torturous hot pain that makes me gag.

The man drops. I hear the crunch of him hitting the ground. Hot sticky blood trickles around my ear as I peer over the edge of the platform. My entire body shakes as I gulp in the frigid night air, terrified by what I'm about to see.

▼ XXVI ▼

There's just enough light from the fires on the island and the stars in the sky for me to see him. He's mewling in agony as a throng of bodies slowly descends on him. A few drops of blood drip from my fingers into the mass below and as one they raise their heads to me, mouths wet and smeared red.

They stumble to the wall and scrape their fingers against the stone, their nails cracking and skin shredding as they push against a wall that I know in my heart can't hold them back forever.

A few more stumble from the darkness. They tumble around each other, try to crawl over one another. And all of them stare up at me with milky blue eyes. Their mouths open. Their fingers reaching for me. As if I'm the only one who can save them.

I force myself away, slap my hands over my ears and shake my head, but I can still hear them. The sound is everywhere.

Tentatively, I reach up to my head and run my fingers over

the ragged edges of what's left of my once-long hair. The cold night air feels strange against the back of my ears and neck, my face too exposed without the curtain of my bangs. I gather handfuls of snow, using it to numb the throbbing pain of my scalp, and then I pull the Recruiter's scarf from the railing and twine it carefully around my head.

It's all I can do, so I stand up, hunch my shoulders against the cold and start making my way down the platform. Just then I see a figure walking along the shore. In the darkness it could be an Unconsecrated, except its steps are so purposeful that it must be a living being—but someone would have to be insane to walk on the wrong side of the wall with no protection from the dead.

I pull back into the shadows, curling tightly into a ball as the figure comes closer to the platform. I realize it's more than one person—it's a small group—and all of them wear dingy gray tunics underneath their coats. Soulers, their faces haggard and drawn.

It doesn't make sense for them to be out here—for them to be on the island at all, much less on the wrong side of the wall. They each carry what looks like a shovel with a sharpened head and focus intently on the group of dead under the platform. As they approach the Unconsecrated they attack, lashing out to force them to the ground and then severing their heads from their bodies.

Their movements are brutally efficient as one by one they silence the moaning. When they get to the Recruiter he struggles a bit more, trying to call out, but he's lost so much blood that he's too weak to protest much.

He's not dead yet. He hasn't turned. Two of the Soulers shrug and move down the beach, nudging the Recruiter toward the river as if the frozen water could hasten his death. The third Souler crouches and watches the Recruiter flounder and choke, blood oozing from his mouth.

I watch him too. He was cruel to me. He'd have dragged me down with him or worse, and yet seeing him like this is almost too much. It's almost too merciless.

As if it makes me as bad as they are.

"Stop it," I call out.

The Souler stands, turning to look up at me. My heart stutters as my mind cycles to place the familiar face. And then I remember him: He was the boy with Amalia. He was the one who tried to protect her from the Recruiters.

"What are you doing? What's going on?" I ask, crawling to the edge of the platform so that none of the other Recruiters hears us.

His eyes are dead, his shoulders slumped. He looks back at the Recruiter floundering in the frigid water, his skin turning blue. "Waiting for him to die and Return so I can kill him," he says flatly.

I want to ask him why he doesn't just do it now—why he's waiting—but there's still a line between the living and the dead, between mercy killing and murder, and I can understand someone not wanting to cross it.

"How long have you been out here?" I wonder how I could have missed this small group combing the shore, how I could have been so wrapped up in my own world.

He glances up at the stars, the weak light from the fires down the wall making his cheeks recede in the darkness. "Since this morning?" He says it as a question. "Recruiters kept us inside most of the day—said they'd only send us out at night so other people from the City don't get ideas of coming over and swarming them."

"But how did you even get here? Where did you come from?"

"We were in the Neverlands—stranded on a roof—and some guy told us we'd be safe if we came with him. He's the one who brought us to a boat and got us across."

A sick dread creeps into my stomach. "What was his name?"

He frowns, thinking. "Trapper? Caesar . . . It was something like that."

"Catcher."

He smiles, just barely. "Yeah, that's it."

I dig my nails into my palms, thinking about Catcher bringing these people across the river. Giving them false hope to lead them here and then abandoning them just outside the walls. Using them to keep the shores swept clean of Unconsecrated—letting them take the risk so that the Recruiters wouldn't have to.

"You need to come inside," I tell the boy. I move around to the ladder, reaching my hand toward him. "It's freezing out here. You need food and sleep."

He stares at my outstretched fingers and I see something flicker in his eyes. There's a spark of hope and life. But then he shakes his head. "They'll find me and throw me back over the wall," he says. "The only way for us to earn a permanent spot on the Sanctuary is to serve our time. Keep the shore swept clear so the dead don't pile up."

"That's absurd," I tell him. "They can't do that to you. Come on, I'll take you home with me." I curl my hand, beckoning him.

I know he wants nothing more than for me to pull him up and take him away. To tuck him into a bed piled with blankets and fill his stomach with warm food and hot tea. And so I know how amazingly difficult it is for him to turn me down. "I can't," he whispers. "I can't leave the others. It wouldn't be fair."

"You can't trust the Recruiters," I implore, but he stands firm, refusing my offer.

I'm afraid to know the answer but I have to ask: "Is Amalia with you?"

A brief movement of pain flashes across his face. "She's already gone," he says. Before I can ask more he walks out into the shallow water where the Recruiter lies still, floating among the shards of ice. I hadn't even noticed him die. He'd been utterly alone in the last moments, not that he deserved anything better.

The dead sometimes scream when they Return, a horrid eerie cry. That's what happens now, a plaintive wail that's cut short as the boy's blade slices through the Recruiter's neck and severs his spinal cord. His head tumbles into the shallows while his body bobs in the gentle waves.

In the distance someone shouts, the sound of the Recruiter's cry still echoing. One last time I try to convince the boy to come with me, but he just turns back along the shore after the others, and I push myself away down the platform and run for home.

Once I'm there the events of the night hit me. There's no way I can sleep, and the air inside feels stale, like a cell. Leaving the scarf wrapped around my head, I retreat to the roof.

The storm from earlier's blown past, wisps of clouds still stuck to the stars. The rising moon's almost full and its glow sets everything around me into an eerie bright stillness.

The muscles along my jaw feel tight, as if I've been trying to hold back a scream, and I remember the infected woman on the roof that night that seems like several lifetimes ago. I think of what it felt like to dip my fingers in the colored stains

she'd left behind—the feel of release without words, screaming in images.

I grab a few chunks of wood from a long-ago fire and use
them for charcoal, long black streaks crumbling under my
touch. I shut everything else off but the feel of my body moving, the joy and need of it. Leaving the smallest part of me to
listen for anyone approaching, the rest of me indulging in the
release of creating.

I draw out lines, shade in contours. Sore muscles along my
arms and shoulders protest and I push them harder.
Underneath my fingers shapes begin to form, faces and bodies straining against the wall. Sweat breaks out on my neck
and down my back and I lose all track of time and place. I forget the pain along my scalp, the way the cold air seeps against
the back of my ears.

It's just me and the wood and the wall. Images that flash in
my mind and are translated by my fingers before I can see
them and piece them together. It's like I'm not even involved,
just a conversation between hand and subconscious. I sweep
lines out and then smudge them with my wrist: a woman's
hair tangling in the breeze. I sketch a child's lips around a
crack: a perpetual scream.

As I step back, I realize what I've been drawing. Etched
along the length of the wall is an army of people, stretching
from side to side and deep into the distance. They shuffle
toward me, fingers outstretched and pleading.

The moonlight makes them look almost real. Spirits of
people from long ago breaking through the crumbling bricks,
needing what's left of our world.

I've drawn myself in there, the shadow of scars along my
left side, my hair in angry spikes. My sister next to me, perfect
and free, her fingers entwined with Elias's. Recruiters tangled

with the Soulers in their tunics. Everyone I've ever known—all of us gone.

All of us shells.

Except for one. Standing in the middle of the crowd is Catcher. The only one with his arms loose by his sides. The only one with his mouth closed, just standing in the midst of it all.

I stare at my drawing of him. I've captured the way his eyebrows curve, the slight slant to his eyes.

The loneliness and despair inside him.

Slowly I walk back to the wall. I pull out a thin strip of wood with a sharp black point. Painstakingly, I begin to scratch the bars of a fence over the mass of Unconsecrated. Needing something to hold them back.

Their fingers curl around the links, their faces against the fence. But when I get to Catcher I can't stand to draw over him. I place the tip of the wood on my lip, thinking.

Using my fingertips I begin to add new details to the drawing, the chalkiness of the black dust gritty under my touch. To the left of Catcher runs the fence, but to the right I add other details. Rather than clutching the links, the Unconsecrated hold flowers, and balloons tug them to the sky. They wear bright hats and absurd makeup. I make them smile, as if they're laughing rather than moaning.

I stand back from the mural, my breath still coming fast from the explosion of effort. Steam rises in wispy clouds from my cheeks and I'm panting for breath. I stare at the plague rats writhing against the fence, at the ferocious need of them. A complete contrast to the people on the other side, ridiculously happy. And in between is Catcher, as if he belongs with both and neither.

I cross my arms over my chest and stare at the image of him, feeling myself falling for him even more with every heartbeat. It's stupid and I know it. I even hate myself for it, trying to find any reason to explain away the blaze of desire in my chest.

He's gone.

I pushed him away.

And I pushed hard enough that he left.

My mind conjures images of my legs wrapped around him in the tunnels, of how he held me as we escaped from the City and how he swept me into his arms in the snow as if I were beautiful.

Every memory stings, reminds me of what I gave up. My mind screams for me to stop remembering, to just be done with the pain of it, but my body still warms, wanting Catcher.

▼ ▼ ▼

They bang on the door at dawn the next morning, not even caring if someone answers before breaking it down.

"What's going on?" Elias bellows.

I hear him trying to stop them but he can't. They go from room to room until they shove open my door and I'm standing there dressed, already pulling on my coat.

My sister pushes past them and as soon as she sees me she gasps and screams, "Annah! What happened? What's going on?"

I'd already seen my reflection in the window: a thin line of scabs arching behind my ear, a bald spot where the hair ripped free. I'd gone ahead and cut the rest of it before going to bed, preferring not to feel the remnants of my hair against my cheeks knowing it's no longer enough to cover my scars.

Conall stands at the head of the crowd of Recruiters. I glare at him and he grins, coldly. "You're gonna pay." He raises his hand as if to hit me and Elias jumps forward, grabbing his arm.

"What's going on?" Elias shouts, trying to regain order, but other Recruiters have pushed into the room and are clutching me, pulling me into the hallway. "What is this?"

I don't fight them but they drag me anyway, grinning at my grunts of pain. I hear Conall explaining to Elias and my sister about the man I killed last night and Elias bellows that he'll talk to Ox and get everything straightened out.

The joyous malice in Conall's voice is unmistakable when he says, "Ox is the one who ordered this."

XXVII

Moans drift through the air as Conall drags me to the cable-car platform and hands me a shovel with a sharpened end, the same tool the Soulers carried last night. My stomach twists with foreboding but I keep my face placid.

Ox stands by the rope ladder leading to the shore on the unprotected side of the wall circling the Sanctuary. Unconsecrated stumble at the bottom, reaching up for us, swiping at the bitterly cold air. Their knuckles—those who still have any—look red and raw, their faces scraped by ice.

The river's a riot of slush with frozen water cracking and shifting around the edges. I can just see the shadow of the Recruiter's body in the shallows, his skin already distorted and swollen.

A few boats stuffed with refugees from the Dark City float beyond range of the Recruiter crossbows. They no longer shout for help or beg to be let ashore; now they just watch us with desperate eyes. It's impossible to tell how long it will be before the Unconsecrated swell from the Dark City and fill the river until they overwhelm the Sanctuary as well.

Elias races onto the platform, his steps reverberating across the old wood. "What's going on?" he shouts, his face purple with rage. "You can't do this!"

Ox turns to him, a blank expression on his face. He points at the decapitated Recruiter below. "She killed one of my men and there will be consequences."

Elias stops, breath coming out in fast pants that cloud the air in front of his face in the cold morning. His lips are blue. "What? Annah couldn't kill anyone!"

Everyone stares at me. There's no use lying—it's clear they know the truth. I raise my chin defiantly. "He was attacking me," I spit at Ox. "I was defending myself."

My confession is enough for Ox and he pushes me toward the ladder, but I turn on him. "It's not my fault you can't control your men. He practically ripped my hair out—he deserved it."

Ox hesitates and Elias jumps forward, trying to yank me back, so I'm in the middle of a tug-of-war between the two men.

"You can't hurt her," Elias argues. "What about Catcher?"

Below us the Unconsecrated reach and moan, pushing against the wall. A few more wash ashore, bloated bodies almost frozen. They lie there, still and silent. Eventually, they'll struggle to their feet as well, hungering for the living.

I scowl as Elias and Ox argue. I know what the result will be—Ox has already proven more than once that he's not one to show mercy.

"She's not going to be killed," Ox reassures Elias and I snort even as my insides relax with relief. "She's going to be put to work." He swings his hand down to the shore. "We need someone to sweep during the day anyway."

I swallow again and again as fear reaches deep inside me. But I refuse to let anyone know I'm afraid.

Elias starts to protest but Ox shifts forward, leaning his huge bulk against Elias's leaner body. "For what she did to my man it shouldn't even be a question," he growls. "I'd kill her myself if I could. Do you want to argue that she shouldn't be punished? You know me better than that."

Over Elias's shouts of protest Conall drags me toward the rope ladder. I kick at his shins and he pushes me over the edge of the platform until I have no choice but to grab the ladder or fall to the ground below. He holds the shovel out at me and when I reach for it he lets it drop, slipping through my grip and falling where the plague rats trample it.

Unconsecrated fingers brush my ankle, their desperation fevered with me so near. I don't allow myself to scream as I grip the rungs of the ladder, no weapon to defend myself.

Elias leaps forward, shoving Conall out of the way and kneeling on the dock, reaching for me. Before I can warn him, Conall's recovered and kicks Elias in the ribs and there's nothing I can do.

With a grunt and a whoosh of air, Elias's face crumples in pain and he falls to his side, clutching his stomach. He scrapes a hand against the platform, trying to push himself back up, but Conall steps on his fingers, grinding his heel into the wood.

"You questioning a direct order?" Conall asks, bending low so his face is flush with Elias's. I can hear Elias groaning with the pain.

"Catcher won't let this happen," Elias mutters.

Ox laughs and pushes Conall out of the way before dragging Elias to his feet. Elias's body is crooked as he tries to curl around the spot where he was kicked, cradling his injured hand to his chest.

When Ox speaks his voice is deadly calm and serious. "Catcher doesn't control the Sanctuary, I do. We need only one of you to keep him coming back to us—you should remember that next time you want to forget the rules."

Wind swirls around us, flinging snow in my eyes and chapping my fingers that are already numb from gripping the rope ladder so tightly. Long-dead fingernails scrape along the bottom of my leg, trying to pull me down, and I lash out, kicking them away, but they stumble back to continue groping for me.

Elias pants, his arm pressed into his side and his face pale with pain. "Don't do this, Ox," he pleads.

My breath catches in my throat at the agony in Elias's expression. I glance down at the Unconsecrated huddled beneath me. There are only a handful, more slowly making their way down the shore toward us.

If I jump I might be able to get clear of them, but it would be a stupid and risky move. If I twist my ankle or break my leg I'll be useless, unable to get away fast enough. I press my head against my arms, trying to figure out what to do next.

There's a commotion on the platform above me, and as I look up I see my sister elbowing a Recruiter in the gut and pulling the crossbow from him. Before anyone can react she grabs a sling of bolts and skids to her knees just above me.

Closing one eye, she aims at the nearest Unconsecrated clawing at my feet. "I'm not the best shot, so you might want to keep still," she says, and I cringe as she exhales. There's a sharp twang of string and the thunk of an arrowhead penetrating the plague rat's skull, his body crumpling limply to the ground.

She's aiming for the next one when Ox roars up behind her. "You want to join your sister? Fine!" he shouts, jamming his foot into her back just as she pulls the trigger. The bolt goes wide, burying itself in the shallow frozen water along the shore.

My sister teeters on the edge of the platform and I grab her just as she falls, pulling her against me with one arm, gripping the ladder tight with the other. Her feet kick at the empty air, the Unconsecrated below us an utter frenzy.

"No!" Elias screams, jolting toward us. Conall grabs one of his arms and another Recruiter the other. With a jerk of his foot Conall kicks at the back of Elias's knees, forcing him down onto the platform. His face falls a few inches from mine.

His eyes strain with terror and panic. "It'll be okay," I tell him, trying to sound more sure of myself than I am. "We'll take care of each other. I know how to survive."

Next to me my sister's wrapped an arm through the ladder and points the crossbow at the head of the nearest plague rat. Without any emotion or hesitation she pulls the trigger and it collapses, eyes falling slowly shut.

"Get him out of here," Ox grunts.

It takes four men to drag a screaming and fighting Elias away. Through it all Ox stands above us, blocking the cable-car platform. My sister doesn't bother looking at him. Instead she shoots another plague rat, clearing a path for us below.

I wait for Ox to pronounce some sort of sentence but instead he just stares at me, his hands buried in the pockets of his thick coat as if trying to figure out what it will take to break me. I smile at him, cold and mean, thinking, Nothing. I will never break for you.

Ox narrows his eyes and nods his head before turning to the few Recruiters left standing guard by the cable car. "You can let them up at sunset," he says. "Not before."

I have no idea what any of this means, but it can't be good, because one of the Recruiter's eyes go wide and he glances at me, looking concerned. "There's a snowstorm coming in over the horizon. Should be here by the afternoon. We weren't even going to put the other Sweepers out tonight."

Ox shrugs. "Maybe it will get cold enough to slow the rotters down." And with that he walks off, leaving my sister and me clinging to the ladder.

The Recruiter, a slightly older man with gray at his temples, looks at us with a deep furrow between his eyebrows. He stares at my bare hands—I didn't have time to find any gloves. He checks over his shoulder, and when he's sure no one's paying attention he unwinds his thick scarf and drops it to us, saying "Good luck" before turning away.

My sister responds by shooting a bolt into the forehead of the last Unconsecrated reaching for us on the shore. We slip to the ground, a thin sheen of ice crunching under our feet.

I loop the scarf around my sister's neck. "You shouldn't have done that," I tell her, picking up the shovel and testing its weight.

She tugs the scarf tight and pulls a stray bolt from where it lodged in the ground. "I don't particularly like killing them, but if we were going to get off that ladder they had to go."

I try to force a smile—I know that's what she wants. "I mean you shouldn't have helped at all. You should've stayed on the platform where it's safe."

She shrugs but her lips tremble, her hands unsteady as they fit the bolt onto the string. "I'm your sister," she says and her voice is uneven as she clarifies, "Your *older* sister. And it's my job to take care of you."

I want to tell her that I don't need taking care of, that I've done just fine on my own. But that would clearly be a lie. I'd have likely died or gotten infected if she hadn't stepped in.

The enormity of what she's done—what she's sacrificed for me—is overwhelming, and I have to turn away so that she doesn't see my face.

I left her alone in the Forest. She had every right to abandon me as well, and she chose not to. That she didn't means that maybe I can allow myself to rely on her. To actually believe she'll be there for me when I need her.

This thought terrifies me. I'm not used to depending on someone.

That's not true—I used to rely on Elias, but when he left me I promised I'd never trust again.

My sister places a hand on my shoulder, the tips of her fingers pressing lightly on my collarbone in reassurance. Beyond us, down the shore, the Unconsecrated shuffle toward us, slow and inevitable.

With a sigh she drops her hand and stands over the dead plague rats, bracing a foot against each one's head so that she can tug at the bolts lodged in each skull. Her muscles strain until the arrows slide free with a loud *shlurk* of a sound.

We both cringe. I watch the way her tangled hair falls over her face and she absently brushes it away. I think how long it took me to learn not to brush my own hair back from my cheeks, to use it instead as a shield to hide my face.

I reach up to my neck, feeling the absence of my hair.

Wind blows off the river and I shiver, wrapping the scarf I took last night tighter around my head.

"Do you think we'll make it through this?" I ask her, the rush from the scuffle on the platform draining out of me.

She doesn't even look up, just says yes as she jerks free another bolt with a grunt. I hear the resolve in her voice. An unshakeable determination to stay alive. I wish I had her absolute belief in survival. I wish I didn't know how hard it is to do—to struggle through each day only to wake up to a deeper struggle the next. I feel like falling asleep and letting it all consume me. Just letting the Unconsecrated take over.

They're bound to anyway.

"I killed someone." My sister's confession shocks me out of my thoughts.

I jerk around to face her. She's standing right where the ice clings to the shore, clutching the recovered bolts in her hands.

"What?" I choke out. Of all the things I expect her to say this isn't it.

She squats and presses the points of the bolts to the thin frozen water, cracking it. I can't see her face and so I walk over and kneel next to her, the icy shore seeping through my clothes, numbing my knees.

"In Vista. I killed someone. His name was Daniel and he was . . ." She swallows, her lips quivering. "He was going to blackmail me. He was going to make me *be* with him—marry him—or else he was going to get me in trouble and I panicked. He had me shoved up against the Barrier and I couldn't breathe and I didn't know what to do and . . ." She's almost hyperventilating, the words stumbling over one another.

In the distance the Unconsecrated moan, their steps crunching as they slowly wend their way along the wall toward us. I wrap my arm around her and pull her to me, tucking her face into my shoulder and resting my chin on her head. She squeezes me so hard that it hurts to breathe. "It's okay," I tell her but she shakes her head. I can feel her tears on my skin.

"It's not." Her voice is muffled, hard to understand. "It's not okay. His blood was all over me and he was looking at me as he was dying. I just left him there. If I'd told someone . . . If I hadn't let him see me in the first place . . . There are so many ways I could have done something so that he didn't have to die."

She draws in a shuddering breath. "I'm not a horrible person, Annah, I promise I'm not. I didn't mean to. I didn't know what else to do."

I hold her tight. "I know you're not a horrible person, I'd never think that of you."

She sniffs and lifts her head from my shoulder. Her cheeks are streaked with tears and her eyes puffy. "I told you I wasn't perfect," she says as I brush wisps of hair from her face.

"It's okay," I tell her. "None of us is," I add. She smiles just a little and her resolve rubs off on me. I stare at the way the tracks of her tears break across her jaw and along her neck, at how it looks like her face, once shattered, has been carefully put back together. And I wonder if that's what my scars really are: proof that I've put myself back together again.

▼ XXVIII ▼

It's a frigid day. The snowstorm hits in the late afternoon and makes it next to impossible to see across the river as gusts leave us almost blind and quaking with cold. My sister and I huddle against each other in a nook in the wall, pushing our hands under our clothes to try to keep our blood moving.

"You shouldn't be down here," I tell her for the hundredth time. "Catcher won't come back for Elias. You have to tell Conall that. If both of us die, they'll lose Catcher."

My sister shakes her head, the Recruiter's scarf wound tight around her neck and covering her hair. "I'm not leaving you." It's hard to hear her over the whipping wind.

"You can't stay here," I tell her. "Both of us can't freeze to death."

She sets her jaw. "I'd prefer to think that *neither* of us will freeze to death out here." She raises one eyebrow. I know too well how stubborn the blood that runs through our veins is.

I grab her shoulders, the freezing air biting my unprotected fingertips. I propel her toward the platform. "There will be other Sweepers out here later—I met one last night. I'll find them and I'll be fine. I promise."

She shakes her head, digging her feet in. "You won't be fine," she argues.

"You're right, I won't be fine. But I'll survive. I know how to do that."

She ducks under my arms, doubling back until she's facing me. "I don't want to lose you again," she says, her voice cracking.

I pull her closer to me. Moans float through the air, more dead washing onto the frozen shore.

I take a deep breath. "Sometimes you have to leave. Sometimes that's the smartest thing to do." I press my bare fingers to her cheek and she returns the gesture.

"Maybe so," she says. "But you're still not convincing me to leave you alone in the middle of a snowstorm when Mudo are washing ashore around you."

I glare at her. "You're stubborn—anyone ever tell you that before?"

She smiles wide. "I take that as a compliment."

We stand side by side, watching the darkness shroud the black slushy river, white pummeling everywhere. Unconsecrated struggle from the half-frozen water, their bodies tossing over ice that cuts dead skin. Where they're not too deep I wade out and use the shovel, digging it into their necks, pushing down and grunting with the effort of slicing through skin and severing bone. The heads roll a little and it's hard to avoid their eyes.

I wonder if I'm somehow giving them peace.

My sister stares down at one of the empty bodies. "What

would you do if you knew you had only a few days left to live?" she says. Water laps around dead arms and legs, tempting the deep.

A gust of wind rips through my coat and I steel myself against it. I think about the woman on the roof asking the same question. How terrified I was that I'd die like her: alone, no one to mourn my absence. I think about how quickly that's changed. "I'd find a way to survive," I tell her, my teeth chattering.

She tilts her head. "And that's all you want? To survive?"

I shrug, jumping up and down a bit to push the blood through my body. "Seems like a good idea right now," I say, jerking my chin at our surroundings.

She's silent, dancing from foot to foot to stay warm.

"What about you? What would you do?" I tuck my hands up in my sleeves.

Raising one eyebrow, she says, "Nope. I'm not telling you my dreams until you tell me yours." She crooks a smile. "It'll give you incentive to make sure we both survive this mess."

I laugh and lean against her. "We'll survive," I tell her. "I promise you that."

▼   ▼   ▼

The storm intensifies, making it hard to stay standing and difficult to hear the moans of the Unconsecrated or see if any have washed ashore. My sister and I continue to huddle together in the nook of the wall, arms wrapped around each other as we try to stay out of the wind.

My breath comes out in pants, and each inhalation is like ice, its sharpness stinging my lungs. "We need to go back," I shout at my sister. "They can't keep us out here like this."

She nods, her face buried in her thick coat. We struggle down the wall, letting the storm push us against it. I try to hold the shovel out in front of me in case any of the dead are still moving in this weather, but my muscles are so exhausted they shake, trying to wring out what little warmth they can. I'm barely able to keep myself upright. Everything's just so cold. So cold and so hard.

Inside I feel empty. I can't even remember the last time I ate. The last time I slept I cycled through nightmares, feeling my hair being torn from my body over and over again.

A figure stumbles toward me from the direction of the water and it takes me a moment to remember where I am. What I'm supposed to be doing. I swing. Sloppy and uneven, the motion throws me off balance. I take two steps. Three. Fall to one knee and use the shovel to pick myself back up again.

The body lurches, slow and jerky. I can just barely hear the moan. Out of the darkness hair whips through the night, tangled around a woman's face so that it's hard to see anything but her mouth.

She's barely walking—barely moving—but still she almost grabs me. I kick her back, which makes my own footing unstable. I fall, the shovel skittering out of my grasp.

The Unconsecrated woman comes for me again, stuck in time so slow it's like her body's full of half-frozen water. I know I should be frantic—my mind tries to be—but my body won't obey. My hands search the frozen shore, digging through snow to find the shovel, but soon I realize I can't feel anything.

My sister staggers to my side, crossbow jolting as she tries to hold it steady with her shivering arms. The first bolt goes wide and the second only tears into the Unconsecrated woman's shoulder. She lumbers toward me, intent.

My hands are nothing more than lumps. I have no way to defend myself. Except to run. The Unconsecrated woman swings at me, her body jerking at the movement, and I push myself away.

And then her head whips back, the left side of it crushed in on itself. My sister stands with my shovel in her hands, pulling it up for another swing.

It takes all my reserves of strength to get to my feet. I totter a moment, pressing my arm against the wall to steady myself. The world tilts and sways, sparks jumping through my vision as dark spots threaten to swallow me.

"You go!" I shout at her, pulling the weapon from her hands. She starts to shake her head but I shove her forward. "Get help!" I cry. She turns and struggles toward the platform, a black shape in the dark evening.

The Unconsecrated behind me moans and I remember that that sound is bad. Really bad. I shove away from it, stumbling down the beach. I lose my footing more than once. I forget where I'm going. Why.

Nothing seems like a better idea than simply lying down. Curling up. Riding out the storm wrapped around my poor frozen hands, which don't even burn anymore.

Then I hear the moan and I remember again. Moan. Death. Bad. In front of me I see light. Fire. My sister. Good.

There's something I should be holding on to. A promise I made. A feeling. But every time the thought enters my mind it's gone before my frozen fingers can wrap around it.

The fire's farther away than it looks. So so far. Too far. I don't have the energy anymore.

Something tangles around me as I stumble against the snow. I fight but my arms are stuck and I can't get them free.

It looks like it could be rope but it doesn't make sense that there would be rope just dangling here.

I scrunch up my face trying to figure it out but it's too hard to think. I let my body weight fall against it and it holds me. That's much better. My legs don't hurt anymore. I can lie here tangled in the rope. Just for a moment until I can remember what I'm doing and have the energy to do it. Sleep will help. That's all I need.

A noise keeps bothering me and when I look down I see that there's a person huddled at my feet. Her shoulders shake and I think I should be doing something. I should have a weapon. I think I remember that much.

I push at the body with my foot, not wanting it near me. It rolls and I'm confused because it's me on the ground. But I'm not on the ground, I'm tangled in the ropes—and then I remember my sister.

A shock of fear jolts through me, focusing the moment. My sister. I fall to my knees and grab her coat. "Abigail!" I shout. Her eyelids flutter. I scream at her, my throat raw with the force of it, until she looks at me.

"Gabry," she mumbles, and I shake her again.

I get right in her face when I yell, "Fight!"

"No." She bats at me and I slap her. I don't even feel it, my fingers are so numb. Her eyes open and she frowns.

"Go away." She tries to pull out of my grasp but I tug at her until she's standing.

Wind howls fierce, blustering over the river and coating everything white. I shove my sister up the ladder, forcefully wrapping her hands around the rope when she wants to give up.

We make it to the platform and it's empty. Sleep—pure

blissful warm sleep—calls to me and I want nothing more than to follow.

"Come on!" I heave her down the platform and across the island, our bodies stumbling into each other as the wind blows at our backs. No one tries to stop us—everything's too howling wind and frozen ice.

Her feet drag and I shake my head to clear it. To focus. It's freezing. It hurts.

In front of me's a tall building and I aim for it. Just one more step, I scream at myself. I can take just one more.

She's limp in my arms now and I'm shaking her to keep us both warm. Finally there's a door. A familiar door and I sag against it, forcing it open. My sister tumbles inside to the darkness and I shut the door and then I slide to the ground.

It's warmer here. No wind. At last, I'm allowed to sleep.

▼ XXIX ▼

In my dream someone's screaming. It's terrifying and I try to run away but the echoes follow me. And then there's warmth. Such wonderful delicious heat that pours through my entire body so bright it's almost painful. I don't open my eyes—I don't need to. This is my dream, so I know who's talking when they beg me to stay with them, when they tell me not to sleep. But why wouldn't I sleep?

It's safe here in the warmth and I was so cold before. I don't want to be cold again.

Catcher's lips press against my closed eyelids and along my ear and my jaw. He touches his forehead to mine and I don't understand why he's crying.

It's my dream. He should be happy like I am. Happy and safe and warm.

Wake up, he begs me. *Please wake up.*

▼   ▼   ▼

I startle awake and every inch of my body burns.

"It's okay," someone says, his voice reverberating through me, and I realize I'm tucked against a body. I can tell by the heat that it's Catcher. We're lying on something soft and it takes me a moment to recognize that we're in my bed, in my room.

Catcher's lips rest lightly against my forehead.

I'm about to ask him what's going on. I'm about to pull away when I remember the shore and the snow with a terror so deep that I feel like I won't ever be able to breathe again.

"Abigail!" I shout, remembering how blue her lips looked, how hard she was shaking.

"It's okay," he murmurs again. "She's in her own bed recovering. She's safe. You're both safe now."

I collapse, turning my head away from him. I try to remember exactly how I got here, but all I recall is the cold and the wind. "What happened?"

Catcher takes a deep shaking breath. "They held Elias in a room all day so he couldn't get you off the shore. When they let him go he ran to find you but you weren't there. He thought you were dead. He came running back here and found you both just inside the door downstairs."

He opens his mouth to say more but then closes it as if he's reconsidering. I feel his arms tighten around me. "All that matters is that you're okay now," he finally says, but I can't truly believe him. I feel like I'll never be warm again, my body shivering with the memories. "I talked to Ox," he adds. "Nothing like that will ever happen again. *Ever*. Not if he wants my co-operation."

I remember Ox's face when he tossed me off the platform. When he let the Recruiter hit me. "He won't care," I say, sighing. "He'll do what it takes to keep order." Reluctantly, I pull away from Catcher. I test my fingers, opening and closing them, but the motion brings with it waves of pain. "We need to find a way out of here," I tell him.

He stands and walks to the window. Outside it's a brilliant blue day, so bright it almost hurts my eyes. He nods. "I know. I've been trying. I've been searching the tunnels and looking for places we can go that might be safe. There's nothing. Not yet. I'm . . ." He traces something over the glass. "I'm sorry I'm the reason you're here."

I untangle myself from the bed, hissing as my swollen feet hit the floor. I walk over, leaving only a thin line of emptiness between us. "It's not your fault."

He shrugs. "I'm the Immune. You're the bait." There's acid in his voice. I can hear how much he hates himself and it isn't fair.

I press my hand to the back of his neck and he winces as if he's not used to being touched. "Thank you for returning. I don't know what would have happened."

A muscle along his jaw twitches, contracting and relaxing as he grinds his teeth. "I was worried. I shouldn't have left you like that." He pauses before softly adding, "I'm sorry."

My cheeks flush when I remember our confrontation. Me grabbing his hand and pushing it against my chest. Him shoving me away when I tried to kiss him. I move toward the bed and cross my arms, feeling the sting of vulnerability all over again.

But that doesn't dissuade Catcher. He takes a step closer and then another. I press my lips together, trying not to hope that he might have changed his mind. That he might touch me.

"I was worried about you, after . . . ," he says. He stops just out of my reach. Keeping me out of his reach as well. "After the other day. After what I said and you said." He glances away and then back to me.

He'd called me beautiful. "Do you take it back?" I ask, breathless.

My heart pounds a million times as I wait for him to answer.

"Never." He licks his lips in a nervous gesture and I can't help staring at them. Imagining the feel of them.

I think about what my sister asked me as we stood huddled together outside the wall. How I didn't know how to answer her. "What would you do if you knew you had only a few days left to live?" I ask him.

He raises his hand to the back of his neck, a nervous laugh brushing over his lips. "You don't have to worry about that, Annah," he says. "I'm going to take care of you. And everyone else. You're safe."

I step forward and place my hand on his arm, feeling his muscle flex beneath my touch. I press against him, pushing his hand from his head, pulling it down to his side, threading my fingers through his. The movement places us even closer together. His chest barely touches mine. Now I can feel his breath on my skin. I can feel his heat wavering between us.

"What would you do?" I ask again, softly.

His eyes become serious and I can almost see the emotions roiling inside him. "I've already been there, remember?" He pulls at his shirt, loosening the buttons and sliding it over his shoulder. Pushing me away in the process so that cooler air drives between us. He takes my fingers and places them against the flesh of his arm, forcing me to feel the two half-moons of red scars.

Bite marks.

I know he's trying to remind me—remind both of us—that he's infected. That he doesn't know if he can infect me. That he'd never take the risk.

"What did you do during those days?" I ask, wanting to understand him.

"I waited," he says, his voice distant. His eyes flicker, a flash of something that disappears.

"Waited for what?"

"To die." That same flicker again. "Alone," he adds in a whisper.

I open my mouth to ask for more but he cuts me off. "I've already had my days of waiting to die," he says. "The question is, what would you do, Annah?"

The same question as last night, except now I actually have an answer. I'm tired of just surviving. I'm tired of waking up each day simply to make it to the next.

That isn't enough anymore. It's been what I've done for too long and when I look back on those strings of days they're all empty. I want more. More than closing myself off, more than being afraid to let someone care about me and me about them.

I want Catcher.

And I'm tired of his fear that he could somehow infect me. So what? I'm already dying anyway—every day I live is closer to death. It's like I told my sister before: what matters is what you do with the time you're alive.

"I'd live," I tell him. Then I step forward, slide my hand from his shoulder to the back of his neck and press my lips into his.

He's so stunned that at first he doesn't react and I take

advantage of his hesitation, deepening the kiss. For a moment—one tiny space between heartbeats—he falls into me. He whimpers slightly, his head tilting to the side as he pushes hard against my mouth and fire engulfs me, races through my veins.

He tries to speak, his tongue forming words that I fight with my own. And then he lunges back, breaking us apart. I step forward, tugging his head to me, but he places his hands on my shoulders and pushes me away.

His eyes are wide, his lips parted and face flushed. He's breathing fast and his hand shakes when he raises it to his neck. "God, Annah, what were you thinking?" With each word his voice hardens.

"I told you . . ." He paces in a tight circle. "God, Annah, I could infect you. I could have already infected you! I can't believe you did that."

He shakes his head, presses a fist to his chin and closes his eyes. Carefully, I shift closer to him, rest a hand on his forearm. "It's okay," I tell him softly.

He explodes. "It's not okay! *This*"—he gestures back and forth between us— "isn't okay!"

Grabbing my head between his hands, he pulls me close, until our lips are almost but not quite together. His breathing is fierce and fast, matching my own. I can tell that he's angry and scared and panicking.

"You could die," he's telling me. "That kiss, it could kill you."

I smile. "Don't you get it, Catcher? With the horde already consuming the Dark City? With the Recruiters and their death cages? I'm already going to die. This Sanctuary isn't safe—nowhere's safe. Even without the horde, one day I'm going to die. Just like one day you're going to die—"

"But that's the difference, Annah! I'm. Not. Going. To. Die. Ever." He drops his hands from my head and paces away from me. I feel the chill of the morning air on every spot Catcher just touched. "One day something will happen to me. My heart will stop working, I'll get stabbed by the wrong person, I'll drown or fall from a bridge or a building will collapse on top of me. And then I'll come back."

He spins to face me. "I could die today right here in your room and I'd come back."

"But it's oka—"

"Don't tell me it's okay!" he shouts. He seems shocked at his own rage and he storms away from me, arms crossed tight over his chest. I approach him slowly.

"Don't tell me it's okay," he repeats, this time more in control. "Because it's not. When I come back, I'll attack you if you're anywhere nearby." His voice is shaking now. "Don't you realize how dangerous that is? Don't you understand there's already that monster inside me, waiting for my heart to hesitate for only a moment before it becomes unleashed?"

He whips around, grabs my upper arms. "I can't do that to you, Annah. I can't."

He starts to pull away but I stop him. "You asked me what I'd do knowing I only had a few days left and that was it," I tell him. "That's what I'd do. I'd stop worrying and being afraid and living in the past. I'd stop trying to keep my emotions safe. You know as well as I do what the horde is doing to the City—how it will eventually come across the river. And if it doesn't, Ox and his men will find a way to kill us anyway. You know my time is limited."

He closes his eyes. "I'm not going to let anything happen to you," he whispers. "I'm going to keep you safe."

"And then what?" I ask him. "I'll survive only to be alone again? To have you slink away? That's not what I want. I want *you*. And I want you to understand that you're not broken."

Taking a deep breath, he presses his lips together until they disappear. I let the silence flow around us. "There's something you need to understand about me," he says. His voice is too even, too devoid of inflection or emotion.

"What?" I ask him, my heart starting to thud.

He reaches out his hand to me, cupping my cheek gently. "Do you think you could ever feel beautiful?" he asks.

I'm so taken aback by his words that I'm stunned speechless. I think about the night Elias made me feel beautiful, remember the touch of his fingers over my scars.

I remember how long I've waited for someone else to find me beautiful. How I push people away before they can see the ugliness. I'm too afraid of the pain that I know comes with losing love.

And I know he was right on the roof. I've been waiting for the validation to come from everyone else, hoping their words can heal the scars that rip through my skin and into my heart.

"I don't know," I answer him honestly. I don't add that I hope so.

"Then how can you ask me to feel unbroken?" he says. I open my mouth to answer but nothing comes out. Because I don't know what to say to him. He's right, how can I ask him to heal himself when I don't know if it's even possible?

XXX

Elias and my sister don't want me leaving the flat. I understand their fear—it's not like the Recruiters don't have enough reasons to cause me trouble. Under normal circumstances I might have listened but I'm not willing to sit around and hope that someone else finds a way off the island.

There has to be another place we can go because I don't see the point of staying in the Sanctuary if it's not ultimately going to keep us safe. And I certainly don't feel safe here anymore.

For the day my sister and I do as Elias asks and stay in bed. My muscles still spasm from the memory of being frozen the night before and my hands and feet are painfully swollen. My head pounds and I have a hard time keeping food down, but Elias is persistent: he will make my sister and me healthy again.

Long after dark, when the flat is silent and I'm sure they're asleep, I pull on clothes dried stiff by the woodstove and find

Elias's machete by the door. I slip it into my belt and sneak down the stairs, wincing until my body gets used to moving again and the ache in my joints subsides.

Outside the night sky's clear and sharp, a million tiny lights exploding overhead—more stars than there ever could have been people in this world.

I think about how fascinated with space Elias always was growing up. How one year I saved every credit I had and traded them all over the months so that on the winter solstice I could present him with an old book mapping the stars. It was the longest night of the year and he spent the entire time on the roof, staring up at the sky and comparing what he saw to the little book in his lap.

It was freezing outside and I'd hauled every blanket we owned up to the roof. While I drifted in and out of dreams, he read to me stories of the stars, origins of their constellations. Over the years I've forgotten most of it, but there's one detail I've always remembered: he told me how long it takes the light from stars to reach through space to us.

How most of the points of light we see actually no longer exist. We're just seeing the remnants of what was—ghosts of what used to be.

I glance at the Dark City across the river, a few buildings still flickering with light as the handful of survivors huddle behind thin curtains slung across broken windows. All of them tiny little stars in their own constellations waiting to fall to infection and become ghosts of what they used to be.

It all seems so worthless. Such a waste of lives. We've spent hundreds of years since the Return buffering the Dark City and trying to maintain it—scraping out a life that will soon be wiped out.

And what of the rest of the world that's already fallen? Stars blinking away, their light slowly fading? Somewhere out there a star's just dying and we'll never know about it. Somewhere another's being born whose light we'll never see.

The Earth will spin, the stars will rearrange themselves around one another and the world will crawl with the dead who one day will drop into nothingness: no humans left for them to scent, no flesh for them to crave. Everything—all of us—will simply cease to be.

They'll finally find peace only when we're all dead.

▼　▼　▼

Once I'm inside the headquarters my footsteps echo down empty hallways, and at first I cringe with every noise, waiting for someone to turn a corner, spot me and cause trouble. But it's a huge building with warrens of twisting corridors, and the ones I walk are dusty and unused.

In the map room I light a few lanterns, knocking the door closed behind me with my foot. It's as I remember: walls covered with faded drawings of the world as it used to be. Pins scattered along the floor, desks piled with neglected stacks of papers and journals.

I flip through a few of the pages—notations from scouts returning from various outings, reporting on enclaves of survivors. There are columns with neatly ordered numbers counting men, women and children. Noting resources and defenses, listing quotas to be met in order to be considered under the Protectorate control.

All this information pulled together and sorted down to one small colored pin on a map. Most of those even gone by now. I wonder how many people mentioned in these pages are dead. I wonder if those who wrote these letters, the ones who traveled to all these places are dead as well.

The reality is that everyone dies. Whether safe in bed asleep or trapped in an alley facing a Returned friend or family member or lover. Whether shot by a Recruiter or just left to float in a boat in the middle of a snowstorm, your body slowly eating itself as resources run dry.

It will happen to me one day. I wonder why I fight so hard against the inevitability of it. What's another day? What's the day after that? Slowly, I walk around the room, trailing my fingers over the wall.

My thumb stops, resting at a green pin. "Vista," I read aloud. My sister's town by the sea. Where Catcher grew up, became infected. Where he survived, broken. There's a thick black line etched along the map just to the west of Vista leading up the coast, and beyond the line there's nothing, but I know it represents the Forest.

And somewhere in that void is the village where I was born, and raised for a few years. I press my hand over it, the scope of the Forest extending past my fingers.

"It's not there anymore," a deep voice says behind me. "Your village."

I cringe, already knowing it's Ox, and reach for the machete at my hip. He doesn't make a move to stop me or even flinch when I pull it from my belt and hold the long blade between us.

"What do you mean, my village?" I ask, cold inside. "How do you know anything about where I'm from?"

Ox leans against the wall by the door, arms crossed casually over his chest. Other than his bulk he appears nonthreatening. But I know better.

He shrugs as if he's not talking about a village. About people. About my father and neighbors. "It's gone."

My eyes go wide, the machete trembling between us. It shouldn't matter, I think. Elias and I had tried to find the village before and we'd failed. We'd given up on it a long time ago. But I'd always preserved that tiny bit of hope that maybe someday we'd make our way back. Everyone we'd left behind would be there with arms outstretched to meet us.

Ox has to see the despair on my face. He has to see how unsettled I am, but he just stays where he is, breathing slowly in and out, face showing no emotion.

"Maybe there was something left of it—the fences were still up and a few buildings looked like they were being maintained. But your friends took care of all that—tearing down the fences to slow Conall and his men." He shrugs again and I want to slap him. "Didn't work," he adds. "And of course they regretted it when they had to fight their way back through to get to Vista."

He squats, riffling around on the floor until he finds a black pin. He stands, knees creaking a little, and walks past me to the map, shoving the pin into it.

I'm staring at the very tip of the machete shaking in the air in front of me. What would it feel like to swing it around, slice it through Ox's neck? I've decapitated enough Unconsecrated by now to know how much force it takes—what it's like trying to saw through the muscle and cartilage and bone.

A part of me would love to hear this man scream. To make him hurt. To see if there's any emotion left inside. But it would be murder, pure and simple, and I'm not sure I'm ready to cross that line.

I'm not sure I'm ready to become a monster like him.

As if he knows what I'm thinking, he smirks but doesn't move out of range of my knife. He just stands there, fingers still hovering over the black pin that represents my village.

"You know"—he smiles, predatory—"Catcher's not the only Immune out there. They're rare, but they exist. We've got people looking—men like Elias infiltrating the Soulers. They know more about Immunes than we do—they worship and protect them, collect them like gods. We bring the Soulers here and eventually one of the Immunes will come to beg for their release. Ask us to trade the lives of all the Soulers—set them free—in exchange for the Immune staying to supply us. It's happened before."

I grip the machete tighter but his glance doesn't waver.

"The second we find a new Immune, you become a whole lot less important. Catcher becomes less valuable and your life becomes about my mercy." He tilts his head to the side. In the small room I can smell his sweat. "And you already know how merciful I can—"

Before he even finishes the statement I swing the machete, aiming for his throat, and then, just as I'm about to feel the blade slice through flesh I stop, letting it hover over his skin. "What about *my* mercy?" I ask through clenched teeth.

I'd wanted a reaction, wanted to see fear, but instead he laughs. "You and I are too much alike for that," he says. "It's that fire I admire in you. If we ever had to teach Catcher a lesson, I'd be sad to see you be the one to go."

He places two fingers on the blade, pushing it away. I resist and the razor-sharp edge cuts into him, thin lines of blood appearing. I know exactly the feel of that pain. It makes my empty stomach turn but he doesn't even flinch. Instead he smiles, hesitating long enough before pulling his hand away that he makes his point.

"We had another Immune once, a few years ago," he says. "We controlled him with his mom—he was a mama's boy, always coming back to her and bringing what we wanted."

My heart begins to beat heavily, my grip on the machete slipping a little as my palms sweat. He pauses, forces me to ask: "What happened?"

This makes him smile as I knew it would. "He felt bad that it was his immunity that made his mom a prisoner, though I thought we treated her fairly well, all things considered.

"Then one day he threw himself off a seven-story building." Slowly, he raises his hand between us, rubbing his thumb over the thin cuts on his fingers, smearing the blood. He considers it a moment before continuing.

"I guess he forgot that, being an Immune, he was still infected. And being infected, he Returned. He couldn't really walk too well, but he could still infect others."

It's silent as Ox wipes his bloody hand over the maps, smearing red across the Forest. I drop my arm to my side, the flat of the machete resting against my knee.

My throat feels tight, making the air in the room that much harder to breathe. "What did you do to him?" My voice cracks.

Ox looks at me hard, his eyes slightly narrowed. "We scraped him up and tossed him in a cage. And then we put his dear old mother in with him."

Even though my stomach lurches at his words, I only clench my teeth—I won't give him the satisfaction of a response. He smiles all the same and then leaves me alone to stare at the bloody maps, trying to figure out what to do next.

▼ XXXI ▼

The next morning I wake up to find a package sitting in the chair by the window. It's wrapped in a worn woven cloth. I look around the room, wondering who was here. The air is freezing and I tug a quilt around me as I climb from bed and pull the bundle into my lap, unwrapping it.

Folded inside is a thick wool coat that looks like it's never been worn before. An intricate pattern is stitched around the edges and I run my finger over it. There's something else tucked inside and I pull free a brightly knit scarf and a matching knit hat. The material of both is so thick and soft that I can't help pressing my face against them, feeling the soft woolen hairs brush my cheeks.

It's too perfect a gift. I look up to find my sister nudging open the door to my room. She sees me clutching the bundle in my hands.

"Was this you?" I ask, wondering how she could have ever pulled it off. I never saw her knitting and don't know where she could have found such amazing materials.

She smiles, eyes bright, and shakes her head. "It was Catcher. He came by in the night and said a woman in the Dark City begged for a way to repay him for bringing her food and keeping her alive. He thought you'd want something." She waves toward my closely cropped hair.

I put on the hat, pulling it down over my ears and luxuriating in the sensation of soft warmth.

"He brought me something as well." She holds out a thick book. I take it from her, running my fingers over the cracked plastic that once protected the cover. I flip through pages of diagrams of buildings and structures that make no sense.

"Architecture," she says, unable to hide the excitement in her voice. "It's about building things." She takes the book from me and sits on the bed, feet tucked underneath her. "I've always wanted to build things and he remembered."

I wrap the scarf around my arms, lift the edge of it to my nose as if I could still catch a trace of Catcher. "He's thoughtful like that." I wonder how he found these things. How long he must have searched. I wonder why he didn't wake me up. Why he didn't say anything to me. I think about him sneaking into my room in the night, of me asleep and never knowing.

He was right here, could have stood at the end of my bed, and he said nothing. It's clear he's avoiding me. I pull the coat on, huddling into the heavy folds as if they could protect me from these feelings.

"Well, what are you waiting for?" she says, swiping at my shoulder. "Finish getting dressed—meet me on the roof! We can see how warm that keeps you."

I'd planned on exploring more of the buildings on this end of the island again, hoping that we missed something in one of the basements. That maybe there's an entrance to the tunnels after all.

I slide from bed and walk to the window. As if she senses my hesitation my sister comes to stand next to me. Beyond the river the Neverlands smolder and the Dark City lies gray and dormant. Dead continue to spill through the streets. They flounder from the docks into the water and eventually will wash ashore on the Sanctuary island.

"Where do you think they're housing the Soulers?" I ask, staring at the wall and wondering how many Sweepers were just on the other side last night, protecting us and getting nothing in return.

"I don't know," my sister whispers softly. "There were a lot of rooms in the basement of the headquarters," she says. "That's where they kept me." She hasn't talked about the time she was imprisoned before the rest of us got here. Even now her face is drawn thinking about it.

"There were others down there too. I knew there were, but . . ."

"But what?" I prod.

"Sometimes they took them away and never brought them back," she finishes. She crosses her arms, shivering at the memory. "I never asked what they were doing with all those people. I didn't want to know."

I think back to the death cages I'd seen my first night here. The frightened man they'd thrown to the Unconsecrated. "Catcher's the one bringing them over," I admit to her.

She winces. "I wondered." She doesn't elaborate.

Which only frustrates me. "I don't understand how he can do it. How he can bring those people here knowing they'll likely die." I push away from the window, walk back over to the bed and stare down at the scarf draped over my pillow.

How can Catcher be both the thoughtful person I care about and the person who gives people a false hope?

"He's doing what he has to." She sounds almost resigned.

"Yeah, but what about *their* survival? Why are we allowed on this side of the wall and they aren't?"

She shrugs. "I guess we're lucky."

Nothing in my life's ever seemed lucky before, but then again, here I am standing inside with food down the hall while Soulers are out there in the cold keeping me safe. "It's not fair," I say, wishing there were something I could do.

My sister crosses the room, takes my shoulders and turns me to her. "It's not fair at all. We're going to find a way off this island and we're going to take them with us." She tilts her head, meeting my eyes, and I nod.

"Now," she says, her voice lighter. "Catcher left books about the Dark City from before the Return. I want to see if we can match up the landmarks and figure out if maybe there's something in there that will help us get off the island and find someplace safe."

"Good idea," I tell her. "I'll meet you up there."

She smiles and bounds from the room.

It takes me a while before I follow, and when I climb to the roof I find my sister standing by the wall at the edge. She's holding up a photograph at arm's length, looking between it and the Dark City spread out before her across the river. Books lie scattered on a blanket at her feet, pages fluttering in the morning breeze.

"What's that?" I ask, pulling my new coat tight around me and retying the soft scarf wrapped around my neck. It's a bright morning, the kind that reflects off the ice and snow and burns the eyes.

She turns back to me, a flush across her cheeks. A small breeze teases the hair along her temples as she holds the little card out to me.

Surrounded by a yellow border is a photograph of a city. Gleaming buildings stretch to the sky, an impossible monstrosity of steel bones. Written across the top in thick yellow letters are the words *New York City*.

There's something about it that tickles in my mind, like I've lived this moment before somewhere else. A flash of a memory when I feel as if I'm in two places and two times at once. "This was . . ." I'm trying to find the words and my sister finds them for me.

"It was our father's," she says. "In our cottage growing up. Don't you remember?" She seems so hopeful but when I try to picture that home all I can see is the crumbling village. All I can hear is the echo of voices hazy around the edges. I shake my head.

"I didn't either," she says. "Until I went back. It was still on the wall. My mother—Mary, who raised me—told me it was hers. Something she'd found a long time ago when she'd fled to the ocean. It was the first real proof that there was an outside world, and she'd given it to our father so he could have something to hold on to. To give him hope."

I close my eyes, desperate to remember. But all I can see are the photos in the makeshift museum I saw when I was younger—similar snapshots of a bright world now dim.

"Anyway," my sister says, a forced brightness to her voice. "I'm trying to line up the landmarks." She pulls me next to her. "See here"—she points at one of the tallest buildings in the picture—"I think that's what that over there used to be." She motions to the stump of a skyscraper in the middle of the Dark City that fell years before either of us was born. Crooked spikes of metal twist from a debris pile, rust turning everything a russet red like dried blood.

"And this," she says, pointing at another set of low buildings in the photo, "is over there." She sweeps her hand back along the island. "In the middle you can see how this green-roofed building lines up along that row where there's the shell of an old glassed one."

She kneels, grabbing one of her books. "And then you can look them up in here and see what they used to be like. Some of them have pretty crazy histories of hidden bars and secret entrances to the underground tunnels, like that green—"

My frown cuts her off as I take the picture from her, twisting it and turning it, squinting and trying to see the city that used to be. "I'm not sure," I tell her. "I don't think it's the same at all." I examine the photo. "What about this one?" I ask, pointing out a slender tower with a dagger-sharp tip. "This has never been there."

She looks up and shrugs. "Maybe it was an old picture even when the Return hit," she argues. "But the river matches up along the side there," she says. "And it just feels right. Don't you get the same feeling looking at this picture as you do looking at the City?"

I can't help it, I laugh. "This?" I ask, flicking the picture against her nose before handing it back to her. "There's nothing the same between them. One's new and bright and shiny and the other's old and dead and forgotten."

She frowns. "Not forgotten," she says.

My breath catches a little at how serious she sounds when she says that. "No, not forgotten," I say, even though I don't believe my words. We forget too fast. Sometimes it's probably a gift, though—we forget the pain also.

She shakes her head, her eyes glistening. "It wasn't supposed to last this long, you know."

"Us?" I ask, confused.

"No, this city. One of the books Catcher brought me talks about what would happen if everything shut down. It says the city would crumble in a few months. Maybe last it out for a few years—a decade or two perhaps. But no one thought it would ever last this long." She's staring at the remains of the city. The steel and glass and concrete still struggling to hold on.

"It's been decades," she whispers. "Over a century and then some. It's stayed alive." She stands to face me. "Don't you see? Don't you understand that if this city that no one had any hope for can do it, then we can too? Look at this," she says, grabbing my hand and pressing it against the photo.

"We've been looking at what's not in this picture. At everything that's fallen. But what about what's still there? What about what's made it through? What about the ones that survived?"

I want to tell her that buildings aren't as fragile as people are. They can't get infected. They don't need to eat and breathe and sleep and love.

"After we're gone this city will still be here, and maybe . . ." She takes in a deep breath. "You know, maybe they can build something we didn't. Maybe they can find a way to make it work that we couldn't."

My sister seems so fierce in that moment that it almost takes my breath away. I realize I've been thinking about her as being my opposite. But seeing her up here like this shows me that she's a fighter as well.

"How can I help?"

She looks at me for a long moment and then glances over my shoulder at the stairwell. Her eyes widen and focus, her lips parting. Wondering what's captured her attention, I turn, hand dropping to the machete at my waist.

"What is it?" I ask, muscles tensed to attack or defend. She takes a step past me and I grab her shoulder, holding her back, not understanding.

"It's amazing," she says, kicking through the snow toward the wall of the structure encasing the stairwell. She presses her fingers gingerly to the charcoal-stained bricks.

Parts of the drawing have been blasted clean by the wind but much of it is still there on the section sheltered from the worst weather.

"Who did this?" she asks, her voice soft as a whisper.

I stare at my feet, cheeks burning, unable to take credit. But she knows—just from seeing me squirm she figures it out.

"I had no idea," she says, mesmerized, her eyes taking in the flow of lines.

I shrug. "It's nothing. Really."

She turns back to me. "No, it's good, Annah. Really good. I could never do anything like this."

I blush harder. "I just . . ." I shrug again, trying to figure out how to explain the night on the roof after the infected woman jumped and I found her powders and stains. How something welled in me like a scream that dulled with the color and movement.

"I guess I never really knew I could do it either," I finally say, just to fill the silence. "I never took the time before."

She presses her hand against the wall. "It's beautiful," she says, staring back at me.

It takes everything I have not to duck my head. Instead I smile and accept the compliment: "Thank you."

▼ XXXII ▼

That night I pull the covers over my head and try to will away the darkness. I'm tangled in nightmares when some part of me feels the mattress sag, feels a body slipping under the blankets.

The Recruiter on the platform immediately rears in my mind and I'm about to lash out when the bright heat of Catcher's body pushes up against my back, his arms wrapping around my waist and his face pressing the nape of my neck.

Before I can say anything, before I can even utter his name, his lips move against my skin. "I can't do it, Annah, I can't," he murmurs, his breath whispering over the tiny hairs along my spine.

"Catcher, what's going on?" I try not to let fear creep into my voice as I turn to face him, but he holds me in place, wrapped around me. He feels so hot, and I can't tell whether it's the natural heat of him or if there's something else causing it.

He weaves his fingers through mine, holding them so

tight it's like he'd be lost if he let go. "I can't save them," he finally says.

"Catcher—" I start to respond, but his body begins to tremble and his voice cracks.

"I tried. I've done everything I know how to do. But they keep dying. The survivors in the Dark City keep dying, and it's my fault. I can bring some here and give them a chance but even that—"

"Shhh, it's okay," I tell him, pulling our hands up until I can press my lips to his burning knuckles. His wrists feel dangerously thin. Every part of him seems fragile.

"It's not okay. I'm the only one who can save them. I'm the only one who can get supplies to them—food and blankets and wood and I just can't. I can't do it. I can't handle it. I've tried and tried and . . ."

He takes a deep shuddering breath. "I don't know what to do anymore. The City's going to die and it's all going to be my fault."

"Oh, Catcher." I grasp his hand tighter, my heart aching for him. "You can't save them all. You're only one person."

"You don't understand what it's like," he says. "What it sounds like when they see that I have food. When I carry it to the cable car to bring here. How they call out to me and the desperation in their eyes. You don't know what it's like to watch them die and know that if you'd just tried harder . . . if you'd just been better . . ."

He swallows whatever he was going to say next. I don't know what to tell him to make it okay. I don't know how to fix this. "You haven't been eating," I say and he doesn't answer me, just presses his face against my back, his tears hot on my skin.

"There was a girl," he finally says. "This morning there was a girl on a fire escape and she called out to me. She had a baby. This skinny little boy who clutched at her legs when she cried for me to stop." He pauses, as if seeing it all in his mind.

Taking a deep breath, he continues. "She told me they were out of food. She said she'd heard about me. That I could cross the horde and bring supplies. She begged me. . . ." His voice breaks. "She begged me," he says again.

His body shakes and he has a hard time catching his breath. I press my lips to his palm, to his wrist, to anywhere I can find to give him comfort. "But I didn't have anything. I could have scavenged for her first but I wanted to find a way to get you off the island.

"It took me longer than it should have to search and when I finally came back . . ." He struggles away from me and sits on the edge of the bed. I turn to see his head in his hands as he tugs at his hair. "When I came back she was dead. And the boy . . ."

I move to sit behind him, circling my arms around his shoulders, holding him together.

"The boy was just sitting there pulling at her and crying for her to wake up. He was tugging at her dead body, sobbing, and I didn't know what to do. They were the only ones in the building. They'd already cut their bridge and there was nothing. No one else around to help them or take the boy."

The moonlight outside casts sharp shadows under his eyes and along his jaw. He gets out of the bed and kneels in front of me, twisting the blankets violently in his fingers. "I didn't know what to do, Annah. I didn't know. I gave him food but he wouldn't stop crying and I didn't know what to do with him. I couldn't leave him there alone. Not without his mother."

He grabs my hands, everything about him desperate. "I

tried to save him. I tried to carry him away. To somewhere they could take care of him. But the Mudo . . ."

And suddenly I know what he's going to say and my heart skips.

"It was so cold I thought they'd be slowed. I thought I could make it. I thought I could run with him and bring him here." Tears course down his face.

"It's been so long since I've had to deal with the Mudo. You have to understand, I'm so used to them ignoring me. I'd forgotten . . ." He shakes his head. "They were on me too fast. There were too many for me to get away. I tried to hold him away from them."

He's shuddering uncontrollably. "Oh, God, he was screaming and crying and I was trying to keep him safe. That's all I was doing was trying to save his life and they got him. They got him."

He buries his head in my lap, sobbing. "I couldn't save him, Annah." His voice is tortured and muffled. "How can I take care of you and Elias and Gabry if I couldn't save that child?"

I bend over him and press my lips to his temples. "It's okay, Catcher, we're safe," I lie.

He raises his head, shaking it slowly. "All I could think is what if it were you? What if you were the one I'd killed?"

He places his hands on either side of me on the bed, pushing himself up. But not away. His chest presses against my knees and then he's leaning over me.

I start to fall back, to shift away but he puts his hand behind my neck, his fingertips grazing my pulse.

"I can't lose you, Annah." His face hovers in front of me. "I won't lose you."

And then his lips are on mine.

It's the warmth I feel first. The pure heat of him when he opens his mouth as if to devour me. There's such urgency—such a hunger between us—born of a need to be something to someone.

His other hand scorches down my back, pressing between my shoulder blades to pull me to him until there's nothing between us, no air or breath to separate us.

I taste who he is and was and together we fall back onto the bed. I shove my hands into his hair, pulling him tighter—always tighter. We breathe each other. We are the other person in that moment—nothing distinct about us except the same desire.

He pulls back and we both gasp for air as he rolls to his side, still pressed against me. With the pad of his thumb he follows the curve of my cheek, the angle of my jaw.

Not my scars, but everything else. Everything whole.

I realize he's shaking. I cover his hand with mine. "What's wrong?" I ask him.

He looks at me, *really* looks at me. "I'm terrified," he whispers. "Of us. Of hurting you."

I lick my lips. "I'm terrified of being hurt," I admit.

Before I can stop him he pushes away and walks to the window, grabbing the back of his neck as he always does when he's worried and afraid. I perch on the edge of the bed, looking at him. At his reflection in the night sky.

"My sister Cira was infected."

Surprised, I suck in a deep breath. "I didn't know," I whisper.

"She was beautiful and I thought she was strong, but then she lost hope and that was it. The end." I can hear the pain in his memory. "Getting infected was just the way she killed herself."

"I'm so sorry." I don't know what else to say.

"And you." He turns to face me. "You're alive. Uninfected. I can't watch the same thing happen to you. I can't go through that again."

"Catcher—" I jump up from the bed but the stiffness in his back stops me from touching him.

"You don't understand," he says. "I exist in this in-between place. In between you and Cira. In between life and death. I don't even know who I am anymore. What I am." He turns and leans against the window so that he's facing me.

"You're not in between," I tell him. He starts to shake his head but I interrupt him. "Do you care about me?" I ask. His eyes go wide. "Me and Elias and my sister. Do you care about us?"

He wrinkles his forehead. "You know I do, but—"

"And the Soulers you brought to the island? And that little boy—the people in the Dark City you take food to?" Now I'm right in front of him.

He flushes red, looking trapped. "I'm doing the best I can with them. I can't—"

"Don't you see?" I cut him off, my voice fervent. "Caring is a trait of the living. Not of the dead."

His expression turns dark. "It's not that easy, Annah."

I lean forward and place my palms on the window on either side of him. "No, it is that easy. You're alive. You're only in that *in-between* state because you choose to be. Because you're afraid to actually live."

"It's not that simple," he protests.

My mouth hovers over his for a moment. "Life is never

that simple. And the fact that it's not that simple to you means only one thing: You're still alive."

He presses against me and I push back, tangling around him as he kisses me. "I am because of you," he whispers in my ear. "Tomorrow I'll find someplace safe for us. For all of us. I'm not coming back before I figure a way out. I promise."

I kiss him again. How do I tell him that I already feel safe in his arms?

▼ XXXIII ▼

I don't even have time to miss Catcher because the next morning my sister becomes crippled with illness, throwing up until there's nothing left in her body and still she heaves and heaves. Her skin's scorching and sweaty as she lies limp on the bed groaning, half delirious.

Elias is on the edge of panic. He goes and talks to the Recruiters, asking for herbs or medicines, but he comes back empty-handed with a rage seeping from his pores.

"They don't care that she's sick," he seethes, pacing around the room. He stops and looks at me, his face drawn. "He said they only need one of us alive to keep Catcher coming back with supplies."

My face drains and I absently raise my hand to tuck my hair behind my ears. Hair that's no longer there. I let my hand fall to my lap and stare at my sister, pale under the blankets. "Maybe Catcher can bring something for us," I say, trying not to let my voice shake because he promised last night that he wouldn't come back until he found someplace safe for us.

And I don't know how long that will take him.

Elias and I alternate shifts, placing frozen strips of cloth on her face and coaxing her to let snow melt on her tongue. I pace by the window through the night, waiting for the cable car to start its way across the river, but it doesn't move.

▼   ▼   ▼

The next morning I'm on the roof staring at the Dark City when Elias joins me. He wrings out a blanket, damp with my sister's sweat, and shovels fresh snow into a bucket to try to cool her fevered skin. And then he just stops and stands there, red raw hands limp by his sides.

"She hasn't eaten or drunk anything since yesterday dawn." He shakes his head slowly as if he's trying to figure something out. "I'm afraid she might stop fighting."

I press my lips together, not knowing what to say, wondering if it's my fault she's sick since she joined me on the shore during the snowstorm. I hate not being able to make her better. I hate feeling so useless.

I kick my foot against the wall, my snow-numbed toes barely registering the pain. Elias glances up at me, his gaze flitting over the bright new hat pulled low over my head hiding the healing scabs.

He narrows his eyes, frown lines cutting across his forehead. I know this look. It's the same one he gave me as the scars from the barbed wire were healing. He feels like he failed to protect me. Like it's his fault. And like it's happening all over again with me and my sister.

Thinking about her downstairs, how hard I'm struggling

to keep her alive, makes me realize what it must have been like for Elias before he left me—the burden of always worrying about someone you care about. It's exhausting. I don't know how long I can keep fighting so hard when it always feels like I'm losing. I sit on the wall, shifting until my feet hang over the nothingness. "Do you ever think it's the dead that have the happy ending?"

He pauses, his head tilted to the side as he thinks, and then he sits next to me twisting a rag between his fingers. "What do you mean?"

I shrug. "Just that they don't have to worry about surviving."

"But they're dead," he says.

"Yeah. That means they don't have to remember anything."

Elias shakes his head. "That means they can't ever love."

I snort. "So they don't know loss."

He stares off toward the Dark City, thinking about this. "Do you think the dead don't know what they've lost? Don't you ever wonder why they seek human flesh? That maybe it's their way of believing again? Of living again—if even for that one pure moment that blood pulses inside their mouths?"

I shudder. "I don't think they know what they're missing," I say. "They don't have to worry about the people they love and what's going to happen to them tomorrow or the next day."

Elias looks confused. "But that's what makes us alive. We make mistakes. We love and lose. That's life."

I think about what it felt like to have the Recruiter pulling on my hair, almost drag me over the wall. The terror inside that Catcher won't make it back. Or that if he does we'll still be stuck on this island forever, however long that lasts. "Don't you think it would be easier without that?"

Elias doesn't answer right away. He climbs off the wall and walks to my drawing of Catcher, staring at it. He raises his hand to his neck, and now the gesture reminds me of Catcher. Now it's somehow Catcher's and not Elias's. "Do you ever think about the night before I joined the Recruiters?"

His back is to me so I can't see his expression, and suddenly I'm a bit unsteady with this conversation. "What do you mean?" I finally ask.

He pauses. "The night you and I . . ." He waves his hand around as if he can't say the word *kissed*.

I swallow, uncomfortable. "Yes." My answer seems too brash. "Maybe."

He turns to look at me, his eyes so intensely light. I'd forgotten how blue they are. How they can almost disappear. "Would you give that up?"

My cheeks are burning, my breath a little ragged. "What?" I don't understand what this has to do with anything. I turn and jump off the wall, start toward the door. But Elias blocks my path.

"Did it hurt?" he asks, stepping closer. "When I left the next day?"

I want space to clear my head and gather my thoughts and stop the spinning. I back away until there's nowhere to retreat to. "No. Yes. Maybe. Maybe it hurt later."

He comes closer so that there's hardly any space between us. And I notice that his nearness brings none of the heat that Catcher's does and nothing inside me wants to draw nearer. "Would you give it up?" he whispers.

Would I give it up? Isn't it the moment I first felt beautiful?

"I don't know." It's the only honest answer I can give.

His expression changes, just a little, as if he's scored some small victory. "If you're willing to give that up and everything else—leaving your sister on the path, struggling in the Dark City, even your scars—everything that makes you *you*, that makes your life yours . . . that's when you walk out into the horde and give yourself over to them."

"It's not that easy," I whisper.

He pulls away from me, giving me distance. "Why isn't it?"

"Because that's not all the same. Those are all different things—different parts of me and my past."

He shrugs. "Exactly. That's what makes you, you. Don't you think you lose *all* of that when you become one of the Unconsecrated?"

I start to shake my head but he grabs my chin. "The Unconsecrated aren't the winners because they died," he says. "*We're* the winners because we get to live. Because we get to survive. Despite the pain of this life, we get to *feel*."

He lets me go and walks over to the edge of the roof, where the Sanctuary is laid out below, cushioned in a blanket of white. "I know you still blame me for bringing us here. But don't you understand that I was only trying to make sure we had a chance to live? I wasn't betraying you or Catcher. I just . . ."

His jaw tightens and I walk toward him, stand next to him looking at the Sanctuary and the City beyond the river.

He takes a deep breath. "We've struggled so hard—both of us. I couldn't have it be for nothing. I had to fight for us—even if that meant bringing us here. It was the only thing I knew to do."

I place my hand over his. His skin feels warm and damp. I glance up and notice his cheeks are flushed.

"Maybe I should be sorry," he says, lifting one shoulder.

"I'm not. . . ." He shakes his head a little, raises his other hand up to press against his eyes. Clearing his throat, he goes on. "I'm not going to apologize for having more time with Gabry. And you."

His fingers clutch mine. "We'll find a way to be safe," he says. He sounds so sure that I can't bear to force him to recognize the reality of our situation. It's easier to let him believe in hope.

A breeze lifts the edges of my scarf, trailing them over my shoulders and flapping them behind me. "If only we could fly," I whisper.

"I flew once," Elias says. His eyes have lost focus and his shoulders hitch as he draws in tight little breaths. "In the Forest. I found a plane—it was the middle of winter and all the Unconsecrated were downed and I sat in it for hours. Below were clouds, above blue sky."

He lets go of my hand and wavers on his feet, then grips the wall to catch his balance. I let him lean into me and realize that he's scorchingly hot. Sweat rolls down the back of his neck even in the frigid air.

"Elias, you have to rest. You have to let me take over for a while. You can't keep pushing yourself." I try to help him sit but he stumbles away from me.

"No," he mumbles, looking around the roof as if he can't remember what he was doing there. "No, I have to take care of Gabry." He finally meets my eyes, his face pale. "She's everything to me." And then he collapses.

▼ XXXIV ▼

I try to catch Elias but only manage to buffer his fall as he
slumps against a deep pile of iced-over snow. I shake him
and call his name and his eyes roll in his head for a moment
before he finally focuses on me.

"I'm sorry," he whispers.

"What are you sorry for?" I ask, trying to get him sitting,
running my hand over his face and feeling the fever of him
seep into me.

"I wanted to love you," he mumbles. "I really did. . . ." His
voice trails off as I freeze in shock. "Promise me you'll take
care of her."

"Elias," I say but he doesn't respond. I shake him again but
nothing happens. "Elias!" I scream but he just lies there motionless, lips parted and chest rising and falling rapidly.

I can't get him to wake up and the ice begins to melt under
him, soaking his clothes. I look around in a panic and then I
run to the edge of the roof.

"Catcher!" I scream even though I know it's useless. Even though I know there's no way he can hear me wherever he is. Below me a few Recruiters hesitate on their way to patrol the wall and glance up. I back out of their line of sight, suddenly wary of drawing their attention.

I rush back to Elias and try to lift him but he's deadweight and my feet slide on the ice. "Elias, please," I whisper to him. "Please please please wake up." He groans and shifts a little and then he starts to heave and I just barely roll him to his side before he begins to retch.

Frustration tears under my skin as I wash his mouth with snow and he tries to push me away but he still won't wake up. He won't listen to me. He starts to retch again and his body shakes as groans tumble from his mouth. I grab the blanket he brought up and wrap it around him and for the moment he stops shuddering.

I know I can't keep him up here. I try to lift him again and manage to half-stumble, half-slide across the roof to the stairwell. Getting him down the steps is almost impossible. I brace myself underneath him and let him slump down each stair in a barely controlled fall. I wince when his elbow slams into the railing but he barely registers anything.

"You can do it, Elias," I murmur to him with each flight, hoping he can hear me but knowing he's probably so deeply lost in fever that my words are meaningless. But I say them anyway because they comfort me and keep me focused.

When I finally get him to our flat I spread a few blankets on the floor and roll him onto them. He retches again but his stomach's empty and nothing comes up. As carefully as possible I peel the frozen clothes from his body, his skin now a chilly pale blue.

He pulls himself into a ball, shivering, and I pile more blankets on top of him and drag him closer to the stove. For now he seems content to let sleep draw him under and I toss wood on the fire and then just stand there, staring at my sister and Elias, wondering what to do next.

Wondering how I'm going to keep them alive.

There's always been sickness in the City. Several years ago a flu raged through, decimating the population. I'd been one of the afflicted and Elias traded almost everything he had— food credits, blankets, his nice boots, oil and a lantern—for the herbs to bring down my fever. He later told me he sat by my bed for a week, his hand against my chest when he slept to make sure I kept breathing.

I look at his body now, at the way his cheekbones angle under the skin. My sister's the same way, skin wan and hair lank. I wonder how either of them can be strong enough to survive this kind of fever for a week.

I let myself fall into a chair and sit, counting the number of times their chests rise and fall. I watch their eyelids flutter and lips mumble words that never become clear. The moaning of the horde swims through the window, wrapping around us all—calling to me.

All I can think is, What happens if I can't save them? What if it's just me in this building alone until I can't survive any longer? Of all the ways I imagined the world would end, this was not one of them.

I lean over, tucking my forehead into my knees, and cover my ears with my hands. I can no longer hold back the tears and I cry, letting the fear shake through me.

I spend the day waiting for Catcher and trying to coax Elias and my sister to drink slushy snow, trying to feed them broth they can't stomach. A few times they wake up but when I talk to them, they don't seem to recognize me.

My sister cries out for her mother, moaning the name Mary, and all I can do is hold her hand and tell her it will be okay even though I'm not sure it will be.

After a while, the flat feels too hot, a sickly sweet smell that mixes with the odor of damp blankets drying by the fire, and I can barely handle it anymore. I was able to haul a mattress into the room and get them onto it and they're both deep asleep, her arm tucked in his.

I drag myself up to the roof, welcoming the freezing air that refreshes my lungs. The night's deep and clear, the moon not yet risen to hide the scattering of stars beating a rhythm of light from millions of years ago.

There are fewer survivors' fires burning on roofs around the City. I try not to think about what this means and light my own small fire, then pull a tub of snow near. As it melts I run my hands over the blankets and quilts I brought to wash, most of the seams frayed and so worn they fall apart in my fingers. I just sit there staring at the scraps, wondering if it's worth trying to rework them into another quilt. Wondering if any of this will even matter in a few days.

Is this what it was like in all those other cities and towns when the Return hit? All the half-finished products of people's lives: laundry still hanging on someone's line, a half-read book tucked into the corner of an old chair, a letter partially written or a painting almost but not quite finished.

I think back to my sister asking me what I'd do if I knew this was the end. I close my eyes and remember the feel of Catcher's lips against mine. That instant when he gave in and let himself fall into me.

I want that moment again. Over and over. I want that to be my life.

I stare at the picture I drew of Catcher on the shed wall, mostly washed away now from the wind and snow. There are still some parts left—the outline of a flower, a hand clutching a bunch of balloons that have all run together.

Pulling a charred stick from the fire, I draw in some of the faded pieces, tracing the edge of a face here, mending the fence there. I start to outline the mass of balloons, to give each one shape again, when I pause.

The charcoal at the end of my stick crumbles under the pressure of my hand, leaving a long dark smudge. If only we could fly, I think.

It seems way too stupid to be a possibility, but even so, I walk back to the fire and the blankets scattered about, running the fabrics through my hands. When I find one with a tight weave that isn't too heavy, I rip apart the seams until I have a decent-sized square.

I pull down the wire we'd used to hang laundry and twist it into an approximation of a ball. After tying the fabric to the wire frame I balance it in my hand, a little hollow balloon open on one end.

Figuring out how to get the hot air inside and keeping it there is more difficult. I stare at the charred embers of the fire for a while and finally I just make a small basket from the leftover wire and stuff a bit of fabric in the bottom. On top of that I pile a few embers and twigs. The entire concoction begins to smolder and spew smoke into the dome of fabric.

I hold my breath, waiting. Slowly at first and then faster and faster the balloon lifts from my hand. The breeze from the river catches it, carrying it through the night sky, and I give a whoop as excitement buzzes through my veins.

It hovers there, a bright spark in the sky like a star. A burst of light in the darkness of the City before the little flame powering it extinguishes and the entire contraption tumbles into nothingness.

Feeling hopeful for the first time in weeks—years!—I gather the unwashed blankets and carry them back down to the flat, plans for getting off the island floating through my mind.

XXXV

In the middle of the night my sister stops breathing. I grab her shoulders and shake her and scream at her that she's not allowed to die, that she promised me she'd survive. As if obeying my command, she sputters and coughs and chokes and resumes her ragged inhalations.

But I can't sleep again. I can't stop staring at her chest, watching the rise and fall of it. Afraid that somehow I'm the one in charge of whether she takes her next breath and terrified that if I look anywhere else, even for a moment, she'll slip away from me.

I pull my chair closer to the mattress, scraps of old clothes and blankets littering the floor around me. Using my sister's quilting box, I sew the lengths of fabric together, stitching the seams as tight as I can, my movements keeping time to the pattern of her breaths.

For the millionth time I wish I were her. Not because of her smooth skin and easy life but because I'm afraid of failing her. I'd rather it be me on the bed slowly letting go of life. Because that means my sister could still hold on to hers.

▼   ▼   ▼

When morning breaks and Catcher still hasn't come, I know he hasn't found a way out of this place. I know he's not coming back anytime soon.

I know what I have to do.

I take the machete and sharpen the blade as best as I can. I make sure both Elias and my sister are tucked tightly under blankets and then add more wood to the stove. It takes a while for me to force myself to leave them but finally, I do.

Outside it's a brilliantly clear blue day, the sky so sharp it stings my eyes. Under my feet the snow crunches, a thin layer of ice giving way to smooth softness underneath. By the time I reach the main building, my pants are damp up to my knees and I'm shivering but I don't care.

Inside my steps echo along cold walls, my breath puffs of clouds leading the way. I pass the map room, pausing only to see if anything's changed, but it still looks the same.

I expected to find the building bustling or at the very least a Recruiter or two wandering the hallways, but there's no one. Just an eerie silence that makes my heart sound too loud. It isn't until I round a corner deep in the bowels of the headquarters that I understand where everyone is.

Then I hear the shouting, the moaning, the sound of someone struggling against metal cages. There are few windows to give natural light so the hall's dim, shadows hovering along the creases between wall and floor. I close my eyes and wait for the scream of surrender. Listen to the pleas for mercy.

I grip the machete tighter, wondering if that's what they'll do to me if they find me. Knowing that my death would mean they'd have to find a way to save Elias and my sister. As they keep reminding us, they need at least one of us alive to tether Catcher. If I die, they have no choice but to save the others.

As carefully as possible, I double back and start searching. I pass barren rooms with nothing but dust and sometimes an old desk or a broken chair. It takes a while and my nervousness causes me to sweat, every sound making me hesitate and my senses tingle. I don't know how long the sacrificed will last in the cage—how much time I have before someone gets bored and stumbles upon me.

Finally I find a storage room, crooked shelves stacked with baskets of food and supplies. I grab an old lantern by the door and light it, start rifling through everything. In the corner I find pouches of dried herbs and plants. One by one I sniff them, pouring the contents into my hands and trying to recall what will bring down a fever. Yarrow? Bloodroot? Coriander? I squeeze my eyes closed tight, trying to remember what Elias purchased for me when I was sick, what it looked and smelled like.

Frustrated, I just give up and shove everything into my pockets, then ease back into the hallway. As I walk to the exit a light sort of fluttery feeling starts to tickle in my stomach—a small sense of relief that everything will be okay.

When the door to the outside appears I get lax and stop straining for every noise. And so I'm utterly surprised when fingers clamp around my arm, twisting me back until I thump against the wall.

It's a tall broad-shouldered Recruiter with brown hair

tucked behind his ears and dark eyes. He smiles, a dimple appearing in his cheek. "This is unexpected," he says, his light tone almost flirtatious.

"I was looking for something," I say nonchalantly, trying not to sound guilty.

He tilts his head to the side. "What's that? Or should I say who's that?" He winks almost awkwardly. I start to relax, thinking maybe I'm not going to be in trouble. That maybe I can talk myself out of this. After all, it's not like I'm not allowed to wander around the island, I just haven't that often.

"A few supplies for Elias," I say with a shrug, hoping the mention of another Recruiter will ease my way out of here.

He nods and is about to push open the door for me when he notices the machete gripped so tightly in my hand that the skin around my knuckles is white. Before I can say or do anything he jerks his knee into my wrist, slamming it hard against the wall. There's a bright pain and then my fingers tingle, go numb. The machete clatters to the floor and the Recruiter places his foot over the flat of the blade.

"It's not polite to bear weapons indoors," he says, grabbing my arm.

I glance at the doorway leading outside, my escape so close. "I—I just—"

He jerks me from the wall and shoves me down the hallway so hard that I stumble, falling to one knee. As I start to right myself, one of the packets of herbs slips from my overflowing pockets and lands on the floor with a quiet thump.

He leans in, trying to see what I've taken, and I kick out, catching the side of his knee with my foot and feeling it buckle. He screams, eyes clenched shut and hands reaching for his leg, then I swing my arm at his face. His head whips back and slams against the wall, and he slides to the ground, whimpering and dazed.

His knee's bent at an unnatural angle and I back away from him, shocked at my own violence. At what I've done. I'm just squatting and reaching for the packet of herbs when a voice calls out.

I look up. Conall's running toward me. My heart sinks and I push myself into a sprint, bolting for the exit.

He shouts for me to stop, and right when I reach the door he throws his weight at me, flinging me outside into the blinding cold. I topple to the ground and I'm already trying to reason with him. "My sister and Elias are really sick." I'm shaking my head. "I need to bring down their fevers. I need—"

Conall's staring at the packets of herbs spread out around me. My machete's still inside where the other Recruiter knocked it from my hand. I'm defenseless and Conall's eyes are murderous.

I throw up my hands protectively, knowing he likes to see me cower. "Look, they're sick and I—"

He cuts me off again, pawing at me until he's pulled more herbs from my pocket, all of them falling to the ground. His eyes are wide, rage shimmering from them. "I can't believe you'd just come in here and steal from us. After all we've done to take care of you." He grabs my arm and shoves it up behind me, dragging me back inside the headquarters.

I struggle against him, trying to bash his face with my head and lashing out with my feet. "I'm just trying to take care of them," I shout. "I didn't know what I'd need. I wasn't going to take it all."

But he either isn't listening or doesn't care. He drags me

down the twisty hallways and my stomach floods with apprehension when I hear the echoes of chants and cheers growing louder. Beads of sweat trickle down my chest as I fight harder against his grasp and he only grips me tighter.

"I didn't mean anything," I beg, truly terrified of what he's about to do to me. "I'm sorry. I really am." I hear my voice cracking and hate the sound of my own weakness.

He doesn't hesitate but slams me through the door into the auditorium. The benches are emptier than they'd been the last time I saw this place. A few have Recruiters stretched out on them, somehow sleeping through the surrounding chaos.

About a dozen men are still awake, clapping and shouting as a clearly exhausted short-haired Souler woman stumbles around the cage while two Unconsecrated men doggedly follow her. Blood covers the woman's arms and tattered gray tunic and pools over the floor, making a squishy splash with each step she takes.

Some of the Recruiters look up at us as Conall leads me down the stairs. Their eyes are blurry and I realize they've probably been awake all night. "Save her for later," one of them calls out, waving a hand limply in the air. "It's time for bed. This one's getting boring." He and a few others stumble up the stairs, leaving.

I bite my bottom lip, trying to keep from screaming in helpless rage. I knew there was a chance that if I was caught stealing, I'd end up dead. But it was a risk I was willing to take because if I die, Elias and my sister have to live for the Recruiters to keep Catcher under control.

Conall marches me down the steps and toward the side of the room where there are three tiny cages, more like kennels for holding a dog than anything else. He opens the door of one of them and forces me to my knees so that I have to crawl inside as he kicks at me.

Before I can even turn around I hear the click of metal on metal. He's locked me in.

▼ XXXVI ▼

I jam my fingers through the thin metal bars. "Please," I shout at him. "You don't understand. If you do this to me you have to go make sure my sister and Elias are okay. If you don't—if all of us die—Catcher won't ever come back. You'll starve to death. You have to go find my sister and take care of her."

I'm desperate. This can't have been for nothing—I can't stay stuck down here while my sister and Elias die. "Please!" I scream after him, tearing my throat raw. "You can't do this!"

He turns to walk away and I crash my fist into the cage door as hard as I can. "You have to make sure they live or else all of you are going to die!"

But it's as if he doesn't hear me. I watch him walk across the room and confer with a few of the Recruiters still there, pointing down at me once or twice, and then they all leave. He doesn't even glance at me as he closes the door to the auditorium behind him. My heart's pounding so furiously that I don't know if it will ever calm down again.

My cage is tiny, so small I'm forced to stay on my hands and knees. The walls close in tight around me, making it impossible to breathe, and I start to hyperventilate and gag. I try to retch but nothing comes up and I realize I haven't eaten since Elias got sick.

I slam my hands against the door, twisting to angle my fingers through the narrow slats to work on the lock, but I can't reach it. All I can do is bang on the cage walls, pulling and pushing and hoping that maybe the tired old metal will give way. My arm jams into one of the rusty hinges and I hiss at the pain as blood begins to well.

And then a tired voice says, "It's not going to budge." I look up and see the woman in the large cage dominating the center of the room. She's standing there, one hand hooked through the links, blood crusted around her fingers. "I tried for over a week."

Behind her, one of the Unconsecrated—a skinny bald man in a ratty white tunic—lunges for her but she easily dodges him, backing away to the center of the cage. The Unconsecrated man raises his face to the air, black eyes searching for the scent of my uninfected blood and then he moans, trying to reach through the cage for me and breaking his index finger back as he does.

The other Unconsecrated shambles around to join him and I gasp when I see his face. It's the boy from before. The one from the Neverlands; the one on the shore who wouldn't let me take him away.

I shudder looking at him, wishing I'd tried harder to convince him to come with me that night. Knowing I had a chance to save him and I didn't.

The woman limps to the far side of the cage, and when it

looks like the Unconsecrated are more focused on me, slowly slides down until she's sitting, pulls her tunic over her knees and wraps her arms tight around her legs. She looks small and helpless, sweat dripping from her close-cropped hair. "What's your name?" she asks me. She sounds exhausted. So ready for all of this to be over.

"Annah," I tell her softly.

She nods. "I'm Dove." She raises a limp finger and points to the two Unconsecrated. "And that's Noell and Jonah. They're . . ." She passes a hand over her face, leaving a streak of blood along her cheek. "They *were* . . ." She pauses, looking for the right word. "Friends." Her voice cracks.

I look away from her, not able to handle the expression of loss on her face. "I'm sorry," I say but it's not enough. I don't think there could ever be words for this moment. The two Unconsecrated rattle the large cage, trying to find a way through it to me, to the uninfected blood slowly dripping from my elbow.

She sniffs and wipes at her eyes. "They wanted this, I think." She leans her head back so that she's staring out through the top of the cage, as if she could see the sky if she just tried hard enough. "They're Soulers. Well, I was a Souler too, I guess." She sighs and then coughs and I notice a red smear around her lips. I wonder how much time's left before she either bleeds out or her weakened body gives in to the infection.

"They thought this would be eternal life. Resurrection." She closes her eyes. "How stupid is that?"

"It's not stupid," I tell her. She glances at me, clearly not believing me. "I mean, I've wondered about that before. If there's something more to them."

"There's not," she says matter-of-factly. "Noell was my husband. He's the one who really believed in all of this. There's nothing left inside him anymore. I'd know if there were." Her voice sounds so flat, so lifeless. As if everything she's ever believed has died.

I want to say something to give her comfort. "There could still be something . . ." I struggle for words and end up lamely offering, "More."

She shrugs again but doesn't protest.

"How long have you been here?" I ask, not sure I want to know the answer.

"Weeks? I don't know. Doesn't really matter. Noell and I were down in Vista when the town revolted. They wouldn't let us keep our dead and the Recruiters promised to protect us." She laughs softly. "They brought us here. Caged us and have slowly been killing us off since. Not enough resources to feed us all—not enough entertainment for them." She waits a moment before adding, "I guess I'm lucky that they just threw me in here and didn't do anything else to me."

Weeks. I press my forehead to the bottom of my cage. I knew about the fights and what the Recruiters were capable of. I knew about the Soulers being used as Sweepers. How many people suffered because I didn't do anything?

I was too selfish. "I'm sorry," I tell her again.

She watches the way her husband moans, the way his teeth clack together. "Doesn't really matter, it'll be over soon. If there's something to their belief in Resurrection, then I guess I get to be with them after all. And if there isn't . . ." She closes her eyes again and I see that her fingers are trembling as she wipes a tear from her cheek.

For a while we sit in silence.

Eventually, she says, "Do you think people were this cruel before the Return?"

Her question surprises me. "I don't know."

"They take so much pleasure in suffering. I don't understand it."

I swallow, stare down at my hands. "I don't either. Maybe *they* don't understand."

"Maybe," she says. "I just wonder sometimes if that's why all this happened. If there wasn't enough good in the world and that's what caused the Return. People got greedy and selfish with their lives and were unwilling to let it go in the end when it was time."

"I don't know what caused the Return," I say. "If what they wanted was eternal life, they didn't do a good job of it. Who wants to live like them?" I wave my hands at Noell and Jonah. "And who wants to live like us?"

She coughs again, loud and vicious. Noell wanders back over to her. "And to think," she says, hauling herself to her feet so that she can evade him. "All the times in my life when I pushed my husband away and fought with him over something petty, I should have been pulling him tighter. I should have been thankful each day to have him healthy and by my side."

I close my eyes, unable to watch what's happening in the cage. Yet I can still hear her quiet whimpering. Hear the sound of her husband's moans and the tangled shuffle of their feet. How much longer can she go on like this? Because he'll go on forever.

I hear a crunch and snap and I look back up at her.

She's in the middle of the cage standing over Noell. One of his knees is bent at a wrong angle, crooked out to the side with the lower part twisted and dangling. She's openly sobbing now. "I'm so sorry, honey, I'm so sorry." She brings her foot down against the back of his neck, screaming in agony as she does it.

It takes a few times but eventually, with a snap, his neck breaks and he goes silent and still. She limps to the other Unconsecrated, who's still pawing at the cage for me, and brutally, efficiently, she snaps his knee and when he falls she breaks his neck as well.

I'm barely breathing, my hand covering my mouth as if I can hold inside the sound of bones cracking.

She falls to her knees, laces her fingers through the cage. She's not that far away from me now and I can see the tracks of tears cutting through the dirt and blood on her face. I can even see some of the bite marks along her arm.

"I couldn't leave them like that," she says, as if seeking absolution from me. "I couldn't see them like that any longer."

"It's okay," I tell her, because I know they're the words she needs to hear.

She nods, but whether it's at what I said or a conversation taking place in her own head, I don't know. "They wanted to be like that. All Soulers do eventually. But I couldn't watch it. I couldn't let them hurt anyone else. They were both so . . ." She leans her head on her arm as if she doesn't have the strength to hold it up anymore. "Gentle," she finishes.

With her other hand she grabs the fence and shakes it, the sound echoing around the empty auditorium. "They were good men," she shouts. "You have to remember that, Annah. They were decent and loving."

"I will," I tell her, my voice seeming so small against her tempest. "I'll remember them." There are so many people to remember, I think.

She says nothing else. Just continues to kneel there, letting the cage hold her up as she stares at what used to be the man she loved.

XXXVII

I'm not really sure how one should spend the final moments of one's life. I don't know if I should pray or reflect back, if I should weep or catalog my various failures and accomplishments. Should I be sad that I never got to tell my sister, Elias or Catcher good-bye? Should I be relieved that I no longer have to worry about surviving?

I lie on my side in the kennel, knees tucked to my chest, and I stare up at Dove in her own cage. She sits in the middle, legs crossed, her lips moving but not with any sound or words that I can hear. Every now and again she'll crawl toward Noell and grasp his limp hand in hers.

Eventually, she lies down with her back against his chest, tucking her head under his chin and pulling his arm across her.

I have to look away. I can't watch that, the way his broken neck hangs crooked. I wonder how long she survived in there with the Unconsecrated. I wonder how long I'll survive. How much fight I have left in me.

I'd like to think that I won't beg, but I'm worried that in the end I'll scream for mercy just like everyone else.

▼　▼　▼

There's no ceremony to the whole thing. Conall strolls into the auditorium, the side of his face creased as if he's just woken up from a nap. He stands at the edge of the large cage in the center of the room and stares at Dove for a while.

"She still alive?" he asks, and I guess he's directing the question at me.

I don't answer. I don't want to give him the satisfaction.

Another Recruiter comes walking down the steps. "Looks like she killed the plague rats," he says, standing next to Conall.

"You were supposed to leave someone here to make sure that didn't happen," Conall growls.

The other one shrugs. "If she isn't turned yet, she will be soon enough. Might be interesting to see the two girls duking it out." The hint of leering suggestion in his voice disgusts me.

Even from here I can tell that Conall's angry and then finally he just throws up a hand. "Whatever," he says. "We still have those other three from before. We can bring them out when we get tired of watching these two run around each other."

I'm shocked at how calmly they're discussing my fate. And the inconvenience they face because Dove defended herself.

Conall comes over to my kennel and kneels. "How's it going in there?" he asks.

I glare at him. "My sister—have you gone to make sure she's okay?"

"I'll take care of it," he says, but of course I can't trust him.

"Catcher won't come back if they're dead," I remind him. "If you want to survive, you have to make sure they're okay."

He stops fiddling with the lock on my cage and stares at me for a moment. "I'm not sure it's their survival you should be worried about," he says. "And if you're not going to put up a decent fight up there, then I'll find someone who will. Even if I have to go get your friends."

"You stupid arrogant bas—"

Before I can finish the insult he slams against my little cage, shoving it over and tossing me around inside. He spits on the floor by the door before stalking off.

I laugh, which causes him to trip, which only makes me laugh harder. He doesn't have to know about the tears burning my throat. That if I don't laugh I'll break down into terrified sobs.

A few more Recruiters stumble into the room, rubbing eyes, some carrying plates of food. The ripe smell of their bodies combined with the gamey smell of their dinner and the omnipresent stench of blood makes my stomach cramp.

"Let's get this going," one of them calls out. His fingers are slick and shiny with grease. Of the many ways I imagined dying, this wasn't one of them, some dinnertime spectacle for a group of monsters.

"Not everyone's here yet," Conall says.

The other one grunts. "They'll get here at some point. Always takes a while to wear them down anyway. That gets boring."

I choke on my breath as Conall unlatches the kennel. My death, boring? He reaches into the cage and I back away to the farthest corner, but of course there's nowhere for me to hide. I really wanted to face this without causing a scene, but now that the time's come I can't help but fight.

I kick at his hands, gratified when I connect and he roars, holding up a crooked finger. But my small victory is short-lived, because he dives in through the kennel door and wraps his other hand around my ankle, yanking me so hard that I feel as though my hip dislocates.

I struggle to grab on to the walls of the kennel, to keep myself tucked safe inside, but his strength's too much and he's able to pull me free. I've been bent over for so long in the cramped space that my muscles spasm when I try to stand and I collapse again.

I try to scramble away from him on my hands and knees, but he hauls me up by my clothes, my feet barely even touching the ground. A seam on my shirt pulls and rips and I feel a gust of cold air along my ribs. One of the Recruiters cups his hand around his mouth and hoots at me, causing my skin to blaze.

I'm punching and screaming and kicking and twisting and fighting as Conall carries me the short distance to the cage. "You can't do this to me!" I yell. But this only encourages the men to chant and cheer, reveling in my panic-fueled struggles.

For a moment Conall fumbles with the lock and I'm able to break his grip slightly. I claw my fingernails down his arm and he flinches. A tiny burst of hope catches in my mind, but just as I'm trying to run he swings the cage gate open and throws me inside.

The door closes with a bang and even though I beat on it, he's able to turn the lock.

That's it, then. I'm trapped in this cage with an infected woman who could Return at any moment.

"Should we bring out another plague rat?" Conall asks the small crowd, rolling his sleeve over the scratches along his forearm.

"Nah," one of them responds. "Let's see what she does. Wait for the others before we up the ante." And then they go back to their meal and their gossip, flitting their glances up at me only occasionally.

I press my back against the cage door, threading my fingers through the links of the gate. Only a few feet away Dove lies spooned with her dead husband. My eyes blur with tears of frustration and fear and I wipe them away angrily as I study her chest.

Several heartbeats go by and she's so motionless I'm convinced she's Returned. I start to taste panic crawling up my throat, my mind reeling with too many thoughts at once—to run, to stay put, to shout, to cry, to do anything to make this stop. I'm practically clawing at the cage gate trying to find a weakness that someone before did not. Trying to escape where no one has before.

And then I see Dove's chest rise and fall, just slightly, and I know she's not gone yet. There's still time.

Tentatively, I walk over to her and kneel so that I'm blocking her face from view of the Recruiters.

"Dove?" I say. "It's Annah." I slip my hand into hers; she barely grasps mine back.

Her eyes flutter open. "I'm sorry," she says. Her voice is a dry husk, like her body. There's so much blood drenching her skin and the floor now that I don't understand how she can still be alive. "I'm sorry for what's going to happen to you. I'm sorry that I won't know what I'm doing. That I can't stop it."

"It's okay," I tell her. Because none of this is her fault.

"I wish they had some kind of memory," she says. "I wish they could understand." Whether she's talking about the Recruiters or the Unconsecrated, I don't know.

"Boo!" one of the men yells. "Hurry up and die already!" I feel something wet splash against my back and when I turn I see one of the Recruiters tossing an empty tin mug at the cage, where it hits and rattles to the floor.

It's too much and I snap. Jumping to my feet, I rush the fence, slamming at it with my fists. "Shut up!" I scream at him. "You don't deserve the air you breathe, you dirty plague bag, and I hope you all die deaths as ugly as you are!" And even though my mouth is dry, I spit at him as best I can.

The Recruiter watches me with a vicious approving smile. "You found one with fire, Conall."

I turn away, fists clenched, knowing that my outburst only makes this more fun for them. I squeeze my eyes shut and try to breathe deeply and calm my thoughts. Dove's sitting and watching me, her body wavering with exhaustion and pain.

She's still fighting to stay alive and so will I. I spin back to face the Recruiters. "You have no idea what you're messing with here," I shout at them.

One of the Recruiters boos and throws a handful of his food at me. I wipe it from my arm, some sort of watery foul-smelling slop that makes my stomach turn.

I square my shoulders and narrow my eyes, directing every bit of hate and rage into my voice. "Are you so stupid that you don't realize that I mean something to Catcher? *He's* the one out there keeping you alive. What do you think he's going to do when he comes back and finds me in here? What are you going to do if he finds me dead or Unconsecrated?"

My words finally seem to crack the surface and they all

glance at one another before turning to Conall for guidance. He rises from his bench and walks slowly down the stairs until he's just on the other side of the cage. "I say let him come."

I'm so focused on the Recruiters that I don't even notice another body slip into the room. I don't notice him making his way along the edges of walls. It's not until he opens his mouth that anyone realizes he's there.

"That can be arranged," Catcher calls out, a machete gripped tightly in his fist.

▼ XXXVIII ▼

For a moment there's silence and then my heart starts to race. A relief so pure floods my system that I'm practically dizzy. Most of the Recruiters just sit there frozen, food-filled hands raised halfway to open mouths, watching as Catcher strides toward the cage.

He looks almost calm but I can see the way his body vibrates with rage. I press my lips shut, resisting the urge to call out to him.

"You do realize your lives mean nothing, right?" I can hear the storm in his voice as he speaks. He looks impossibly menacing and for the first time I understand what he meant about there being a monster trapped inside him.

"You know that I can kill each one of you, right here, right now, and no one would care." He looks at the Recruiters, piercing them individually with his gaze. A few of them stumble to their feet and trip over one another in their haste to leave. He doesn't stop them.

But Conall continues to stand with arms crossed, blocking

the gate to the cage. "Just because you're immune doesn't mean you're invincible," he says.

Catcher laughs, an awful sound full of bitterness and fury. "As far as you're concerned it means I'm *God*." He starts to advance on Conall with his head down, jaw clenched. "I get to decide who eats and who doesn't. I decide who lives and dies. I'm the one who gets to pass *all* judgment."

Conall opens his mouth to protest but Catcher doesn't let him. "You want to challenge me? You want to go to Ox and tell him what's going on here? Tell him why none of you will ever get food or supplies from the mainland again?"

"Ha!" Conall rolls his eyes, refusing to back down. "You bring supplies because of your stupid women. You can't bring them food without bringing it for us. If you refused, we'd no longer offer them protection."

"And what kind of protection is this?" Catcher shouts, kicking out at a bench and causing it to topple over, the old wood cracking. "You don't think I can kill you right here? Sever your spine and leave your body for the others to clean up?"

Conall shakes his head but I notice how his face drains of color.

"Explain to me," Catcher continues, still moving forward, "why anyone else would bother to try to stop me if I killed you. Explain to me why I should care anything about you at all. Do you really think you mean anything to them? Do you really think that given the choice between me and you, they'd choose you?"

Catcher's now standing inches from Conall, staring at him through the top of his eyes like an animal hunting its prey. The Recruiter has no weapon, no way to defend himself but still he curls his hands into fists.

"You saw what happened when one of yours killed one of

ours," Conall retorts. "You know Ox always sides with his men. He'll side with me."

Catcher snarls. I can see the wrath written in every part of him.

"Catcher," I say softly, as a warning, not wanting him to do anything he'd regret later.

"This is the woman I love," he says, raising his machete to point at me. "She is my *life*, and when you harm her you harm me." His breath is loud and I can see the way he fights to control himself.

"Catcher," I say again, trying to tether him to my voice. Trying to get him to step outside of the anger that's clouding his judgment. Trying to make him understand what he's doing—that this would be murder.

And then Catcher's shoulders relax, just a little. But Conall must notice this too and think he's safe because he cracks a small smile. "This is *our* world now," he says. "You should get used to it."

Catcher stares at him. "No it's not," he says sadly. "You don't deserve Annah's mercy and you won't have mine." The muscles on his arm jump as he swings the machete at Conall's throat. The blade's sharp and the cut is clean, severing his arteries, windpipe and spine. I scream and cover my face with my hands, looking away too late.

I'm standing like that, eyes squeezed shut with the feel of the dead Recruiter's blood on my exposed skin, when Catcher unlatches the gate and wraps his arms around me. He pulls me away and it's not until we're outside the cage that I look up and see Dove still sitting by her husband.

She struggles to stand but is unsteady, one leg giving way so that she falls back to her knees. She holds a hand out to me.

I catch my breath.

"Annah, please," she says, her voice so hoarse it's more like a whisper. "Please don't leave me here. Not like this."

I stare at her. At Conall on the floor, his body draining of blood. I know Dove's as good as dead. The infection's blazing inside her, shutting down her organs. It will kill her if she doesn't die from blood loss first, and either way she'll turn Unconsecrated.

She'll hunger for me and the living on this island just as her husband did. Just as they all do. I think of how I felt locked in the kennel, terrified I'd never see the sky again or breathe fresh air.

I know she feels the same, but if I let her go free I'm setting that loose on the island. I'm putting everyone including my sister and Elias in danger.

Yet I can't kill her. Not now. She's still alive. She's still human. It's a line Catcher's crossed but that I never have. Not even to grant mercy.

"Annah," she whispers again. Her arm trembles with the effort of keeping her hand raised, held out for me to grasp.

I've never considered myself a cruel person. Apathetic and ambivalent, maybe, but never outright inhumane. I've tried to take care of those around me or at the very least, tried not to cause them harm.

And yet here there's no easy answer. There's no easy choice.

"Annah?" Catcher asks softly, standing next to me. He holds out the machete, its blade still slick.

My breath burns hot inside me and my heart pounds in my ears. It's not fair that this all falls to me. I'm not supposed to be the one deciding someone else's fate. I'm not the judge of what's right and wrong.

I imagine slipping my fingers into Dove's. Her pulse under mine, the life still flowing inside her. But it's not her hand I'm gripping, it's the cold metal of the cage gate. When I swing it closed, the hinges protest and cry and it latches shut with such an indifferent jolt that I wince.

Dove lowers her hand. She kneels in the middle of the locked cage, staring at me. I want her to understand this decision. I want her to understand that in this world there are no easy choices, only choices that have to be made.

"Don't leave me like this, Annah," she begs.

I start backing away from her. Once you begin determining someone else's fate, how can you ever stop?

"Annah." She tries to shout but her voice cracks. "Don't let me be like them! Annah! Don't do this! Don't leave me here! Please, Annah! Please!"

Her voice follows me as I stumble up the steps. "They're going to turn me into a monster, Annah! Don't do this to me! You have to help me! Annah!"

She's right, of course she's right. And I'm so undone by my inability to fix things for Dove that Catcher has to carry me from the building, striding swiftly down the dim hallways. We pass a few Recruiters, who shuffle back into the shadows, their narrowed eyes tracking us.

I press my face against Catcher's chest. I wish the touch of him brought me comfort. I wish it made me feel whole. I wish I could remember the determination on his face when he told Conall that I was the woman he loved.

But all I can hear are Dove's pleas. The sound of the gate crashing shut. All I can think is that I'm not the person I thought I was. I'm selfish and horrible and cruel, just like the Recruiters.

I wonder if that's what it takes to survive in this world, and if that's the case, whether any of us deserve to live after all.

▼ ▼ ▼

"Do you think they'll come after us?" I'm standing over the woodstove steeping herbs into an infusion for Elias and my sister. I've been forcing them to drink this stuff all day and already they're looking better, sleeping more peacefully.

Catcher's at the window, looking down on the Recruiter headquarters. "I don't know," he says.

I nod, watching the water in the pan turn dark and murky. We both know they will, after what happened with Conall. I wonder if Dove's alive. If she's still in the cage screaming for me. Beating her fists against the gate. I wonder if she'll ever forgive me.

I wonder if I'll ever forgive myself. I notice a few traces of dried blood caked along my nails. Dove's blood. Dove, whose pain I chose to ignore. I wonder how often Catcher is forced to make similar choices.

"I found a ship." He says it so quietly and calmly that it takes a moment for the magnitude of the statement to sink in.

"It's beached, not too far away. Big enough for us to live on for a while. For a lot of us—anyone else who can get off the Sanctuary and out of the Dark City. I think it belonged to the Protectorate. There were some Mudo on board, but . . ." He waves a hand in the air as if they're no longer a problem.

"A ship?" I whisper. I let my eyes close and dream about it. Nothing but water surrounding us. Free of the Recruiters.

He smiles, a small lopsided grin. "I saw the curve of a roller coaster off in the distance when I was out scavenging."

He tilts his head toward me, his eyes glinting with joy. "I grew up next to an amusement park. That's where . . ." He swallows, the smile dimming a bit before he shakes his head, clearing away whatever was bothering him.

"Anyway, it reminded me of home and so I decided to go check it out." He laughs softly. "I climbed to the top of one of the coasters. It was the most amazing sensation being alone out there staring at the horizon." His eyes lose their faraway look. "That was when I saw the ship. It was beached in the shallows down the shore a ways."

He shrugs. "I just wish I knew how to get us there. I can stock it with food and water, but what good is that? I can't get it up the river to the Sanctuary by myself, and I can't figure out how to get you and the others there safely."

I poke at the bag of herbs, letting it bob and sink in the water. Watching little dried pieces of leaves tremble along the surface. Floating. It makes me think of the other night when I heated the air in the fabric bag and sent it drifting away. How I haven't told Catcher my thoughts on how to escape.

How maybe I can get us to his ship. "I think I have a way off the island," I say hesitantly.

Catcher freezes, his breath held as if he isn't sure he heard me correctly.

I pause, a bit uncertain about how to voice my thoughts. "The other night I was on the roof and I made a balloon out of a cloth bag and hot air from the fire. I was thinking about balloons from the before time—pictures I saw in a museum when I was a child—and I wondered if I could make it work. I think . . ."

I walk over to stand next to him by the window, staring at the darkness outside. "I think we could make them big enough to carry us off the island. It could be really dangerous and stupid but . . ." I look up at him, at the hope in his eyes. "But I think it might be worth the risk."

Reaching out, I trace the shape of a balloon where my breath fogs the window. "We'll need more supplies." I draw the lines, the basket, a cauldron for the fire. "We can seal the seams with fat or oil. We need ropes and wires and light wood to make the basket. Something big to hold the fire."

I look around the room, trying to take stock of what we already have. "Some of this stuff we can scrounge up here, but you might need to get the rest in the Dark City. And you have to tell the people over there how to make their own so they have a shot at escape as well. We'll have to hurry."

He stares at my crude diagram. "I can't leave the three of you alone again. Not so soon with the Recruiters and Ox. Not after what I did to Conall. They're going to want some kind of revenge."

I thread my fingers through his. "You're never going to be able to be here all the time," I tell him. "Someone's always going to need you somewhere else. There's nothing either of us can do about it. You're not a person who can ignore other people's pain. I wouldn't want you to be."

"You don't understand, Annah." He grips me so tightly I can feel the tips of his fingers imprinting my skin. "I almost lost you." He kneels, wrapping his arms around me. "I walked into the auditorium and I saw you in that cage and I died. All that blood—I thought you were infected."

He looks up at me. "At that moment I realized I'd made the biggest mistake in my life. I realized that I'm nothing without you. That there's no point in being alive if I can't love you."

I catch my breath but he's not finished. "I love you, Annah. And if you're willing to risk everything to be with me, then I'm willing to risk everything to be with you. I'm going to keep fighting for you, every day of my life. If you'll have me."

I sink to my knees until our foreheads are touching. Amazed at how in this tiny little room in this corner of a dark and forgotten world I can feel so alive.

"Yes," I whisper against his lips. I kiss him and he kisses me back, fully and wholly and without reservation.

And for a moment there's no death in the world, no pain or infection or despair. There's only us and life and something between us so impossibly pure that it consumes us both.

▼ XXXIX ▼

J ust as we feared, there's a knock on the door that night as I'm helping my sister drink another cup of the herb tea. Already color flushes her cheeks and she's able to stay awake for small stretches of time. She's still weak—they both are— but they're not on the edge of death any longer.

Someone pounds on the door again, insistent. Elias struggles to push himself from the bed but I nudge him back down under the quilts. "Catcher's here, he'll take care of it," I tell him but he frowns, clearly wanting to stand between us and them—to protect us.

I tiptoe into the hallway, my back pressed against the wall so that I can watch as Catcher opens the door, machete clutched in his hand. Ox stands on the threshold, alone, and my entire body tenses.

That voice—the casual impassive tone. That allowed a man to hit me. That ordered me to be thrown over the wall. That told me my childhood village no longer existed. I ball up my hands in useless rage, wishing I could storm down the hall and punch him but knowing he'd only strike me to the ground.

"The men aren't happy about what you did, Catcher," Ox says. "Conall was a good friend to many of them, and the second in command."

"I wasn't too happy about what they were doing to the woman I love," Catcher responds evenly.

"I'm not kidding around." Ox's voice is menacing, but also exhausted. "You don't have any idea what it takes to keep so many people alive, do you? Any idea how much it takes to keep order? It takes rules, and to have meaningful rules you have to have consequences for breaking them."

He leans against the doorframe, wiping a hand over his face. There are dark circles under his eyes. "Regardless of what you might think, I'm not evil, Catcher. But you can't get away with what you did. And since we can't punish you directly . . ." His voice trails off and he sighs. "They wanted to take the women."

My stomach lurches. A storm of horrible images flashes through my mind and I shove them away, anger building inside me.

"You know you can't allow that," Catcher growls. "*I* won't allow it."

Ox throws up his hands in exasperation. "This whole thing's gone too far. These men want blood."

I close my eyes, press my hands to my temples. There has to be a way to fix this. To make it stop.

Catcher fires back, "They're your men, Ox, control them. You're in charge of them. You shouldn't have allowed things to get to where they have."

"Maybe so," Ox counters. "But that doesn't change where we are now. Someone has to pay for Conall's death. They wanted both your women. I convinced them to take only one. You have to hand one of the girls over and I'm not going to stop them. What you did was wrong—"

And before I know what's happening, Catcher slams his fist into Ox's face and Ox staggers backward. I race down the hall, throwing myself between them with a hand pressed against each chest to keep them apart.

"Stop it!" I yell.

"What *you* did was wrong!" Catcher shouts over me. "What I did was justice."

Ox stares at me a moment, an expression approaching pity in his eyes. He's different from Conall in that way. Conall loved blood and fear. Ox is just trying to maintain some sort of order on the island—a way to keep his men alive.

"Conall would have found a way to get himself killed one way or another," I tell Ox. "He went too far." It's clear he sees the truth of my words but doesn't care.

He raises a few fingers to his nose, wiping away blood. "What's done is done," he tells Catcher before looking at me, almost apologetically. "I've convinced them they can't have both women. They don't care which of them you hand over, they just want one. I'll do my best to keep them from hurting her too badly."

I stand there dazed, trying to let his words sink in. Catcher's face pales and his hand clutching the machete trembles. "You allow that and I'll never supply your men again."

Ox takes a deep breath and I can hear the weariness in his voice. The same weariness we all feel. "You don't have an option, Catcher. They patrol the walls and cable car—they know there's no way to get your friends off the island. And they know that so long as your friends are still here, hurt or not, you have to supply the Recruiters as well.

"I'm sorry about this, I really am. I'd hoped . . ." He pauses and for a moment he looks lost in thought. Then he shakes his head and turns away. "Look, I can keep them in check for a day, maybe two. Give you a little time to sort it out, decide. But I can't make any promises, Catcher," he calls out over his shoulder as he disappears down the hallway.

I just stand there, one hand on Catcher's chest and the other touching emptiness.

Catcher slams the door and then he punches it again and again until I pull him back, his knuckles raw and bleeding. He doesn't stop me as I tug him out of our flat toward the stairwell. He lets me lead him to the roof, where my sister and Elias can't hear us and where I can press snow to his bloody fingers.

He stares at where the ice melts to pink water trailing down his arm. "I don't know what to do anymore," he says. "I don't know how to protect you."

"It's not your job to protect me," I tell him, ignoring the frozen air that envelops us.

He reaches out with his uninjured hand and runs a finger along my lips. "I can't let anything happen to you," he says. "It will kill me."

I try to hold his gaze but I can't and end up looking over his shoulder at the dark clouds on the horizon pulling close to the City. I can hear the sound of ice freezing along the ground, the small quiet groans of the water forcing itself into cracks and expanding. Tearing our world apart degree by degree.

"I should just smuggle Mudo onto the island and infect all

the Recruiters. It wouldn't be hard for me to take care of them right after they turn."

I shake my head. It would be a brutal and cruel way to kill them all and I'm not sure it's what they deserve. "The Recruiters would probably kill you and the rest of us if anything went wrong—if they caught you trying to smuggle Unconsecrated onto the Sanctuary. It'd be a risk." I stare at my hands for a moment. "Besides, that makes us as bad as they are. We can't kill them like that."

"But they don't deserve to live," Catcher says in frustration. "Didn't you hear what Ox said?"

I bite the inside of my cheek. In my mind I see Catcher's blade slicing through Conall's neck, hear his last breath, the gurgling of blood in his lungs.

"What you did . . ." I hesitate, trying to figure out what I'm feeling and how to put it into words. "Conall was a monster," I say. Catcher's back stiffens.

"I'm not saying your killing him was wrong, I just . . ." I take a deep breath and lean my hips against the low wall circling the roof. "I don't think we can be so indifferent to life," I finally finish. "I'm not sure we should be the ones judging."

Catcher opens his mouth to defend himself, his jaw tightening, and I rest my hand over his to cut him off. I press my lips together, knowing I have to say this but afraid of how he'll respond. I push forward anyway.

"You terrified me back there, Catcher. You've talked before about how you feel caught in between the living and the dead because of being immune, but you're going to have to choose which side you want to be on. It's the Unconsecrated who take life indiscriminately. It's the living who strive to preserve it—even for the worst among us."

He lets his chin drop to his chest, his hand snaking to the back of his neck and pulling at the taut muscles lining his shoulders. "He was about to kill you, Annah. I couldn't let that happen. He wouldn't have stopped coming after you."

I tug on his arm until he lets go and I can press his fingers against my chest, over the thumping of my heart. "I'm still alive," I remind him. "You're not an evil person, Catcher. But that doesn't make it okay to kill the rest of the Recruiters. Maybe it's not fair—but we have to be better than they are. We can't sink to the worst of them."

I lay my other hand on his face, tilting it back until the light of the night splays across his cheekbones, his eyes. "Killing them would make us monsters. What's the point of working so hard to get off this island if we're going to turn into monsters anyway?"

Catcher pulls me to him and together we stand there staring up at the sky, the heat of him keeping me warm against the winter chill.

"We have a little time to figure something else out," I tell him. "I've already made progress quilting together material for the balloon. You just need to make sure the people left in the Dark City will have what they need and be ready on time as well." I turn and face him.

"We can make this work. I know we can." I wonder whether if I say it often enough, with enough force, I can make it true.

He pulls my head to his chest and I listen to the beat of his heart. "Do I still scare you?" he asks and I can sense the fear and uncertainty in his voice.

"Always," I tell him. He catches his breath and I lean away until I can see his eyes. "I'm scared of losing my heart to you. But I think it's a risk I'm willing to take."

I'm kneeling on the floor, sifting through the scraps of quilts my sister's already sewn together, when she shuffles into the room. Her hair's greasy, hanging around her face limply, but her eyes are no longer dull, her cheeks no longer fever-flushed.

"What's going on?" she asks, a little out of breath from walking down the hallway. She's weak from the illness and slides down to perch on the edge of a nearby chair, her muscles trembling slightly.

"I had no idea you'd quilted this much," I say, organizing the fabric into different piles: what looks strong enough to bear our weight and what doesn't.

She shrugs, picking up one of the strips of intricately pieced cloth. "It gave me something to do. I like putting things together—making something out of nothing."

Another detail I didn't know about my sister. There's still so much for us to learn about each other. "We're trying to sew a big fabric bag—sort of like a balloon—in less than two days," I tell her.

She looks at me, eyebrows raised. "You figured out how to fly?"

I blush a little, wondering if Catcher's getting the same reaction from the survivors in the Dark City—he went to tell them about our plan this morning. "Maybe. It might not work but . . ." I shrug. "Catcher's found a ship not too far away. We just have to make it off the island and down the mainland a bit."

She presses a finger against her lips, thinking. "Any idea how to steer it once it's up there?"

Cringing, I shake my head. "That's a detail I hadn't gotten to yet." I twist my fingers in the fabric spread around me, suddenly wondering if this is a stupid idea after all. I clearly haven't thought through how it all works. What if I end up killing us?

"Elias!" my sister calls out. We hear him grumble in the other room as he pulls himself out of bed and comes to stand in the doorway.

I can't help but see my sister's playful grin as her eyes slide down his body. It's evident they're feeling much better after being so ill. I glance away, the moment too intimate for me to watch.

"Annah's making a balloon to carry us to a ship Catcher found," my sister says as if it's old news. "She needs a way to steer it. You're good with flying things—think you can come up with something?"

His eyes light up. "How big a balloon?" he asks.

I shrug, gesturing at all the fabric. "That big."

He walks to the window and looks out over the river. "How far?"

I shrug again. "Down the coast. That's what Catcher says."

"I'll draw up plans." Excitement laces through his words. "You know, I was in a plane once."

My sister rolls her eyes at me. "We know," she says, giggling.

He shoots her a mock-stern look. "But after that, when I needed a place to spend the night, I slept in an old library. They had books about flying and I read everything I could. I never thought about a balloon, but it could work."

He's almost jumping with energy. He begins to pace and mumble, calculating surface area and lift, and my sister and I go back to the piles of fabric.

I push the sewing box toward her. "Think you have enough strength to tackle all this?"

Grinning, she settles back into the chair, pulling out a tarnished thimble and slipping it on her finger. She picks up haphazardly sewn rags. "Who stitched these?" she asks, looking at one of the crude seams.

I glare at her and she laughs, obviously enjoying making fun of me. We get back to work, me struggling to keep pace with her speed and Elias muttering as he sketches designs for some sort of propeller.

▼ XL ▼

Later, after Elias goes off to search through the building for some gears and soft metal he can bend into blades, my sister stands and stretches, then sets a kettle on the wood-burning stove.

"When you were in the Forest with Elias when we were kids," she says, staring out the window into the darkness, "did you think you were going to die?"

I'm so startled by her question that I don't know what to say. I think back on that time, remembering each moment.

"Yes," I tell her. "Every day."

She nods, seeming lost in her own thoughts. "But you kept pushing?"

"We didn't have a choice."

She pauses for a moment, shifting so that she can see our reflections in the window, her head tilted to the side as if she's trying to figure something out about me. Her eyes trace over my scars but I don't feel judgment and pity—it's more like a sculptor trying to fit the pieces of a puzzle together.

"You and Catcher?" she asks, one eyebrow raised suggestively.

I feel myself turn a bright red and she smiles, that being all the confirmation she needed. "I thought so. He's a really good person." She says it almost wistfully.

"I know." I stare at the strips of fabric in my lap. All these different pieces of cloth ripped apart from clothes and blankets that became worn and useless but now have a new purpose. I run my hand over one of the uneven seams, feeling the bumps of stitches.

Broken things can be made whole again. Perhaps not as they were before, but maybe stronger this time.

"You asked me on the shore what I'd do if I had only a few days left?" I venture.

My sister nods and pours herbs into the hot water, suffusing the room with an earthy scent.

"I decided that I'd live," I tell her. "I decided I'm tired of being scared and waiting for other people to make up their minds about what they want—I'm going after what *I* want." I pull another pile of fabric toward me. "And what I want right now is off this stupid island."

My sister laughs, bringing me a mug of tea. She curls back on her chair, legs tucked underneath her. "I want to build something," she says, getting a faraway look in her eyes. "Recently I've had this idea of a village." She sounds hesitant, as if waiting for me to make fun of her. But I hold myself still, barely breathing, wanting to hear more.

After a while she goes on. "There would be these beautiful buildings all connected with bridges—everything would be off the ground. It would be a part of nature—not trying to change it but to meld with it." She smiles. "It would be safe. We wouldn't ever have to worry again."

It's silent in the room when she's done. Down the hall we hear Elias throw open the door, a clanking of metal as he drags in supplies for his steering contraption. My sister and I glance at each other, dreams of possibilities still floating in the air around us.

She pulls the lantern closer to her lap and picks up where she left off, focusing on her hands guiding the needle in and out, in and out. Everything about this moment feels so content, so right.

▼　▼　▼

"I think they're ready across the river," Catcher says. We're standing on the roof in the darkness before sunrise, the clear air frozen around us. Catcher came back from the Dark City a little while ago after helping the remaining survivors put together the necessary materials. He stands beside me, gripping my hand as Elias buzzes around a crudely constructed box he built from wood from the walls of one of the abandoned flats. It's open on the top, a thin metal cauldron in the center to hold the fire and bags of fat-soaked wood strung around the sides.

It's tiny—we'll have to squeeze together inside—but it looks sturdy enough. Lying next to it is a simple-looking propeller attached to a hand crank that can be shifted to any side of the box to steer us.

My sister flutters around attaching thickly braided ropes reinforced with wires to the box and making sure they're secured to the fabric of the balloon, which is folded at the edge of the roof.

Once we start the fire and direct the smoke into the balloon there's no turning back. If the Recruiters see us before we can get it inflated enough, we're in trouble.

I stand by the wall around the roof with Catcher, watching the Sanctuary below to make sure no one sees us. It's frigid outside and I lean against his body for warmth as he goes over the last-minute details.

"The survivors I found were able to pull everything together pretty quickly. They'll be looking for the signal just before first light. There's also a group of Soulers at the other end of the Sanctuary—they've been working on one too. It's going to be harder for them: I've been smuggling supplies to the shore but they said the Recruiters might have found them and confiscated everything."

I press my lips together, rocking back and forth on my feet to keep the blood pumping through my body as dread boils in my stomach. "Is this going to work?" I ask, probably for the hundredth time.

Catcher squeezes my hand in his but doesn't answer because the reality is we don't know. "Did I tell you about the night I climbed the roller coaster back in Vista?" he asks, trying to distract me from all the ways I imagine this whole thing failing.

I frown at him, trying to remember, and shake my head.

"It was after I'd been infected. I was alone, living out by that amusement park. I'd always been afraid of heights and I sat there and stared at the roller coaster and I realized that I was going to die. In a few days, I'd be dead."

It hurts to hear him talk about what that time was like. How alone he must have felt.

"And so I climbed it. If I was going to die, let me die doing that—something interesting."

I raise an eyebrow. "Are you trying to tell me that if all this fails, at least it will be interesting?"

He grins, pressing a finger to my lips to quiet me. "No, I'm telling you that it was this amazing feeling." The light from the fire dances over his face. "I'd accepted that it was the end and I just sat there, staring out toward the darkness of the ocean and the starlight flashing off the crests of waves and knew that we were all part of this bigger whole. That somehow I mattered in the course of things and a part of me would always have left its mark on this world."

He stares at me for a long while. "The funny thing is, once I realized I was immune and wasn't going to die in a few days, I became scared of heights again. Scared of life and losing it. But for just that moment when I thought the infection would take me, I realized that life isn't something to be scared of. That you don't have to hold on so tightly that you can't breathe."

He leans his forehead against mine. "Don't be scared. This is going to work—you'll make it," he whispers.

I squeeze his hand, never wanting to let go of him.

Eventually, my sister and Elias finish their prepping and we stand, the four of us, staring out into the darkness. I know what happens next: Catcher will leave to go light the fire in the big empty field not too far from the ship so that the smoke will guide us where to steer when we're airborne after first light.

"It's getting close to dawn," he murmurs.

I grip him tighter. What if something goes wrong and this is the last time I see him? I close my eyes, willing the sun not to rise. Just this once.

Elias turns to stoke the large bonfire and my sister holds up the mouth of the balloon while he fans smoke into it, the fabric unfolding as it fills.

Catcher faces me, cups my cheeks in his hands. "I'll see

you soon." He says it as a statement, not a question. The look he gives me is pained and I know he doesn't want to leave me as much as I don't want him to go. But he has to.

And I have to let him go. Just for a little while, I tell myself.

He presses his lips to mine softly and then urgently, and I wrap my arms around him, digging my fingers into the muscles along his back to draw him tighter.

When he pulls away his forehead barely touches mine. "Be safe," he commands.

"You too," I tell him. He nods and then nods again.

I search for anything I can say to keep him close, to stop him from going, but I know there's nothing.

Except this: "I love you," I whisper. It hurts to say the words, to know that he now carries my heart with him and that I have to trust him with it.

He kisses the tip of my nose, my mouth, my cheek. "I love you," he says back, and then he turns and is gone.

The fire burns at my back, the smoke drifting and swirling around me as I watch him leave the building and cross to the cable car. As I watch it whisk him away from me.

On rooftops across the City I see other fires. Other sparks of light like stars. I try to shove my emotions down so I can focus on what needs to happen to keep us safe.

Behind me the balloon fills more and more. I help my sister keep the mouth of fabric open, astonished that it's actually working. The seams hold, the oiled fabric capturing the hot air inside. I start to get a giddy rush in my chest. We just have to get off the Sanctuary and down the river a bit—not even half a day's walk.

The horizon begins to lighten, a strip of pink vibrating along the curve of sky. "Should we give the signal to the others?"

Gabry asks. Her cheeks are flushed, her eyes bright with excitement.

I nod and turn toward the structure enclosing the stairwell. Most of my drawing of Catcher is gone, just a few bold slashes of charcoal left. I press my hand against what used to be his face and then climb to the roof, where there's a long strip of bright red cloth tied to the end of a tall pole. I lift it, letting the ribbon unfurl in the frozen morning breeze.

It snaps out, catching the wind. Telling everyone in the Dark City that now's the time to fly. This is it. A lightness fills my body, a rush so intense I want to combust with joy. The fabric balloon's starting to lift. Elias throws more logs onto the fire. It won't be long before it will carry us away. When we'll be free.

That's when I hear the shouts. I leap down and sprint to the wall. A Recruiter stands outside the headquarters, pointing up at us as if trying to figure out what's going on. As the balloon lifts higher behind me he turns and runs back inside and before long there's a stream of them racing toward our building.

"Go!" I shout at Elias. "They're coming!"

My sister's face pales as she joins Elias by the fire, fanning the smoke into the bag as hard as she can. It raises from the ground but not enough to carry the weight of the basket and us.

"They're at the door downstairs," I yell.

"It's not going to fill in time," Elias mutters under his breath and my sister knocks him with her elbow, telling him to shut up.

I look around the roof, searching for anything to buy us time. We'd used melted fat to coat the fabric and still have a vat of that and a few bags of oil for the lanterns. I grab them both and drag them to the stairwell.

In the center of the roof the envelope's filling, the seams starting to strain and the basket lifting more. I can already hear the Recruiters shouting as they spiral up the steps. We're running out of time.

Collecting pieces of fabric and wood, anything we won't need anymore, I throw them all into the stairwell and then light the bag of oil and toss it down after. There's a concussion and *whoomp* of air as the oil ignites, spreading along the steps and eating at the walls, bathing the hallway in flame. I slam the door.

"I guess you weren't planning to need those stairs if this didn't work," Elias grouses as he lifts my sister into the box. She starts to stoke the fire in the center cauldron.

"It's not going to burn long," I tell him. There's the sound of something popping and a high-pitched sucking sound as below us one of the windows explodes. I can't help cringing, thinking about the awful waste of the destruction.

"Let's go," Elias says, holding out a hand to me. I let him help me into the box and the balloon jerks us from the roof, Elias still lifting his leg over the side.

The balloon struggles at first, skimming across the roof, and then it pulls free and hovers, dragging us up into the air as the door to the stairwell slams open and flames leap out. Men in black uniforms chase us on the ground, but we're rising higher and higher and their sounds are lost to the wind. Elias points us toward the river, trying to clear the airspace over the Sanctuary as Recruiters scramble for crossbow bolts.

For the first few heartbeats that we're airborne my body revolts, desperate for the feel of solid ground as the tiny box jerks and sways. Air curls up my legs and the sensation is entirely wrong—unnatural.

The men chasing us grow smaller, the buildings less imposing as they recede below. I hold my breath, terrified that any movement will cause the balloon to spiral out of control, will split the seams and send us plummeting to a certain death.

"We're flying!" Elias shouts as if he can't believe it, the dawn wind ruffling his short hair. He throws his hands out wide in the air like wings and I clutch the edge of our small vessel, waiting for it to tear apart.

But it doesn't. The balloon continues to rise, the propeller steering us out over the river and away from the Sanctuary, while other balloons climb out of the Dark City—at first only one or two and then more and more. They're different colors, different sizes, but they all spring into the air, carrying the survivors away from the dead-choked streets.

We did it. My chest feels lighter than air, as if I alone am pulling us into the painted dawn sky.

▼ XLI ▼

The sun's just rising over the horizon, the morning wind shifting, pushing us across the river and over the edges of the Dark City. Behind us more Recruiters surge toward the Sanctuary wall but they're distracted by a group of dingy gray balloons rising on the south end of the island: the Soulers.

I whoop and cheer; Elias and my sister grab for each other, kissing and hugging. *We did it!* I want to scream at the world. *We're free!*

But the Recruiters won't let us go that easily. They climb the Sanctuary walls and continue to fire their crossbows at us. I hold my breath, watching the bolts go wide or fall short. Every second we're farther away, every heartbeat we're drifting out of range.

The balloons careening away from the south end of the Sanctuary aren't as lucky. A flaming arrow pierces the fabric of one of them, fire racing along the fat-soaked seams and crumbling the material to ash almost instantly.

I avert my eyes but not quickly enough to escape the sight of bodies plummeting to the frozen river below.

And then a loud ripping sound races down my spine—the sound of fabric tearing, splitting apart, and I look up to see a small flap of the material snapping in the wind. It takes a few seconds to lose enough air but suddenly the envelope buckles and we drop, fast. I scream from the shock of it, grabbing for my sister.

I struggle to add more fuel to the fire to refill the balloon, but my fingers fumble as the basket whips and jerks around. Hot air rushes into the envelope but we're still dropping. Sweat pours from our faces, every inch of our skin glistening from being so close to the flames.

The lightness I'd felt earlier solidifies into something dense as panic teases my mind. I force it away, needing to focus.

"Weight," I shout. "We have to drop everything we can."

My sister scrambles for the bags at her feet—supplies for the journey ahead—and tosses them over the side. Our descent slows but we're still not rising and the wind's taken over, shoving us faster in the wrong direction—toward the shore of the Dark City.

Elias cranks the propeller, trying to steer us away from the ragged buildings, but the balloon is too heavy and it's difficult to control. We might not even make it over the first one. "Maybe we can just land and repair the seam," my sister says, pointing to a long rooftop ahead. I glance up at the envelope, at the way it strains.

"We'd never find enough fuel to fill it again," I shout as I shovel more wood onto the fire.

Recruiters bellow in the distance. I look back and see them scrambling into the cable car, and slowly it starts to move across the river right underneath us. But the shore at the other end still teems with Unconsecrated: It's suicide for them to come after us.

"Look." I point down at them as Elias shifts the propeller, trying to turn us away from the tallest buildings. Heat billows into the balloon from the fire, a trail of smoke seeping out from the tear.

My sister heaves the last of the supplies over the side and then stands there with a book held in each hand, staring at the covers. I'm sick knowing she's willing to throw away things that mean so much to her.

She glances at me trying to fill the envelope with as much hot air as possible, and at Elias, who's trying to steer us, but there's just too much weight.

We're blown over the edge of the City, buildings passing by so close we could almost touch them. She tosses the books, watching them fall to the roof just below us, pages fluttering like broken wings.

But it's still not enough. We're still not rising.

In that moment I'm thrown back in time. I'm standing on the path and staring at Abigail, who's crying and begging Elias and me not to leave her behind. She's scared and alone and bleeding. I'm back in my little girl body, trying to decide what to do.

Except this time I can't choose between them. I don't have to choose between them.

"I love you," I say. They look at me, confused. "Both of you."

"We'll make it out of this," my sister says.

I reach out and cup Gabry's face, feeling her smooth skin under my thumb. "Build a world for me," I tell her.

And then I jump.

From the air I can hear Gabry shout and I can see Elias throw himself against the other side of the basket to keep it balanced. I'd watched the books fall and I know it's not that far a drop. I try not to scream because I don't want to scare my sister, but even so, when I hit the roof and tumble into a roll to break my momentum, I can't help but cry out.

I pivot to my feet, staring up at the balloon pulling them up and away from me. I tell myself I have to be strong. I've survived alone before and I can do it again, but still a penetrating isolation filters through me.

Gabry and Elias lean over the basket and shout down to me frantically and I wave them on. I can only stand and watch as Elias steers them south, other balloons drifting by high overhead.

They look like dandelion seeds on the wind, off to create a new world. To fall in the fields, burrow into the soil to grow and eventually bloom.

I scurry across the roof to my sister's books, plucking them from the wet snow. Even from where I stand the walls of the building I'm on look old, the bricks crumbling in some places. I can already hear the moans from the streets, plague rats shuffling below, pushing against the structure.

I won't be safe here long.

Far off in the distance to the south I see a thin plume of smoke. Catcher. My eyes blur thinking about him out there, expecting me to come flying toward him. I know he'll look for me when he finds out what I did, but I also know I can't wait for that to happen.

Not if the Recruiters are still crossing the river. It would be stupid of them not to turn back. Crazy.

Except that something moves in the distance—a figure lumbering across a roof several blocks down. I squint, trying to make out who or what it is, hoping it's just Unconsecrated shuffling after me.

But the figure runs hunched over, weaving around obstacles. Others follow, their black uniforms almost blending in with the dull morning light. I let out a long low breath like a hiss as I watch the Recruiters race for a bridge to the next building, making their way toward me.

Somehow they made it into the City. They've found access to the roofs and they're coming after me.

A frozen wind needles into me. All I have is the small knife in my pocket—no real weapon—which means my only option is to run. Dread fills my blood. I drop my sister's books and am headed toward the closest bridge when something flutters from the pages.

I plan to ignore it, the need to escape overpowering, except that I recognize the bright yellow banner, the block letters spelling out NEW YORK CITY across a photo of this city as it used to be.

It was the object that gave my father hope when he was lost in the Forest as a child. Something my sister carried with her when she came looking for me. The last remnant of my life from the village.

I can't leave it and I stoop to pick it up, to slip it into my pocket, when I remember standing on the roof in the Sanctuary with my sister as she tried to locate landmarks in the picture. When she told me about the secret histories of the buildings in the photo—underground rooms with hidden access to the tunnels.

Over my shoulder the Recruiters bear down on me,

finding a way through the maze of broken bridges that leads to where I stand. Already I can hear snatches of them shouting for me.

The streets are filled with dead. The bridges will never take me across the island—too many of them have been cut and I'll always be in sight of the Recruiters. If I want any hope of escaping them, there's only one option: the subway.

I have to make it to the tunnels.

Sacrificing even a few moments is stupid, but even so I hold the postcard up, turning it back and forth. With each thump of my heart my fingers waver, panic-fueled blood racing through my body.

And then everything lines up perfectly. There's the skeleton of what used to be a tall glass skyscraper and beyond that the building with the green roof and the arching windows.

But which one has the secret rooms? I clench my eyes shut, trying to put myself back in time with my sister as she was telling me about these places, but all I can recall is my frustration and skepticism.

I drop to my knees, tossing my sister's books around me and flipping frantically for anything that will give me a clue as to which one has the access. Nothing.

The Recruiters race toward me but there's no direct route; they keep having to detour when they encounter cut bridges. There are only a handful of them, and even though I might be able to take them, it would be insane to try. If I got hurt, if they overpowered me—I'd have no hope of finding Catcher again.

I'm about to give up and start running when I notice tiny numbers imprinted on the postcard, so small they almost fade into the background. I hold the card up to the sky, tilting it toward the morning sun until I can make some of them out: page numbers.

My sister made a key.

Trying to keep my breath steady, I turn to the corresponding pages in the book that held the postcard. I scour the history of three buildings and want to scream in frustration when something catches my attention.

A diagram of the subway. A picture of a rusted-out sign over an old metal door. An arrow pointing to the green-roofed building that's just down the street from me. A footnote about a ghost station in the basement.

I tuck the postcard into my shirt and start running across the roof to the next building and then the next, vaulting the short walls in between. I might be a fool for believing what the book says. It's my sister who believes parts of this city have truly survived since the Return—that there are still places rooted in the before time.

But it's a chance I have to take. If I stay up here the Recruiters will eventually catch up to me, overpower me. Take me back to the Sanctuary, where Catcher and I will be trapped forever.

I can't do that to him. I'd rather risk myself than see him turned back into their lackey.

The morning wind gathers around me, pushing balloons lazily across the sky high over my head. All of them chasing a strip of smoke on the horizon leading to Catcher and safety. All of them so close but beyond my grasp.

Under my feet the bridge jostles and jumps as I cross, one of the boards splitting when I land on it, my leg breaking through. I grapple with the rope railings, twisting my wrist through one to stop my fall.

My breath comes in jerks and I close my eyes for just a moment, the muscles of my arm straining to hold me up. Slowly I ease my way onto the next board, testing its strength before transferring my weight.

Already I can hear the Recruiters shouting behind me, closing the distance. My body begs to run, but I force myself to take even steps, testing each section of the bridge before moving across it, agonizingly slow.

I can't stop glancing over my shoulder, watching the uniform-clad bodies weave their way nearer and nearer. Unable to keep the need to run from taking over, I leap from the end of the bridge onto the roof of the green-roofed building, my feet slipping on a patch of ice when I land.

Without pausing, I sprint to the fire escape and bolt down the stairs two at a time. In the street below the plague rats sense me and turn their faces up, their mouths gaping wide. There are so many it's like looking at a writhing mass of maggots twisting and wriggling in the body cavity of a dead animal. They scratch at the old bricks, pressing against brittle-looking wood blocking the large entrances on the ground level.

At the first open window I come across, I duck inside, grateful to be away from the sound of the dead. I'm met with a long narrow hallway, the floor stained and walls cracked. The only light filters in from the window behind me and for a moment I don't want to leave its safety.

Ahead of me is nothing except dim shadows, but I know the Recruiters are behind me. I have no other option but to press forward. Taking a deep breath, I square my shoulders and start throwing open every door I come across, looking for a stairwell. I desperately want some sort of weapon larger than my little knife—my hands feel useless without one.

Most everything's picked clean, though, and I spiral down the staircase at the end of the hall, barely noticing the remnants of the before time—old wallpaper clinging to plaster, a painting tacked up here and there.

Finally, toward the bottom floor I find an apartment that looks like it was lived in not too long ago, the smell of stale food hanging in the air. I bust open the door and it's a room with a crude table and bench under a window. A machete's casually propped against the far wall. I step inside and grab it, happy to have the heft and weight of it in my hand.

I'm about to leave when something makes me pause, a tingling on the back of my neck. I tilt my head, listening. From outside I hear only the moans of the dead, the shuffling of their feet. There's nothing to indicate the Recruiters have made it to this building yet.

"Hello?" I ask the emptiness. I push farther into the flat, knocking open a cracked door. It swings slowly, revealing a sagging bed with a pile of blankets on top, a lump clearly visible. Everything's coated with dust and a thin layer of grime, the boarded window admitting barely any light at all.

A lantern and flint rest on a crate next to the bed, and carefully I move into the room and reach for them. But I can't stop staring at the bed and something makes me grasp the edge of the blanket and tug—unveiling the tip of a skull, the remains of hair and tattered clothes.

Two long-dead corpses, more desiccated skeleton than anything else, lie intertwined, the arm of one over the other as if they lay down one night to sleep and never woke up.

My eyes burn and I hold back tears. I toss the blanket back

over their bodies, giving them peace. They already gave me what I needed anyway. Shoving the flint into my pocket and taking the lantern in one hand, the machete in the other, I race back down the hallway and start down the stairs to the ground level, wondering what it would be like to die in the arms of the one you love most.

▼ XLII ▼

The bottom floor is a chaos of noise: the sound of so many bodies beating against the walls, the wails and moans, the creaking of old wood about to give way. There are thousands of dead surrounding the building now, clawing and beating and shoving—all sensing me. All needing me.

Brick and mortar are only so strong. Already I can feel the vibrations through the building, hear the strain of it trying to stay standing. It's just a matter of time before they force themselves inside.

I find my way to a huge empty room. Thin streams of light filter through boarded windows, over enormous faded pictures of half-clad boys and girls in sunnier days that crumble from the walls. My only thought as I race past them is how vulnerable they look—how naive to be so unprotected in a world with so much danger.

Frantically, I search for another stairwell leading down, figuring that any access to the tunnels has to be underground.

Against the back wall I find a narrow door blocked by a web of rusted bars. I growl with frustration as I yank at them, the sharp end of one slicing along my forearm when I pull it free. I fling the bars over my shoulder; they make a hollow sound when they clatter to the floor.

I can barely squeeze through into a dark hallway that smells of mold and decay. I fumble with the lantern I took from upstairs, lighting a low flame that sputters and sways.

All around, shadows threaten to swallow me whole, and once again I have to remind myself that I can survive—I can find my way out of this mess.

There are a dozen doors lining the hallway and I throw open each one. Every time my heart freezes, terrified something's trapped behind it. My mind conjures up the worst sort of nightmares, until I'm almost convinced that just by thinking them true they'll exist: bodies with nothing but mouths and teeth and infection.

I want to take a moment for a deep breath, to ease the thundering of my heart and calm the images racing through my mind. I know that acting frantic is an easy way to end up dead or infected, but my body screams at me that I don't have any time to spare.

The Recruiters will find me soon. They can't be that far away.

I'm drenched in sweat and my breath is shaky as I reach for the last doorknob. This one's stuck, the wood swollen, and I kick at it several times until there's a crack wide enough for me to see inside.

Holding my breath, I hope for stairs only to find a tangle of bones draped in stained strips of tattered cloth. What used to be fingers and teeth are scattered across the floor. Their tomb is my dead end. I spin away, needing to figure out where to search next.

For a heartbeat I think about crawling through that last door and hiding behind the skeleton. Just wishing the Recruiters would never find me. But I know that even if they didn't, the dead would. The Unconsecrated will inevitably push their way inside.

I sprint down another dark hallway, the wrinkled and rotting carpet tearing underfoot as I run. There are several more tiny empty rooms, and as I race past I wonder if this is what the rest of my life will be: dark hallways, empty rooms, terror.

Just then I stumble into an alcove and find a large metal door with rust spots bubbling up through flaked white paint. I throw all my weight against it. I shout at it as if it were human, as if it can grant me mercy and let me in.

With a loud protest of rusted hinges, the door pops open. I'm greeted with a gust of cold musty air. The darkness is deeper here, older, and my lantern fights to illuminate it. There's a set of stairs leading down, and just as I'm about to follow them I hear a loud crack. A cascade of shattering follows.

I hesitate, trying to locate the noise, and then I hear men shouting. Moans filter through, no longer muffled by the hasty barriers over the windows and doors. A deep voice booms, "Run! They've breached."

My throat closes. They're here. The Unconsecrated and the Recruiters, both catching up. I have to push forward, it's my only hope. I throw myself into the dark, forcing the door closed behind me. I practically fall down the steps and stumble into a smaller room. As I turn the corner a figure clutching a lantern lunges at me from behind a long gleaming slab of wood.

I cry out, stumbling over a broken table as I wave my machete wildly.

The figure falls back as well, disappearing, and I blink several times before I realize there's a mirror. I clutch my chest, trying to ease the terror-fueled pain. When I stand back up I see my reflection, hunched and small, my hair spiked short and wild around the bright band of the hat Catcher gave me.

My eyes are fierce and determined. Almost feral. And in the mirror I see another door behind me, intricately carved, with raised paneling. I spin around and race to it. This one opens smoothly, easily, to another stairwell. My heart pounds with each step and the air grows thicker as I descend.

Shouts and the sound of feet hammering against stairs chase me. I propel myself faster, stumbling and sliding over the steps until I hit the landing and slam into another door. I'm panting, not even caring that the sound of my choked breathing echoes loudly, giving me away.

I'm trapped.

My heart screams as I wrap sweaty fingers around the knob, the metal of the door freezing cold. It rattles uselessly and I jerk at it, trying to force the lock to catch, and finally it clicks. The door swings open. A blast of frozen air hits me in the face along with a darkness so pure it seems as if it's never known light.

Taking a deep breath, I push the lantern through the opening and am greeted with the most beautiful sight I've ever seen: blackness that goes on forever.

Escape.

I jump out onto the subway platform, the chasm of two

long black tunnels stretching out to either side. The desire to cry with relief is so strong that I have to swallow again and again, pushing the stinging fear back into my stomach.

I feel rather than hear the footsteps of someone chasing after me and I throw the door closed, banging at the knob with my machete, hoping to bend it out of place. Someone slams against it from the other side and I leap back.

He pounds and screams for me, shouting my name over and over again like a howl and I recognize the fury of Ox's voice.

For a moment I'm still, my breath clouding around me. Of course it would be Ox coming to claim me and drag me back to the Sanctuary to lure Catcher. He would never let me go that easily. Which makes my escape that much more desperate.

In ten steps I'm at the edge of the platform and I shimmy over, dropping to the tracks below. The darkness spreads to either side of me and I don't know which way to go.

I close my eyes, trying to concentrate. Trying to think. Softly, I feel the trace of dank air along the left side of my body, skimming over my scars. The draft has to be from somewhere—there has to be an opening in that direction.

My muscles shout that I have to go. Now. I have to run run run. Behind me the pounding grows louder and then I hear a different noise. I look up to see fingers reach through a grate in the wall next to the door. My lantern glistens off eyes and I stumble back.

Out of time, I turn to my left and start running.

It's freezing down here, each breath searing my lungs with what feels like ice-cold fire. My body protests as I struggle to go faster, my feet stumbling along the rotted wood spaced along the tracks.

Usually the worst thing you can do when you're being chased by Unconsecrated is run. It wears you out fast, and any distance you might gain is only lost while you recover and they keep coming.

But that's the problem. I'm not being chased by Unconsecrated. At least, not *just* them. And the living can move much faster than the dead.

Shouts echo after me, bounding from the walls so that it's almost impossible to tell which direction they're coming from. I ignore the pain in my legs and lungs and try to run faster. I fall and skin my knee but I get up and go on.

Time in the darkness is meaningless, measured in gasping breaths and pumping heart. The sound of men shouting morphs into the noise of the dead: moans of every timbre combining into an almost-choir.

Sweat rolls down my face; I don't know how long I can push. But I also don't know what else to do.

The walls holding me in splay open, the ceiling soaring as I scramble into another station. The platform stretches along next to me and I slow my steps. If I climb up, can I hide?

But then what? I'm still faced with the same impossible scenario: I can hide from the Recruiters, but no one can hide from the dead.

So I keep running, the tunnel beginning to curve to the right. My lantern swings with each step, the light bobbing almost like a boat on water as I race past marks on the wall—some of them official-looking stamps designating locations and emergency exits, others bright puffy scrawls and pictures.

An emergency exit sounds like the perfect thing right now. Climb a ladder, find a hole, escape from this life.

The reality is that I'd just end up in the streets facing the horde. They'd find me. So many would devour me I wouldn't even get a chance to Return.

The moaning becomes like a tidal wave behind me, a wall of water pressing me forward. I just have to let it push me, not get dragged under. The cold numbs my ears, radiating down my neck and trailing under my clothes.

Something catches my foot and I fall, dropping the lantern. I stare at it as it rolls to a stop, cursing my stupidity for not being more careful. "Come on," I grumble, watching the flame choke and sputter.

It flickers out, dousing me in nothingness that is so absolute I'm not sure air exists. The darkness amplifies every sound—the scrape of breath up my throat, the whisper of my fingers as I fumble in my coat pocket for the flint, the wheeze of air drifting along forgotten walls.

On my knees, I strike at the flint, my fingers shaking now with urgency. Each failed try is the Recruiters growing closer; every spark that dies, them gaining on me. They can't be that far back, not anymore. The ground vibrates, traces of the pursuing footsteps thumping like summer rain.

With the lantern finally relit I notice that the tunnel is partially caved in ahead, boulders, rocks and twisted steel beams strewn every which way. I groan in frustration for a moment before I pull myself together. Almost madly I attack the debris, pulling at the smaller stones, wrenching free broken metal rods and digging as hard as I can, knowing that I'm losing time.

Steps volley behind me, any sense of distance lost to the echoes. Moans meld with the Recruiters' voices calling for me, all lost in the growing thunder of noise.

Finally I've dug a narrow path and I shove the lantern

through, crawling after it. It's a tight squeeze in some places, and I have to wriggle, cringing as icy rocks grate over my ribs. At least this will hold back the dead, I reassure myself with each scratch.

Just as I make it through, I catch sight of movement chasing behind me at the edge of my lantern light. I kick at the hole I've created, shifting debris until it falls back in on itself, blocking my pursuers.

"Annah," the man calls out, and it's Ox. He stops on the other side of the web of broken beams, woven tightly enough to keep him from coming after me but loose enough that we're standing almost face to face.

"Leave me alone," I growl, picking up a rock and flinging it at him. He dodges but it hits the Recruiter behind him in the face, scratching his cheek. In the weak light of my lantern I can see there's already blood dripping from the man's mangled fingers.

I cough and choke on the frigid air, wondering if any of them got infected when they landed in the sea of dead that is what's left of the Dark City. I step back once and then again, putting more distance between us.

Ox wraps a massive hand around one of the beams, his knuckles bruised and raw. "You don't understand, Annah. We need you! The Sanctuary will fail without you and Catcher. They'll all die." He tugs at the metal, picking apart the debris, and I kick at the pile again, shifting the rocks to narrow the gaps he's creating.

Behind them shapes flicker, deeper grays in the black darkness. The dead. My heart stutters and then races. I step back again, the light cast over the Recruiters growing weaker.

"You should have thought of that before," I shout at him.

The two other men start pulling at the boulders, and they're so much stronger than I am that it won't be long before they've dug a way through.

Not that they have much time before the Unconsecrated will overwhelm them.

I start running. "I know these tunnels," I yell back at him, following the curve of the tracks as they meet with another set. I stumble over the metal rails but manage to catch myself. "You won't find me!" It's a lie but he doesn't have to know.

My muscles have already cooled and they pull and strain as I run harder, gasping for air. I don't care about the pain. I can live with that if I can get distance. I need to lose them.

I know the smartest thing would be for me to drop the lantern, that it must be easy for them to follow the light, but then I'd be blind. Every time I tripped they'd draw closer. Every time I had to hesitate over my footing, they'd gain on me.

Besides, I'm not that desperate. Yet.

I lose sense of everything in the almost-darkness: who I am, where I've been, how much time I've been down here. I just run: one step illuminated, then the next, and always the moans and Ox's shouting behind, constant, grating.

I think about pressing myself into a crack in the wall and holding my machete tight, waiting for Ox to thunder past and then striking. I'd slice along the back of his leg first, nicking the tendons and hobbling him. Then I'd kick him onto his face and make the final blow against the back of his neck.

My own vicious thoughts make me shudder. Could I really do that? Take his life?

He deserves it, of that I'm sure. But as I run I think about the sound of Catcher's blade slicing through Conall's spine.

It was murder. A brutality that still weakens me. Because where do I go when I cross that line? I'm not ready to make such a decision, and so instead I keep careening into the darkness, since as long as I'm moving I'm still safe.

Or at least, that's the illusion I promise myself.

Eventually, the feel of the air in the tunnel shifts and I notice a glow around the bend ahead that looks almost like daylight. My heart pounds faster. A point of desperate hope spreads through me—it could be a way out.

And then reality crashes down, pulling me to a standstill. If there's an opening, it will be filled with Unconsecrated. There could be a swarm of them just ahead. Moans already fill the tunnel, making it impossible to figure out whether they're in front of me or behind.

I hold the machete in one hand and the lantern in the other as I scurry forward, ready for anything. After a dozen more steps the ceiling arches away from me, soaring up in a graceful curve over my head, and the walls swing wide, revealing a short looping platform dusted with snow.

It's like walking into someplace sacred, the way the ice crystals shimmer in the air. Recessed in the ceiling, windows with intricate patterns gaze down on me, most of them blocked by thick leaden grids but a few still full of colored glass. There's a hallowed stillness to the station, to the joining and breaking of vaulted domes that collect the sound of my pursuers and dissipate them into a meaningless chorus.

To run feels profane but I have no choice. I press my back against the inner curved wall and shuffle my way along it, my gaze sliding over the brown and green tiles interlocked along the arches and then fixing on the windows above.

Already I see them straining. See the cracks. Who knows

how many hands pound against them? Ahead of me another tunnel looms, a black abyss ready to swallow me, but before I step into it Ox calls my name.

It's not that he's there that surprises me. What surprises me is that he's alone, one hand pressed to the edge of the platform and the other to his chest. He just stands there as if he's sure that I won't run.

Or that even if I do, he'll catch me.

▼ XLIII ▼

"Go away!" I scream as I keep walking backward from him. Drifts of snow shimmer in piles around the platform and along the tracks, fallen through the broken windows above.

Blood pounds through my body, keeping me warm—but my ears still burn with cold, my throat raw and sore.

"I can't," he says, hand clutching his chest. Every breath comes out as a cloud, blurring his features. "I promised the men I'd keep them alive and I need you to do it."

I'm shaking my head. "Even if you dragged me back I wouldn't let you have Catcher," I spit at him.

"That's not the way it works," he says. "He's proven enough times he'll do what we ask to keep you alive. How do you think we knew which one of you to threaten when we needed to remind him to keep working for us?"

"What?" I stumble over a rotted chunk of wood and pause, ready to run or fight—whichever will keep me alive longer.

He rubs his hand over his bald head, wicking away

glistening sweat. "Throwing you over the wall. The cage. Not that I approve of the way Conall handled himself, but it worked. Before we knew about you we thought your sister would be more useful for controlling him." He shrugs. "I was wrong. Once you were in the picture we had to figure out which sister he cared about more. Turns out it's you."

I think of all they put me through—the torture and agony of it! "You're worse than the Unconsecrated," I hiss. "You're a monster."

"It worked," he says evenly. "I told you when we met that I'd do anything for my men. You should have believed me."

"You're crazy and stupid." I wave my machete in the air, dismissing him. "You're the one who said there was nowhere else to go! You're the one convinced we're all that's left."

He shakes his head, sliding his hand from the edge of the platform, and takes a step toward me. I square my shoulders, raising my chin, ready to attack. He stops. "It's not for me to decide," he says. "I don't decide we're the last ones. I just keep the people safe. They'll determine whether to start a new generation."

I snort. "There are only men on that island."

He tilts his head. "We have Souler women too. They'd have learned to make a life with some of my men."

My stomach lurches at the thought. At creating a generation by force.

"Do you ever wonder about the very first people?" he asks. "About what it must have been like for them? To find themselves so unprepared for this dangerous new world?"

"You mean after the Return hit?" I take another two steps back. It won't be long before the tide of Unconsecrated sweeps into the station, and every moment we stand here unmoving is a moment they're drawing closer.

He laughs, the sound out of place in these tunnels. "No, I mean the very first living. What would happen if they'd simply given up?"

"I guess humanity wouldn't have been worth it then," I say. Above us more cracks race across the glass, the lead grates shuddering under the weight of so many undead bodies. I retreat farther down the tunnel until it's as if Ox is just speaking to the empty tomb of a station.

"Does the fact that we ended up here and now with little hope mean that everything that came before was meaningless?" he calls after me. "The rise and fall of empires? The families and wars and loss and growth and knowledge and striving for something better? Is it always about the end and not about the beginning? Is it always about the conclusion and not about the path to it?"

He's looking for meaning where there is none. He should have learned this by now. "I'm tired of paths," I shout past the edge of my lantern light. I glance behind me at the endless tunnels beckoning. "Sometimes they lead nowhere."

My words are drowned by a massive shattering sound, glass splintering against the platform like icicles. I press myself against the wall, far enough into the tunnel that the shards merely scatter at my feet.

Ox, still standing by the curve of the platform, drops into a crouch, throwing his arms over his head as chunks of broken lead latticework crash in from the ceiling. The old windows arching across the station buckle and break, allowing a wash of moans to roll over us. There's a massive grating sound of metal on metal before something gives and bodies begin to fall.

The first few land with sickening thuds. Their bones crunch, puncturing skin with sharp gleaming fractures of white. Yet, oblivious to the almost complete destruction of their bodies, they're still desperate for Ox.

I retreat back along the tracks as the dead crawl forward, leg bones scraping over the concrete with a horrible high-pitched scratch, fingers swiping the air.

Ox's eyes meet mine for a helpless moment as bodies rain around him. One fractures its thighbone, another splits its head and lies motionless. They just keep coming. More and more, falling on one another, piling up so that those on the bottom cushion the landing of those on the top. They roll and writhe until they find their footing and start to stumble forward.

The sound of so many Unconsecrated becomes deafening.

I turn and run. The last thing I see is Ox standing there, the dead a downpour between us. Already the Unconsecrated move after me, filling the tunnels like water, flooding behind me.

▼   ▼   ▼

I don't stop running. If anyone deserved to die it was Ox, but still, to see him there with so many dead—they'd have pulled him apart.

I shake my head, trying to erase the thought, and instead focus on what to do next. I can't just keep running randomly through the tunnels. The Unconsecrated will continue to pile up behind me, their numbers becoming a tidal wave that will drown me if I don't stay ahead of them.

If I accidentally hit a dead end or double back . . . I'll be in the same situation as Ox. It's too much of a risk.

At the next station I drag myself up onto the platform, scouring walls for any clue about where I am and where to go. How to make it out of here alive.

I've seen maps down here before, back when I used to explore after going to the museum, and I desperately need to find one now. My heart thunders in my chest, panic squeezing my lungs as dingy bare walls stare back at me.

Finally the weak lantern light illuminates dull colors barely visible under layers of dirt and grime. Frantic, I scrub the heel of my hand against the wall until the lines of a map appear. It's faded, making it almost impossible to distinguish the various twisted lines and tunnels, and my eyes skitter everywhere at once until I see sharp letters stating YOU ARE HERE with an arrow pointing at a white circle.

I place a trembling finger over the spot like it's an anchor holding me firm. I know where I am, now I just have to figure out where I'm going.

Behind me the moans in the tunnel grow stronger, pushing me to move, to run, but I know I have to think first.

My body shaking from the cold and strain of the day, I start tracing the lines that spread away from where I'm standing, tunnels curving and twisting back under the Dark City or out past the island, sometimes doubling back or just ending.

It's like a maze, and I keep getting lost and tangled where the lines intersect into knots before untangling and breaking out again. There are too many options. I don't know where to go. I beat my fist against the wall, pouring out my frustration and forcing myself to focus.

I refuse to die down here alone. I didn't give up when I fell into a pit of barbed wire and I won't do it now. There's always a way to survive. The trick is finding out how. Survivors aren't always the strongest; sometimes they're the smartest, but more often simply the luckiest. I close my eyes and take a deep breath, clearing the panic from my mind, and then I open them and start tracing the lines on the map again, knowing there's something I'm missing.

That's when I see, at the edge of the map, a picture of a roller coaster, and I almost laugh at the simplicity of the solution. Catcher told me about a roller coaster—he said that was how he found the boat.

Now I just have to find where that is. With the lightness of hope screaming through my body, I rub more of the grime away and uncover an arrow pointing from the picture of the coaster to a round dot at the bottom edge of the map— another station.

My teeth chatter, the cold closing in around me as I track the lines on the map, figuring out how the tunnels connect and how to get there. It's far away, and my body wants to sag at the thought of covering such distance, but it's still hope. At least now I know where to go so that I'm not running in aimless circles, waiting for the dead to bury me.

For the briefest moment I allow myself to think about Catcher waiting for me. To think of the boat and the water and my sister and the sky. These are the thoughts that drag me back to the edge of the platform. That propel me down to the tracks and push me to stumble through the tunnels.

The moans wash behind me, almost a physical force that screams at my body to move faster, but I know better. This time I don't run. It's a long way to the roller coaster and I can't exhaust myself. I'm more cautious with my steps, keeping the lantern in front of me so I don't fall—I can't afford any more scrapes or cuts. Any more blood.

The only problem is that my body doesn't generate as much heat walking, and soon I start to lose feeling in my fingers and toes. I pull my new coat tight, try to remember the feel of the fire on the roof earlier, when we were inflating the balloon.

Try to remember the heat of Catcher's skin against mine.

I shiver just thinking about it.

I feel like a tiny lightning bug lost over the ocean—a tiny bright light surrounded by dark so deep the world might as well not exist. Time and distance become distorted and I find myself counting steps just to know that I'm moving forward.

I can't remember the last time I ate. I find myself pulling ice from the walls for water. It's nearly impossible to raise my feet, so I drag them along, the Unconsecrated thundering after me.

Eventually, the ground becomes slick, and I press my hand against the ice-coated wall to keep steady. My footsteps alternately crunch and slip, making it easy to lose my balance. Every time I crash to my knees it takes longer for me to push myself up again, and the dead get closer.

Every time I hesitate, that's distance lost between me and the dead.

I'm so tired. My body's exhausted. Spent.

This is the true brutality of the Unconsecrated. My body tires and theirs don't. My muscles cramp and lock up and theirs don't. My mind screams to rest for just a moment and they know only the hunger that will keep them stumbling after me forever.

Every heartbeat I'm not moving, the Unconsecrated are.

And eventually I *will* have to stop. To sleep. To eat. To drink. To catch my breath.

I can't walk forever. The dead can.

Knowing this should break me. It should have broken all of us long ago.

But it didn't. Not my mother or my father. Not their parents or the generation before that.

And if I've learned anything surviving on my own it's that I can take another step. That's all I have to promise myself: one more step, and then I can worry about the one after that.

One more morning: that's all I have to focus on.

So that's what I do. Behind me the dead follow, the empty sound of their moaning making me nauseated and dizzy. I begin to hum, a wavering sound as the muscles in my arms and across my chest clench from the cold.

My throat's sore, mouth parched dry, so I run my hands across the ice on the wall, bringing the drops of water to my lips to keep them from cracking. It tastes old and stale. Metallic, like blood.

A minute or an hour or a day or a week may have passed, for all I know. I just know one foot and then the other. I know the feel of the frozen wall under my half-numbed hands to keep balance. I know the feeling of my feet sliding—that moment I think I'll catch myself just before I slam to the ground.

And I know pushing myself back up, bruises blooming on bruises. Moans chase me, the sound such a constant that it feels as necessary as breathing.

The tunnel slopes deeper underground, which makes the ice underfoot grow thicker. It starts to fill the tunnel until I'm forced to walk stooped over so I don't hit my head on the ceiling. Keeping my balance on the slick surface becomes difficult, and finally I fall with a thud that forces the air from my lungs and sends the lantern flying.

As I lie there trying to coax myself to breathe again, shadows whisper at the edge of the feeble light.

I roll to my knees, recognizing the shapes: twisted arms, splayed fingers, gaping mouths. Eyes still open, sightless. Ice burns on my knees and palms. My teeth chatter and I have to clench my jaw hard to make them stop.

Bits of the bodies jut from the ice, frozen in time. Fingers like blades of grass coating a field, an elbow like a broken tree branch. They're everywhere, surrounding me. My lantern's trapped in a nook a few arm's lengths away, and slowly, careful to avoid the snags of protruding bodies, I crawl toward it.

The ceiling grates against my back, the space so narrow I almost have to lie flat on my stomach to reach the lantern. I'm forced to rest my cheek on the ice, facing the bared teeth and clawing hands.

Some of the dead look like they're asleep—like they collapsed down here, with no more living flesh to tempt them, and have been trapped ever since.

As I crawl I feel the top layer of ice beginning to melt under my touch. A tiny puddle already rests under the divot where the lantern rolled to a stop. Moans from the dead chasing me slip around the narrow space, bathing the frigid air with a sense of intense loneliness.

Stretching my arm as far as possible, I feel my fingers slide over the heated glass bulb of the lantern, knocking it just out of reach. Something brushes my foot and I glance over my shoulder, see fingers wrapping around my ankle. Teeth straining from the ice. All around me ice crystals sparkle and shimmer in the light and then there's a sputter, a last gasping wheeze from the lantern, and everything goes black.

▼ XLIV ▼

I scream. I can't help it. The darkness hits with such a star-
tling intensity that I'm stunned. I clamp a hand over my
mouth, silencing myself. Listening for the sound of another
body moving.

The image is still imprinted in my mind. The
Unconsecrated, half her body trapped in the ice. Reaching for
me nonetheless, her movements agonizingly slow.

I kick and kick again, dragging my knees to my chest until
I'm wrapped in as tiny a ball as possible. Sound is basically
useless in the tunnels. It hits the walls and runs over the ceiling, making it tricky to judge direction or distance. A trace of
air whispers up my back and my mind conjures the worst—
dead lips against my skin—and I have to force myself to focus.

I listen to my breathing and then I stretch my senses beyond that. I hear water melting down icicles dripping to pud-
dles collecting under my body. And then I hear a body
unfolding. The pop of a joint stretching. The wheeze that
comes before the moan.

I knew there were pockets of dead trapped in these tunnels. I knew it was only a matter of time. Twisting onto my side, I grab my machete and swing it toward where I last saw the lantern, hearing the blade clank across the metal, the glass rolling over ice.

Panic claws at my senses, desperate to overwhelm me and shut me down, but I refuse to crumble. I feel the tip of the machete hook the lantern, then slide it toward me and fumble in my pocket for the flint.

I strike. A tiny flicker of light that illuminates mouths and eyes a short distance away. I whimper.

Strike again.

Hands stretching toward me.

I lash out with the machete, swinging it wildly around me and finding only air and ice. I kneel, strike the flint again and again, twisting my fingers against the wick of the lantern until there's a hiss and a sizzle and the flame sputters to life.

The moans are almost whispers, Unconsecrated bodies so close to being frozen that their movements are dulled, as if trapped under thick sludge. But still they come for me.

Clawing at the ice, sliding across its surface, they slither through the narrow gap near the roof of the frozen tunnel.

The few moments I took to light the lantern allowed them to come closer. I see the details now—the curve of cheekbones, angle of jaws, arch of eyebrows. The hollow desire.

When the first one is within range I strike out, piercing her eye with the tip of the machete, bracing my foot against her face for the leverage to pull the blade back and strike again.

I clear a narrow path between them. Feel the trace of their fingers along my leg as I crawl past. But I'm not moving fast enough. There are too many surrounding me.

My movements become frantic as I wave the machete in tight circles, warding off their touch, but it's not enough. Suddenly I hear a high-pitched keen, and then without warning there's a loud crack and something shifts underneath me. I roll to the side, digging the tip of the machete into the ice and wrenching myself forward.

It takes both my hands to hold on, and I'm forced to toss the lantern aside. It feels as if the ground's given way, opened up and swallowed the world. Massive sheets of ice tilt and collapse, dumping the weight of the dead into the depths as a wave of frigid water washes over the bottom of my legs.

Kicking hard, my feet connecting with a body and gaining traction, I scramble forward, sliding on my stomach across the rest of the ice until I can finally stand.

The lantern sputters again, out of my reach on a ledge of ice surrounded by the dead. It throws a guttering light over the thrashing bodies, some of whom still fight toward me, fingers reaching. Their moans warble and fade, swallowed by the water.

I don't want to leave the comfort of the light. But I know that beyond this pocket of dead there are more—hundreds more, if not thousands, spilling into the tunnel. I turn back to the darkness, stumbling into the abyss.

As my numb feet carry me forward I start feeling like the dead behind me are calling my name. Like instead of moans they're calling "Aaaaannnaaaahhhh" over and over again, like a choir from the end of the world singing for my death. Sometimes bodies will rise in front of me, their steps staggering toward me, and all I can do is flail at the noise with my machete, slicing through whatever bits of them I can reach until they fall silent and let me pass.

For what feels like hours, days, months, I'm in the darkness. I become the darkness; it seeps into me and tries to eat its way out. It lulls me with promises of sleep and rest. It whispers to just give in. That it will protect me forever.

I ache to believe in it. I'm trembling from exhaustion, unable to feel my fingers or toes or knees or ears or lips from the oppressive cold and ice. There's nothing inside me anymore. I'm just a body that jerks and shivers as time folds and crumples. For a moment I feel as though I'm on the path as a child with Elias. My sister is behind me, crying and begging me to come home to her.

Elias is reaching out a hand to pull me forward, but his fingers constantly slip through my own. I call out for Catcher. For anyone. For help. But the only response is the moaning. The stench of stale air.

I stumble to a stop and turn around. I wonder if this is it. If this is how the world ends. I wonder about all the other people who have faced this moment. I think of Catcher telling me about the night he climbed the roller coaster, when he lost all fear of heights because death was already eating away at him. He had nothing more to lose.

And I realize that's the difference. I realize that I still have everything to lose. The possibility of my sister and Elias and Catcher and my future. I'd lose sunrises and stars and the feel of Catcher's heat against my lips. I'd miss the taste of snow and the smell of the first flower of spring.

I'd miss laughing and crying and all the moments in between.

I stumble back into the darkness and keep walking. Knowing that the pain I'm feeling now is because my body is alive.

I can tell by the echo of sound and the feel of the air when the tunnels open up into stations, when the path branches in front of me. I just keep my hand on the wall and push forward. I fall into such a repetition of steps that I'm stunned when I stumble against a massive pile of rubble.

I don't even know how to process this information, I'm so surprised, and it takes a moment for me to realize that this is it. I can't go any farther. I stand in the darkness, the vibration of the air behind me bristling with the ever-constant presence of moans.

I'm sure the Unconsecrated aren't that far behind me; I've barely been able to walk. All I know is that I have to get past this and continue on. I shove the machete into my belt and start to feel my way along the debris, pulling at smaller rocks, when I notice something.

I can hear a slight whistle of air. I lean into it—it feels warmer and smells fresh and clean and like the outside.

A ball of excitement coils in my stomach, energizing me. I run my hands over the cave-in, feeling for loose pieces and prying at them. Sharp corners bite my fingers but I don't care anymore. I have to keep moving.

It's agonizing, trying to find a weak spot and dig away at it, and when I'm finally able to clear an opening wide enough to reach my arm through, rubble collapses in on itself. Behind me I hear the Unconsecrated shuffle along the tracks, knowing that soon they'll stumble around me in the darkness.

I take a shuddering breath and shove my shoulder against a large slab of concrete, trying to shift it away, but my feet slip over the ice-slicked ground and I fall.

It's impossible in the darkness. I can't see how the pieces all fit together. Frustration rages through me. I don't want to take the time to build a fire but I'm afraid that's my only option. I skitter back down the tunnel, hands sweeping for anything dry, but everything's still crusted with ice. I press my fists against my temples, trying to figure out what I can burn.

My fingers brush the edge of the hat Catcher gave me and the matching scarf wrapped around my neck. I tear them off and crumple them into a ball by the wall of debris. Over and over again, I strike the flint above it. Sparks dance down but won't catch.

The moans grow louder, swelling around me. My heart pounds so hard that it feels like the world is pulsing. Quickly, I use the machete to slice a chunk of what's left of the hair from my head and drop it on top of the scarf.

Breath held, I strike the flint. It sparks but still nothing catches. I strike it again. Nothing. But the third time, one of the sparks falls into the nest of hair and blazes—the flame spreads to the edge of the scarf and ignites. I swallow back the ache of watching Catcher's present to me burn, the soft bright colors dissolving into ash and smoke.

Once the tiny fire sputters and flares I step back and stare at the debris pile, trying to figure out how to pull it apart. I find a slab of concrete bearing most of the weight and I dive toward it, scratching at the pebbles packed underneath it, digging my way through.

My hand reaches the outside air and I shove harder at the shards of concrete and stone, doing everything it takes to widen the little gap. I just need a bit more space. I squeeze and pry, and then I hear someone call my name.

XLV

"You're kidding me, right?" I ask simply, pulling myself back into the tunnel. In the guttering light of the flames I see Ox standing about twenty feet away. He looks terrible, blood soaking his uniform, bites peppered along his hands and arms. Skin pale. "You're supposed to be dead," I add.

He smiles. "Not yet. Soon. And then I'll Return, of course."

I drop my chin to my chest, not able to believe this is happening. I take a deep breath before facing him again. "You should have turned around and run back there," I tell him. "You could have saved yourself."

He shrugs. "I got infected the moment I stepped off the cable car." He stumbles over to the wall and slides down until he's sitting on the tracks. The light of my tiny fire barely reaches him. He removes his shirt and tosses it toward the flames, making them burn even brighter. His chest is covered in scars—some thick and ropy and others tiny flecks of white.

I don't want to think about what caused them. What the pain must have been like. I don't want to feel sympathy for this man.

"Stupid," I mutter. "What a waste. I wasn't worth the hassle, you know." I kick at more of the debris to clear it.

He looks up at me, his eyes big and dark. "There are people who believe the undead are eternal life. That they are a higher form of existence."

"Yeah," I scoff at him. "The Soulers. You imprisoned them, remember?"

He breathes deep. He's lost a lot of blood. He may not have long to live but it's hard to tell. I'm sure he'll hold on as long as he can.

When I realize he's not coming closer I crouch back down toward the hole I've been working on, shifting and pulling at the rocks again to widen the gap.

"Think about it," he says, ignoring that I'm not paying attention. "What makes us frail? Stupidity, love, anger, hope. The undead have none of that. All they are is eternal existence."

"They have no life," I shout back at him. "Literally," I add, which makes him smile. His teeth gleam in the darkness and it saddens me that this is what his last moments have come to.

He tilts his head. "That's the question, isn't it? What's life and what's existence?" He takes another deep breath and another, as if he can't get enough air. I scramble at the rocks, knowing that once he dies he'll Return and that behind him even more dead are coming. "Which would you choose?" he asks, his voice gravelly and wet.

I set a rock aside in case I need to use it against him. I

make sure my machete's within easy reach. The sound of the dead approaching rumbles and roars, making my work take on a frantic edge.

"It's a fool's choice, that's what it is," I tell him. "One brings you pain and the other numbness."

He smiles wider, enjoying himself. "Isn't that the question of life?"

I don't answer. I dig.

"I know you think I'm a bad person, Annah," he says softly. I glance back at him. He's rolled almost onto his side. He's gulping for air. I'm the last person he'll ever talk to. The last person he'll ever see—at least when he's alive.

"I think we all make choices," I tell him quietly.

And then he stops breathing.

I scramble for the machete and start running toward him, hoping to end it before he can Return, but when I'm halfway there I realize just how deafening the moaning through the tunnels has become. I recognize the beating under my feet, so constant that I'd grown accustomed to it. The air swells around me, and when I look up I see their eyes first.

They're coming for me, a wall in the distance. I glance back at Ox, my grip on the machete so tight that my knuckles ache. He's already twitching; his mouth opens and he screams loud before his vocal cords collapse and he's struggling to his feet.

Terror wells inside me, as frigid as ice water. It threatens to paralyze me but I break against it, sprinting back to the debris pile.

They come after me, shuffling and stumbling and thundering with their moans. I tear at the rock wall, try again to shove myself through the gap. It's still too narrow.

I can't stop glancing back, some sick part of me needing to know just how much time I have left. Ox lumbers toward me, the rest of the horde closing in around him. He raises his arms, reaching for me.

I hack at the stones again with the machete. Anything to make this gap a little wider. For a brief moment I even consider taking the machete to myself—cutting off an arm so that I could fit through the opening—but I know it would be useless. I'd bleed to death before I ever made it outside.

That's when the last gasping flames of my fire sputter out, plunging me into darkness once again. There's just a tiny glow of gray light from the gap I've made, a shaft of something brighter cutting through the black like a knife.

Something moves next to me and I shout, swinging the machete wildly. At first it only cuts through the air but I swing again and feel it connect with Ox's flesh.

The moans continue. More bodies stumble along the tracks toward me. They keep coming. There's no escape. There will never be escape.

They'll smother me and then I'll wander aimlessly like them until there's no flesh left to eat. Trapped here forever.

Screaming in rage at the thought, I slice the machete through the air in a wide arc, feeling it dig into a body. I shove the body back as hard as I can and then I dive through the darkness to the debris.

This time I know it's my last chance. I either squeeze through the gap or become Unconsecrated. I kick my feet against the ground, not caring about the rocks tearing at my ribs and shredding the skin over my hips.

But I'm still too big. I reach for anything on the other side to hold on to, but all I feel is rock and earth and ice.

Something grabs my foot. Dead fingers wrap around my ankle and I know that any second I'll feel the hard ridge of teeth and I kick violently, jerking to the side as much as possible.

Around me the rocks shift and give just the tiniest bit. But it's enough. My hips slide free and I'm pulling myself along the ground. When I get through I run my trembling hands over my body to make sure I wasn't bitten. To wipe away the feel of those fingers on my cold pricked flesh.

Arms reach after me through the opening—Ox's arms, with fresh bites still marking the skin—but he's too big to get out. He'll be stuck there reaching for me until eventually they all down or the force of so many bodies against the debris shifts it, pushing back the barrier and spilling them out into the world.

I stare at Ox's hand. Minutes ago he was alive. Three days ago I pressed my palm against his chest to stop him from fighting Catcher. And now this is all that's left.

Outside the night glimmers, the darkness just before dawn so much brighter than the emptiness of the tunnels that I can see a few shapes stumbling toward me in the shadows.

As much as I'd love to collapse and weep, I'm not safe. Not yet.

Beside me a trestle of the track juts from the ground, and I test my weight on its braces before starting to climb. At the top, the rails from the tunnel continue into the distance. It's deserted up here, and I sit, pulling my knees to my chest, allowing myself a moment of rest.

That's when I let the tears come. I can still feel the fingers of the dead on me, still hear their moans. Every inch of me is bruised and battered, my muscles so fatigued they don't even protest anymore.

But I survived.

And now it's time to live.

I scour the horizon. To my left a band of light teases the sky, the smallest hint of morning. But it's enough that I can see the path of the tracks stretching forward, and I push myself to my feet, determined to find Catcher and the others.

I can barely walk in a straight line after being trapped in the tunnels for so long, the cold eating into me. But the trestle is narrow and some of the boards are rotted, and it takes all my concentration to put one foot solidly in front of the other. A few dead stumble along the ground below me, pawing at the braces, and yet without the horde rumbling after me it feels quiet out here in the fog-coated morning.

The tracks take me past expanses of barren land, charred bricks chewed over by weeds. A long low cemetery fades out of view to be overtaken by a graveyard of rusted-out train cars. From all of these places the dead come, trailing behind on the ground as I make my way past overhead. They moan and reach and I ignore them all.

Eventually, as the sky lightens, a structure begins to rise from the mist in the distance. Elegant curves and twists fading in and out of the tumbling clouds. I rub my eyes, wondering if my mind's playing tricks on me.

It's almost too painful to hope. I swallow, pressing my fingers to my lips as tears blur the outline of what has to be the roller coaster from the picture on the map.

The roller coaster Catcher told me about.

I want to call out, to scream for joy as my body aches with the possibility of relief, but I still can't believe it. I move forward slowly, waiting for the world to crash in around me again.

Because I can't believe this could be it. I can't believe I've made it this far.

As I draw closer, the trestle branches toward a bridge crossing a vine-choked road, and I climb over it, dodging a few Unconsecrated who wander too close. I stumble through hip-high weeds, tripping over old roots and stones. With every step I want to stop, but I just promise myself one more and then one more again. My eyes never leave the coaster; I crane my neck as I draw closer.

The top of it is shrouded in the early-morning mist, a frozen white fog clinging to the dips and curls of the ride.

Something shifts along the curve of the tallest hump and I freeze. It's a shadow. A person.

My heart starts to pound.

Just then a breeze blows from the water, curling the mist away from him.

The arch of his neck, the set of his shoulders. Everything inside me stops.

Catcher.

He sits with his back to me, staring out past the beach at the ocean.

It takes me a moment to find my voice. "What are you looking for out there?" I call up. And then I start to climb, a fresh energy sweeping through me.

Catcher jerks and reaches out to steady himself. He looks around and I know the instant he sees me. His body goes still, his eyes wide open and his mouth caught on a sound he can't force out.

Before I even reach the top he's grabbing and pulling me up. He runs his hands over my body, along my arms and legs and then over my shoulders and up my neck until he's cupping my head.

I pull his face to mine and I kiss him, tasting his heat and fire and need.

"You're alive," he says.

"You're here," I say.

"You're not hurt or infected?" I see the terror in his eyes.

I shake my head. "Well, not infected anyway," I say, smiling.

This breaks the tension of the moment. We're laughing and crying and he crushes me to him, burying his head in my neck, and I tilt my head back as the morning sky swirls around us in a hundred million colors, brighter than any I've seen.

He traces a finger along my jaw, the heat of him so familiar now. So much a part of me. "My Annah," he murmurs, pulling my head back so that he can look into my eyes.

I'm so happy at that moment that I don't know what else to do or say. I just know that I love this man. And more than anything, I want to live my life with him—truly live.

"Mine," I whisper, twining my fingers through his, holding him closer. Knowing that this is what it means to live. That this love, this need is what drives us to push and fight and build and grow. That as long as there's hope and love in this world, there will always be the living.

For this moment it's just us and the breaking day, the promise of something new. We sit pressed against each other and stare out at the limitless horizon.

"What now?" I ask him.

He smiles, an excited flicker in his eyes. "That," he says, turning and pointing. I follow his gaze and draw in a sharp breath that I let out with a laugh. Down the coast a peninsula juts into the water with a fenced field teeming with hot-air balloons of all different colors and sizes. They're like wildflowers bobbing and twisting in the breeze. People huddle around them in groups, shaking hands and hugging.

"And there," he says, pointing toward the shallows, where a large ship sits serenely, deck bustling with activity as smaller boats ferry back and forth from the shore. "Gabry and Elias are already on board, making sure there's enough room and supplies for everyone. We'll go to Vista first and then . . ." He pauses, pulling me tighter, fitting us together as one. "Then we'll search for other survivors. If we can survive, others have as well."

I shake my head, not ready to believe it.

"You made it," Catcher whispers into my ear. He draws back, his forehead resting against mine.

I think about the moment in the tunnel when I didn't believe I'd make it out. When I was willing to just curl up in the ice and sleep—let the dead take me because it was too hard to keep fighting against them. "I almost gave up," I admit, unable to put force in my words because it makes me feel weak.

He pulls away, his gaze serious as he meets my eyes. He trails his finger along my cheek, following the path of a tear. "But you didn't."

I stare past him at all the people in the field, at those on the boat scrambling to fill it with supplies. They didn't give up either. Not in the face of the Recruiters or the Rebellion or the horde. All those sparks of light, stars burning brightest in the darkness.

"And I won't," I reassure him, knowing it deep inside as truth.

Catcher pulls me to him and I feel his heart thrumming through me, matching the rhythm of my own. I close my eyes, listening to the sound of the ocean, the constant brush of water against shore.

My father, Jacob, used to tell me about the ocean when I

was a child. Stories whispered to him on the endless path through the Forest when desperation lay thick like ash. He said it was a place where possibilities were endless and hope stretched as far as the horizon. And now, staring at the pure endlessness of it, I know it to be true.

ACKNOWLEDGMENTS

I'm incredibly grateful that I'm lucky enough to spend every day doing what I love: making up stories and writing them down. Thank you to all the readers, booksellers, librarians, teachers and book lovers who have made my dream a reality!

There are so many people involved in getting a book from idea to shelf, and I'd be lost without each of them. A huge thanks to my agent, Jim McCarthy, who is just fantastic beyond words, and to my editor, Krista Marino, whose insight and patience continue to astound me. Beverly Horowitz and the entire team at Delacorte Press have been wonderfully supportive in every way imaginable: Meg O'Brien, Jessica Shoffel and Kelly Galvin, my publicists, have worked tirelessly on my behalf with amazing results. I'm so thankful to Jocelyn Lange and the subsidiary rights department, as well as all the sales associates who've shown such enthusiasm for my books: Lauren Gromlowicz, Deanna Meyerhoff, Tim Mooney and Dandy Conway. Once again my book designer, Vikki Sheatsley, has outdone herself creating a gorgeous package, and Colleen Fellingham and Barbara Perris showed such patience combing through the details.

I feel so lucky to have the support of so many amazing friends who were willing to brainstorm, give advice, critique and procrastinate with me. A massive thanks to Diana Peterfreund, Saundra Mitchell, Sarah MacLean, Aprilynne Pike, Sarah Cross, Sarah Rees Brennan, Ally Carter, Kami Garcia, Margaret Stohl, Holly Black, Jackson Pearce, Maggie Stiefvater, Kristin Finlon, the 2009 Debutantes and everyone else who has been so generous with their time and support.

As always, research for this book took me in some fascinating directions, and I'm indebted to Dr. Gavin Macgregor-Skinner, whose work with USAID and the CDC helped inform my understanding of the progression and effects of global pandemics, and to Dr. Jason Davis for discussing the biological possibilities of zombies—any mistakes regarding such things are entirely mine. Thanks also to Kelly, Jessica and Krista, who tromped through the New York Transit Museum with me, and Sarah MacLean, who indulged me on some rather long subway rides.

Without the hospitality of the Dilworth Coffee Shop, Kebob Restaurant and 300 East I'd have never been able to leave the house and continue to work, and of course, big thanks to Dennis for giving us Jake and to his partner, Scott, for marrying JP and me.

I owe my family an extra-special thanks for all the times I had to sneak away during the holidays over the past year to get a few more words written in order to meet my deadlines. My parents; Tony Ryan; Bobby and Doug Kidd; my sisters, Jenny Sell and Chris Warnick (and their husbands!); and my new family, John, Jane and Jason Davis, continue to humble me with their constant love and support.

And finally, for my husband (yay!), JP: Even during the times that I lost faith in myself, you never lost faith in me.

ABOUT THE AUTHOR

Born and raised in Greenville, South Carolina, Carrie Ryan is a graduate of Williams College and Duke University School of Law. *The Dark and Hollow Places* is the third book in the Forest of Hands and Teeth trilogy. Look for the first two books, *The Forest of Hands and Teeth* and *The Dead-Tossed Waves,* both available from Delacorte Press. Carrie Ryan lives and writes in Charlotte, North Carolina. You can find her online at carrieryan.com.